Praise for *What You Wish For*

An Indie Next Great Reads Pick for July 20

"A lovely novel about moving through grief and choosing to find joy wherever you can." —Cathy Berner, Blue Willow Bookshop

A LibraryReads pick for July 2020!
Voted one of the top ten reads of the month that librarians across the country love!

What You Wish For tops the *Philadelphia Inquirer*'s list of Romance Book Recommendations for a Stressful Season!
"Funny and moving, *What You Wish For* will have you engrossed until the end."

What You Wish For tops the list of We Are Bookish's July 2020 Must-Reads!

One of:
People's "Books of the Week"
Refinery29's "17 Brand New 'Beach' Reads for Summer"
Parade's "30 Best Beach Reads"
Real Simple's "Best Books"
POPSUGAR's "30 Best New Books to Dive into This Summer"
She Reads' "Best Beach Reads"
Medium's "9 Compelling Books to Pick Up"

"This charming, often lighthearted novel touches on serious issues and celebrates the power of joy to trump fear and despair." —*People*

"[A] fast-paced tale steeped with whimsical plot points. This is one for the beach bag." —*Publishers Weekly*

"The story's message, that people should choose joy even (and especially) in difficult and painful times, seems tailor-made for this moment. A timely, uplifting read about finding joy in the midst of tragedy, filled with quirky characters and comforting warmth."

—*Kirkus Reviews* (starred review)

"In Katherine Center's *What You Wish For* . . . even in hard times, joy is at our disposal." —*Real Simple*

"Katherine Center excels at writing gentle, beautifully crafted romances."
—POPSUGAR

"*What You Wish For* is a bona fide explosion of happiness packaged in book form. A compassionate story of grief and resilience, *What You Wish For* is also a vital reminder that joy is not just something that happens to us but also something we have the power to choose. . . . Center has created for her readers a quirky confection that celebrates life in all its imperfect glory and delivers a much-needed dose of optimism."

—*BookPage*

"*What You Wish For* has Center's signature sprightly style and is a bubbly tonic to chase away the blues." —*The Augusta Chronicle*

"Katherine Center's new novel, *What You Wish For,* might be exactly what you're, well, wishing for. Sweet, charming, and funny."

—Bookreporter

Praise for *Things You Save in a Fire*

"Oh, how I love Katherine Center's writing . . . and her newest novel is a gem . . . a story that reminds us that the word 'emergency' has, at its heart, a new beginning. Just read it, and thank me later."

—Jodi Picoult, *New York Times* bestselling author of
A Spark of Light and *Small Great Things*

"A novel as vibrant as its cover." —*Bustle*

"[*Things You Save in a Fire*] is not only delightfully romantic, but also courageous and inspiring." —*The Christian Science Monitor*

"An emotional story of self-discovery and forgiveness." —Fresh Fiction

"*Things You Save in a Fire* is a profound tale of how a woman makes it in a man's world." —*New York Journal of Books*

"A wonderful exploration of personal vulnerability and strength that takes the reader along on Cassie's journey . . . *Things You Save in a Fire* is sure to be a hit." —*Shelf Awareness*

"I don't even know how to explain how much I adored this book. . . . This is a story of love, of family, and of learning how to be vulnerable— and trust me, Cassie's life journey is one you don't want to miss." —Siobhan Jones, Book of the Month

"A love story full of courage, forgiveness, and steamy chemistry." —*Woman's World*

"This book is so good! Loved the juxtaposition of the hero's and heroine's roles. She's the expert, and he is the rookie. Fabulous forgiveness theme. Humorous and touching!" —Leigh Davis, *USA Today*

ALSO BY KATHERINE CENTER

What You

Wish For

KATHERINE CENTER

ST. MARTIN'S GRIFFIN

NEW YORK

Published in the United States by St. Martin's Griffin, an imprint of St. Martin's Publishing Group

WHAT YOU WISH FOR. Copyright © 2020 by Katherine Pannill Center. All rights reserved. Printed in the United States of America. For information, address St. Martin's Publishing Group, 120 Broadway, New York, NY 10271.

www.stmartins.com

Designed by Devan Norman

The Library of Congress has cataloged the hardcover edition as follows:

Names: Center, Katherine, author.
Title: What you wish for / Katherine Center.
Description: First Edition. | New York : St. Martin's Press, 2020.
Identifiers: LCCN 2020002696 | ISBN 9781250219367 (hardcover) | ISBN 9781250219381 (ebook)
Classification: LCC PS3603.E67 W48 2020 | DDC 813/.6—dc23
LC record available at https://lccn.loc.gov/2020002696

ISBN 978-1-250-21937-4 (trade paperback)

Our books may be purchased in bulk for promotional, educational, or business use. Please contact your local bookseller or the Macmillan Corporate and Premium Sales Department at 1-800-221-7945, extension 5442, or by email at MacmillanSpecialMarkets@macmillan.com.

First St. Martin's Griffin Edition: 2021

10 9 8 7 6 5 4 3 2 1

For my editor, Jen Enderlin.

And for my agent, Helen Breitwieser.

Thank you both—so much more than I could ever say—for believing in me.

one

I was the one dancing with Max when it happened.

No one ever remembers who it was now, but it was me.

Actually, pretty much everything that night was me. Max and Babette had gone on a last-minute, two-week, second-honeymoon cruise around the boot of Italy that they'd found for a steal—and the return date just happened to be two days before Max's sixtieth birthday party—smack in the middle of summer.

Babette had worried that she couldn't book a trip with an end date so close to the party, but I stopped her. "I've got this. I'll get everything ready."

"I'm not sure you realize what a big undertaking a party like this is," Babette said. "We've got the whole school coming. Three hundred people—maybe more. It's a huge job."

"I think I can handle it."

"But it's your summer," Babette said. "I want you to be carefree."

"And I want you," I said, pointing at her, "to take a dirt-cheap second honeymoon to Italy."

I didn't have to twist their arms. They went.

And I was happy to take charge of the party. Max and Babette were not technically my parents—but they were the nearest thing I had. My mom died when I was ten, and let's just say my dad was not my closest relative.

Actually . . . technically he *was* my closest relative.

But we weren't close.

Plus, I didn't have any siblings—just a few scattered cousins, but no family anywhere nearby. God, now that I'm laying it out like this, I have to add: no boyfriend, either. Not for a long time. Not even any pets.

I did have friends, though. Lest I make myself sound too sad. Especially my friend Alice. Six feet tall, friendly, and relentlessly positive Alice, who was a math specialist and wore a T-shirt with a math joke on it every day to work.

The first day I met her, her shirt said, NERD SQUAD.

"Great shirt," I said.

She said, "Usually, I wear math jokes."

"Is there such a thing as math jokes?" I asked.

"Wait and see."

To sum up: Yes. There are more math jokes in the world than you can possibly imagine. And Alice had a T-shirt for all of them. Most of which I didn't understand.

We had almost none of the same interests, Alice and me, but it didn't matter. She was a tall, sporty, mathy person, and I was the opposite of all those things. I was an early riser, and she was a night owl. She wore the exact same version of Levi's and T-shirts to work every day, and every day I put together some wildly different concoction of clothes. She read spy novels—exclusively—and I read anything I could get my hands on. She played on an intramural beach volleyball team, for Pete's sake.

But we were great friends.

I was lucky to be a librarian at a very special, very legendary elementary school on Galveston Island called the Kempner School—and not only did I adore my job, and the kids, and the other teachers, I also lived in Babette and Max Kempner's garage apartment. Though, "garage apartment" doesn't quite capture it. The real term was "carriage house" because it had once been the apartment above the stables.

Back when horses-and-buggies were a thing.

Living with Max and Babette was kind of like living with the king and queen. They had founded Kempner, and they'd run it together all these years, and they were just . . . beloved. Their historic mansion—that's right: real estate is super cheap in Galveston—was just blocks from school, too, so teachers were constantly stopping by, hanging out on the porch, helping Max in his woodshop. Max and Babette were just the kind of people other people just wanted to be near.

The point is, I was glad to do something wonderful for them.

They did wonderful things for me all the time.

In fact, the more I thought about it, the more it seemed like a rare opportunity to really astonish them with the greatest party ever. I started a Pinterest board, and I went through magazines for décor ideas. I got so excited, I even called up their daughter Tina to see if she might like to do the project together.

Ironically, their daughter Tina was one of the rare people in town who *didn't* hang out at Max and Babette's all the time. So I didn't know her all that well.

Also: she didn't like me.

I suspected she thought I was trying to take her place.

Fair enough. She wasn't totally wrong.

"Why are *you* decorating for my dad's party?" she said, when I called—her voice tight.

"You know," I said, "just—timing." It's such a disorienting thing when people openly dislike you. It made me a little tongue-tied around her. "They're on that trip . . ."

I waited for a noise of recognition.

"To Italy . . ."

Nothing.

"So I just offered to get the party done for them."

"They should have called me," she said.

They hadn't called her because they knew she wouldn't have time.

She had one of those husbands who kept her very busy. "They wanted to," I lied. "I just jumped in and offered so fast . . . they never got the chance."

"How unusual," she said.

"But that's why I'm calling. I thought maybe we could do it together."

I could feel her weighing her options. Planning her own father's six-tieth birthday party was kind of her rightful job . . . but now, if she said yes, she'd have no way to avoid me.

"I'll pass," she said.

And so the job was mine.

Alice wound up helping me, because Alice was the kind of per-son who was always happiest when she was helping. Babette had been thinking streamers and cake, but I couldn't leave it at that. I wanted to go big. This was *Max*! Principal, founder, living legend—and genuinely good-hearted human. His whole philosophy was, *Never miss a chance to celebrate*. He celebrated everybody else all the time.

Dammit, it was time to celebrate the man himself.

I wanted to do something epic. Magical. Unforgettable.

But Babette had left an envelope on her kitchen table labeled "For Party Supplies," and when I opened it up, it held a budget of sixty-seven dollars. Many of them in ones.

Babette was pretty thrifty.

That's when Alice suggested we call the maintenance guys to see if we could borrow the school's twinkle lights from the storage facility. When I told them what we were up to, they said, "Hell, yes," and offered to hang everything for me. "Do you want the Christmas wreaths, too?" they asked.

"Just the lights, thank you."

See that? Everybody loved Max.

The more people found out what we were doing, the more every-body wanted in. It seemed like half the adults in this town had been Max's students, or had him for a baseball coach, or volunteered with him for beach cleanups.

I started getting messages on Facebook and texts I didn't recognize: The florist on Winnie Street wanted to donate bouquets for the tables, and the lady who owned the fabric shop on Sealy Avenue wanted to offer some bolts of tulle to drape around the room, and a local seventies cover band wanted to play for free. I got offers for free food, free cookies, free booze, and free balloons. I got texts from a busker who wanted to do a fire-eating show, an ice sculptor who wanted to carve a bust of Max for the buffet table, and a fancy wedding photographer who offered to capture the whole night—*no charge.*

I said yes to them all.

And then I got the best message of all. A phone call from a guy offering me the Garten Verein.

I'm not saying Max and Babette wouldn't have been happy with the school cafeteria—Max and Babette were pretty good at being happy anywhere—but the Garten Verein was one of the loveliest buildings in town. An octagonal, Victorian dancing pavilion built in 1880, now painted a pale green with white gingerbread. Nowadays it was mostly a venue for weddings and fancy events—a *not-cheap* venue. But several of Max's former students owned the building, and they offered it for free.

"Kempner class of '94 for the win!" the guy on the phone said. Then he added, "Never miss a chance to celebrate."

"Spoken like a true fan of Max," I said.

"Give him my love, will ya?" the Garten Verein guy said.

Max and Babette were too jet-lagged by the time they came home to even stop by school, so the change of venue took them completely by surprise. That evening, I met them on their front porch—Babette in her little round specs and salt-and-pepper pixie cut, forgoing her signature paint-splattered overalls for a sweet little Mexican-embroidered cotton dress, and Max looking impossibly dapper in a seersucker suit and a pink bow tie.

They held hands as we walked, and I found myself thinking, *Relationship goals.*

Instead of walking two blocks west, toward school, I led them north.

"You know we're going the wrong way, right?" Max stage-whispered to me.

"Don't you just know everything?" I teased, stalling.

"I know where my damn school is," Max said, but his eyes were smiling.

"I think," I said then, "if you stick with me, you'll be glad you did."

And that's when the Garten Verein came into view.

An arc of balloons swayed over the iron entrance gate. Alice— amateur French horn player and faculty sponsor of the fifth-grade jazz band—was already there, just inside the garden, and as soon as she saw us, she gave them the go-sign to start honking out a rendition of "Happy Birthday." Kids filled the park, and parents stood holding glass champagne flutes, and as soon as Max arrived, they all cheered.

As Max and Babette took in the sight, she turned to me. "What did you do?"

"We did not go over budget," I said. "Much."

We stepped into the garden, and their daughter Tina arrived just behind us—looking svelte and put-together, as always, with her third-grader, Clay, holding her hand. Babette and Max pulled them both into a hug, and then Max said, "Where's Kent Buckley?"

Tina's husband was the kind of guy everybody always called by his first and last name. He wasn't ever just "Kent." He was always "Kent Buckley." Like it was all one word.

Tina turned and craned her neck to look for her husband, and I took a second to admire how elegant her dark hair looked in that low bun. Elegant, but mean. That was Tina.

"There," she said, pointing. "Conference call."

There he was, a hundred feet back, conducting some kind of meeting on the Bluetooth speaker attached to his ear—pacing the sidewalk, gesticulating with his arms, and clearly not too pleased.

We all watched him for a second, and it occurred to me that he probably thought he looked like a big shot. He looked kind of proud of how he was behaving, like we'd be impressed that he had the authority to yell at people. Even though, in truth, especially with that little speaker on his ear, he mostly just looked like he was yelling at himself.

A quick note about Kent and Tina Buckley. You know how there are always those couples where nobody can figure out what the wife is doing with the husband?

They were that couple.

Most of the town liked Tina—or at least extended their affection for her parents to her—and it was a fairly common thing for people to wonder out loud what a great girl like that was doing with a douchey guy like him. I'm not even sure it was anything specific that folks could put their finger on. He just had a kind of uptight, oily, snooty way about him that people on the island just didn't appreciate.

Of course, Tina had never been "a great girl" to me.

Even now, beholding the party I'd so lovingly put together, she never even acknowledged me—just swept her eyes right past, like I wasn't even there. "Let's go in," she said to her mom. "I need a drink."

"How long can you stay?" Babette asked her in a whisper, as they started toward the building.

Tina stiffened, as though her mother had just criticized her. "About two hours. He's got a video conference at eight."

"We could drive you home, if you wanted to stay later," Max said then.

Tina looked like she wanted to stay. But then she glanced Kent Buckley's way and shook her head. "We'll need to get back."

Everybody was setting out their words carefully and monitoring their voices to keep everything hyper pleasant, but there were some emotional land mines in this conversation, for sure.

Of course, the biggest emotional land mine was the party itself. When we stepped inside and Max and Babette beheld the twinkle lights, and the seventies band in their bell-bottoms, and the decorations, and the mountains of food, Babette turned to me with a gasp of delight and said, "Sam! It's magnificent!"

In the background, I saw Tina's face go dark.

"It wasn't just me," I said. And then it just kind of popped out: "Tina helped. We did it together."

I'd have to apologize to Alice later. I panicked.

Babette and Max turned toward Tina for confirmation, and she gave them a smile as stiff as a Barbie doll's.

"And, really, the whole town's responsible," I went on, trying to push past the moment. "When word got out we were planning your sixtieth birthday party, everybody wanted to help. We got deluged, didn't we, Tina?"

Tina's smile got stiffer as her parents turned back to her. "We got deluged," she confirmed.

That's when Max reached out his long arms and pulled us both into a bear hug. "You two are the best daughters a guy could have."

He was joking, of course, but Tina stiffened, then broke out of the hug. "She is not your daughter."

Max's smile was relaxed. "Well, no. That's true. But we're thinking about adopting her." He gave me a wink.

"She doesn't need to be adopted," Tina said, all irritation. "She's a grown woman."

"He's kidding," I said.

"Don't tell me what he's doing."

But nothing was going to kill Max's good mood. He was already pivoting toward Babette, snaking his arm around her waist and pulling her toward the dance floor. "Your mama and I need to show these whippersnappers how it's done," he called back as he walked. Then he rotated to point at Tina. "You're next, lady! Gotta grab you before you turn into a pumpkin."

Tina and I stood at a hostile distance as we watched her parents launch into a very competent set of dance moves. I spotted Alice across the way and wished she would come stand next to me for some emotional backup, but she made her way to the food table, instead.

Was Alice's party attire jeans and a math T-shirt?

It was.

The shirt said, WHY IS 6 AFRAID OF 7? And then, on the back: BE-CAUSE 7 8 9.

I was just about to walk over and join her, when Tina said, "You didn't have to lie to them."

I shrugged. "I was trying to be nice."

"I don't need you to be nice."

I shrugged again. "Can't help it."

Confession: did I want Tina to like me?

I absolutely did.

Would I have loved to be a part of their family—a real part of it? I would. Even if the most Tina could ever be was my bitchy big sister, I'd take it. My own family was kind of . . . nonexistent.

I wanted so badly to belong somewhere.

I wasn't trying to steal her family. But I would have given anything to join it.

But Tina wasn't too keen on that idea, which seemed a little selfish because she was never around, anyway. She and Kent Buckley were always off hosting charity galas and living a fancy, ritzy social life. You'd think she could share a little.

But no.

She didn't want them, particularly, but she didn't want anyone else to have them, either.

She resented my presence. She resented my existence. And she was determined to keep it that way. All I could think of was to just keep on being nice to her until the day she finally just gave up, held out her arms for a defeated hug, and said, "Fine. I give up. Get in here."

It was going to happen someday. I knew it was. Maybe.

But probably not tonight.

After a very long pause, I said something I thought she'd like. "They adore you, you know. And Clay. They talk about you both all the time."

But she just turned toward me with an expression that fell somewhere between offense and outrage.

"Did you just try to tell me how my own parents feel about me?"

"Um . . ."

"Do you honestly believe that you're qualified to comment on my relationship with my own parents—the people who not only brought me into this world but also spent thirty years raising me?"

"I . . ."

"How long have you known them?"

"Four years."

"So you're a librarian who moved into their garage four years ago—"

"It's a carriage house," I muttered.

"—and I am their biological child who's known them since before I was born. Are you trying to compete with me? Do you really think you could ever even come close to winning?"

"I'm not trying to—"

"Because I'll tell you something else: My family is not your place, and it's not your business, and it's not where you belong—and it never, ever will be."

Sheesh.

She knew how to land a punch.

It wasn't just the words—it was the tone of voice. It had a physical force—so sharp, I felt cut. I turned away as my throat got thick and my eyes stung.

I blinked and tried to focus on the dance floor.

An old man in a bolo tie had cut in on Babette and Max. Now Max turned his attention back toward Tina and swung an imaginary lasso above his head before tossing it over at her to rope her in. As he pulled on the rope, she walked toward him and smiled. A real smile. A genuine smile.

And I—resident of the family garage—was forgotten.

Appropriately.

It was fine. I never danced in public, anyway.

That night, Max mostly danced with Babette. It was clear the two of them had done a lot of dancing in their almost four decades together. They knew each other's moves without even thinking. I felt mesmerized, watching them, and I bet a lot of other people did, too.

They were the kind of couple that made you believe in couples.

Max lassoed a lot of people that night, and one of them, eventually, was me. I was surprised when it happened—almost like I'd forgotten I was there. I'd been watching from the sidelines for so long, I'd started to think I was safe—that I could just enjoy the view and the music without having to join in.

Wrong.

As Max pulled me onto the dance floor, I said, "I don't dance in public."

Max frowned. "Why not?"

I shook my head. "Too much humiliation as a child."

And that was true. I loved to dance. And I was actually pretty good, probably. I had good rhythm, at least. I danced around my own house constantly—while cleaning, and doing laundry, and cooking, and doing dishes. I'd crank up pop music, and boogie around, and cut the drudgery in half. Dancing was joyful, and mood elevating, and absolutely one of my very favorite things to do.

But only by myself.

I couldn't dance if anyone was looking. When anyone at all was looking, the agony of my self-consciousness made me freeze. I couldn't bear to be looked at—especially in a crowd—and so at any party where dancing happened, I just froze. You'd have thought I'd never done it before in my life.

And Max knew enough about me to understand why. "Fair enough," he said, not pushing—but not releasing me, either. "You just stand there, and I'll do the rest."

And so I stood there, laughing, while the band played a Bee Gees cover and Max danced around me in a circle, wild and goofy and silly—and it was perfect, because anybody who was looking was looking at him, and that meant we could all relax and have fun.

At one point, Max did a "King Tut" move that was so cringingly funny, I put my hand over my eyes. But when I took my hand away, I found Max suddenly, unexpectedly, standing very still—pressing his fingers to his forehead.

"Hey," I said, stepping closer. "Are you okay?"

Max took his hand away, like he was about to lift his head to respond. But then, instead, his knees buckled, and he fell to the floor.

The music stopped. The crowd gasped. I knelt down next to Max, then looked up and called around frantically for Babette.

By the time I looked down again, Max's eyes were open.

He blinked a couple of times, then smiled. "Don't worry, Sam. I'm fine."

Babette arrived on his other side and knelt beside him.

"Max!" Babette said.

"Hey, Babs," he said. "Did I tell you how beautiful you are?"

"What happened?" she said.

"Just got a little dizzy there for a second."

"Can somebody get Max some water?" I shouted, and then I leaned in with Babette to help him work his way up into a sitting position.

Babette's face was tight with worry.

Max noticed. "I'm fine, sweetheart."

But Max was not the kind of guy to go around collapsing. He was one of those sturdy-as-an-ox guys. I tried to remember if I'd ever seen him take a sick day.

Now Max was rubbing Babette's shoulder. "It was just the long flight. I got dehydrated."

Just as he said it, a cup of ice water arrived.

Max took a long drink. "Ah," he said. "See that? All better."

His color was coming back.

A crowd had formed around us. Someone handed Max another cup of water, and I looked up to realize at least ten people were standing at the ready with liquid.

He drank the next cup. "Much better," he said, smiling up at us, looking, in fact, much better. Then he lifted his arms to wave some of the men over. "Who's helping me back to my feet?"

"Maybe you should wait for the paramedics, Max," one of the guys said.

"You hit the floor pretty hard there, boss," another guy offered, as an answer.

"Aw, hell. I don't need paramedics."

The fire department was maybe four blocks away—and just as he said it, two paramedics strode in, bags of gear over their shoulders.

"Are you partying too hard, Max?" one of them said with a big grin when he saw Max sitting on the floor.

"Kenny," Max said, smiling back. "Will you tell this batch of worriers I'm fine?"

Just then, a man pushed through the crowd. "Can I help? I'm a doctor."

Very gently, Max said, "You're a psychiatrist, Phil."

Kenny shook his head. "If he needs to talk about his feelings, we'll call you."

Next, Babette and I stepped back, and the paramedics knelt all around Max to do an assessment—Max protesting the whole time. "I just got dehydrated, that's all. I feel completely fine now."

Another medic, checking his pulse, looked at Kenny and said, "He's tachycardic. Blood pressure's high."

But Max just smacked him on the head. "Of course it is, Josh. I've been dancing all night."

It turned out, Max had taught both of the paramedics who showed up that night, and even though they were overly thorough, everything else seemed to check out on Max. They wanted to take him to the ER right then, but Max managed to talk them out of it. "Nobody's ever thrown me a sixtieth birthday party before," he told them, "and I really don't want to miss it."

Somehow, after they helped him up, he charmed them into having some snacks, and they agreed to give him a few minutes to drink some water and then reevaluate.

They took a few cookies, but even as they were eating, they were watching him. Babette and I were watching him, too.

But he seemed totally back to his old self. Laughing. Joking around. When the band finally started up again, it was one of Max's favorites: ABBA's "Dancing Queen."

As soon as he heard it, Max was looking around for Babette. When he caught her eye about ten feet away, he pointed at her, then at himself, then at the dance floor.

"No," Babette called. "You need to rest and hydrate!"

"Wife," Max growled. "They are literally playing our song."

Babette walked over to scold him—and maybe flirt with him a little, too. "Behave yourself," she said.

"I'm fine," he said.

"You just—"

But before she could finish, he pulled her into his arms and pressed his hand against the small of her back.

I saw her give in. I felt it.

I gave in, too. This wasn't a mosh pit, after all. They were just swaying, for Pete's sake. He'd had at least six glasses of water by now. He looked fine. Let the man have his birthday dance. It wasn't like they were doing the worm.

Max spun Babette out, but gently.

He dipped her next, but carefully.

He was fine. He was fine. He was absolutely fine.

But then he started coughing.

Coughing a lot.

Coughing so hard, he let Babette go, and he stepped back and bent over.

Next, he looked up to meet Babette's eyes, and that's when we saw he was coughing up blood—bright red, and lots of it—all over his hand and down his chin, drenching his bow tie and his shirt.

He coughed again, and then he hit the floor.

The paramedics were back over to him in less than a second, ripping his shirt open, cutting off the bow tie, intubating him and squeezing air in with a bag, performing CPR compressions. I don't really know what else was going on in the room then. Later, I heard that Alice rounded up all the kids and herded them right outside to the garden. I heard the school nurse dropped to her knees and started praying. Mrs. Kline, Max's secretary for thirty years, tried helplessly to wipe up a splatter of blood with cocktail napkins.

For my part, all I could do was stare.

Babette was standing next to me, and at some point, our hands found each other's, and we wound up squeezing so tight that I'd have a bruise for a week.

The paramedics worked on Max for what seemed like a million years—but was maybe only five minutes: intensely, bent over him, performing the same insistent, forceful movements over his chest. When they couldn't get him back, I heard one of them say, "We need to transport him. This isn't working."

Transport him to the hospital, I guessed.

They stopped to check for a rhythm, but as they pulled back a little, my breath caught in my throat, and Babette made a noise that was half-gasp, half-scream.

Max, lying there on the floor, was blue.

"Oh, shit," Kenny said. "It's a PE."

I glanced at Babette. *What was a PE?*

"Oh, God," Josh said, "look at that demarcation line."

Sure enough, there was a straight line across Max's rib cage, where the color of his skin changed from healthy and pink to blue. "Get the gurney," Kenny barked, but as he did his voice cracked.

That's when I saw there were tears on Kenny's face.

Then I looked over at Josh: his, too.

And then I just knew exactly what they knew. They would wipe their faces on their sleeves, and keep doing compressions on Max, and keep working him, and transport him to the hospital, but it wouldn't do any good. Even though he was Max—our principal, our hero, our living legend.

All the love in the world wouldn't be enough to keep him with us.

And as wrong as it was, eventually it would become the only true thing left: We would never get him back.

A PE turned out to be a pulmonary embolism. He'd developed a blood clot sometime during the flight home from Italy, apparently—and it had made its way to his lungs and blocked an artery. Deep vein thrombosis.

"He didn't walk around during the flight?" I asked Babette. "Doesn't everybody know to do that?"

"I thought he did," Babette said, dazed. "But I guess he didn't."

It didn't matter what he had or hadn't done, of course. There would be no do-over. No chance to try again and get it right.

It just was what it was.

But what was it? An accident? A fluke? A bad set of circumstances? I found myself Googling "deep vein thrombosis" in the middle of the night, scrolling and reading in bed in the blue light of my laptop, trying to understand what had happened. The sites I found listed risk factors for getting it, and there were plenty, including recent surgery, birth control pills, smoking, cancer, heart failure—none of which applied to Max. And then, last on the list, on every site I went to, was the weirdest possible one: "sitting for long periods of time, such as when driving or flying." And that was it. That was Max's risk factor. He'd sat still for too long. He'd forgotten to get up and walk around during the flight—and that one totally innocuous thing had killed him.

I couldn't wrap my head around it.

An entire lifetime of growing up, learning to crawl, and then to toddle, and then to walk, and then run. Years of learning table manners, and multiplication tables, and how to shave, and how to tie a bow tie. Striving and going to college and grad school and marrying Babette and raising a daughter—and a son, too, who had joined the Marines and then died in Afghanistan—and this was how it all ended.

Sitting too long on a plane.

It wasn't right. It wasn't fair. It wasn't acceptable.

But it didn't matter if I accepted it or not.

People talk about shock all the time, but you don't know how physical it is until you're in it. For days after it happened, my chest felt tight, like my lungs had shrunk and I couldn't get enough oxygen into them. I'd find myself panting, even when I was just making a pot of coffee. I'd surface from deep sleep gasping for breath like I was suffocating. It left me feeling panicked, like I was in danger, even though the person who had been in danger wasn't me.

It was physical for Babette, too.

When the two of us got home from the hospital, she lay down on the sofa in the living room and slept for twelve hours. When she was awake, she had migraines and nausea. But she was almost never awake. We closed the curtains in the living room. I brought in blankets, and a bottle of water, and a box of tissues for the coffee table. I fetched her pillow off the bed upstairs, and some soft pajamas and her chenille robe.

She would sleep downstairs on that sofa for months.

She would send me to get anything she needed from their bedroom. She would shower in her kids' old bathroom down the hall.

I mean, she was Max's high school sweetheart. Can you imagine? They'd started dating in ninth grade, when their math teacher asked her to tutor him after school, and Max had been right there by her side ever since. She hadn't been without him since she was *fourteen*. Now she was almost sixty. They had grown up together, almost like two trees growing side by side with their trunks and branches entangled.

Suddenly, he was gone, and she was entangled around nothing but air.

We needed time. All of us did. But there wasn't any.

Summer was ending soon, school was starting soon, and life would have to go on.

Three days later, we held Max's memorial service at the shore, on the sand, in the early morning—before the Texas summer heat really kicked in. The guys from maintenance built a little temporary stage in front of the waves, and in a strange mirroring that just about shredded my heart, Max got a whole new set of offerings from all those people who loved him: The florist on Winnie Street offered funeral wreaths and greenery.

The photographer from the party gave Babette a great photo of Max to feature in the program. A harpist, who had gotten a D in his civics class but had loved him anyway, offered to play at the service.

There were no balloons this time, no fire-eater, no fifth-grade jazz band.

But it was packed. People brought beach towels to sit on, I remember that—and there was not an open inch of sand anywhere.

It's amazing how funerals even happen.

The party had taken so much work and planning and forward momentum, but the funeral just . . . happened.

I showed up. I read a poem that Babette gave me—one of Max's favorites—but I couldn't even tell you which one. It's crumpled in my dresser drawer now along with the program because I couldn't bear to throw either of them away.

I remember that the water in the Gulf—which is usually kind of brown on our stretch of beach from all the mud at the mouth of the Mississippi—was particularly blue that day. I remember seeing a pod of dolphins go by in the water, just past the line where the waves started. I remember sitting down next to Alice on her beach towel after I tried, and failed, to give Tina a hug.

"She really doesn't like you," Alice said, almost impressed.

"You'd think grief would make us all friends," I said, dragging my soggy Kleenex across my cheeks again.

After the service, we watched Tina walk away, pulling little Clay behind her in his suit and clip-on tie, Kent Buckley nowhere to be found.

Once we were back at the reception in the courtyard at school, Alice kept busy helping the caterers. I'm not sure the caterers needed help, but Alice liked to be busy even on good days, so I just let her do her thing.

I was the opposite of Alice that day. I couldn't focus my mind enough to do anything except stare at Babette in astonishment at how graciously she received every single hug from every single well-wisher who lined up to see her. She nodded, and smiled, and agreed with every kind thing anybody said.

He *had* been a wonderful man.

We *would* all miss him.

His memory would definitely, without question, be a blessing.

But how on earth was Babette doing it? Staying upright? Smiling? Facing the rest of her life without him?

Tina had her own receiving line, just as long, and Kent Buckley was supposed to be in charge of Clay . . . but Kent Buckley—I swear, this is true—was *wearing his Bluetooth headset*. And every time a call came in, he took it.

Little Clay, for his part, would watch his dad step off into a cloistered hallway, and then stand there, blinking around at the crowd, looking lost.

I got it.

I didn't have a receiving line, of course. I was nobody in particular. Looking around, everybody was busy comforting everybody else. Which freed me up, actually. Right then, surveying the crowd, I had a what-would-Max-do moment.

What *would* Max do?

He would try to help Clay feel better.

I walked over. "Hi, Clay."

Clay looked up. "Hi, Mrs. Casey." They all called me "Mrs."

He knew me well from the library. He was one of my big readers. "Tough day, huh?" I said.

Clay nodded.

I looked over at Kent Buckley, off by a cloister, doing his best to whisper-yell at his employees. "Wanna take a walk?" I asked Clay then.

Clay nodded, and when we started walking, he put his soft little hand in mine.

I took him to the library. Where else? My beautiful, magical, beloved library . . . home of a million other lives. Home of comfort, and distraction, and getting lost—in the very best way.

"Why don't you show me your very favorite book in this whole library," I said.

He thought about it for a second, and then he led me to a set of low shelves under a window that looked out over downtown, then over the seawall, and out to the Gulf. I could see the stretch of beach where we'd just held the service.

This was the nonfiction nature section. Book after book about animals, and sea life, and plants. Clay knelt down in front of the section on ocean life and pulled out a book, laid it out on the floor, and said, "This is it," he said. "My favorite book."

I sat next to him and leaned back against the bookshelf. "Cool," I said. "Why this one?"

Clay nodded. "My dad's going to take me scuba diving when I'm bigger."

My instant reaction was to doubt that would ever happen. Maybe I'd just known too many guys like Kent Buckley. But I pretended otherwise. "How fun!"

"Have you ever gone scuba diving?"

I shook my head. "I've only read about it."

Clay nodded. "Well," he said, "that's almost the same thing."

Talk about the way to a librarian's heart. "I agree."

We flipped through the pages for a long time, with Clay narrating a tour through the book. It was clear he'd absorbed most of the information in it, and so all he needed was a picture to prompt conversation. He told me that the earth's largest mountain range is underwater, that coral can produce its own sunscreen, that the Atlantic Ocean is wider than the moon, and that his favorite creature in the Gulf of Mexico was the vampire squid.

I shivered. "Is that a real thing?"

"It's real. Its lower body looks like bat wings—and it can turn itself inside out and hide in them." Then he added, "But it's not really a squid. It's a cephalopod. 'Squid' is a misnomer.'"

"I'm sorry," I said, "did you just say 'misnomer'?"

He blinked and looked at me. "It means 'wrong name.' From the Latin."

I blinked back at him.

"Clay," I asked. "Are you a pretty big reader?"

"Yep," Clay said, turning his attention back toward the book.

"I don't think I've ever met a third-grader who knew the word 'misnomer,' much less anything about its Latin origins."

Clay shrugged. "I just really like words."

"I'll say."

"Plus my dad does flash cards with me."

"He does?"

"Yeah. My dad loves flash cards."

Honestly, I'd never worked very hard to get to know Clay. He was in the library a ton—almost whenever he could be—but he knew his way around, and he didn't need my help, and, well . . . he was reading. I didn't want to bother him.

Plus, yes, also: I was afraid of his mother.

It's true in a school that even the kids who need help don't always get it—so a kid who *doesn't* need help? He's gonna be on his own.

At least, until now. Clay was going to need some love this year, and it would be right here waiting for him in the library, if he needed it.

I don't know how long we'd been gone—an hour, maybe—when Alice came running into the library, breathless, her face worried. She had on a black skirt and a black blouse—one of the only times I'd seen her not in jeans—and she almost didn't look like herself.

"Oh, my God," she said, when she found us, bending over to breathe for a second before grabbing Clay by the shoulders and steering him out. "They're looking for him everywhere! Tina Buckley is freaking out."

Oh. Oops. Guess we'd lost track of time.

"Found him!" Alice shouted as we strode back into the courtyard, shaking Clay's shoulders for proof. "Got him! He's right here!"

Tina plowed through the crowd to seize him in her arms.

"I'm sorry," I said, catching Babette's eye as I arrived behind them. "We went to the library."

Babette waved me off, but that's when Tina stood up and glared at me. "*Really?*" she said, all bitter.

I lifted my shoulders. "We were just looking through Clay's favorite book."

"You couldn't—I don't know—mention that to anyone?"

"Everybody seemed pretty busy."

"Clay's father was watching him."

Um. Sorry, lady. His father was not *watching him. His father was taking business calls on his cell phone. At a funeral.* "I'm sorry," I said again.

"You bet you are."

"I just wanted . . . to help."

"Well, you can't help. But here's one thing you can do. You can leave my family alone."

Leave them alone?

What did that even mean? I lived with Babette. Clay was about to be in my third-grade library class. "How would that even work, Tina? I live on your mother's property."

"Maybe you should find somewhere else to live."

But whatever this weirdness was with Tina, it had gone on too long. "No," I said.

She frowned. "No?"

"No. That's ridiculous. I'm not doing that. I love my carriage house—"

"Garage apartment," she corrected.

"And I'm not leaving. Why would you even want me to? Would you really rather your mom be all alone in that big house than have me nearby?"

We both looked over at Babette, who was back in her greeting line, now with her arm around Clay, who was watching us with his big eyes.

"She wouldn't be all alone," Tina said.

"Who would be with her?" I demanded. "You?"

Across the courtyard, Kent Buckley was back on another call.

I saw Tina's eyes flick from Babette to Kent. I saw her take in what he was doing. I saw her nostrils flare—just the tiniest bit, enough to ripple across her composure for a second. I knew she was suppressing some rage. Her husband was *talking on his cell phone during her father's funeral reception.* It wasn't just inappropriate, it bordered on pathological.

In a different context, I could have felt very sorry for Tina Buckley.

But not today.

She'd married that dude, after all—and no matter if it was a mistake, she chose to stay with him. Yes, I should have been more compassionate. But what can I say? I was grieving, too—and she'd done nothing all day but make it worse.

When her eyes came back to mine, I jutted my chin in Kent Buckley's direction, and then I said, "You think he's going to let you look after your mom? He didn't even let you out of the house when Max was alive."

Too much.

Too soon.

Tina went rigid. I saw her angry eyes turn to ice. And if I'd thought her voice had ever sounded vicious before, I now realized I hadn't known the meaning of the word. All that rage about her husband she was suppressing? She found a place to release it.

"Get out," she said, like a snake. "Get out of here."

I wasn't sure how to respond.

She stepped closer and her voice was all hiss. "Get out—or I will absolutely fucking lose it right now."

Now the ice in Tina's eyes had turned to fire. Crazy fire. Did I doubt that she would lose it? Did I think she was bluffing?

I did not.

I looked over at Babette—lovely, wise Babette, who was using every micron of strength she had left to hold it together. In the past decade, I knew, she'd lost her parents, a son, and now her husband. Did I want Tina Buckley to make things worse? Did I want to reduce the funeral of Max Kempner—the final punctuation mark on his long and extraordinary life—to a single image of his daughter screaming like a banshee in the courtyard?

No. On all counts.

And so I left.

And that's the story of how I got kicked out of the funeral of my beloved landlord, best-ever boss, and closest thing I'd had in years to a father.

two

Just over a week after the service, Kent Buckley called an all-faculty meeting to "detail our school-wide plan for moving forward."

I guess I should mention that, in addition to being Tina's husband, he was also the chairman of the board of directors at the school. Honestly, I'd almost forgotten, myself—until he called us all in for a meeting by announcing that he was going to name Max's replacement.

Max's replacement?

Um. That would be Babette.

When the king dies, power transfers to the queen, right?

I didn't see why the meeting was necessary.

We gathered in the cafeteria at the appointed time. Babette, normally a front-row lady, took the very last seat in the back row, and sat slumped in a chair, her eyes looking dull, like it was all she could do just to be there.

Alice came up front and plopped into the seat I'd been saving for Babette. She was wearing a shirt that said, I'VE GOT 99 PROBLEMS. *JEALOUS?*

We waited for the meeting to start in an eerie, deflated, heartbroken silence.

Kent Buckley wound up striding in fifteen minutes late, still talking on that damned Bluetooth, and even though he said, "Gotta go—gotta go—I'm taking the stage," and hung up as he turned to stand in front of us, he left the Bluetooth in place on his ear.

I swear: he left it there the whole time.

Then he began. "We've all had a shock. Max's sudden passing was a tragedy. This community is grieving," Kent Buckley said, sounding like he'd just looked all those words up in a thesaurus. He'd contorted his face into such a bad facsimile of sympathy, I couldn't look at him.

He paused dramatically, so we could all feel moved.

"But," he said then, "life has to go on."

I looked around to meet eyes with Babette, but her eyes were trained on Kent Buckley.

"We have an opportunity here to make the most of this . . ."

I could see him mentally searching for a synonym for "tragedy."

"Tragedy," he finished.

Oh, well.

"But we're going to need someone to take us into our next phase. We need someone to step into Max's shoes and lead us forward. And I'm proud to report that I have found that person."

Why all this buildup for Babette? Kent Buckley didn't even like her.

"He's been quite the rising star the past two years in Baltimore."

Wait—what? *He? Baltimore?* I turned to look at Babette. She snapped her eyes to mine, face totally stoic, and gave me a tiny, barely there head shake, like *Don't freak out.*

And then, before I had even turned back to Kent Buckley, I heard him announce to the room the name of Max's replacement.

"The new principal of the Kempner School will be . . . a rising star in the world of independent administration . . . a guy we were unbelievably lucky to get at this late date on such short notice . . ." Kent Buckley paused as if we were all having fun. As if a drumroll might magically come out of nowhere. Then he said, "Duncan Carpenter."

I don't know if Kent Buckley was expecting cheers or clapping or what. But there was just silence. That name was just a name. It didn't mean anything to anybody.

Anybody except me.

I knew that name.

At the sound of it, I stood straight up in the middle of the room.

Just popped right up.

Just . . . *burst* upward, like a reflex. Like a leg at the doctor's office.

But then, unlike a leg, I stayed up—my brain frozen.

Everybody stared at me. Including Kent Buckley, who was not exactly pleased.

There was no universe where Kent Buckley would have been a fan of mine, given that I was his wife's nemesis. But he really, especially detested me ever since the time he'd overheard me calling him a "douchebag" at a school function.

In my defense, he *was* a douchebag, and I bet you nine out of every ten people would pick that exact word. But I guarantee you none of them would say it to his face.

Not even me.

Kent Buckley wanted me to sit back down. That much was clear.

But I couldn't.

The name he'd just spoken was holding me suspended in shock.

"I'm sorry." I shook my head, as if to clear it. "Did you just announce Max's replacement . . . and tell us that it would be . . . that it would be . . ."

I paused at the impossibility of it.

Kent Buckley had zero time for this. "Duncan Carpenter," he repeated, like he was talking to a dumb kid.

So many questions. I didn't know where to start. "Do you mean *the* Duncan Carpenter?"

Kent Buckley frowned. "Is there more than one?"

"That's what I'm asking you."

The whole room was watching. Was this a conversation that needed to happen right now?

Um, yes.

"Tall and lanky?" I asked Kent Buckley then, lifting my hand way above my head. "Sandy hair? Super goofy?"

Kent Buckley's voice was clipped. "No. Not 'super goofy.'"

Maybe we had different definitions of that phrase. I tried to clarify. "Like, wearing crazy golf pants?" I went on. "Or a tie with rubber duckies on it?"

I was on borrowed time. "Just a normal suit," Kent Buckley said.

I paused. *A normal suit. Huh.*

The whole room could tell I was having a moment. I don't know a word, or even a category, for what I felt at the sound of that name, but it was more like a cocktail of emotions than any simple substance. Equal parts horror and ecstasy, with a twist of panic, and a little zest of disbelief—all poured over the cold ice of comprehension about what Kent Buckley's announcement meant for my immediate future.

It wasn't good.

The clock was ticking on everybody's patience—Kent Buckley's the most. Before I could ask another question, he pointed decisively at my seat, like *We're done here.*

I sat. More out of stupefaction than obedience. Then I stayed still, trying to will the adrenaline out of my system.

Could there be more than one Duncan Carpenter in the world? I guessed it was possible. The world was a big place. But . . . more than one Duncan Carpenter in the world of independent elementary education?

Less likely.

The reality of the odds hit me.

Duncan Carpenter was coming here. To my sleepy little town on Galveston Island. To replace my beloved principal and run my beloved school.

The Duncan Carpenter.

"He's a stellar candidate," Kent Buckley continued to the room at last, glad to have his rightful stage back. "An assistant principal that took a nightmare of a school and pulled it together in the course of one year. They counteroffered several times to keep him, but he needed a change of location for personal reasons, and he's ours now. He's going to get in here and shake things up. Give this place the kick in the pants it's needed for so long."

Did our sweet little utopia of a school need a kick in the pants?

No. Not at all.

Of course, we would need somebody to be in charge. But why wasn't it Babette? I guarantee every single teacher in that room would have voted for Babette.

But this was Kent Buckley. He wasn't asking us to vote.

As far as he was concerned, his vote was the only vote that mattered.

Are you wondering how it's possible that Kent Buckley was the chairman of the board even though absolutely nobody liked him? Because, seriously: nobody liked him. Nobody liked his scheming, or his striving, or his ill-informed opinions on "what you people need."

But when I say nobody, I really mean the faculty and the staff.

Let's just say, we weren't charmed by his BMW.

He campaigned hard to get voted chairman, and while Max was alive, it wasn't that much of a job. Max made all the decisions, anyway—and this school was as much a cult of personality as anything else.

Max had known that Kent Buckley's values were not in line with the school's. But he just wasn't too worried about it. "Just let him be the chairman. He wants it so bad."

So they let him be the chairman. And then, less than a year later, Max died on us. And now Kent Buckley, of all people—a guy who had never liked Max, or the school, and who only sent his kid here because it was the one thing his wife had ever insisted on in their entire marriage—was suddenly in charge.

What. The. Hell.

And his first decision was to hire Duncan Carpenter as our new principal.

Which was . . . unexpected.

I would have expected Kent Buckley to hire somebody weaselly and petty, like himself. But he'd hired Duncan Carpenter. *Duncan*

Carpenter. Probably the most Max-like person I'd ever met . . . besides Max himself.

It had to have been a mistake somehow.

In the wake of his announcement, Kent Buckley got some IT guys to project a photo of Duncan Carpenter up on a screen for us all to see. At first, I felt a buzz of relief.

For a half-second, I thought: *Never mind.*

The Duncan Carpenter I'd known had a lopsided smile, and perpetually mussed-up, shaggy hair—and he did something crazy in his official school portrait every year: deely boppers, or a fake punk-rock mohawk, or a giant stick-on mustache. The Duncan Carpenter I'd known had never taken a serious photo in his life. He had an irrepressible streak of joyful, anti-authoritarian naughtiness that he brought to every photo.

Not this guy.

No way was this guy Duncan Carpenter.

This guy had perfectly trimmed hair, styled up in front in a neat, businessman's coif. And a gray suit with a navy tie. And he was just . . . *sitting there.* He wasn't even smiling.

The guy in this photo was a stiff.

But once my eyes adjusted, once I accounted for the missing mop of hair, and the missing Hawaiian-print tie, and the missing mischievous smile, I had to admit . . . the face was essentially a lot like Duncan Carpenter's face. Different, somehow—but the same.

His nose. His eyes. And definitely his mouth.

I felt an electric buzz—part agony, part thrill—at the moment of recognition.

It was him, after all. It was Duncan.

I'd thought I'd never see him again, ever. I'd *planned* to never see him again.

But now there he was.

Sort of. Though he looked so wrong. So unlike himself. He looked like he was in costume. And that was the most likely explanation, actually: that he might really be in costume—that he'd taken a *parody* photo of a hard-ass administrator, and Kent Buckley, in all his humorlessness, had thought it was real.

Because it *couldn't* be real.

"Meet your new principal," Kent Buckley said then to the room. "He knows a thing or two, that's for sure. He starts next week, so you'll have to be ready to hit the ground running when he arrives."

What was this guy even talking about? We didn't take orders from him.

Alice raised her hand. "We all thought Babette was going to take over."

Kent Buckley's eyes flicked over in Babette's direction.

Babette was our art teacher at the school. She was the lady responsible for all the painted tiles in the courtyard. And the mosaic stepping-stones. And the painted lanterns. And the friendship quilt that hung in the office. And pretty much every inch of color or whimsy in the place.

But she wasn't just the art teacher. Max and Babette had been a team of wise and kindly co-parents since the beginning.

"Babette," Kent Buckley declared, "is grieving. She's in no state to run a school."

We all looked over at Babette.

She didn't argue . . . but she didn't agree, either.

For months following that moment, there would be a raging debate among the faculty over why Babette hadn't been given the job. Most people got the sense that Kent Buckley had snubbed her and withheld her rightful position.

The conventional wisdom would become that Kent Buckley had refused to even consider Babette. That her power and devotion from the community was threatening to him. That he'd used technicalities to keep her from her rightful place.

But a second theory would also take root: that *she* had turned *him* down. One look at her confirmed she wasn't doing well. If she'd eaten anything since the funeral, I couldn't tell you what. And her hands, I noticed every day, were still shaking. She was listless and deflated.

Despite all her years of wisdom and strength, looking at her now, it was possible that losing Max was more than she could handle.

Anyway . . . fair or not, right or not, it was happening.

Under Kent Buckley's leadership, we were suddenly about to bring a total stranger into our stunned, lost, grieving school family.

Except—not a total stranger to me.

I stared at the photo while Kent Buckley talked on and on, building up to a genuine rant about how the American school system had gone soft, and how we all needed to toughen up, and how if we weren't careful, these kids were going to be a generation of hippies, nerds, and weaklings.

This to a group of teachers made up exclusively of hippies, nerds, and weaklings.

Yet another reason Kent Buckley was unlikable.

He had no idea how to read a room.

As he brought his rant to a close, and before anyone could respond, or even ask a question, Kent Buckley's Bluetooth rang—and he decided to take the call. He turned his attention back to his ear, announced, "Meeting adjourned," and walked on out of the room, berating whoever was on the other end of his earpiece with, "Dammit, that's not what we told them to do."

What was Kent Buckley's job, again? Some kind of "business." I thought maybe he did commercial real estate. I felt like he built minimalls. How important could that call possibly have been?

But there it was. He was gone. And we were left with a new principal.

In the wake of that moment, nobody moved.

Everybody stayed put, looking around, as the room filled up with murmurs. *What the hell had just happened?* everybody wanted to know—and nobody more than me. I sat still, blinking at the floor, trying to let it all sink in.

Duncan Carpenter was coming here.

My Duncan Carpenter.

And it was, somehow—at the exact same time—both the best and the worst news I'd ever heard.

three

"Who the hell is Duncan Carpenter?" everybody demanded later that night—much later, when we'd gathered in Babette's backyard for an emergency meeting under the bulb lights.

It was both our Friday-night gathering place and the default meeting spot for emergencies and nonemergencies alike—had been for years.

This was, of course, an emergency.

Usually, Babette didn't mind. It was a BYO situation—and people let themselves in and out of the side gate. No trouble at all. It had become a standard gathering, and almost, if I'm honest, a kind of weekly group therapy. With alcohol. Even in the summer.

At this point, Babette couldn't have stopped us if she'd wanted to.

Especially tonight.

I didn't expect her to join us. She'd done almost nothing but sleep since the funeral.

I understood that this was part of the process. I'd lost my mom when I was ten. I wasn't a stranger to grieving, to the way it drowned you but didn't kill you—only kept you submerged for so long you forgot what air and sunshine even felt like. I knew that grief set its own timeline, and that the only way out was through.

I got it.

But she did join us, in the end, and I was so grateful to see her there. We'd all lost Max—but I'd lost them both, in a way.

Max and Babette and I had always been the last ones to leave the iron table in the backyard on Fridays . . . talking, overprocessing school politics, psychoanalyzing the kids and their parents, and spitballing ideas for solving everybody's problems.

They really had been my dearest friends.

Slash mentors.

Slash surrogate parents.

The meeting centered, naturally, on Duncan Carpenter, and how nobody'd even heard of him, and what was the deal with that overly serious photo, and didn't we get any say at all in the hiring process, and what was happening, and *why the hell wasn't it Babette taking over?*

"Kent Buckley's not wrong," Babette said. "I'm hardly in a fit state to take over the school."

But who was this new guy? And why hadn't anyone been consulted? And what kind of psychotic break had I experienced in the meeting today?

So I told them everything I could confess to publicly. "We used to work together," I explained, "in California, at Andrews Prep—my last school before I came here. He was a teacher then—fourth grade and gym—and he was . . . kind of a legend. Everybody loved him. I'm telling you, he was something really, really special. He was Max-like."

I glanced over at Babette.

She gave a nod, like *It's okay. Go on.*

"He just had a warmth about him. He was funny and goofy and crazy. He was playful. He was hilarious. Kids followed him around. Hell, *adults* followed him around."

Emily Aguilo from the second-grade team said, "Why would Kent Buckley hire a guy like that? That's not Kent Buckley's thing. He just lectured us for an hour on how this school needs to toughen up."

I shrugged. "Maybe he doesn't realize?"

Carlos Trenton, our hipster science teacher with a beard long enough that he could braid it, said, "No way is Kent Buckley paying any attention to this guy's teaching philosophy."

We all agreed. Kent Buckley had no interest in pedagogical theory. He cared about one thing: status. If Duncan was a rising star, and he'd poached him from another school, then Kent Buckley was happy.

But that's when Donna Raswell, who'd had Clay in the second grade last year, jumped in: "Kent Buckley pays attention to everything. I've never met a bigger control freak in my life. He counts the pencils in his kid's pencil bag."

I shook my head. "He may pay attention—but not to the right things."

"But why would he hire another principal like Max?" a kindergarten teacher asked. "He's been trying to undermine Max from the minute Clay started in kindergarten."

Carlos actually snorted. "Unsuccessfully."

True. Max had viewed Kent Buckley as an annoying, ankle-biting dog that he had to shake off his pants cuff from time to time.

But one he couldn't get rid of entirely. Because of Tina. And Clay.

In truth, we all knew Kent Buckley would have no interest in our hippie school if his kid didn't happen to be a student. And his kid never would have become a student if his wife hadn't wanted their child to attend the school founded by her parents. And so now Kent Buckley was forced to watch his son attend a school that, in his opinion, was doing everything all wrong.

And it wasn't Kent Buckley's way to just *let* people disagree with him.

So while Max dying was a crushing loss for everybody else, for Kent Buckley it was—as he'd kind of confessed in the meeting today . . . an opportunity.

Right now, with everybody reeling, if Kent Buckley could stay focused and push through a new head of school more to his liking, he could impact how things were done around here for years to come.

And so he'd moved quickly, and quietly—and he'd brought in someone new before we could focus enough to protest.

But the joke was on Kent Buckley. He had just accidentally done the opposite of what he'd meant to: he'd hired a new principal almost exactly like the old one.

A part of me had to be happy about it. Given our sudden, unbelievable situation, Duncan Carpenter was a stroke of impossible luck. Bringing him here would be the best possible thing for the school.

Even though, given my history with him, it might well be the worst possible thing for me.

Later, after Babette had gone to bed, and most folks had gone home, as I rinsed cans and bottles for recycling at the kitchen sink, Alice leaned against the counter and said, "What's going on, Sam?"

Her shirt today said, GRAPHING IS WHERE I DRAW THE LINE.

Even though Alice was a year younger than me—twenty-seven— she was also six inches taller than me, and so she had a big-sisterly vibe. She was engaged to her college sweetheart, Marco, who was in the navy and went on long deployments. They rented a little 1920s bungalow a few blocks down. When he was gone, I saw a lot of her—and when he was here, I saw almost nothing of her.

Fair enough.

He had shipped out a week before Max died, and though I wouldn't want to say I was glad Alice was alone these days, let's just say I was grateful to have a friend.

She knew me pretty well. Well enough to know something more was up than I'd confessed to the group.

"So," she said, like she'd been waiting all night for all the other bozos to leave. "What did you leave out?"

I met her eyes, and I said, "Duncan Carpenter is the Guy."

"What guy?"

I pursed my lips and leaned in to intensify my look. Then I said slowly, "*The* Guy."

Alice frowned a second, then said, in recognition, "*The Guy?*"

I gave an unmistakable nod, like *Bingo.*

"*The* the Guy? The one who drove you out of California?"

"I beg your pardon. I drove myself."

"But he's the one from your old school? That you were obsessed with?"

"Not *obsessed.*"

Alice squinted at me. "Pretty obsessed."

"It was not an obsession. It was a healthy, red-blooded American crush."

Now Alice was trying to remember. It had been a while—a lifetime, really—since we'd talked about it. "Didn't you snoop in his diary?"

"I wasn't snooping, I was feeding his cat while he was out of town."

"But you read his diary."

"Well, he left it lying open on the kitchen table. You could argue that on some unconscious level, he *wanted* me to read it."

Alice gave me a second to decide if I could stand by that statement.

"Plus," I went on, "it wasn't a diary. It was just a notebook."

"A notebook full of private thoughts."

"We all have private thoughts, Alice," I said, as if that was somehow a good point.

"You shouldn't have taken that cat-sitting job in the first place," she said.

"What was I supposed to do? Let his cat starve? It was declawed and missing a tail."

"It wasn't even his cat. It was the girlfriend's cat."

"I didn't know that at the time."

Alice gave me a look then that was part affection, part scolding, and part *Give me a break.*

Anyway, there was no point in continuing the denials. She knew the whole story. I *had* read his notebook that day all those years ago while he was on vacation in wine country about to get engaged—or that was the rumor anyway. And I hadn't just read the one page that was facing up on the table, either. I had grabbed a pair of kitchen tongs from the drawer—as if *not touching the pages with my fingers* somehow made it less awful—and used them to turn every single page, searching for clues to his soul like some kind of love-struck Sherlock Holmes, and careful, like a crazy person, not to leave any fingerprints.

What can I say? It was a low point.

A very low point.

And, actually, it became a turning point.

Before that moment back then, I'd been infatuated with Duncan Carpenter for two solid years. Big-time infatuated. Hard-core infatuated. Infatuated the way teenage girls get infatuated with pop stars. If he'd had song lyrics, I'd have memorized them; if he'd had merch, I'd have bought it; and if he'd had a fan club, I'd have been the president.

Of course, he wasn't a pop star.

But he was, you know . . . a celebrity of sorts. In the world of private, secondary-school education. In our tiny little sliver of humanity, he was a big deal. He was the pop icon of our teaching colleagues, for sure.

And for good reason.

He had a big, friendly smile filled with big, friendly teeth. He was handsome without trying. He had a magnetic quality that was almost physical. If he was in a room with other humans in it for any amount of time, there'd be a group of them gathered around him by the end. He emitted some kind of sunshine that we all wanted to soak up.

Me included.

Me especially.

But I was terrible around him. I was the worst possible version of myself. All the longing and desire and electricity and joy I felt whenever he was anywhere near me seemed to scramble my system. I'd freeze, and get quiet and still and self-conscious, and stare at him, unblinking, like a weirdo.

It was uncomfortable, to say the least.

When I'd first met him, he was single—and he stayed that way for one long, beautiful, possibility-infused year as I tried to work up the nerve to sit at his table at lunch. A year that slipped by fast, and then suddenly, before I'd made any progress—*boom!*—a perky new girl from the admissions office just brazenly asked him out.

Their assigned parking spots were next to each other, apparently.

It was front-page teacher news, and the grade-school faculty were by and large offended. Wasn't it a little *uppity* to just swoop in and start dating whoever she wanted?

Apparently not.

Soon, they were exclusive, and then they were serious, and then, barely a year to the day after she'd first asked him out, they were moving in together. Rumor had it she'd been the one to ask him. A move I would've admired for feminist reasons if it had been any other couple at all.

The consensus among the female teachers was that she was too conventional, too small-minded, and too ordinary to be a good match for him—mostly because he was the opposite of all those things.

Frankly, I agreed—but I also knew my opinion was based largely on one short interaction, when, awkwardly trying to make chitchat at a school function, I'd said to her, "Admissions! That must be tough! How do you make all those agonizing decisions?"

And she just blinked at me and said, "It's just whoever has the most money."

Then, reading my shocked expression, she shifted to a laugh and said, "I'm kidding."

But was she, though?

Nobody was sure she deserved him.

Of course . . . it didn't follow that I *did*.

I couldn't even say hi to him in the elevator.

Anyway, it was not five minutes after I'd heard the moving-in-together news—from a librarian who'd heard it from a math teacher who'd heard it from the school nurse—that, as I was making my way outside to gulp some fresh air . . . he asked me to cat-sit.

I'd just rounded the corner of the hallway, and there he was. Wearing a tie with dachshunds all over it.

"Hey," he said.

"Hey," I said, panicking at the way he'd . . . just materialized.

Then, of all things, he said, "I've heard you're a cat person."

A cat person? Nope. But, not wanting to kill the conversation, I shrugged and said, "I'm more of a dog person, actually."

He blinked at me.

"I mean," I went on, feeling like I'd said the wrong thing. "I'm not *opposed* to cats . . ."

"Don't you have a bunch of them?"

"Um. Nope."

He frowned.

"I don't have any cats," I added, just to be clear. "At all."

"Huh. Somebody told me you had like three cats."

Wow. The only thing he knew about me . . . and it was wrong. Or maybe he thought I was somebody else entirely.

He looked as disappointed as I felt.

I reminded myself to breathe.

"I don't *dislike* cats," I said then, to cheer him up. "I don't wish them harm or anything. I'm just . . . neutral."

He nodded. "Got it." Then he started to turn away.

"Wait!" I said. "Why?"

He paused. "I'm looking for a cat sitter. For the weekend. Just one night, actually."

And then, truly, without even considering how pathetic it would be for me to be cleaning the litter boxes of my true love while he was off on a romantic weekend with his new live-in girlfriend, I said, "I'll do it."

"Really?"

"Sure. No problem at all."

Next thing I knew, there I was in his apartment, snooping—and doing unspeakable things with his kitchen tongs.

So what was I looking for, exactly, as I tong-flipped those pages in that notebook? What could I possibly have been hoping to find? Some note-to-self that he didn't really want to be with the woman he'd just decided to live with? Some daydream doodle of a face that looked remarkably like mine? Some secret code only I could break that spelled out H-E-L-P M-E?

Ridiculous.

Anyway, there was nothing like that.

There were grocery lists. Reminders. A half-written letter to his mom. A circled note to get his baby niece a one-year birthday present, with the words "baby biker jacket" scratched out and replaced with: "Something cool." Doodles (mostly 3-D boxes), and to-do lists, and a whole bunch of tally marks on the cardboard of the back cover. Nothing special, or memorable, or even private. The normal detritus of a perfectly not unhappy life that had nothing at all to do with me.

And that's when, flipping the pages back into position, a very important word came into my head: "Enough."

I heard it almost as clearly as if I'd said it out loud. And then I did say it out loud.

"Enough."

Then I shook my head. I couldn't keep living like this—stealing glances, brushing past him in the hallways, sitting near—but not too near—his table at lunch, pausing to watch him leading kindergarten dance parties on the playground. Yearning.

Enough.

I had to shut it down. He'd chosen somebody else. It was time to move on.

And even though I did not always, or even often, follow the life advice I gave myself—on that day I did. I put the tongs back in the drawer, walked out, locked the door, drove straight home, and got on the Web to start looking for a new job.

Anyway, that was how I'd ended up in Texas, of all places—though that was how almost everybody wound up in Texas: *love or money.*

I'd come to this island by chance, but I'd found a real home here, way down at the bottom of the country in this wind-battered, historic town. I loved the painted Victorian houses with their carpenter Gothic porches. I loved the brick cobblestone streets and the tourist T-shirt shops. I loved the muddy, soft sand and the easy waves of the Gulf lapping the shore. I loved how the town was both humble and proud, both battered and resilient, both exhausted and bursting with energy, both historic and endlessly reinventing itself.

Most of all, I loved our school. My job. The life I'd built.

A post-Duncan Carpenter life that—really—the Guy himself had no place in.

"What are the odds?" I said to Alice, turning on the kettle for tea. "That of all the people in the world Kent Buckley could have hired . . . he picked *him*?"

"Do you really want me to calculate the odds?" Alice asked.

"Maybe not," I said.

But Alice was off and running. "Challenge accepted! There are a multitude of variables to consider here. You've gotta take the square root of the independent schools in the Southeast and then factor in the ones with administrators looking to make a sudden move right before the start of the school year, and then solve for the X-Y axis."

For half a second I thought she was being serious.

She went on, with a slight smile peeking through her deadpan expression. "It's basically the same equation you use for escape velocity for the gravitational field. Minus alpha and omega, of course. Times pi."

"I feel like I'm being teased."

"I've seen that photo of him," she concluded, now openly grinning. "Once you factor in the slope of that jawline, the coefficient there just skews the whole curve."

I flared my nostrils at her. "Thanks so much for your help."

"He does have a good jawline."

I sighed. "Doesn't he?"

The thing was, it seemed like such a shallow thing to fret about—especially in light of what Babette was going through. So an old crush was coming back to haunt me. Big deal.

"I guess the odds don't really matter now," I said next. "It happened."

"Atta girl," she said.

"You see my point, though," I said. "It puts me in a very strange situation."

Alice studied my face. "I can't tell if you're devastated or thrilled."

"I am ninety-nine percent devastated and one percent thrilled," I said. "But it feels like the other way around." You'd think those two feelings might cancel each other out, but they just seemed to amplify each other.

Alice nodded. "So . . . you are devastated because . . . ?"

"Because! Because I have a history with this person, even if he doesn't know it. A history that I'd done a pretty competent job of dealing with and moving on from, only to find it boomeranging back at me with no warning. He was the entire reason I left my old school—it was *one hundred percent* to get away from him—and now he's coming here. *Here.* I can already see how this story ends. He'll drive me away from here, too. And then I'll have to get a new job someplace far away and I'll have to start all over—again—but I know no new school could be as awesome as this one, so that means I'm doomed to spend the rest of my life in exile, pining for—this place, my friends, everything."

"I guess that's one possible scenario," Alice said.

I leaned down and banged my forehead against the table. "I don't want him to take my home away from me."

Alice frowned. "You think he's going to fire you because you had a crush on him a million years ago?"

"I don't think he's going to fire me," I said. "I just think he'll make me so miserable I have to quit."

"You think he's going to be mean to you?"

"No," I said, feeling my body sink in defeat. "I think he's going to be nice to me."

Alice tilted her head, like *Huh?*

"I think he's going to be really nice," I explained. "Too nice. Totally irresistibly nice."

She lifted her head, like *Got it.* "You think the crush is going to wash back over you."

"Like a tsunami."

"So you think it's going to be the same situation as before."

"But worse. Because now they'll be married and have like forty kids and the life I wanted so badly but was too chicken to try for will parade itself around endlessly until it breaks me."

Very gently, Alice said, "Maybe it'll shake down some other way."

But I'd accepted my despair. "No. That's it. That's what'll happen."

But Alice wasn't giving up. "So what if he's married now? So what if he's got a whole litter of kids? That could work in your favor! You'll hardly see him. He'll be exhausted. He won't be drinking beers out in Babette's backyard, that's for sure."

"It doesn't matter," I said, shrugging. "I'll see him enough. A little goes a long way."

An image appeared in my head of Duncan in the courtyard of our school, wearing a pair of his crazy pants—maybe the red ones with lobsters—surrounded by a crowd of cheering kids while he juggled beach balls.

"You look sick," Alice said, watching me.

"I feel sick," I said. And that's when I noticed it was true. Of all the equilibrium-shaking things that had happened lately, this one was throwing me off the most.

"Maybe it won't be as bad as you think," she said. "Maybe he'll show up here and you won't feel anything. Crushes fade all the time. It's been years. Maybe he'll seem middle-aged and unappealing. Maybe he'll have sprouted a bunch of hair on his ears. Or maybe, like, one of his teeth turned weirdly brown. Or"—she brightened, like this was her best idea yet—"maybe he has really bad breath now!"

"Maybe," I said, but really just to be polite.

"I'm just saying," Alice said, "that photo in the meeting was not exactly irresistible."

I couldn't explain the photo. "Yeah," I said. "But it didn't capture him."

"Let's hope not," Alice said.

"You're going to love him," I promised, "despite yourself. We all are. You can't not love him. On hot days, he used to bring squirt guns to car pool. He invented Hat Day. He started a pancake-eating contest. He talked the kids into doing a terrible flash mob on the playground. One time, he rented a cotton-candy machine without telling anyone and put it in the cafeteria. On the last day of the school year every year, he'd wear a purple velvet tuxedo to class, and then he'd take off for the summer in a limousine."

"Okay," Alice conceded. "Fine. He's got *joie de vivre*."

"He's got it," I said, "and he shares it. You can't be around him without catching some."

"So that'll be . . . good for the school."

"Not just good—*great*," I said. "It'll be *great*. For the school."

Alice nodded and finished my thought. "And it'll be kind of awful for you."

"The irony is," I said, "after I moved away, I regretted it. I missed him so much after I was gone. I used to fantasize all kinds of reasons to see him again. I used to long for a reason to be around him."

"Exactly," Alice said, like she really got it. "Be careful what you wish for."

I nodded. Then the kitchen fell quiet, and we stared at our half-drunk tea mugs.

And in that little pause, I realized some other worst-possible-bad news for me. I did feel sick. Physically sick. Sitting in Babette's kitchen talking about Duncan Carpenter was making me nauseated.

But not just any kind of nauseated. A very particular kind. The kind of nauseated that can mean something's going on neurologically. The kind of nauseated that I sometimes got . . . when I was on the verge of having a seizure.

Which happened from time to time.

Occasionally. Once or twice a year.

Fine. I'll just say it. I have epilepsy.

Mild epilepsy.

A touch of epilepsy.

Just enough to know for sure, as I sat there and felt all the sensations inside my body, that I was having an aura.

Which is actually a type of seizure in itself—it just doesn't feel like one.

I felt the nausea gather in my stomach like storm clouds. I sat up a little straighter and I pushed back my chair from the table an inch or two.

Alice noticed. "You okay?"

"I just feel a little . . . off," I said.

"Are you having an aura?"

Alice was one of the very few people who knew.

I made an O with my lips and blew out a controlled, frustrated sigh, and said, "Probably." Like *Of course. Of course this is happening.*

Stress was a risk factor. Ironically.

I'd had it bad as a kid—really bad. Bad enough that my third-grade best friend had disinvited me from her birthday party after witnessing a particularly bad one in the cafeteria. Then it had gone away in middle school—and stayed gone for so long, I thought I was cured.

But then, not long after I moved here, it came back.

Just a mild case. Not bad, really, in the bigger picture. I tried to remember that. But just . . . the idea of it? The knowledge that it was back? That a seizure *could* happen at any moment? Knowing that I wasn't cured? That I was still the same person who might get uninvited to a sleepover?

It was enough to shift my whole conception of myself.

But that wasn't something I talked about—ever, if I could help it. It was just something I carried around like a little ice cube of fear in my chest.

And so Alice attacked the symptoms over the cause. "Maybe you should start dating someone."

"Dating someone?" I asked.

"You know. Preventatively."

"Who?" I demanded. "Raymond the security guard?"

"What about that guy in IT with the earlobe rings?"

"Earlobe rings are a deal-breaker for me."

"What about that guy Bruce who does tutoring?"

"He's married to the girl who runs the coffee shop on Post Office Street."

"Didn't the new fifth-grade science teacher just get divorced?"

"Oh, my God, Alice!" I shrieked. "He's, like, *forty*!"

Alice didn't endorse the hysterics. "You'll be forty someday."

"In *twelve years*."

"The point is," Alice went on, "if you could just fall in love with somebody—anybody—real quick, then your heart would be too happy to care about any of this."

"I'm no expert on love," I said. "But I don't think that's how it works."

It was preposterous. I hadn't dated anyone since the seizures came back. Partly, yes, because the pickings on the island were slim. But also, I liked stability. More than that, I *needed* stability. Especially now. Stasis. Routine. Even if it were possible to "fall in love with somebody real quick," this particular moment of emotional chaos would be the worst possible time to choose. Plus—and I had never admitted this to anyone, maybe not even to myself—I'd already given up.

Because there was a persistent, unanswered question at the center of my life. One that had come back into my head when the seizures returned. One I didn't even fully realize I kept asking. One I wasn't sure I even wanted to answer.

Who could love me now?

I'd never even thought it in words, much less said it out loud.

And I wasn't going to start today.

four

I did not have a seizure that night—or the next night, or the next.

Sometimes they threaten but never come.

But they sure can sharpen your focus. In the wake of it, I just tried to settle, and adjust, and *not have a seizure*.

So much easier said than done. Especially when you start stressing about the fact that you aren't managing to de-stress.

The truth was, I had more to do than it was possible to get done. I hadn't worked in the library all summer. Not since Max died, for sure— but even before that, when I'd been so happily planning his party, thinking I'd get to my cataloguing later. Then, after the funeral, I'd fussed over Babette: organizing the service, doing her laundry, baking her blueberry muffins that she never ate, watering her garden, and stacking the unread condolence cards in alphabetical order.

Summer was my time to get organized: to catch up and to plan ahead. But this summer, I hadn't done either. And now summer was almost over.

So: No more messing around. It was time to handle it all—the shock, the grief, the dread, the anticipation, the anxiety—the old-fashioned way: like a workaholic.

Convenient. Because I really did have a ton of work.

It takes long hours and late nights to gear up for the start of a school year, even in a normal year—cataloging all our new books, stamping them (I'm a title-page and edge-of-the-pages stamper), bar-coding them, wrapping the jackets in plastic covers, and getting them all on the shelves. Plus: decorating, organizing, lesson planning, Marie Kondo-ing my cabinets, checking in on teachers' upcoming lesson plans, and stocking books to tie in with study units and book reports. It's a lot of planning, but it's also a lot of physical work, and it can only go so fast.

I'm always astonished at the number of people who think I just "hang out" in the library all day. Not to mention the number who think all I do is read. Plus, of course, the kids—who literally think I live there.

Like, they think it's my actual home.

I do read—constantly—but not during the workday. During the workday, I'm helping kids find the books they need and then teaching them self-checkout. I'm teaching classes on how to find books, and how to be good library citizens, and why stories are important. I'm reading books to every grade level, even the big kids. I'm training volunteers to help restock the shelves, and poring over catalogs to find new books for the library, and weeding old books from the stacks. Plus: lunch duty, faculty meetings, author visits, planning classes, and let's not forget, in the spring, countless hours of inventory.

It's more work than people think it is.

It's more work than even I think it is.

Plus, this year, I'd bought—with my own money—a multicolored hanging sculpture made up of brightly painted recycled bicycle parts. It had looked so soothing on the website where I'd found it, and I'd gotten mesmerized by a video of it gently spinning . . . but when the box arrived, and I saw the random bags of at least a hundred pieces to assemble—I'd closed it again right away.

Nope. Never mind.

It was going to take me a million hours to put together, at minimum.

As far as my to-do list went, assembling that sculpture would have to be dead last.

Workaholism worked and it didn't work at the same time.

In the abstract, when I think of "de-stressing," I think of bubble baths, and page-turning novels, and naps under fuzzy blankets—and the truth was, I didn't have time for any of that. But chipping away at all my piled-up work did have a stress-reducing effect, and not only because I felt a little less panicked with each to-do item I scratched off: it kept me from looking at the big picture. It kept me from thinking about the past, and it kept me from trying to imagine the future, and it let me stay focused on whatever tiny next step was right in front of me.

There is something comforting about tunneling down your focus like that. It was kind of a can't-see-the-forest-for-the-trees effect. And in certain moments of relief, I forgot about the forest entirely.

Which is how, the night before our first scheduled faculty meeting with Duncan, Alice was able to shock me like she did. I knew it was Sunday—but I'd just kind of lost track for a little bit of which Sunday it was.

I was walking over to the grocery store to stock up for the week, when I got this pretty standard text from Alice: "Great news!"

"What???" I texted back.

"I thought of the title for my autobiography."

"Thank God!"

"I know, right?"

"What is it????"

"Do the math."

"Please never tell me to do math."

"No! That's the title!"

"???"

"*Do the Math: The Alice Brouillard Story.*"

"Ah."

"Perfect, right? I'm going to make it my catchphrase, too."

"You have always needed a catchphrase."

"Agreed. And thanks in advance."

"For?"

"Being my ghostwriter."

All fairly standard texting for Alice and me. We threw in a few GIFs, too, and then just when I thought we were done, I got one last *ding*, and Alice added, "Can't wait to meet the Guy tomorrow!"

And that's when I dropped the phone.

Tomorrow. It was suddenly about to be *tomorrow*. As in *the* tomorrow. The one I'd been dreading so hard I'd lost track of time. The one where I would see Duncan Carpenter again, for better or for worse, as I stepped—willingly or not—into the rest of my life.

I couldn't believe it.

It just didn't seem possible.

None of it seemed possible, in fact.

De-stress, I reminded myself. *De-stress*.

But it was good timing. I always found grocery stores pleasantly anesthetizing.

I grabbed a cart and took deep breaths as I curved my way around the magazines and mass-market paperbacks, then up and down the aisles. I considered buying a beach towel with unicorns all over it—on sale for $7.99. Did I need a blender? A coffee grinder? A new muffin tin?

I had only managed to put one thing in my cart—the most essential of all essentials: coffee—when, suddenly, I saw him.

Duncan Carpenter.

He was here. Just like that. In my grocery store.

I caught a glimpse—one glimpse—of him walking past the far end of the aisle, and it was enough to make me drop down into a squat, hiding behind my cart.

Slowly, every sense on high alert, I stood back up, and pushed my cart to the edge of the aisle where I'd just seen him, and peeked around the corner.

There he was, at the far end of the wide center aisle, in a white oxford shirt and gray suit pants, striding along with his cart like it was no big deal. Like it was totally normal. Like people named Duncan

Carpenter just . . . wandered around grocery stores in Galveston all the time.

Yep. Definitely him.

I couldn't see his face, but I'd know that walk anywhere: the way his legs swung forward and his feet struck the ground. I know you're thinking, *Yeah. That's how walking works*. But the point is, I knew his particular way of doing it. The angles, the rhythm, the sway. I recognized it. Some things had changed, but the essentials were the same. The posture, the gait, the back of the head: all Duncan. I glanced a little farther down.

Yep: confirmation on the butt, too.

With that came a jolt of panic.

I wasn't ready. I couldn't do this.

I had to get out of here.

I'd been working in the library all day, wrapping book jackets in plastic and cataloging on the computer, and then I'd gone straight to Babette's and made a splattery mess of pasta and tomato sauce for her dinner—much of which was on my shirt—and then I'd stayed to do dishes. My eyes were tired, and puffy, and my shoulders were tight. I hadn't showered that morning, I knew that for sure—and now I couldn't even remember if I'd put on deodorant. Or brushed my hair.

Nope. This was not the time to meet Duncan Carpenter. Again.

I had to get out of there.

I bent low behind my cart and started following him, figuring it was better to keep him in my sights as I moved toward the checkout aisles. All mindless shopping was now forgotten. He was here! On the island! *My* island! In my grocery store, of all places!

I can't tell you how shocking it was to see him. Looking back, I should have just abandoned the coffee and slipped off into the night.

But I actually was out of coffee. Something I couldn't face the start of school without.

I didn't want to look directly at him, for fear he might feel it and turn around, so I looked at a spot a few inches to his right, and I kept my eyes there until he took a left at the frozen foods, and I hooked a right into the first available checkout aisle. Then I waited while the clerk scanned a stack of what had to be every single frozen dinner in the place for an old man on a walker.

Should I have had compassion for the old man? Of course.

Was it likely he was a widower, now fending for himself after losing the love of his life—the way Babette was? Or possibly doing a weekly shop for some pals who just needed sustenance? Or maybe he was ill, and microwave meals were all he could accomplish? Everybody had a story. But I didn't have time for sympathy. I had to get out of there. I stood behind him impatiently—actually, literally tapping my toe—as the frozen boxes glitched the bar-code scanner again and again, my anxiety rising.

Can I just add that the clerk was about as sharp as a marble? He didn't think—or didn't know how—to manually enter the item numbers, and so when the scanner didn't beep, he'd just scan it again, and again, and again. Then he'd wipe the scanner off with his shirt hem, or blow on it, or talk to it in a stern voice.

Seven thousand frozen dinners later, I wanted to bang my head against the conveyor belt. But I held still. Absolutely still. Because it was just as the old man was finally all rung up and counting out his exact change—in ones and nickels, for the love of God—that I heard a cart rolling up behind me. Heard it, and then felt it—because it slammed into my butt.

"Whoa. I'm sorry," the pusher of the cart said, now just feet behind me.

Duncan Carpenter.

I hadn't heard that voice in over four years, but I knew it in an instant.

When I'd identified his gait in the aisle, I'd been 90 percent sure it was him. When I'd taken a glancing ogle at his butt, I'd bumped the percentage to 99. And now, with the voice, we could make it an even 100. It was him. No doubt. No wiggle room. There was not even the slightest possibility that here, in my sauce-splattered shirt, I'd just been butt-bumped by someone else.

I only knew one thing in that moment.

I wasn't turning around.

I would leave my coffee behind before I'd turn around. I'd shove that old man on the walker out of the way before I'd turn around. I would get down on my hands and knees and crawl my way out to the parking lot before I'd turn around.

When I didn't respond to "I'm sorry," he tried again with, "Didn't quite hit the brakes fast enough."

Guess what I wasn't going to do? Turn around.

I just lifted my hand and flicked it, like *Whatever*.

Then I stood there. And just ignored him.

When it was time to pay for my one can of coffee, I didn't even turn—just faced straight ahead, only shifting my eyes sideways to acknowledge the clerk—and as soon as he'd rung me up, I snaked my arm around the coffee tub, flicked a five-dollar bill at the clerk, and hightailed it out of there.

"What about your change?" the clerk called after me.

"Keep it," I called back, without even turning my head, as I blew past the little old man.

Outside, on the sidewalk, I leaned against a post for a second, then I kept staggering on like some kind of fugitive—ready to get myself the hell home before anything else had a chance to happen.

One block away, as the panic subsided, it hit me at last.

This was happening. This was really happening.

Duncan Carpenter was moving here—had already moved here.

It was real. I was going to have to go to work every day and see him. I was going to run into him on the beach, and walking around town, and, as we now knew for certain, at the grocery store.

Of course he'd be married now to that dull admissions lady from Andrews. Of course he'd have a family. How many kids would they've had time for in all these years? Three? Four? A gaggle, at the minimum. Possibly a flock. Of course, of course. He'd be a great dad—carrying them around on his shoulders and giving them airplane rides. And she'd have organized all the kids' activities on a color-coded family calendar. She'd be a reliable cook, and she'd have exactly one glass of wine every night with dinner . . . and she would take all her blessings for granted.

I thought of all the school functions where I'd have to look at them, being adorable. At her, good-naturedly tolerating his antics as he walked on his hands, or juggled hot dogs, or fired up a karaoke machine at the back-to-school faculty picnic.

Before I knew it, what had started as an attempt to lean in to the inevitable gave way to a sting of dread so acute I found myself walking faster, like I was trying to get away from myself. Just the idea of it . . . of being trapped there with them, endlessly bearing witness to their familial bliss as my life fell so tragically short by comparison on every single count . . .

Oh, God. It was going to be worse than I'd thought.

I had escaped him before. I had given everything up, and moved away, and built a new life. A good life. And now, walking—or maybe more and more like *stomping*—back, I resented the hell out of Duncan Carpenter for blithely just coming here and ruining it all. And Kent Buckley, for that matter—for hiring him. And Max, too, while I was at it—for leaving us in this situation to begin with.

By the time I'd made it back to the carriage house, there was no escape.

This was my life.

Now, all I could see ahead was misery, as Duncan charmed everybody and filled Max's shoes as our new favorite guy. Duncan everywhere. Every day. Forever. What would that do to me? Would I wilt? Would I collapse? Would I turn bitter and desiccated and small?

And then it just seemed clear: something had to give.

I may not have had a choice about what Duncan Carpenter did, or Kent Buckley, or even Max. But that didn't mean I didn't have any choices at all.

I didn't have to stay here, passively waiting until the situation became too excruciating to bear. I didn't have to stand still while my life crumbled away around me. I could do something, could leave sooner rather than later. Skip over the worst of the worst—and fast-forward to the part where I got to start feeling better.

That felt like a great idea.

I could leave.

I didn't want to leave my life. But I didn't want to *have it taken from me* even more.

And that settled it.

Given my choices, this idea looked pretty good. I'd put myself out of my own misery. I'd go into school tomorrow, sit through Duncan Carpenter's introductory meeting, follow him back to his office. And then I'd take my future into my own hands . . . and I'd quit.

It was the most heartbreaking good idea I'd ever had.

But there it was: problem solved.

five

It felt like a great idea at the time.

It felt like a great idea the next morning, even, when I woke up by accident two hours before my alarm.

Just—*ding*—woke up.

I wasn't powerless. I didn't have to go into work every day as the misery of unrequited love embalmed the joy out of me.

I'd just resign—like a boss.

People did it all the time.

Of course, I'd never abandon my kids at the library. I'd stay until a suitable replacement could be found. And, of course, in the bigger picture, quitting was the worst-case scenario because it meant giving up my entire life here. But I wasn't looking at the big picture. I was looking at this one part of it: Did I want to be powerless—or take charge of my own destiny?

Distilled down to that one question, the answer was easy.

And easy answers always feel good.

The idea of escape unclenched my heart and just pumped relief through my body. I had choices. None of them were particularly *good* choices . . . but that was beside the point.

I'd start over. Not impossible. I'd done it before, and I could do it again.

I'd start looking for school-library positions in adorable small towns. Maybe Babette would even come with me. She could probably use an escape, too. And if Babette was going, Alice might come. Hell, we could start a whole new utopia in a historic fishing village in Maine, or a forgotten ghost town in Colorado.

There was no going back to sleep now. I sat up in bed and flipped on the light. It was still dark as night outside.

I felt better. And not just better: *invigorated*.

I was taking back my life.

Now all I had to do was just endure seeing Duncan again for a little while. How long could that meeting possibly last? An hour? I'd grit my teeth for one hour, and then I'd set myself free.

I'd made my decision. The hard part was over.

Though I still had one decision left: what to wear.

It's a big deal to see someone you were once in love with again after so many years—for anybody. But for me it would be an extra-big deal.

Because I had changed so much.

When we'd worked together before, I'd been mousy. By choice. I'd been . . . hiding. But I wasn't hiding anymore. Now, in fact, I did the opposite.

That first seizure I'd had after my epilepsy came back?

I'd been *driving* when it happened.

I'd crashed my car into the side of a 7-Eleven.

I'd wound up in the hospital with a broken arm, a black eye, sixteen stitches across the top of my head, and a bald patch where they'd had to shave it.

No one else was hurt, thank God . . . but I hadn't set foot inside a 7-Eleven since.

After the accident, on the morning when it was time to go back to school, I just couldn't. I got all dressed, and I worked to cover my bruised eye with makeup, and I put on a little gray stocking cap to cover my bandage. Then I put my satchel on my shoulder, picked up my car keys, caught my reflection in the mirror . . . and started crying.

I was still crying after second period when Max called to see why the library was still dark.

I wound up taking a personal day, but that night he showed up at the carriage house with a present for me: a hat covered all over with tissue-paper flowers.

"This is certainly . . . very bright," I said.

"It's Babette's," Max said. "I asked her if I could give it to you."

I let Max in, and we sat on my sofa. I could not even imagine what I would do with a Technicolor flower hat like that. I didn't know what to say. "It's really got . . . a lot of flowers."

"I think you should wear it to school tomorrow," Max said.

I eyed the hat, not wanting to be rude. "It's . . . a little bolder than my normal look."

"Yes, it is," Max said. "And that's why you'll spend the whole day talking about the flowers, rather than talking about the seizure."

I nodded. I got it. "Or the stitches."

He gave a little shrug. "Or the 7-Eleven."

I studied the hat a little longer.

"What's your hesitation?" Max asked.

"Have you ever seen me wear anything like this?"

"Flowers are very joyful," Max said.

"I'm not really feeling joyful."

"Yeah," Max said. "That's what the flowers are for."

I shook my head at the flower hat. "I'm just not sure I can pull this off."

"Just give it a try," Max said, nodding at it, like *Go on*.

And so, gently—as much for the paper flowers as for my stitches—I put it on and turned toward the mirror, and suddenly, I didn't look like a sad, frightened, disappointed, relapsed person who had almost just died in a car accident of her own making. I looked like I was headed out for a parade.

And then I burst into tears again.

I couldn't even have told you exactly why.

Because of everything. Because my stitches hurt. And because I missed my mom. And because I didn't want to go back to school—ever. And because after well over a decade of being cured, I suddenly wasn't cured anymore. But also because of the unrepentant beauty of those paper flowers. And Max's kindness. And that stunning, ridiculous, marvelous hat.

He put his arm around me and just let me cry. Just stayed right there until I'd run out of tears. And then, when I finally quieted, he said, "I want to tell you something smart I've figured out about life."

"Okay," I said.

"And I want you to make a mental note, 'cause this is a good one."

"Okay."

"Ready?"

Now I was smiling. "Yes!"

"Okay. Listen close. Pay attention to the things that connect you with joy."

It wasn't what I'd expected him to say. I leaned away and turned to frown at him. "What does joy have to do with anything?"

"Joy is important."

Was it? "I don't know. Not having car accidents is important. Joy seems pretty expendable."

But Max just smiled. "It's one of the secrets to life that no one ever tells you. Joy cures everything."

I flared my nostrils. "*Everything?*" I challenged, pointing at the bandage over my stitches."

"Everything emotional," Max clarified.

"I don't think you can cure emotions," I said.

But Max just nodded. "Joy is an antidote to fear. To anger. To boredom. To sorrow."

"But you can't just decide to feel joyful."

"True. But you can decide to *do something joyful.*"

I considered that.

"You can hug somebody. Or crank up the radio. Or watch a funny movie. Or tickle somebody. Or lip-synch your favorite song. Or buy the person behind you at Starbucks a coffee. Or wear a flower hat to work."

I shook my head. "One flower hat can't fix all my problems."

"No, but it can sure help."

I sighed.

"It's not about fixing all your problems, anyway," Max said. "You'll never fix all your problems."

"Well, that's encouraging."

"The point is to be happy anyway. As often as you can."

I let out a shaky sigh.

"I know you're scared," Max said, squeezing my hand. "But you're going to get up tomorrow and put on that crazy hat and walk over to school . . . and no matter what, you'll be better for it."

I wanted to believe that. "How do you know?" I whispered.

"Because," Max said, "courage makes everything easier next time. And I'm not going to let you live your life in fear."

The next day, I wore the hat to school.

And—just as predicted—all anybody noticed was the hat.

The kids were beside themselves with delight—and so were the teachers. I could see it in their faces when they saw me—the happy surprise of it. People lit up when they saw me—and stayed bright as they walked away, carrying that feeling off to whatever they were doing next, and whoever they'd see, passing it on.

Nobody talked about the car accident, or the seizure, or the fact that my life had just collapsed in on me. We talked about the hat. Where had it come from? What was it made of? What did it feel like to wear it around?

"Fabulous," I'd say, and I meant it.

Did the hat solve everything? Of course not.

But it brought me flashes of joy every time I saw it ignite joy in someone else. It shifted my ratio of "okay" to "not okay" just enough that I could function, and go to work, and do my job.

It wasn't a lifeboat, exactly—maybe more like a preserver. Just enough to hold on to.

But it worked.

That realization changed my life. My whole way of dressing and being in the world. My quiet wardrobe of tans and navies was gone within the year—replaced by polka dots and stripes, beads and fringe, and bright pinks, oranges, and blues. While I waited for my hair to grow back, I took to wearing headscarves, and big polka-dot sunglasses, and flowered leis as necklaces.

I got so addicted to color that, once I had hair again, I dyed my bangs cotton-candy pink.

I'm telling you: The year after that first seizure, I had a *renaissance*.

A fashion renaissance.

Mostly at Target, of course. (*Right?* I wasn't going to Paris on a school-librarian's salary.) A budget-conscious renaissance, but a renaissance all the same: scarves, purses, necklaces, striped knee socks, platform sandals, circle skirts, lipstick. The crazier and more colorful, the better. All the color I'd spent my entire life avoiding came flooding back in—as well as the fabrics, the movement, the textures.

I may have gone a little bit overboard. It's possible I tilted a bit more toward "circus clown" than fashionista that first year. But it didn't matter. The transformation saved me. It gave me something to do—something to look forward to and get excited about. It gave me a way to call attention to myself that was positive.

In a situation full of downsides, it was undeniably an upside.

I might never drive again, but dammit—I had a fun wardrobe.

And, to be truthful, through all that, the memory of Duncan Carpenter was kind of my inspiration.

He was definitely fashion-fearless.

I thought of him a lot during that year—his collection of pants and ties alone was great food for thought. If there was a crazy pair of pants in the world, he owned it. He had plain cotton pants in every color from red to green to purple, as well as seersucker, and a whole collection of patchwork madras. He had pink pants with flamingos, blue pants with palm fronds, and yellow pants covered in pineapples. Honestly: American flags, hibiscus flowers, hamburgers, dalmatians.

Not to mention his rule that he'd wear any tie any student ever gave him, which gave rise to a whole collection of doozies: rubber ducks, flying pigs, ice-cream cones, Frida Kahlo, and even Einstein sticking out his tongue. The kids got competitive, trying to find him the craziest, most shocking ties. And from dollar bills to Homer Simpson to cans of Spam, he wore them all. On picture day every year, he wore a tie with his faculty photo from the year before printed all over it for a picture-within-a-picture infinity effect.

And don't even get me started on his socks.

It was more about the surprise of it than anything. The whimsy, and the naughtiness, and the rule-breaking. It had an effect on other people. Kids teased him about his fashion choices, and so did adults, and he *liked* it. It was something he did for himself—but also something he did for others. It was a way of making his own rules—but doing it so cheerfully that nobody minded. It started conversation after conversation in the loveliest, most self-deprecating way.

It disarmed people. It relaxed them. It put them in a good mood.

I mean, this was a guy whose permanent faculty name tag, which should have just listed his name and department, like, "Duncan Carpenter/Kindergarten + Athletics," every year, mysteriously came back with a "typo" so that it read: "Duncan Carpenter/Defense Against the Dark Arts."

That was Duncan: a human mood-enhancer.

Wearing the flower hat to school that day did many great things for me—but I never expected it to give me a taste of what it felt like to be Duncan Carpenter.

It felt pretty good.

In the wake of that flower-hat day, the number one question I started asking myself when getting dressed in the morning became, "Is it fun?"

Later, I would read a bunch of books on color theory and the psychology of joy that would explain exactly how bright colors and whimsy create actual, neurological responses of happiness in people. But back then, I didn't know any science. I just knew that wearing a red dress covered in flowers to work with polka-dot sandals made me feel better.

And I'd really, really needed to feel better.

Now, this morning, I had many, many complex feelings about seeing him again—but one of them was definitely excitement. I couldn't help it. I wanted to see him again. And I wanted him to see me again—or maybe even see me for the first time—all new-and-improved, no longer mousy, no longer invisible, no longer trying so hard to disappear.

Which made my choice of outfit this morning extra critical.

This was a way of standing up for myself. A way of saying I'd had all this color inside me all along. He hadn't chosen me back then, but back then, I'd been hiding.

I wasn't hiding anymore.

I was a lady with a flower hat now.

Faced with darkness, I had chosen flowers. And polka dots. And light.

And if anybody on earth would appreciate the hell out of that, it was Duncan Carpenter.

And then—finally, at last, and way too soon—it was eight forty-five. Time to head over for the nine o'clock meeting.

Since waking up, I'd changed outfits no less than seven times— finally settling on an apple-red shirtdress, a pale blue polka-dotted scarf around my neck, stewardess-style, and blue open-toed platform sandals that matched my blue pedicure. Nowadays, my hair was down past my shoulders—mostly for the fun of braiding it and wrapping it up in wild buns.

I'd kept the bangs pink, though.

Pink bangs had kind of become my signature thing.

I added hoop earrings and red lipstick and subtle winged eyeliner that gave a retro Mary Tyler Moore vibe. Alice had given me a little pack of edible tattoos in cupcake flavors for my birthday with little empowering sayings, like, I REALLY DON'T NEED YOU, BECAUSE I SAID SO, and I WOKE UP LIKE THIS. I went ahead and applied one—YOU GOT THIS—to the outside of my bicep, even though my sleeve covered it. I could smell its faint caramel scent through the fabric.

You got this.

I wanted to be amazing. Not something as ordinary as "hot" or something as common as "pretty." I wanted to be *astonishing*.

Kind of a tall order for a Monday morning faculty meeting.

Before I left, I put my hair in two high buns and stuck little paper flowers in them, Frida Kahlo-style.

Then I pulled my bike and its flower-covered basket out of the garage, and I got on.

It was the longest three-block biking commute in the history of time.

I couldn't wait to see Duncan Carpenter again exactly as much as I hoped he would never show up. I longed for the moment to arrive as plainly as I dreaded it. And, just as I had since the moment Kent Buckley had spoken Duncan Carpenter's name, I thought about his arrival fully as often as I refused to think about it.

Which was constantly.

What would it be like to see him again?

In that photo Kent Buckley had shown us, Duncan had cut his hair . . . so that would be weird. The Duncan I'd known and loved had sported the very definition of bed head—some different configuration every day. A lovable mess.

In the photo, Duncan had seemed undeniably different: more grown up, more serious, better at shaving. But I couldn't think of Duncan as a *guy in a suit*.

I knew who Duncan was.

He was a *guy in a Hawaiian shirt*.

The anticipation woke up all my senses, raised my awareness of everything—the feel of the wind over my skin, the sounds of the cars going by, the color of blue in the sky, the flock of pelicans gliding by overhead. My insides were tingling with nervousness—in good ways and bad.

Would he be glad to see me? Would he remember me right away—or would I seem so different it would take him a second? Would he like my new vibe? There was always the possibility that he wouldn't. How would I respond to him if he told me to tone it down? Would I be the old me and nod meekly, eyes downcast—or would I get sassy, lift my eyebrows, and say something like, "Says the man in the flamingo pants"?

Would it be joy or would it be agony? There was no way to tell.

But my money was most definitely on both.

I arrived right on time, expecting to find Duncan handing out donuts, or arm-wrestling somebody, or doing the robot on the stage. Expecting the fun would've already started.

But when I stepped through the doorway, Duncan wasn't there yet.

The way our historic school building was set up, the cafeteria did double-duty as a theater. A kitchen at one end, and a stage at the other. This was why all large school meetings took place in the cafeteria—and why we could never hold assemblies at lunchtime.

My nervousness crescendoed as I stepped through the doorway, but then it subsided.

The chairs were full of teachers.

But no Duncan.

I was both relieved and disappointed at the same time

I blinked. Scanned again. And then I decided to leave the room quickly and come back later.

Look, this was *Duncan Carpenter.*

I couldn't be just a dot in an audience the first time I saw him again. I needed to stride into the room, tall and resplendent in my red outfit like a slightly funky and very Technicolor goddess, *thankyouverymuch.* This was the biggest crush-slash-heartache of my life, and I had a lot to prove and a whole new paradigm about myself to set up—right before I quit forever.

This had to be a heck of a moment, and I wouldn't get a do-over.

I needed to make an entrance.

Was that so unreasonable?

Answering my own question, I threw myself in reverse—lifting a finger like I'd forgotten something, then backing up and spinning around, figuring I'd take a lap around the cloisters and come back in five for a second grand entrance attempt.

But guess what?

Duncan himself was right behind me—striding through the doorway just seconds after I had. So when I stopped, spun around, and reversed direction—all in the span of one second—I ran smack into him.

Or maybe he ran into me.

Either way, we collided—hard—and I'm pretty sure I stabbed him in the gut with the pen I was carrying. I know for sure that my jaw slammed into something hard, most likely his collarbone—and as we reverberated back from the impact, Duncan dropped his laptop on the industrial-tile floor.

It hit with a clatter, and the whole room let out a collective "Oof!"

Then somebody shouted, "That's gonna leave a mark!"

It all happened so fast that I forgot myself.

For a second, I forgot entirely where we were, and who we were, and all I thought about was that I had just stabbed somebody—and without thinking it through at all, I looked down, slid my hand inside his suit jacket and pressed it against his stomach, murmuring something like, "Oh, my God! Are you okay?"

The whole thing happened in seconds.

What was I even doing? Checking for bleeding? Making sure my pen wasn't impaled in his abdomen? It wasn't until my hand was already there, already pressed against him just above his belt, feeling his warm skin through the cool cotton of his shirt, that I felt the muscles in his stomach tense into some kind of six-pack situation as he recoiled from the unexpected touch.

The shock of what I'd done hit me at his reaction—I had just *reached inside his suit jacket* and *pressed my hand to his stomach*—and I snatched my hand back. But then, as I lifted my eyes toward his face, intending to say I was *so sorry for all of it*, I noticed something else: a dark red smear—oh, God, of *lipstick*—on his white shirt from the moment my mouth had just collided with it. And at the sight, still not thinking—my brain still several steps behind my actions—and maybe just wanting to make something right in this whole disastrous situation, I found myself reaching up to rub the stain, as if I could wipe it off with the pads of my fingers, even though that's not how lipstick works.

That's right. I followed my accidental pressing-my-hand-against-his-stomach with an only slightly less accidental rubbing-his-collarbone-with-the-pads-of-my-fingers.

Tallying it up, I'd say the moment totaled five very unfortunate seconds.

At last, I stepped back, my mouth open, my whole jaw still smarting like I'd been punched, and he looked down at the laptop's carcass.

When he bent to pick it up, moving slowly, like there might still be some hope, it rattled.

"I'm so sorry," I said, leaning closer to get a look at the damage.

He rose and stepped back, his eyes wide and astonished, blinking at me like I was some kind of she-devil. Like I might attack again.

And then time seemed to warp and slow down as I took in the sight of him for the first time since the grocery store, when I'd been too panicked to really take it in.

There he was.

After all these years.

Him, but not him.

Him, but altered. Bulked-up. Groomed. Short hair, coiffed up and back, almost like a cross between a buzz and a pompadour. Pressed and neat. Professional. Adult.

That was it: he looked like a grown-up.

And I'm not going to lie—it was definitely a new kind of sexy.

I'd been hoping that the sight of him might not do much to me—that after all this buildup and dread and worry and anticipation, that the actual moment when I saw him again might fizzle. That I'd see him again after all this time and think, "Oh. You. Whatever."

But . . .

Nope.

The opposite. The most electric, physical, breathtaking opposite.

The fact of him—right there, so close—sent ripples of awareness buzzing and crackling through my body. It almost hurt a little. But in a good way.

Duncan Carpenter was six inches away from me.

Looking really, really good.

It was like he'd amplified all the most masculine parts of himself.

Even his jaw seemed squarer. How was that possible?

It was him, no question . . . but nothing like the goofy guy whose memory was stored away like a keepsake in my heart. It was him, but with a totally deadpan expression. It was him, but wearing—and I'm not joking here—a three-piece suit.

A *gray* three-piece suit.

With a navy blue tie.

Had I ever seen anyone, ever, in a three-piece suit? Did they even make them anymore? Wasn't that only for dads in reruns of midcentury sitcoms? It would have been so bizarre for anybody my age to be wearing that suit—but *Duncan Carpenter,* the guy who used to teach juggling classes barefoot because you had to "massage the earth" to "get your rhythm"?

Impossible.

I blinked a couple of times, like that might help it all make sense.

I couldn't read his expression. I hoped like hell that when he drew in his next breath to say something, it would be, "Samantha Casey? From Andrews Prep?" And then, heck—as long as I was writing dialogue for him, he might as well also say, "You look amazing! I never realized how stunning and fabulous you were!" And then maybe—*why not?*—he'd relax into a big smile and stretch his arms out wide for a hug, and announce to the room, "I regret all my life choices!"

I wouldn't have said no to a moment like that.

Instead, he looked at me and—just like he might have to any other total stranger in the room who had just slammed into him, broken his laptop, rubbed his belly, and then weirdly caressed his collarbone—he said: "Have a seat, please. It's past time to get started."

As he turned and walked off toward the stage, cradling his broken laptop, I accepted several truths at once. One: Duncan Carpenter was really here, in my school, about to become the guy in charge. Two: I was not immune to the sight of him in any microscopic way. And three: he had no idea who I was.

That last one smarted, I'm not going to lie.

Not even a flash of recognition. Not even a tiny frown of déjà vu. Nothing.

I knew I'd changed a lot. Almost everything about me was different now. The bangs, the glasses, the lipstick—the colors. I'd expected he might not place me at first.

But I'd been so looking forward to the big reveal—when I'd get to say, "It's Samantha Casey! From Andrews! Except I'm fabulous now!"— and watch all the recognition click into place.

In truth, I didn't even realize how hungry I'd been to experience that moment until it *didn't happen*. I hadn't been an ugly duckling before, exactly . . . but maybe more like a mousy mouseling. What would it have been like to see his face when he realized that the mouse had been transformed into a . . . a . . . a really stylish librarian in a polka-dot scarf?

There's nothing better than a before-and-after.

But he didn't remember the before. So that pretty much killed the after.

It was deflating, to say the least. It was also a moment I could have processed straight through until dinnertime with Alice if there had been time to drag her off to the ladies' room.

But there wasn't.

In seconds, Duncan was up at the podium and I was seated meekly in the last empty chair—right in the front row, next to Alice, who was wearing a navy blue T-shirt that said: EAT. SLEEP. *MATH*. REPEAT.

Alice was a front-row kind of person, and so was I.

Though maybe less so today.

I snuck a look at Duncan, now looking down at the red lipstick blotch on his shirt.

He rubbed at it himself for a second. Then he gave up.

He turned to the room, and my eyes felt magnetized to him.

He looked even bigger on the stage, and so *wrong* in that plain, dull, gray suit—but also—okay—undeniably handsome. To me, at least.

"Hello," he said at last, into the microphone, even though there were only about forty faculty and staff there. He didn't exactly need it. "My name is Duncan Carpenter, but you can call me—"

And here, I fully anticipated one of his old nicknames from Andrews: Duncan Do-Nuts, Big D, Dunker, Dig-Dug, or just plain D, before remembering that he was in administration now and revising my expectation to maybe just his plain-old first name.

That's when he finished with, "Principal Carpenter."

I let out a funny little squeak.

Duncan ignored it. "I am your new head of school."

Where was the comedy? Where was the mirth? I waited for something fun to happen—anything. A balloon drop, maybe. A karaoke moment. Maybe that suit would turn out to be a rip-away.

But nothing.

"The Kempner School," Duncan went on, in a dull, serious voice, "is a paragon. Its national reputation for nurturing creativity and diversity is unparalleled. For thirty years, this institution has been innovating, uplifting, and leading with its child-centered models for growth and learning. You've inspired a whole generation of educators, and it's a great honor for me to be here, stepping humbly into Principal Kempner's oxfords."

Okay. All right. Fair enough. This was a serious occasion. I could give him a few minutes of gravitas.

But his sentences sounded so formal and so stilted, more like he was reading written remarks than talking to us. More like a newscaster reading a teleprompter than a colleague. More like a robot than a human.

He went on for too long, doing most of the things that administrators do at the start of the school year—running down the perfunctory checklist of Topics to Cover.

Just as I looked over and saw Alice stifling a yawn, his tone shifted and he seemed to start building toward something. "You've been a leader for so many years in education—especially in areas of diversity and creativity. During my tenure, I hope to make Kempner known for leading in one more area. One that's so often tragically overlooked. One where I have much expertise."

Suddenly, I got it. All this stiff, bureaucratic nonsense? It was all a setup for an awesome payoff.

I knew what he was going to say.

A smile broke across my face—teeth and all.

What area did Duncan Carpenter have expertise in?

Play.

He was the king of play. Back at Andrews, he'd founded the Donut Society, invented a game called Goof-Ball, and started a club called Fits and Giggles that was basically a semester-long laughing contest. He'd started the annual faculty pie-eating competition. He'd dressed up on unannounced days in costume as, randomly, a hamster, a sandwich, and a saguaro cactus—for no reason. He'd been the instigator of countless lunchtime conga lines, sing-alongs, and food fights.

If this guy had one area of "much expertise," it was play.

I felt a kind of brightness in my chest at the anticipation. Of course this serious-dude stuff had been a setup. Of course he must be wearing some kind of Captain America costume under that suit. Of course a disco ball was about to drop from the ceiling.

The real Duncan Carpenter had to be in there somewhere.

Something was about to happen. I could feel it.

I nudged Alice, like *Get ready.*

Then I turned back to look up at Duncan on the stage, my eyes already shining with admiration for whatever it was he was about to do. This was the moment when he would show everybody what I'd meant when I'd promised them that he was awesome.

He was about to redeem us both.

Next, he said, "Get ready, because . . ."

I lifted my hands, poised to clap.

And that's when he reached inside his suit jacket and did something that I still can hardly believe to this day.

Totally unbelievable—even now.

Duncan Carpenter—one of the sweetest humans I had ever known—stood on the cafeteria stage of our little school in front of the entire faculty and staff, reached inside his suit jacket, and pulled out . . . a pistol.

He lifted his arm.

He pointed it at the ceiling.

And then—over the choked gasp of the entire crowd—he said, like it was some great piece of *Die Hard*–like dialogue: "We are going to lead the nation in campus safety and security."

six

Spoiler: it was a squirt gun.

Not that that makes it any better.

Duncan had spray-painted a clear plastic water gun metallic gray.

Like a psychopath.

He'd done a great job, too. It looked frigging *real*.

He paused for one second of terror. Then, before people could start screaming, or fainting, or dying of heart attacks, he pulled the trigger and squirted several little harmless fountains at the ceiling before dropping his hand to glare at us.

There was a long pause before he spoke.

Then he said, "Scared?"

The crowd did not respond.

He set the water pistol down on the podium. "Because you should be."

Nobody knew what to do. We all just sat there, frozen by fear.

Who *was* this guy? Did Duncan Carpenter have an evil twin? The Duncan I knew would have been juggling rubber chickens by now. I waited, hoping that any moment a marching band was going to come filing into the auditorium.

But, nope.

Duncan just held up the gun again.

Even knowing it was fake, we all winced.

"For all this school's prestige," Duncan said, looking genuinely angry at us, "for all its brilliant innovations, and groundbreaking programs . . . it's got a long way to go."

He set the gun down again, and we all sighed. "I walked right in here with that. Anybody care to guess how I did it?"

He blinked at the group.

The group blinked back.

Finally, I couldn't stand it—for him, as well as us. I raised my hand as I called out: "Because you're our new principal and we trusted that you were not a homicidal maniac?"

Duncan nodded at me. "That's exactly my point: never trust anyone." He surveyed us all then, nice and slow, and he said it again. "Never. Trust. Anyone." Like it was going to be our new school motto.

Alice looked over at me, like *You've got to be freaking kidding me*.

And all I could do was give her the same look back.

What was going on? Was Duncan doing good cop/bad cop—but without the good cop?

"The security at this school," Duncan went on, "is appalling." Then he started ticking problems off on his fingers. "Nobody looked. Nobody checked. The gate to the courtyard was standing wide open. Nobody asked me who I was or required that I get a security badge. The security guard was *fast asleep in a folding chair with a fishing magazine over his belly*."

Alice and I shared a glance—and a head shake. *Raymond*.

Duncan kept going. "I've just completed an assessment of your security practices. Do you know that the school's emergency plan has not been updated in seven years? Did you know that half of the posted emergency instructions in the classrooms are missing or obscured? Did you know that a third of the surveillance cameras are nonoperational?" He held up a yellow notepad. "I could go on for hours. For a school of this caliber to care so little about its students' safety is a disgrace. This school is a national embarrassment. It's a nightmare."

I looked around at our sunny cafeteria. Its tall, bright windows. Its cheerful yellow checkerboard floor. The kid-painted paper lanterns strung from the ceiling. The bulletin boards already papered in orange and red and yellow, just waiting for some kindergarten self-portraits to fill them. Not to mention the wall mural of giant butterflies that Babette and I had lovingly painted a few years back—colorful and whimsical and joyful.

I wouldn't exactly call it a *nightmare*.

"What I don't understand," Duncan went on, "is how things could be this bad? What current-day school doesn't lock its gates during the school day? Or require that visitors show ID? Or have security guards that are conscious?"

We assumed these were rhetorical questions, but then he waited for an answer.

Finally, Carlos shrugged and said, "Because we've never had a problem before?"

Duncan nodded and pointed at him. "Exactly." Then he addressed the room. "No one ever has a problem—until there's a problem. The state of things at this facility is, frankly, an insult. An insult to you, and to me, and to the children who come here every day. You're begging to be attacked."

I wouldn't say *begging*.

Did Duncan have a point? Probably.

Were security practices a little too lax at our breezy island school? Maybe.

But was he alienating everybody in the room right now? You betcha.

What could he have been thinking? This was our *very first* meeting. Even people with terrible people skills didn't have people skills this terrible. Why wasn't he charming everybody and being awesome? There was no way he didn't know what we'd all just been through with Max. What exactly about scaring the hell out of everybody with a fake gun and then calling our sweet, sunny school "a nightmare" seemed like a good idea?

From the looks on all the faces in the room, everybody was as lost as I was. We knew the new guy wouldn't be Max—who could ever be?— but nobody had expected . . . *this*.

If nothing else, Duncan Carpenter had had people skills. He was—or at least had been—a genius with kids. And with grown-ups. And with animals, too, while we're at it. Basically, if you were a living thing, Duncan knew what to say to you, and how to interact, and how to encourage you to be the best version of yourself.

Not anymore, apparently.

Max had taught us all to care desperately about the school. To be invested. To participate—actively and deeply. Nobody here was dialing it in. Most of us worked extra hours on a weekly basis. Most of us had found a dream job here—where our opinions were valued, and we were admired for whatever gifts we brought to the table, and we were encouraged to have a stake in what the place was and how it was run.

That was all Max. He'd set up a culture of admiration and support.

And he'd spoiled us all terribly.

This *Twilight Zone* version of Duncan didn't see any of that. All he saw was what was wrong. Which was the absolute opposite of the Duncan I'd known—who had been the best person I'd ever met at seeing what was right.

Duncan stepped closer to the edge of the stage and stood up taller in some kind of He-Man power stance. "I want you to know that I understand Principal Kempner was pretty much the heart and soul of the school."

Along with Babette, I wanted to add.

"But I'll tell you something right now," he went on. "If he wasn't looking out for your physical safety, then he was no better than a fool."

I felt the entire room catch its breath.

No. He. Did. Not.

Quick reminder: the man he was talking about had died right in front of us.

Babette went white, but she didn't move.

"I want you to know," Duncan went on, "that I'm excited to be here. Principal Kempner's criminal neglect of your safety has given us the chance to make some epic improvements. Now it's time to lead the nation in our next phase. The phase that will ensure the safety and security of every member of this school community and show all of America how it's done."

We stared at him.

He stared at us back.

Finally, he gave a little nod and said, "Thank you very much."

And he was finished.

At least, I guess he was finished.

He hadn't met anyone in the room, or asked us anything about this new place he was supposed to be in charge of, or interacted, or bonded, or, you know, done even one thing that he should have . . . but, no matter, he was picking up his broken laptop and walking off the stage.

Maybe three people clapped out of politeness.

Then the clapping stopped, and we all listened to the tapping of his shoe heels as he finished crossing the room, and walked, at last, out the door.

seven

As soon as the door clicked closed, everybody freaked out.

"What the hell was that?" Carlos demanded, just as Donna and Emily both said, in unison, "That guy is crazy!"

A coach named Gordo stood up then and gestured at the empty podium. "Did that guy just stand up *in the auditorium of an elementary school* with a gun?"

"A squirt gun," I felt compelled to point out, almost like I had to do a little PR for Duncan . . . for old times' sake, if nothing else.

"Looked pretty damn real to me," Anton, the recently divorced science teacher, said.

"Until it squirted water," I said.

Why was I defending Duncan? I was as horrified as anyone else.

"More importantly," Carlos demanded, "did he just *insult Max*?"

The room descended into murmurs of abject bewilderment tinged with outrage—with phrases like "What the hell?" and "Who does that?" breaking the surface over and over.

"Maybe he just wanted to get our attention," I said.

"With a gun?" Anton demanded.

I sighed. The whole morning was unfathomable. I couldn't explain it, and I sure as hell couldn't defend it.

Duncan—or whoever that had been—was on his own.

But I couldn't disavow myself so easily.

I had stood up for him just now, but I had also been vouching for him all along, promising that Kent Buckley had accidentally hired us the best principal we could have hoped for. I'd sworn up and down that Duncan was going to blow their minds.

Unfortunate phrasing, in hindsight.

Either way, I'd established myself as the resident authority on Duncan, and now the room wanted answers. The panic turned accusatory. "You said he was amazing," Emily said, turning to me.

"He *was* amazing," I insisted. "I swear he was."

"That was *not* amazing. That was psychotic," Emily said.

"He painted a squirt gun to look real! Who does that?" Carlos added.

The outrage built to a din.

"Maybe it's his evil twin," the school nurse said, shaking her head.

I blinked and shook my head. "Maybe he was having an off day?"

"An off day!" They were indignant.

"I don't know!" I said. "I'm as baffled as everybody else. Whatever that was—it's nothing like the guy I used to work with. The guy I knew dislocated his shoulder testing out a Jell-O Slip 'n' Slide for the school carnival—twice! He wasn't obsessed with safety. He didn't care about safety at all."

Babette just sat in her chair, watching us. Normally, she'd be the person fielding everybody's worries. But nothing about life was normal anymore.

Finally, I stepped up. "Okay," I said. "That was not the meet-the-new-principal moment anybody was expecting."

"That's an understatement," Coach Gordo called out.

"But," I said, trying to instill that one word with an optimism I didn't quite feel, "it was just one meeting. Maybe he was nervous. Maybe he was given some bad advice. Maybe he wasn't feeling well. We don't know. All we can do right now is go back to our classrooms and finish getting ready for the start of school."

"That's not *all* we can do," Anton said.

I sighed. "I will go talk to him and try to figure this out. Let's meet at Babette's tonight and I'll report back."

One of the teachers offered to get the school's bylaws to figure out just exactly how much hiring power Kent Buckley had. Could he just pick any crazy person he wanted? It seemed unlikely, but, on the other hand, when Max and Babette were in charge, none of this had mattered. It was possible, at least, that some weird rules had gone unnoticed.

As we considered that possibility, I pulled a little teacher move. "Eyes on me," I said. "We're not going to freak out. We're going to choose to believe everything's okay until we have evidence to the contrary."

It was some of my favorite Babette advice. She gave it to me all the time.

"Um," the nurse said. "I think we got our evidence to the contrary when he pulled out that fake gun."

"Okay," I said, like *Fair enough*. "But this was his first day. We can give him one do-over."

We could, and we would. We had work to do, rooms to organize, a school year starting up next Monday, ready or not. There was no time to do anything else. This plan would have to do for now. People started gathering up their things.

They weren't going to panic, and neither was I.

Not, at least, until I figured out what the hell was going on.

Walking over to Max's office—now Duncan's—I struggled to wrap my head around pretty much every single thing about seeing him again. There was so much to wrestle with—from the fake gun, to his utter tone-deafness with the group, to his rude comments about Max.

Not to mention that he hadn't recognized me.

Now that the full-on crazy of the meeting was on pause for a minute, that was the part that came rushing back.

He had stared right into my face with zero recognition.

How was that possible? *Was* that even possible? Physiologically, I mean?

It wasn't like it had been twenty years. I did the math as I walked along the cloister past the courtyard. I had left Andrews to come to Kempner four years ago in May, so it had been four years and three months since Duncan Carpenter had seen my face. Could you forget the face of someone you'd worked with for two solid years in that amount of time? Someone you'd sat across from in faculty meetings, passed in the hallways, eaten across from in the cafeteria?

I know I'd been trying to stay invisible back then, but *come on.*

Nobody's *that* invisible.

Are they?

As I thought about it, I realized that I was always near him, but never right in front of him. I was always aware of him, but it didn't follow that he was aware of me, too. If I was camouflaged in the background, maybe he didn't remember me. Maybe I had just been a generic version of a girl he worked adjacent to—with never enough specific details to register. Some kind of navy blue, nonspecific female smudge in his memory.

There were plenty of people in the world that I didn't remember.

Most of them, in fact.

Still, I was offended.

Of course, I was wildly different now. The trappings of me, at least. Maybe that was all he could see.

Or maybe he just wasn't even really looking. Maybe he was so busy trying to adjust to his new job and step into Max's shoes and scare the hell out of everybody that he wasn't focused on his visual surroundings. Maybe he was tired from being up all night with a sick baby, or two. Or maybe he wasn't wearing his glasses.

Did he even wear glasses?

Good. Something I didn't know about him. One thing, at least.

Because I really knew too much in general. I knew his birthday, for example: May the fourth—and he'd always worn a Luke Skywalker costume to school that day with a button pinned on it that said MAY THE FOURTH BE WITH YOU. How lopsided was that? I knew his birthday, and how he liked to celebrate it, and exactly how good he'd looked in that Luke Skywalker costume. I carried a full visual of him brandishing a light saber stored in my memory at all times . . . and he didn't even know who I was.

It wasn't fair.

But he certainly wasn't carrying a light saber now. What the hell had happened to him? Was it that he'd married that boring admissions girl? Had she told him he needed to grow up and stop being fun? Or maybe it was becoming a parent. Or maybe some mentor had given him the very bad—and very wrong—advice that he had to change his entire personality to be successful.

Or maybe he was just having an off day. It was possible.

But an off day that was *that* off?

I couldn't fathom it. And I didn't want to.

When I reached Mrs. Kline's desk, her little reception area was stacked to the ceiling with boxes. She was dabbing at her eyes with a tissue.

"It's all Max's stuff," she said, as I took in the sight. "I spent the weekend boxing it up."

"Oh, Mrs. Kline," I said, getting a little teary myself. "I bet that was hard."

"Better me than Babette," she said, and I had to agree.

I nodded. "I guess he really had a lot of stuff."

"Thirty years'll do that."

"Yes," I agreed.

"I'm just going to have maintenance take it to storage."

I nodded. Good plan.

Then Mrs. Kline took a slow breath and shifted gears. "Are you here for"—she checked her appointment book—"your ten-thirty meeting?"

I glanced at the wall clock above her head. It was nine forty-seven. "Yes," I said.

"Would you care to wait?"

"Not really," I said.

She tilted her head toward Max's closed office door. "Principal Carpenter said he didn't want to be disturbed."

"Okay," I said.

I didn't want to be disturbed, either. None of us wanted to be disturbed.

I looked at the closed door, hesitated for one second total, and then I marched over and knocked on it.

Loudly.

No answer.

I knocked again. Nothing.

But I knew he was in there.

Finally, I just started knocking and didn't stop. Short, insistent raps: *tap-tap-tap-tap-tap.* Like a woodpecker. A loud, you-better-come-open-this-door kind of woodpecker.

Mrs. Kline just watched, her eyes wide with disbelief.

Finally, Duncan yanked the door open, growling: "Mrs. Kline, I said I'm—"

When he saw me, he stopped.

Then he finished with, "Not here."

He looked a little breathless. Almost a little sweaty—like he'd been . . . exercising, maybe? His jacket was off, and so was the vest. His tie was off, too, and his collar was open. What was he up to?

"But you clearly are here," I said, determined not to be fazed.

Mrs. Kline stood up. "Principal Carpenter, this is our librarian, Samantha Casey. Most people call her Sam."

And then I couldn't help it. "Unless we've all had a few margaritas," I said to Mrs. Kline, like *amiright?* "Then it's more like Saaaam, or Samster, or Sammie."

What was I doing? I didn't even drink. I didn't have any nickname but Sam. But Duncan didn't know that. Because, as I may have mentioned, *he had no idea who I was*.

"I need to talk to you," I said.

"I'm in the middle of something."

Clearly. "It's urgent."

"I'm unavailable."

"But I have an appointment."

Duncan checked Mrs. Kline's wall clock. "In forty-one minutes."

He wasn't wrong. But there was no possible way I could wait for forty-one minutes.

"It really can't wait," I said, walking right past him into his office. A very ballsy move that, for a minute at least, made me feel quite I-am-woman-hear-me-roar.

That is, until Duncan—less impressed than I'd have liked—watched me situate myself opposite him in his office, ready to face off. Then he seemed to give a kind of mental *oh, well* shrug, and then he kneeled down to the floor, leaned forward onto his hands . . . and started doing push-ups.

For a second, I just watched him. It was so unexpected. And he was kind of mesmerizing, too—straight as a board from his heels to his head, pumping up and down with absolute vigor, like it was easy. Great form.

"What are you doing?" I finally asked.

"I told you I was busy."

"Isn't this the kind of thing people usually do at the gym?"

"Some people, I guess. I like to space them out through the day."

It was so off-putting. It threw me off. "Should I . . . wait for you to finish?"

"I thought you said it couldn't wait."

Fair enough.

Looking back, the fact that I thought I was about to quit really impacted how that moment played out. I wasn't thinking of myself as

Duncan's employee, or trying to keep my behavior professional, or even worried about my job. I had one foot out the door, anyway.

Besides, this guy had just pulled out a gun at a school. A fake one, but still.

All bets were kind of off.

When this office had been Max's, it was full of keepsakes. Plants, kid art, and photos had covered every shelf, wall, and surface—including his desk, at least the parts of it that weren't covered with ever-changing stacks of papers.

The same office—now belonging to Duncan—was the opposite.

Of course, Duncan had just moved in. Most of his things were still in the boxes stacked in the corner. But it wasn't just that he hadn't un-packed. He'd changed everything. When facilities had repainted—which the room had needed—Duncan had chosen a cold gray to replace the warm, creamy white from before. The tan carpet had also been replaced with gray. Max's warm, Stickley-style furniture had been replaced with— you guessed it—cheap, gray office furniture. With a little black for variety.

The paint smell wasn't helping, either.

I'm not here to debate the merits of tan carpet over gray.

It was just a very different vibe.

"This place . . ." I said, looking around. "It's like the Death Star."

If Duncan heard me, he decided not to engage.

I took in the sight of him, still going strong—down, then up, then down, then up—with the push-ups. No faltering, no variation. Like a piston firing in a factory.

No wonder his shoulders were so much . . . *shoulderier.*

"So," he said, from below me, in the most conversational tone, as if anything about this moment was normal. "What is it that can't wait forty-one minutes?"

Good question. What was it again?

I was so disoriented, both by what was happening right now and by what had happened at the morning's meeting, that I couldn't figure out where to even begin.

My original goal had been to meet with Duncan this morning, tell him it was nice to see him again, give him a few pointers, and then pleasantly quit my job.

But it *wasn't* nice to see him again.

It was many things, but definitely not *nice*. It was highly disturbing. And worrying. And panic-inducing. And so now I was here to—what? Give him a talking-to? Shake him by the shoulders? Find out why he was acting so weird?

And how, exactly, do you follow all that by saying, "Oh, and P.S. I quit"?

But, of course, I wouldn't be quitting now. Not anymore. I couldn't. How could I possibly quit now—and leave everybody I loved behind with no one to protect them from this guy?

My half-an-hour-ago goals had all been nullified—but now I wasn't totally sure what my new ones were.

"We need to talk about that meeting," I finally said.

Duncan straightened a crease on his sleeve. "What about it?"

"It was . . . really odd."

No response. Duncan just kept pumping up and down.

"Is there any way at all you could pause your exercise routine? Doing push-ups while I talk to you is kind of super rude."

"Barging in here without permission is also super rude."

"So," I said, "we're even."

Duncan seemed to slow while he thought about that. "Fair enough," he said, and then he shifted back onto his feet, stood up, and turned toward me, looking . . . extra tall.

"Okay," he said, resting his hands on his belt. "Let's talk."

But what to say? Where to even begin? I wanted to say, "What the hell was that?" Or, "Who the hell are you?" Or maybe even, "Did you eat the real Duncan and assume his identity?" That's how weird things were in my head.

In the end, I went with plain old: "What just happened?"

But I really amped up my tone of voice to compensate.

Now that I finally had his attention—now that we were alone, and face to face—I couldn't help but wonder if, away from the audience and the stage, he might recognize me then. I hoped he might say something like, "Hey—do we know each other?" Or, "Hey—you look a little bit like . . . ?"

But nope. He just said, like he'd say to a total stranger, "I don't know what you're talking about."

And here's where my ego got in the way of my goals. Because if he didn't recognize me, then I sure as hell wasn't going to admit that I recognized him. Which eliminated some of the most insightful things I could have said. "I'm talking about the meeting," I said.

"What about it?"

"It was a disaster."

"I disagree."

"Do you have any idea what this school is dealing with right now? We've just lost our principal. Our beloved principal—and founder. Not last year or even last spring. *This summer.* Everybody in that room was grieving and raw and lost and scared—including, I'll add, his wife, who was sitting in the back row like a statue."

"None of that has to do with me," Duncan said. "I didn't cause any of that. And I can't fix it, either."

"Maybe you can't fix it. But you can try like hell not to make it worse."

"People die," Duncan said then. "It happens all the time. The best we can do is move on. *That's* what I'm here for."

"Nobody is ready to move on."

"I'm not sure that matters. School starts on Monday."

"Yes. Exactly. And we need a plan for facing that. What we don't need is a dude walking in here with a water gun."

"I did what I needed to do."

"But you didn't do what anybody else needed you to do. You didn't meet anyone, you didn't talk to anyone, you didn't interact at all or bond."

"I'm not here to bond."

"You most certainly are. Do you think you can run this school as a stranger?"

"Do you think you can walk in here and tell me what to do?"

He knew better than this. "Look," I said. "I'm trying to help you."

"I don't need your help."

"You didn't know Max. So let me just tell you that he never ran this place as a dictatorship. That's not how things work here. It's always been consensus and discussion. This is a highly engaged, very passionate group of people—and part of what makes this school so legendary is everybody working together. Whatever it was you just did in that meeting is not going to fly—not here."

"What Principal Kempner did or didn't do isn't really relevant anymore," Duncan said then.

"I'm trying to tell you how things work."

"Things work the way I say they work."

"If you keep acting like this, you're going to lose them."

"What are you saying? That they'll quit?"

"These are amazing teachers—the best of the best. They could be teaching anywhere."

"That sounds weirdly like a threat."

"I'm not threatening you. I'm telling you how it is. They came here to be part of a very special school culture. One that's all about creativity and encouragement and making learning joyful."

Duncan was unfazed. "Well, it's a new culture now."

He wasn't taking me seriously. "You have no idea how much you just freaked the entire faculty out."

"I think I have some idea."

"And don't even get me started on the gun."

"Here it comes."

"What the hell was that?"

"A *water* gun," he said. "And it got their attention, didn't it?"

"Not in a good way."

"I'm not here to coddle them."

"Why are you here?"

"To get this place on track."

"It's already on track. It's one of the best elementary schools in the country. It's famous for being amazing."

"It's also a death trap. And I'm here to fix that. And if they don't like it, they're more than welcome to quit—every last one of them. Yourself included."

But no way was I quitting now. "I can't quit," I said.

"Sure you can," he said, in a tone like *I dare you*. Then he met my eyes and said, "There is nothing more expendable than teachers."

Rude. And insulting. Max had spent decades filling this school with superstars—the best of the best of the best. Teachers were anything but expendable. The best teachers lifted kids up with excitement and drive and curiosity—and the worst teachers did the opposite. And no one on earth should have known that better than Duncan Carpenter.

I looked down for a second to try to regroup. What was I even trying to accomplish here? I wanted him to snap out of it. I wanted him to be his old self again. I wanted him to reach his potential. But I didn't have any leverage. Was he bluffing? If he really didn't care if everybody quit, I wasn't sure what to do.

And that's when I saw something sticking out from under Duncan's desk.

Something furry.

Something that looked like a paw.

I stepped closer and leaned around to get a better look.

Curled up under the desk was a large, gray, very furry dog—fast asleep.

In this entire sleek, gray, cold office, the dead-last thing I would've expected to see was a fluffy dog—and, of course, the gray fur against the gray carpet had camouflaged it.

"Is that a poodle under your desk?" I asked.

"It's a labradoodle," Duncan said, like it was obvious.

I leaned a little closer. "Is it . . . yours?"

"It's a security dog," Duncan said, all business. "A guard dog."

"It doesn't look very on guard right now."

"Even security animals have to rest."

"Fair enough. What's its name?"

Duncan stood up a little taller. "Chuck Norris."

I let out a laugh. Then my face fell. "Oh. You're serious."

"He's in training," Duncan said, unamused.

"I guess I would have just expected a German shepherd or something. Something scary."

"This dog is plenty scary," Duncan said, as we stared at the not-at-all-scary pile of snoozing fluff. "Or at least, he will be when I finish with him."

"Are you going to squirt him with the water gun?"

Duncan's face was dead serious. "That's not the protocol for training working animals."

"If you say so," I said. I actually liked the idea of having a dog on campus. I'd just read an article about how dogs had a soothing impact on humans. I could hear my voice softening as I looked at Chuck Norris. "He's going to keep us safe, huh?"

"He's not the only thing, but yes."

That got my attention. "He's not the only thing?"

Duncan stood up a little straighter. "I'm looking at enacting many new safety protocols, from improving visibility issues, to training teachers, to making use of new technologies. I'm eyeballing some very high-tech, very top-of-the-line changes. It'll be expensive, but so worth it."

I'm telling you: this guy—*this* guy—once broke his wrist at Andrews during a skateboarding race through the school hallways.

But then a question occurred to me. "Where's the money coming from?"

Duncan blinked. "There's room in the budget."

I didn't know that much about the budget, but I knew enough. "Not sure there is," I said.

Duncan looked away. "You can always find room in a budget, if you're creative."

What an amazing nonanswer answer. I stepped closer to peer at him. His face was a mixture of determination, defiance, and just a hint of guilt. Taking it in, I just knew.

"Please tell me we're not talking about the empty lot."

He stepped closer to his desktop and fixed his eyes on it. "What empty lot?"

But my body knew the answer before the rest of me did. I stood up straighter. My muscles tightened. "The empty lot for the playground."

"What playground?" Duncan asked then.

Was it possible that he really didn't know? Building that playground was all set to be the main attraction—the defining feature—of the coming school year. We had plans and a contractor lined up already. It was on the schedule.

But he'd just gotten here. Things lately had been rushed, to say the least. Maybe he hadn't been updated. I stepped closer to his desk and, never letting him out of my sight, I leaned down over his phone, pressed the intercom button like I'd done so many times with Max when we were goofing around, and in a careful, cautious voice said, "Mrs. Kline, could you please bring in the plans for the playground?"

Two seconds later, she appeared, efficient as ever, with a stack of file folders—rubber-banded together, stuffed and overflowing with brochures, sketches, plans, notes, Post-its, doodles, ideas and suggestions— and set the stack on Duncan's desk with a *whomp*.

"Meet the Adventure Garden," I said to Duncan, as Mrs. Kline swished back out. "Two years ago, we bought the lot next door from the city. One year ago, we started a capital campaign that raised a hundred thousand dollars to build the coolest, most creative, joyful, surprising, and multisensory playground in the history of the world. And, this year, at last, in the face of everything, we're going to build it."

Duncan blinked at me for a second, and I got the feeling he was sizing up what kind of an adversary I was going to make. Then, in a tone of voice that let me know exactly what he'd decided, he said, "Yeah. That's all canceled."

I felt like I couldn't get enough air in to make the word. "Canceled?" It came out like a gasp.

"Yep," Duncan said, all matter-of-fact, smacking his hand down on the top of the files. "We're going to need that money for other things."

I pulled the files closer to me, protectively. "Other things? What kind of other things?"

"Well, I'm not at liberty to get into details just yet, but there's a lot going on."

"You can't cancel the Adventure Garden!"

"Why not?"

"Because it was Max's idea."

"Max isn't here, though, is he?"

"But . . ." What was happening? I shook my head. "You can't."

"Sure, I can," Duncan said pleasantly, walking to his office door and putting his hand on the knob, like we were done here. "You should read my contract. I can do anything, pretty much. I could serve hot-fudge sundaes for every meal. I could declare that the school uniform was Halloween costumes. I could fire the entire faculty and hire a troupe of circus clowns."

"The board would never let you do that stuff," I said.

"The board is a complicated place," Duncan said.

"What is *that* supposed to mean?"

"It means I can rearrange the budget in whatever way I deem necessary for the good of the school."

What the hell was happening? We'd spent a year planning this place. We'd had committees, done research, read articles and watched TED Talks.

It had been Max's baby. He was the one who'd had the idea—and convinced the board to use some of the endowment to buy it. When the sale had gone through, Max encouraged everyone to submit ideas for how to bring it to life. Then, over the summer—a summer that now felt like a thousand years ago—Max, Babette, and I had gone through the plans and ideas, culling through the articles and concepts, consult-

ing with designers, finalizing the budget, and getting things rolling in
earnest.

This was what we usually did with our summers, anyway—starting
with the summer we'd painted the butterfly mural all over the big
wall in the cafeteria. The next year, we'd yarn-bombed the playground
in the courtyard with brightly colored crochet spirals and webs and
flowers. Last year, we'd gone crazy with paint: adding bright yellow,
orange, and baby blue stripes all around the lockers and hallways,
roller-disco-style, and clouds and flowers and rainbows in all sorts of
unexpected places.

It hadn't even occurred to me that Duncan might not want to keep
the project going.

Duncan, after all, had hung a disco ball in the cafeteria of Andrews
Prep. He'd kept a class hedgehog. He'd once tried to build a zip line off
the gym roof.

How could Duncan kill plans for a playground? He *was* a playground.

The Adventure Garden had been a massive, school-wide project
that we were unanimously excited about, and now we needed it more
than ever. I started pulling off rubber bands and pulling out file folders, frantically looking for the best parts so I could show him what
I meant. "But the Adventure Garden *is* for the good of the school!
Let me just show you the plans. It's epic. It's magical. You won't even
believe—"

"I don't need to see the plans," Duncan said.

"It's like nothing you've ever seen," I promised. "It's going to have a
tree house, and a lily pond, and a ropes course—"

He opened the door then, and held it open, waiting for me to leave.

But I hesitated. Then I had to ask. "Are you here to destroy the
school?"

Then, in a slightly softer tone that seemed to acknowledge that he at
least registered all the crushing, life-altering anxiety hiding behind that
question for me, he said, "I'm not here to destroy the school."

I let out a deep sigh.

Then he added, "I'm here to fix it."

One thing was clear after that: I was more trapped here than ever.

When I'd first found out Duncan was coming, I'd thought he was going to make me miserable by being so likable I'd have no choice but to fall in love with him again—but now it looked like the opposite would be true: he'd make me miserable by ruining my school, and, by extension, my life.

I wasn't sure which one was worse—but, either way, I was miserable.

My emotions were moving around like numbers on a slide puzzle, but I wasn't getting any closer to a solution.

That was my takeaway: somehow, for some reason, Duncan Carpenter had become completely deranged, and I couldn't leave until I understood why. Leaving to save myself was one thing. But leaving a whole school behind in the hands of a madman was quite another.

It left me wondering if Duncan had an evil twin or something. Because, truly, weren't people's identities fairly consistent over time? People didn't just wake up one morning with completely different personalities. Something had happened to him—but what? Traumatic brain injury? Amnesia? Witch's spell?

It had to be something epic.

Seriously. He was a monster now.

And that's exactly what I told everybody that night at Babette's.

I was kind of hoping that the shock of the morning meeting might wake Babette up and stoke her into action. Not that there was anything wrong with grieving. She was allowed to grieve, of course. But I wasn't really a leader, per se, and so I wouldn't have minded at all if Babette had suddenly lifted her head, realized what was happening, and stepped into her rightful shoes as the commander of the resistance.

But not tonight.

She'd gone to bed with a headache and wouldn't come down.

Instead, I wound up reminding myself not to overthink it. "Leading" was really just talking, planning, and making people pay attention.

Three things I was perfectly good at.

I told the group about everything Duncan had said in his office, and everything I'd learned: That the morning meeting had not, in fact, been a fluke. That this legendary warmhearted goofball had somehow mutated into a militaristic dictator. That he didn't care if the faculty all quit. And that he was canceling the Adventure Garden.

Each piece of news elicited progressively louder groans of outrage, but the news about the Adventure Garden was the clincher.

"That was Max's project!" Anton shouted.

"What about the tree house?" Carlos demanded.

"What about the vegetable patch?" Emily and Alice asked.

Everybody wanted to know what we were going to do.

I told them I didn't know. We'd just have to figure it out as we went along. Then I looked around. "Mrs. Kline?"

She raised a hand. "Present."

"Can you please find a copy of his contract? And the school-board charter, while you're at it? Let's figure out exactly how stuck with this guy we are. Also . . ." I looked around. "Does anybody know our school policy on dogs?"

"On dogs?" Rosie Kim asked.

"He's got a security dog," I told them.

This touched off a whole new wave of outrage. *What kind of dog? Was it big? Was it scary? Was it trained? What was it doing at school? What about kids who are afraid of dogs? Who was going to keep an eye on it? What kind of person brought a dog to a campus full of little kids? What about dander? What about allergies? Were dogs even allowed? Could somebody find out?*

I did not tell them that the dog's name was Chuck Norris. Nor did I tell them that Duncan had declared it was "scary."

Finally, when the worrying reached a crescendo, I stood up.

I might not know how to be a leader, but I did know one thing: we were going to protect our school. We weren't all this awesome for nothing.

And that's when I made my voice loud and gave us all the pep talk that everybody needed to hear—including me.

"I don't know exactly what we're going to do," I said. "I've never been faced with anything even vaguely like this. But I know what we're *not* going to do. We're not going to panic. We're not going to let fear make us lose sight of who we are. We're here for a reason—right? To look after all these little souls we've been entrusted with. We're not going to forget that. We're here for them—and for each other. Kids first—and we'll worry about this Duncan Carpenter situation later. I don't want anybody doing anything stupid—Anton, I am looking at you. No graffiti, no threatening notes, no angry posts on social media. The most important job we have for the next few weeks is helping the kids. Right? We need to help them understand that death is a part of life, that Max is gone but not forgotten, that we can keep him with us by carrying his warmth and his kindness forward. They need all the stability we can give them for now. So let's hunker down, do our jobs, help the kids through this transition, remember who we're here for . . . and do everything we can to make things better, not worse."

eight

Chuck Norris, the security labradoodle, did not turn out to be scary.

He did, however, turn out to be a massive pain in the ass.

Soon, impossible as it was, school started again.

The building flooded with kids and backpacks and lunch boxes. Every single kid, it seemed, wanted to know where Max was. Even kids who'd been at the party.

I felt pretty much the same way.

Where *was* Max?

For my part, I just put my head down and tried to focus on what was right in front of me: kids and books and paperwork and planning.

Sometimes, in quiet little moments, when I looked up from my desk in the library and saw the place filled with kids reading on the sofa, and in the beanbag chairs, and in our reading fort, I could almost pretend that everything was the same as always.

But the new security dog wasn't really having that.

In fact, he turned out to be a book eater.

Not once, but twice on the first day of school, he found his way into the library and chewed up books. First, a Mo Willems boxed set. Then, after lunch, *The Secret Garden.*

Both times, I walked him back down to Duncan. "Seriously?" I demanded, holding out the mutilated *Secret Garden*—now missing a full third of its binding.

"I think he might be teething. I found a tooth in the carpet earlier."

"Not okay. Get him a chew toy."

Duncan nodded, like that was actually a good idea. "I will."

"And don't let him just roam around school."

"It's looking like he can open my office door."

"And the library doors," I added.

"I thought he was napping," Duncan said.

"Well, he wasn't," I said. "He was roaming around loose."

"I'm sorry about the books. I'll pay for them."

"Great," I said, all deadpan. "I'll put them on your tab."

That dog, in fact, made quite a name for himself on the first day of school. By car pool, he'd climbed up on Mrs. Kline's desk, eaten a whole box of tissues, chased a squirrel across the courtyard, gotten his collar caught on a tree branch, barked at his own reflection in the office doors for a full five minutes, peed on the carpet in the kindergarten room, chewed a hole in Coach Gordo's gym bag, and stolen a whole bag of hot-dog buns from the cafeteria.

Not to mention when he tried to take a flying leap into Alice's arms during recess and knocked all six feet of her down to the ground.

Alice didn't mind. She was a dog person. But Coach Gordo was none too happy about the gym bag. "What the hell, man?" he'd said, after Duncan handed him back a decapitated sock and a drool-soaked pair of boxer briefs.

"He's still in training," Duncan said.

Anyway, that was the moment that prompted Duncan's first faculty-wide memo of the day.

Memos are never good things in the world of education—or maybe anywhere. If nothing else, they're usually dull, and repetitive, and, as Max always put it, TLTR—Too Long To Read. Max had banished memos entirely before I even arrived—replacing them with IOMs— Instead Of Meetings. These were basically . . . memos. But Max enforced a strict, hundred-word length, limited them to Fridays (when we were "almost free"), and emphasized that he was only sending them so we could avoid an MSM—a Meeting that Should've been a Memo.

Context is kind of everything.

Max's guiding principle was to respect us as teachers—our ideas, our input, and, most important, our time. Memos, in Max's view, were the very worst waste of all of those things.

But Duncan, as they say, hadn't gotten the memo on that.

And if Max knew the value of calling actual memos by other names, Duncan did the opposite: He called an email that wasn't even a memo . . . a memo.

Five minutes after the Sock Incident, there it was, in all our inboxes. And it read:

From: Duncan Carpenter
RE: MEMO—SECURITY DOG

Many of you got a chance to "meet" the Kempner School's new security dog, Chuck Norris, when he stole a box of donuts from the faculty lounge and made an epic escape attempt— which was thwarted by security guard Raymond when he got tangled in the leash. Fortunately, no one was hurt, though I regret to report that none of the donuts survived.

In future, all members of the school community must stay aware that Chuck Norris is still in training and will need our help to succeed. Please do not pet, play with, scratch, talk to, coo at, or in any way agitate Chuck Norris while he's on the school campus. All forms of human affection are a distraction from his duties as he learns to watch over our campus and keep us all safe. For his benefit, as well as everyone else's, all interaction with Chuck Norris is expressly forbidden.

Two minutes after I got that email, through the library window that overlooked the cloisters, I saw Chuck Norris steal a kid's lunch box, and then get chased across the courtyard by a whole class of second graders, his fur undulating and his fluffy face and bright black eyes loving every minute of everything.

Then I watched Duncan come out, scold the dog, return the lunch box to its owner, and sternly point the kids toward the lunchroom. Leave it to this new version of Duncan to bring an adorable dog onto campus and then forbid all forms of affection.

Anyway, the man and the dog were not the perfect match.

Once the kids were gone, I watched Duncan practicing obedience commands with Chuck Norris for about five minutes before Chuck Norris ran out of patience and rose up on his hind legs to lick Duncan all over the face.

Were we worried about the *kids* agitating *Chuck Norris*—or the other way around?

Anyway, that wasn't the last memo we'd get from Duncan that day—only the first of a deluge:

From: Duncan Carpenter
RE: MEMO—NAME TAGS
Please note that all faculty must report to the security department today to register for new, digitized security name tags. Tags will be delivered next week. Faculty must wear their name tags at all times or risk disciplinary action.

From: Duncan Carpenter
RE: MEMO—PARKING SPACES
Please note that all faculty must report to the security department today to register for a new numbered parking space. Once numbers are assigned, they cannot be changed or traded. Faculty must park in their designated spaces at all times or risk disciplinary action.

From: Duncan Carpenter
RE: MEMO—SECURITY QUESTIONNAIRE
Please note that all faculty must check in online today to fill out a new standardized security questionnaire and screening. All surveys must be completed by Friday—no exceptions. Faculty who do not complete their surveys before the deadline risk disciplinary action.

Risking disciplinary action was a big thing with him.

We got maybe nine of these memos before lunchtime. Most teachers I bumped into that morning stopped reading after the first two or three. Which meant by the time "*From*: Duncan Carpenter. *RE*: MEMO—CAMPUS TOUR" came around just before car pool, only the most obedient members of the faculty were still paying attention. I was one of them, of course. I read everything. It turned out Duncan needed somebody to walk him around the school, give him the inside scoop, and familiarize him with everything he needed to know.

As I was skimming the memo, I'd said, out loud, "Not it."

But then every single person who responded nominated me.

Unanimous.

Fair enough. After car pool, I went to Duncan's office, once the school had emptied out.

He was in another gray suit today. One exactly—down to the weave of the fabric—like the one he'd been wearing before.

Same pants. Same vest. White shirt. Navy tie. And—even though it was August in Texas, which meant it was going to be a minimum of one hundred degrees out—a suit jacket. Buttoned.

Was there a tiny part of me that had been hoping he'd show up on the first day of school in checkerboard pants and a SpongeBob tie?

Absolutely.

But only a very small part.

For contrast, I'll mention that I was wearing a navy blue polka-dot blouse, an orange pencil skirt, and hot-pink, open-toed sandals. I also wore a long necklace with heavy white beads and I had a pale pink hibiscus flower tucked behind my ear that exactly matched my pink bangs.

I'd worked extra hard on this outfit that morning. To make it, shall we say, memorable.

"We match," I said, when I showed up.

Nothing about us matched.

"Navy," I explained, touching the navy part of my blouse, "and navy." I pointed at his tie.

He knew I was teasing, but he didn't smile. Just looked me over, taking particular note of the flower over my ear.

So I looked him over right back, taking particular note of the fact that *nobody in our generation wears three-piece suits*.

But I can't deny that he wore that suit well.

He just . . . wasn't Duncan.

I'd hoped that Chuck Norris would be with him, for comic relief if nothing else. But I guess he'd tuckered himself out, because when I arrived, he was conked out, belly-up, on Duncan's new, gray, office sofa.

Duncan sighed. "Let's do this."

I sighed back. "Fine."

I had one goal as we started the tour—to *not* show him the library.

Because I already knew how this whole thing was going to go. I was going to show him every whimsical, surprising nook and cranny of our beloved campus, lovingly turning his attention to the colorful, fluttering bunting flags we'd strung above the courtyard, the fairy houses the first-graders had been making for the garden, the collection of driftwood sculptures Babette had amassed in the art room, the mural the fifth-grade girls had painted last year on a blank wall across from their bathroom that said, BE YOUR OWN KIND OF BEAUTIFUL, and on and on . . . and he'd be uninterested, inattentive, and unimpressed.

Or worse.

I mean, I hoped he'd prove me wrong. But I also knew he wouldn't.

The library was special. The library was mine. And I had no interest in watching him undervalue it, insult it, or say something like, "These books are a fire hazard! Get rid of them."

It wasn't out of the range of possibilities.

So I decided to take him to the library last, keep the pace of the tour nice and glacial, and hope that we'd run out of time to ever get there.

We started in the courtyard.

"It's a historic building," I said, as I caught up behind him. "Built as a convent in the 1870s, and the nuns lived here for a hundred years before their numbers dwindled so much, the church sold the property to the city. It sat empty for another twenty years before Max and Babette"—I always made sure to give her equal credit on feminist principle—"founded the Kempner School and renovated it. Fun fact: did you know that our school is named after Babette?"

Duncan looked at me like that didn't make sense.

"Babette *Kempner*," I said.

"But wasn't Max's name also Kempner?"

"Sure," I said. "But he was thinking of Babette when he named it."

We kept walking.

"The cafeteria used to be the chapel," I went on.

"I read that in the manual."

"We have a once-a-week assembly with the kids where we bring in speakers and programs from all different faiths and philosophies—plus performances. Singers, drummers, belly dancers, fire-eaters."

"Fire-eaters?"

"It's kind of an anything-goes situation."

I could almost hear him mentally typing: MEMO—RE: FIRE-EATERS.

I pointed up at one of the second-story rooms. "That's where the ghost lives."

Duncan glanced sideways at me, though he never actually met my eyes. "The ghost?"

This was a good story. "One of the nuns fell in love with a sea captain whose boat went down in a storm in the Gulf. She couldn't believe

he was dead, though, and she locked herself in this room, watching the
ocean, refusing to come out until he came back to her . . . but he never
came back, and she died of heartbreak. They say she's still here, waiting. Sometimes people see her, still waiting by the window, watching
for him, never giving up hope."

Duncan frowned again. "Do the kids know that story?"

"Of course."

"Does it scare them?"

"Well, yeah. But in a good way."

Duncan looked back up toward the room. For a second, I thought
he was thinking about the ghost, but then he said, "Roof needs to be
replaced. And that window paint is peeling like crazy."

I'd known he was going to look at the place like that. But it still bothered me. I wanted him to be impressed. I wanted him to fall in love.

"This building survived the Great Storm of 1900," I said then. "Do
you know about that storm?"

"A little."

"It's the worst natural disaster in U.S. history," I said, "*to this day*.
Ten thousand people died in one night. Winds were more than a hundred and fifty miles an hour. People's clothes were ripped right off their
bodies, corsets and all—that's how strong the winds were. But this
building stood steady. All the nuns survived—as well as a hundred people who found their way here and sheltered overnight. There's a whole
museum about the storm. And a documentary."

Duncan nodded. "Sidewalk needs to be fixed," he said then, pointing at an uneven spot. "That's a tripping hazard."

The old Duncan would have taken my hand and dragged me upstairs to look for the ghost. The old Duncan would have walked right
out of school to buy tickets for the documentary. The old Duncan would
have fallen in love with this breathtaking, stately, remarkable stone
building and everything it had survived.

But the new Duncan just said, "Insurance on this place must be a
nightmare."

Nightmares were a big thing for him, too, apparently.

As we continued the tour, I got limper and limper. I showed him our butterfly garden, but he said it had too many bees—a liability. I showed him Babette's art room, but he said it was too overstuffed with supplies—a fire hazard. The brightly painted hallways were "visual chaos." The hopscotch pattern we'd stenciled on the hallway floor was a "tripping problem." The bulb lights in the faculty lounge were "a mess."

Everything awesome about our school—everything that made it special and unique and joyful—was problematic to Duncan. It was like he refused to see anything good. He was hell-bent on only looking for trouble.

And his *demeanor.*

Good God, he was like a prison warden.

Which would have been alarming to witness in any new school principal, but given that this was *the* Duncan Carpenter, it was utterly destabilizing. There were no jokes. There was no laughter. I did not even count one smile.

If I'd had any indication—at all—that he even vaguely remembered me, I might have asked him about it. Part of me wondered if he would recognize me eventually, if something might trigger his memory. And part of me thought I should just go ahead and say something.

But I couldn't bring myself to say it.

Frankly, it was insulting. If he'd forgotten me so thoroughly, it was pathetic for me to remember him. Pretending not to know him, either, became a way of saving face, even if only to myself. He didn't remember me? Fine. I didn't remember him, either.

It was worse than if I hadn't known him at all.

I'll tell you something: I'd known all along that Duncan coming here was going to break my heart. But this was worse than what I'd braced myself for. It wasn't just the agony of wanting someone I couldn't have. It was like the guy I'd loved so much for so long *no longer existed*—even though he was standing right next to me.

It was more like grief than heartbreak.

There was an upside, though. The old Duncan had been intimidatingly awesome.

That was not a problem anymore.

The tour took us two hours—hours when I should have been making dinner for Babette, or organizing library shelves, or putting together that dumb hanging sculpture I'd ordered.

Over and over, I tried to tell Duncan about the building's history—how a famous bank robber had tried to hide here in the 1890s before being apprehended, and how it had been used as a military hospital during World War II, and that it had been a set for a movie with Elizabeth Taylor in the 1950s. And over and over, he countered those amazing stories with questions like, "Why don't any of the classroom doors have locks on them?"

I give myself credit for doing an epic job of stalling, pausing to call his attention to big things and minutia alike—from our painted rock garden to our rain-collecting barrels. I showed him the back staircase where we'd painted a number on each step going up, and then added the English word for that number, the Spanish word for it, and the number in braille dots. I showed him how the rubber "floor" of the playground was patterned in Fibonacci spirals. I showed him the fifth-grade science room that had a periodic table painted on the ceiling. I took him past Alice's room, where she had drawn a semicircle of angles on the floor under the spot where the classroom door opened.

I kept thinking, as the tour went on and on, that he'd finally tell me that he needed to get back to his office. But he didn't. Finally, when there was nowhere left but the library, I made an attempt to just cruise by.

"Wait," he said, pointing at the library doors.

"Ah," I said, as if I'd forgotten the very place that I was in charge of. "Of course."

Duncan opened the door for me, looking impatient.

When Max and Babette had renovated the building thirty years before, they'd been dead split over putting the library down on the lower level, near the entrance, so that kids had to walk right past it to get in and out of the building—or on the higher level, so it had views to the ocean and felt like a tree house. In the end, they compromised and did . . . *both*. The main entrance to the library was down low, off the courtyard, but they'd busted a hole in the ceiling and built a staircase to the room directly above it, making it two stories tall.

When I'd arrived, Babette had helped me paint the stair risers like a stack of giant books, and it was the first thing you saw when you walked in.

It was exactly what a library should be, in my view. Whimsical. Inviting. Infused with possibility. Not to mention sunny, comfortable, and homey. I wanted kids to come in and out all the time. I wanted the doors to be open from the moment the first kid arrived on campus in the morning until the very last kid left.

I kept a collection of crazy pens in a cup on my desk to entice the kids to come see me: pens with troll hair, and googly eyes, and pompoms. One pen had an hourglass embedded in it, one looked like a syringe filled with blue liquid, and one was shaped like a very realistic bone. I had pens in the shapes of feather quills, and pens with bendy mermaid tails, and pens that told fortunes like a Magic 8 Ball. I had sloth pens, unicorn pens, and pens with pom-poms.

I had other toys on my desk, too—a fancy kaleidoscope, a Newton's cradle, a set of magnetic sculpture balls, and a collection of spinning tops. I had a Rubik's Cube, too, although it didn't work as well as it used to since one of the first-graders had decided to solve it by peeling off and rearranging the stickers.

All to make the circulation desk feel like fun.

All to let the kids know they were safe with me.

I wanted to make sure that if kids felt an impulse at any moment to pop by the library, there'd be nothing to stop them. It was the best way I knew to turn them into readers: to catch those little sparks when they happened and turn them into flames.

I loved my job, is what I'm saying.

The second floor was like a magical land. We kept reference books, how-tos, and nonfiction downstairs—but upstairs was all fiction. From picture books to chapter books, that floor was all about getting lost in imaginary worlds. We had reading nooks tucked around every corner, beanbag chairs all around, and even a big reading "nest" that the kids could climb into like baby birds, fashioned out of wood and papier-mâché. We had a tunnel made out of books. We had a loft by the window where the kids could climb up and read next to a view of the Gulf.

It was bright. It was whimsical. It was special. And it was mine.

I didn't want Duncan telling me it was a fire hazard.

But I went in with him anyway. What choice did I have?

The first thing he saw as we stepped in were the book-spine stairs.

"Cool stairs," he said, seeming to forget his no-praise policy.

It was the first nice thing he'd said all afternoon. "Thank you," I said. "Babette and I painted them."

That got his attention. He met my eyes for the first time all day. "You painted them?"

"Babette did the hard stuff. I just filled in the colors."

"They really look like book spines," he said then, studying them, the wonder in his voice softening it and making him sound the tiniest bit like the old Duncan.

"She figured out the shading to make them look three-D."

Duncan read the spines out loud. *"Charlotte's Web. James and the Giant Peach. How to Train Your Dragon. Harriet the Spy. Harry Potter and the Sorcerer's Stone."*

Was he going to read them all? "We let the kids vote on their favorites."

"Of course."

It was the first—the only—moment all day that had felt anything like a normal, pleasant conversation and it confirmed what I'd always believed about whimsy—that it found a way past people's defenses.

At the top of the stairs, we found Clay Buckley lying on the reading-circle rug surrounded by stacks of *Archie* comics.

"Hey, Clay," I said.

He rotated, chin on his hand. "Hey."

"Doing some reading?"

"I'm not allowed to read these at home."

"Gotcha," I said with a wink, just as Duncan said, "Shouldn't you be in after-care?"

"I'm waiting for my dad," Clay said.

But Duncan didn't seem to get who his dad was. "Still. You shouldn't just be roaming around campus like a—"

"Like a labradoodle?" I offered.

"My grandmother lets me come to the library," Clay said, like that settled the issue.

Duncan looked at me, like *Who's his grandmother?*

"His grandmother is Babette," I said. Then I added, "Kempner."

"So," Duncan said, piecing it together. "If Babette is his grandmother then that must make him . . ."

"Kent Buckley's son," I said with a nod.

And that seemed to settle it. This kid could read all the *Archie* comics he liked.

The tour was almost over. I was ready to be done. The stress of being around someone who looked like Duncan Carpenter but acted like the opposite of him was wearing me out.

As I walked him toward the exit, past the circulation desk, he noticed the disassembled mobile spread out all over it. "What's this?" he asked.

"It's a hanging butterfly sculpture made of old bicycle parts I got this summer. I thought it would be great right there." I pointed at a spot on the ceiling. "But when I opened it and saw all the pieces, I panicked."

At that, Duncan actually smiled—not at me, but down at all the pieces. I saw his cheek move and the side of his eye wrinkle . . . but then, he dropped it, almost as if smiling by accident had startled him, and when he looked up again, his face had returned to blank.

"You're not going to put it together?" he asked.

I gave a little head shake. "Not today."

"When, then?"

I'd ordered that thing in the summer—a whole lifetime ago. "I don't know," I said. Then I shrugged. "How about never?"

nine

That first month of school was such an onslaught that I almost forgot about Duncan Carpenter. All my voracious readers were all over me—wanting to know what was new, wanting to check out ten books each, or the biggest books they could find, or looking for book three in whatever series they were hooked on. It was like a circus in there.

A book circus.

I was glad for it. Glad for an escape from those strange, heartbreaking final weeks of summer. Glad for the rhythm of the school year to pull me along. Glad for the library full of readers.

I loved the energy of their little bodies, and sounds of their voices, even when they got too loud. I was not a librarian who went around shushing kids—but I did try to help them remember that the library was supposed to be a calming space, a special space, one that left room for the imagination.

Duncan made changes, yes—but incrementally enough that, one by one, they didn't provoke rebellion.

He instituted assigned seating for the kids at lunch, for example. Which actually turned out to have some advantages.

The kids hated it, but that was okay. Kids hated lots of things.

Duncan also started requiring the teachers to take attendance in every class—not just first thing in the morning. His reasoning was that we needed to monitor where the kids were throughout the school day. What if one of them went missing? How would we know?

This change had fewer advantages. The *teachers* hated this one.

Um. How would we know? We would just—you know—*notice that someone was missing*. The implication that taking attendance was the only way to keep our kids from going AWOL was, frankly, pretty insulting. But Duncan wanted a record—an accounting of where every single kid was during the school day. And it wasn't the biggest imposition in the world. Seriously, once we'd seen him hold up that gun, something like taking attendance in class seemed like small potatoes.

In theory, at least.

In practice? Taking attendance is just about the most boring possible way to start a class.

Other little changes that Duncan worked into the schedule bit by bit without ever causing a riot: Shortening lunch by ten minutes. Shortening recess, too. Decreeing that faculty could not cover each other's classes. Decreeing that faculty could not leave campus during the school day.

Not to mention, adding locks and keypads to every gate that let you in or out of school grounds—except for the front entrance, which was guarded by security at all times.

The keypads themselves weren't all that onerous, but what did turn into a serious drag was that they changed the security codes every two weeks.

Maybe this wouldn't be so bad, if you had nothing else to think about.

But teachers always have *everything* else to think about.

It was the worst for people who drove—which was everybody except me—because the parking lot was on the far side of the school's entrance. If you forgot the code, you had to walk all the way around to the front. It made me glad, in a way, that I didn't drive anymore—not since the seizures came back. Partly because I didn't want to be on medication, which was required for a license. But also, if I'm honest, after that first, spectacular reintroduction to my adult epilepsy, I wasn't too eager to get back behind the wheel.

It was fine. There were upsides.

It was a slower pace of life.

Most mornings I just rode my yellow bike—with my supplies tucked into the handlebar basket that Babette and I had hot-glued fake flowers all over—and Chuck Norris would come bounding out of the gates and lick my ankles while I locked it up out front.

Remember how Duncan told us not to pet him?

Yeah . . . I would pet the hell out of that dog.

It was good for both of us.

In fact, I did my best to ignore most of Duncan's changes.

But the one that hit me the hardest was car-pool duty.

He completely overhauled car pool the third week of school—deciding that it wasn't safe for kids to sit outside the building while they waited to go home.

"They're literally sitting ducks," he'd said to Alice.

"Well," she had famously said, "not *literally*."

By royal decree, the kids now had to sit inside in the courtyard for car pool. It took twice as long and required a relay system.

It required twice as many teachers, too.

I got conscripted into it—against my will. Everybody did. So once a week, at the end of a long, draining workday, I got to stand out in the hundred degree heat for more than an hour, breathing carbon monoxide and fielding angry parents who'd roll down their car windows and shout, "I've been in this line for over an hour!"

"At least you have AC," I'd say, taking a swig from my water bottle.

It got so bad, Alice suggested we stick ice cubes in our bras—which I did not go for, though it was tempting. Instead, I found a giant pink parasol at one of the beach shops and used it to create my own personal patch of shade.

Which helped a little. But not enough.

It was close to Thanksgiving before Duncan went nuclear on us.

I'm not sure if he'd been trying to lull us into a false sense of security, or if it just took him that long to get organized, but by the time it happened, we had settled into a comfortable state of discomfort.

I, for one, had found a very unexpected peace with him. As profoundly as his revised personality had disappointed me, for the most part, it had also cured me of my epic crush. I almost thought of them as two different people now. Old Duncan, who I still pined for, and New Duncan, who I most definitely did not.

Old Duncan was still my irreplaceable gold standard for everything lovable.

New Duncan? Was just kind of a dickish boss.

And guys like that were a dime a dozen.

I couldn't have been in love with him now. There was nothing likable there to love.

New Duncan was intensely private—never talking about himself, or his home life, or his past. We hadn't even had one sighting of the wife— or the kids. He kept his home life and his work life completely separate in every way. I guess he really did not want us in his business. Fine with me. Better, in fact. He didn't even have photos in his office—no personal things at all. Just books on pedagogy.

Dull as chalk and half as fun.

It was a relief. My heart was safe. Now if he would just stop meddling with my school, I kept telling myself, things could go back to normal. Ish.

Even though, of course, I knew they never could.

And then, one unremarkable Friday afternoon, we got a doozy of a memo—like no one at this school had ever seen before. *"From*: Duncan Carpenter. *RE*: MEMO—SAFETY AND SECURITY—Effective Immediately."

It was nine single-spaced pages long, and I read every word.

We all did.

It may be the only nine-page, school-wide memo in the history of time that's been read to completion by all of its recipients.

But not in a good way.

As my eyes took in sentence after sentence in horror, I felt a rising sense of panic.

All those things I was so relieved Duncan hadn't done?

He was doing them now.

He'd organized his memo into two sections: On-Campus Security Improvements and Off-Campus Security Improvements.

For On-Campus Security, the following changes would be effective immediately: Our lovely, open archway at the school's entrance would have an iron gate installed over it, and visitors would be buzzed in by a guard—one of three new ones we'd be hiring. Once inside, everyone would clear metal detectors and run their bags through airport-style X-ray machines: students, faculty, administrators, and visitors alike. Bags and backpacks would be hand-searched, as well.

Oh, and P.S.—Duncan had just fired our security guard, Raymond, for "lack of alertness."

On to classroom safety: All rooms on the ground floor would be required to keep their shades drawn and their windows closed and locked at all times. At some point in the future, windows would be replaced with bulletproof glass and/or metal bars would be installed. All the hardwood, historic classroom doors would be replaced with metal ones—made by a company that also made armored tanks—as soon as possible. Transoms over the doors—which we still used on pretty days for breezes, would be boarded up.

To "reduce visual chaos" and "aid visibility" on campus, over the course of the year, the school would be repainting hallways and classrooms a color that Duncan described as a "calming gray." He was also instituting a uniform for the children to wear—also gray—starting in January, and he respectfully asked that teachers try to dress in solid colors, preferably muted grays, browns, and tans. All of this in the service of "increased visibility."

Before I could even react to any of that, my eyes had moved on to the section titled Off-Campus Security—which argued, in essence, that there was no such thing. Because it would be impossible to ensure students' security off campus, we would no longer be taking field trips to the beach, or to the aquarium, or to the amusement park built out over the ocean.

Basically: no field trips at all. Ever. Effective immediately.

I scrolled back up to the top of the email, and I read it again.

Then I read it again.

Especially the "no field trips" part. Because we had a field trip planned for the very next week: our annual beach cleanup for the third-graders, where the class combed a section of beach to collect as much plastic trash as they could. They wore gloves, used rakes and shovels, filled trash bags, and generally felt like they were making a huge impact. You could see the difference on the stretch of beach—and over the years, we'd filled a whole hallway with before-and-after pictures.

It was Max's view that you couldn't teach kids about something deeply depressing—like the state of our oceans—without also giving them hope and a plan of action. This week, as scheduled, the kids had all been watching documentaries about a phenomenon known as the Great Pacific Garbage Patch—a floating collection of plastic, litter, trash, and debris that had been carried by currents from all over the world to collect in a giant, gloppy soup of nastiness that was twice as big as the state of Texas.

Texas is big, y'all.

It's almost 700 miles wide and almost 800 miles long.

It takes fourteen to sixteen hours to drive across it.

So that is one big patch of floating garbage.

We were *islanders* in Galveston. We had the Gulf on one side and the bay on the other. This wasn't theoretical for us. People here made their livings, one way or another, from the water. And so we'd built the fall curriculum around it. Whether the bumper sticker on your car said BOI (Born On the Island) or IBC (Islander By Choice), we were all on this island together. The ocean and everything it meant, symbolized, or impacted was woven through every minute of our days. This wasn't theoretical for us.

This was personal.

Max always felt like learning had to matter. That we had to build our lessons around things kids cared about and make sure they knew the stakes. And so building the third-grade curriculum around the ocean gave a theme to the whole year.

I even had a whole display in the library, and I'd been reading a retelling of *The Little Mermaid* that was slightly more Ariel-positive than the animated version they all knew. We'd compare different versions, usually ending in a lively discussion about gender politics in the mermaid kingdom and how giving up your entire identity for love was generally a bad idea.

"Don't ever give up your voice for anyone," I told the kids every year.

"Or your tail!" the kindergartners usually shouted.

"Especially not your tail," I agreed—and then I had them spend the rest of the period in the maker space, drawing me pictures of their merfolk tails.

In my favorite version of the story, the mermaid finds a magic shell that let her do both—have human legs or a mermaid tail, depending on her mood.

How realistic was that ending? I didn't really care.

If *mermaids* couldn't have it all, dammit—who could?

But I'm getting off topic.

That night, after we'd all received Duncan's epic memo, as we gathered at Babette's, the mood among the teachers was very . . . *villagers with pitchforks.*

I guess you could say that the faculty and staff were not happy.

You could also say that they thought Duncan was the devil.

By the time I arrived, the garden table was stacked high with pizza boxes and at least thirty teachers were stress-eating. And stress-drinking. And somebody had hit the grocery store and cleaned out the bakery—cinnamon rolls, donuts, éclairs. Even a birthday cake that said "Happy Birthday, Stanley" that was on super-special for $1.99 because no one had ever picked it up.

People weren't even using plates with that birthday cake. Just digging in with their forks like desperate raccoons.

Mrs. Kline was trying to keep order, but being in charge wasn't really her thing. She had a yellow legal pad and was taking notes as the crowd got louder, and drunker, and more sugared-up.

Let's just say the canceling of all field trips, all color, all individuality, all creativity, and all fun did not go over too well. It might have been the definitive moment when Duncan fully lost them.

Lost all of us.

"He wants to paint the whole school gray," Alice kept saying.

"He wants to put bars on everything," Sadie Lee from the first grade added.

"He's making the kids wear uniforms," Carlos said.

"He's making *us* wear uniforms!" Anton the science teacher called out

"Where's he getting the money for all this?" Mrs. Kline added.

"How is this happening?" Donna demanded.

"How did he get approval?" the school nurse wanted to know.

As I watched the teachers panicking, I came to a conclusion. Who Duncan used to be didn't—couldn't—outweigh who he had become.

I could not—and absolutely *would not*—let him turn our school into a prison.

He had to go.

We had to find a way to get rid of him.

I took Mrs. Kline's yellow pad and her pen. Then I stood up on the back steps and called everybody to order by shouting, "One! Two!"

"Eyes on you!" they all shouted back.

So easy with teachers.

In the quiet that followed, I said, "That memo today made it clear: Nobody is coming to save us. We're going to have to save ourselves. And save the school." I looked around at all the teachers. There were at least thirty of us there. Then I said, "We have to get rid of this guy."

A wine-and-cake-fueled cheer went up.

Of course, nobody really knew how to do that—but that was what this gathering was going to turn into. A full-panic, no-idea-is-too-dumb brainstorming session.

First idea was to get a petition going.

Second idea was writing a group letter to the board signed by as many faculty as we could get—which would be everybody.

Third idea was to refute each of Duncan's bad ideas, one by one, assigning each to a willing faculty member to do a write-up about why it wouldn't work. I agreed to take the gray walls; Coach Gordo agreed to take the iron bars; Carlos took the security guards; and Alice took the canceling of field trips. Once all the major affronts had been assigned, we went through the smaller changes, from the changing keypad codes to the recent switch of all campus lightbulbs to blue fluorescents, which were cheaper, yes, but which gave off a morgue-like vibe that was bumming everybody out. Unanimously.

Was I sure it would work? No.

But it was a start.

We'd figure this out. We'd work together. I wasn't sure how, and I wasn't sure when, but I knew we'd manage it. We weren't giving up. We weren't chickening out. And we sure as hell weren't canceling our field trip to the beach.

ten

That was another rule of Max's: *Never give anyone bad news without also giving them something to do about it.*

We went to the beach to pick up trash every year without fail.

All to say, when Duncan sent out that email, the buses were already ordered, the teacher teams were already organized, the trash bags and rakes and cleanup supplies were already assembled, and the posters to record and celebrate how many pounds of trash we'd removed were already made.

All ready and waiting.

I'd say, in general, I was a pretty obedient person. I didn't throw recyclables in the trash. I voted every Election Day—even in the tiny ones most people skipped. If a recipe called for a tablespoon of something, I didn't just eyeball it, I measured it out.

But in response to the beach cleanup being canceled, I had a very nonobedient reaction. Some unknown, fiery part of me rose up from some unknown, fiery place in my soul and created this thought in my mind: *I dare you.*

I dare you to stop us.

Duncan Carpenter had no right to cancel that trip. It was a tradition much bigger than him. We did a beach cleanup every year. It had been happening since before Duncan Carpenter was *even born*. Or close enough. It had been Max's idea long before I'd come here, and we weren't going to just let it die now that he was gone.

Was *this* the hill I wanted to die on? Trash cleanup at the beach?

Yes. Apparently, it was.

Here's what I'm saying: We wound up sneaking the entire third grade out of the building.

Just funneled 'em out the south gate and walked them the three blocks to the seawall. We held hands and we sang sea shanties. It was easy. The teachers had already blocked out the time. Carlos drove over with the shovels and the sifters in his pickup truck. It was fine. We'd be back by lunchtime.

I wore a wide-brimmed straw hat to work that day, and a seashell-printed sarong, and I brought my beach bag with extra sunscreen, in case anybody needed it.

The early part of the day was delightful.

I had the adorable Clay Buckley in my group, and he was full of trivia about everything sea related. He was one of those sweet, serious little boys who seemed somehow more like a thirty-five-year-old therapist than like a kid. Maybe it was the too-big glasses with blue camo frames. Maybe it was his gentle manner, or his impressive vocabulary, or the way he was practically an encyclopedia . . . but he mostly seemed like he was narrating a nature documentary.

Wise beyond his years.

The rule for the kids was that they weren't allowed to touch the trash with their fingers. We made them wear gloves and dispensed cheap plastic beach toy shovels and plastic sifters for them to shovel up any trash they saw, sift the sand out, and then dump the remaining trash in the garbage bags. If a kid saw something sharp—a broken bottle, or worse—they had to call a teacher. The kids did pretty well with it—I think, in part, because by this point in the year, they knew so much about plastic in the ocean, they were eager to help.

Clay Buckley and I wound up side by side on our hands and knees that morning for more than an hour, shoveling and sifting bottle caps, balloons, six-pack rings, plastic bags, fishing line, and a million little brightly colored pieces we couldn't identify—and by the end of it, I was officially in the Clay Buckley Fan Club.

Regardless of his mother. Or his dad.

Early on, Clay said to me, "It's ironic that we're cleaning plastic off the beach with plastic shovels."

"It's a little bit like cannibalism," I joked.

But Clay thought about it. "It feels more to me like soldiers collecting their war dead."

"I see that," I said, and kept shoveling.

In that hour, from Clay, I learned more about the marine habitat of the Gulf of Mexico than I ever thought possible. Here's a sample of what Clay had to say: "Everybody's heard about the Kemp's ridley sea turtles, but did you know the Gulf's also got leatherback, logger-head, and hawksbill?" (I did not.) "Did you know that the leatherback has existed in basically its same form since the time of the dinosaurs?" (Again, no.) "Can you imagine what it would be like for your favorite food to be jellyfish?" (Another nope.)

"Spicy!" was all I could think of to say.

Then Clay said something that really shocked me: "Max and I used to go turtle hunting during nesting season."

"Wait—you and Max *hunted turtles*?"

Clay looked up at me. "Not hunting, like *bang-bang*," he said. "Hunting like *click-click*." He clicked the imaginary shutter of a camera.

"Well, that's a relief." I gave him a wink.

I had seen more than a few photos of their outings, actually. You had to watch out, or Max would make you stand there while he flipped through every snapshot on his phone.

"There are whales out there, too," Clay said, pausing to look out at the Gulf.

That didn't seem right. My image of whales was out in the deep ocean, not the shallow Gulf. This time, I meant it: "Really?"

"Twenty-five different species, in fact. Humpbacks, blues, killers, and a bunch of others. One called a Bryde's whale that just got listed as endangered. Oh, plus sperm whales."

I frowned, like *No way.* "Sperm whales? Seriously?"

"Seriously."

"I have never seen a sperm whale around Galveston."

"Well, of course not," Clay said gently. "They're underwater."

"Fair enough."

"Plus," he added, "they're far out, in the deep parts. But ships used to come to the whaling grounds from all over." Then he turned to me and nodded. "And we've got the shipwrecks to prove it. Four thousand of them, to be exact."

"There are *four thousand* shipwrecks out there?" I said, pausing to look out, like I might spot one.

"Yup."

"How do you know all this?" I asked.

Clay looked down. "Max."

Oh. Max.

"Plus," Clay added then, "I want to be a maritime archaeologist when I grow up. And there's a lot to learn. So I have to keep pretty busy."

"I could totally see you as a maritime archaeologist," I said. I wasn't 100 percent sure what that was, but I could see Clay as anything he wanted to be.

"Thank you," Clay said, giving a little bow. He went back to sifting. "Do you know about the shipwreck *La Belle*?"

I shook my head.

"It sank in the 1600s in Matagorda Bay—and archaeologists found it not that long ago and excavated it. They built a wall to hold back the water. They found a crest of a French admiral. They found the hilt of a sword. They found *human bones.*"

"Whoa," I said.

"Max was going to take me overnight to the museum in Port Lavaca . . ." Clay stopped sifting for a second. "But now my dad's going to take me instead."

I tried to imagine Kent Buckley at a museum with his introverted, bookish, deep-thinking child. Clay would be reading every sign for every artifact twice, and Kent Buckley would be conducting some douchey meeting on his cell phone, talking too loud and hurrying Clay along.

It hit me then that, out of all of us, Clay might have been the person who'd needed Max the most.

"The museum sounds amazing," I said, trying to say something true.

Clay met my eyes. "You can come with us if you want." He gave a little shrug. "I'll sleep on the floor."

For some reason, the way he said it made my eyes sting with tears. I blinked them away.

"You just pay close attention," I said, "and then come back and tell me everything."

"Roger that," Clay said.

"Hey, Brainerd," a kid called out to Clay a minute later, "I found a shark's tooth!"

He held up a triangular piece of plastic.

"Awesome," Clay said, refusing to take the bait.

That kid's name was Matthew, but he'd just started telling people to call him "Mad Dog." A few seconds later, I leaned over quietly and said, "What did Mad Dog just call you?"

Clay kept sifting. "Brainerd," he said. "It's a nickname."

I tried to proceed gently. "How did you get that nickname?"

Clay paused. "It's supposed to be insulting. You know: 'brain' plus 'nerd'? But Dr. Alfred Brainerd happens to be one of my favorite rock-star scientists, so the joke's on Matthew."

"Don't you mean Mad Dog?"

Clay wrinkled his nose. "I'm sticking with Matthew."

I couldn't tell how much the nickname bothered Clay. "Do you want me to tell Matthew to stop calling you Brainerd?"

He met my eyes and shook his head. "Nah," he said. "I take it as a compliment."

I nodded, like *Gotcha.*

Whether he did or didn't, this wasn't the moment to take a deep dive into it. He seemed okay—better than okay, actually, as he went back to chattering along about the marine life and general history of the Gulf of Mexico: the dolphin stranding a couple of summers ago, the details from a book he'd read about the 1900 storm, the escapades of various pirates.

"There's pirate gold buried everywhere," Clay promised. "Max and I used to look for it with his metal detector."

Max had loved that metal detector.

"He left it to me," Clay said then. "In his will."

There were those tears again. I swallowed. "Will you take me looking sometime?"

"You got it," Clay said, and dumped a sifted pile of bottle caps in the trash bag.

A minute later, Mad Dog called, "Brainerd! What's this?"

He pulled a nylon fishing net up from under a fine layer of sand. Some teachers came to help. By the time the whole thing was uncovered it was as big as a blanket.

"It's a ghost net," Clay said.

The kids perked up at the word "ghost."

"That's the name for nets that have been abandoned and end up floating free in the water," Clay explained. "They're made of nylon, so they don't disintegrate, and they kill wildlife all the time. Fish, and sea turtles, and pelicans, and dolphins—they all get caught in them and suffocate. Or starve."

"Well, not *this* net," a little girl named Angel said, marching over to Mad Dog with a trash bag. Mad Dog got her meaning and started stuffing the net in the bag. Soon it was disposed of.

"Thanks, Brainerd," Mad Dog said, and then a bunch of other kids chimed in, high-fiving him and cheering the demise of the ghost net.

Such a hard moment to read: the nickname seemed mean, but the thanks seemed genuine. I decided to follow Clay's lead on it—and he seemed happy, so I concluded it was a win.

And just at that moment, when I was feeling glad we were there, and proud we'd snuck the kids to their rightful beach cleanup, and happy to have learned so much beach trivia from my brainy little pal, and maybe just a little triumphant over the disposal of the ghost net myself, I looked up to see a figure standing on the seawall, looking down at us.

A male figure, backlit by the cloudless sky.

Duncan.

He came halfway down the concrete steps and surveyed us all—kids and teachers alike—as if we were the most shameful batch of heartless rule breakers.

"What's going on here?" he said at last, in a low, none-too-pleased voice.

The teachers all looked around at each other. Alice seemed to hunch a little shorter.

Finally, I stepped forward. "Just cleaning up some beach trash." Then I pointed at the trash bag full of the net, and said, as if it would make any sense, "Just being heroes and saving the ocean."

The kids cheered, and Duncan turned to stare at them.

Then he looked at me like I was very naughty. "Didn't you get my memo?"

I nodded.

"Did you *read* it?"

"I did. All nine single-spaced pages."

"So you know that all field trips have been suspended."

"I do."

"You're not here by mistake, is what I mean," like he was offering me an out.

I guess I could have taken it. But I didn't. "We're not here by mistake."

"You knew this field trip was canceled, but you came here anyway?"

"Correct."

Duncan looked me over. "Did you think I just wouldn't notice that *the entire third grade* was missing?"

"I hoped you wouldn't," I said, with a shrug. "If you weren't taking attendance."

Duncan turned to the teachers. "Start packing up. We're going back."

But I motioned to Duncan to come the rest of the way down the steps. "Can I talk to you please?"

When Duncan stepped onto the sand, after taking a second to adjust to the cognitive dissonance of a man in a gray suit, in recently polished black oxfords, standing on the beach, I added, "Privately?"

I started marching away from where the kids were, and Duncan, to my relief, followed.

When we were out of earshot, I said, "Don't do this. Let us finish what we're doing."

He shrugged. "You broke the rules."

"Well, they're bad rules."

"I disagree."

"We're fine," I said, gesturing to the kids. "It's been a lovely day. The kids have learned things and cheered for each other. We've been building toward this day for weeks—the moment when the kids get to do something to help out the ocean. It's been very inspiring for them."

"Irrelevant," Duncan said. "They can't be here."

"Why not?"

"Because field trips have been canceled."

"So uncancel them."

"That's not how it works."

"You can cancel them, but you can't *un*cancel them?"

"Not when people break the rules."

I pointed at the kids. "Look how happy they are. Why not just let them stay?"

"I can't protect them out here."

"You're not the Secret Service. They're just kids on a field trip."

"Not anymore."

He took a step like he was about to go back and round them up.

"Wait!" I said, putting my hand on his arm to stop him.

He looked down at my hand.

"Listen to what you're doing," I said, counting off of my fingers. "You're putting gates on everything and bars on the windows. You're painting everything gray. You're putting the kids—and the teachers, by the way—in gray uniforms. You're hiring a whole new flock of security guards. And you fired poor Raymond—"

"He was asleep all the time!"

"He has sleep apnea!"

We glared at each other for a second.

Then I said, "Can't you see what you're doing?"

He blinked at me.

"Bars? Gray walls? Gates? Guards? You're turning our school into a prison. An actual, literal prison."

It was my zinger. Meant to get some kind of reaction—prompt even some tiny new awareness. Maybe even spark an epiphany and make him realize how astonishingly wrong he'd been all along. Wouldn't that have been nice?

But what's the opposite of an epiphany? A shrug? Duncan said, "It's necessary."

"Says who?"

"I've consulted extensively with security experts."

"How do you know they know what they're talking about?"

"Um. Because they're experts."

"So? Experts are wrong all the time."

"That's fine. But it's my job to keep these kids—and the faculty, by the way—safe."

"That's not your only job."

"That's my number one job."

"They can't learn if they're miserable!"

"They can't learn if they're dead!"

At that, we both fell silent.

The wind was flicking at his hair, and his oxfords were now brushed with sand, but despite how ridiculously out of place he looked on this beach in that suit, he still managed to ooze authority. Duncan Carpenter, of all people, oozing authority. He should have been flying a kite! He should have been doing handstands in Hawaiian-print board shorts. He should have been *helping*.

The wrongness of the whole situation helped fuel an indignant courage in me. Me, in my straw hat, and heart-shaped sunglasses, and a T-shirt with a drawing of an octopus with all its arms stretched wide that said FREE HUGS.

I refused to back down.

And that was the moment—right there—when my need to understand what the hell had happened finally outweighed my need to protect myself. Before he could turn and walk back to the group and round everybody up before they were even finished, I found myself asking the question that had been following me like a ghost net ever since he'd arrived.

"How is it possible that you don't remember me?" I said then, taking a step closer.

Duncan just stared at me.

"I used to work at Andrews Prep in California. We"—I gestured between the two of us, feeling a flash of irritation that I had to explain this—"worked together for two years. I was quieter then, and a lot less . . . colorful. Maybe you didn't notice me. But I noticed you. Everybody did. You were . . ." I shook my head. "You were everything I wanted to be. You were the best possible kind of teacher I could imagine. And when I heard that you were coming here to be the principal of Kempner, I thought you'd be the best thing that could happen to us in the wake of losing Max—and that's saying a lot. But . . . what happened to you? Where are your flamingo pants? Where is your popcorn tie? The Duncan Carpenter I knew wouldn't be canceling field trips! He'd be planning new ones." Suddenly, the anger kind of melted away, and my voice got a little shaky. "I remember who you used to be. I was *so* excited to see that guy again. But it's like he's gone. I don't know where he is. And I don't have any idea at all who you are. But I'd give *anything* to see that guy again."

Duncan kept himself still the whole time I was talking—not moving, his expression totally stoic.

I don't know what I was hoping for. Some kind of explanation, maybe, like *My boring wife told me it was time to grow up and stop goofing around.* Or maybe, *I thought principals had to be hard-asses. Are you saying this place would* prefer *a sweet-hearted goofball?*

I guess in some fantasy version of this moment, I'd be able to show him the error of his ways. I'd be able to give him permission to be who he truly was. It's that fantasy we all harbor when somebody else is completely wrong, and we hope that if we explain it to them, they'll hear us, and go, "Oh, God. You're right. I'm the worst. Thank you for helping me be a better person."

Like that's ever worked.

Anyway: it didn't.

In response to all that—my confession that I knew him, my admission of how much I'd admired him, my accidental, utterly vulnerable, grand finale confession of how much I truly longed to see the former Duncan again—Duncan went with, "We're getting off topic, here."

But no. We were just—finally—getting *on* topic.

I didn't back down. "I remember you," I said, taking a step closer, peering into his face.

Duncan looked out at the Gulf.

"What happened?" I said. "What made you like this? Why did you change?" And then, thinking maybe I was asking the question that would hit the bull's-eye and cause him to admit the truth at last, I said, quieter, in almost a whisper. "Was it your wife?"

Duncan frowned and looked at me. "My wife?"

"She doesn't approve of goofing around, does she? She wants you to be serious all the time. She wants you to be like all the other adults." I shook my head. "She never had a sense of humor. Why do guys always, always go for the pretty girls—no matter how boring they are?"

But Duncan was staring at me.

Oh, God. I'd insulted him. You can't go around calling people's wives boring! I tried to backtrack. "Not your wife, of course—I mean—she's pretty and also . . . not . . . boring." I was so blatantly lying.

But that's when Duncan said, "Who?"

"Your wife. I'm sorry. I'm sure she has many, many great qualities."

But he was frowning. "I don't have a wife."

I froze. "Of course you do." And then, as if I were trying to remind him of something he should already know, I went on, "That lady from admissions? From Andrews?"

"Chelsey?"

"That's it," I said. "The one who asked you out in the parking lot."

"Wow," Duncan said. "Okay. We dated, but . . ."

That didn't compute. "Didn't you . . . marry her?"

"Marry her!" he burst out with the closest thing I'd seen to a laugh from him since he'd arrived.

"Didn't you move in together? Wasn't it really . . . serious?"

He shook his head slowly, like he couldn't imagine why I was asking that. "No."

"There was a rumor," I said, now all accusatory, "that you were thinking about getting engaged."

He looked at me like that was irrelevant. "Still, no."

"A solid rumor," I said. "A convincing rumor."

But Duncan just shook his head.

And despite the fact that we were fighting over the field trip, despite the fact that he had just declared the end of all fun forever, and despite the fact I didn't even like him anymore, my heart, very slowly, just started flapping its wings.

"So . . . you're not . . . married?" I needed to reconfirm. Again.

"No!" he said, like he'd never heard anything so crazy.

"You don't have, like, a whole gaggle of kids?"

Embarrassing, but true: I could not disguise the bizarre feeling of joy that had just appeared inside my body—like a million tiny, carbonated bubbles. I felt positively fizzy.

Duncan peered at me, reading my face.

I smiled. I couldn't help it. Then I put my hand over my mouth.

He shook his head at me, like he couldn't make sense of it all. "It was always casual. Sometimes I think we were really just dating because she wanted it so badly. It was easier to say yes than no. Anyway,

I left Andrews the next year—got offered a job in Baltimore—and she didn't want to leave California, and that was that."

I didn't know what else to do but start laughing. "Just to confirm one more time: not married?"

"Not even close."

I shook my head. "I thought you went home every night to the wife and kids."

"God, no. I go home every night with Chuck Norris—who has totally become the alpha, by the way—and then he bosses me into giving him half my dinner and then sleeps on my head."

"Okay," I said. "So—similar."

"I'm not *opposed* to being married, though," Duncan said. Then he added, "Kind of the way you feel about cats."

Oh, my God.

Wait—*what?*

My mouth dropped open. "You . . . know that?"

"That you are neutral on cats? But more of a dog person?"

I felt like all the air had been sucked out of the sky. "Wait. You . . . remember me?"

"Of course. We worked together at Andrews."

"But . . . have you always remembered me—or just since I started yelling at you?"

His voice sounded a little rough. "I have always remembered you."

"But why didn't you say anything?"

"What was there to say?"

"I don't know. How about 'Hello. Nice to see you again. How've you been?'"

Duncan's eyes seemed softer, somehow. "Hello," he said. "Nice to see you again. How've you been?"

Luckily, I remembered the third-graders nearby. I condensed my voice into a whisper-shout. "I've been *shitty*, thank you!" I said.

"Not entirely, though," Duncan said back, and I was too mad to notice that he sounded almost human. "You love it here." Then he added, "And it seems to love you."

Were we going to talk about something real now? It was completely disarming. I felt dazed. "I did love it here. I loved this job, and this town, and this school. I've grown up, and—you know . . ." I wanted to say "blossomed" but that felt like a weird thing to say about myself.

"Blossomed," Duncan supplied, when I faltered.

I blinked at him.

"But then," I went on, "we lost Max. My hero—*everybody's hero*— and the closest thing to a father, and a mentor, and frigging *Santa Claus* that I've ever known. He died right in front of me. Just as close as you are right now. And then, *boom*! You showed up—and I was so hopeful to see you again, and I thought maybe you could heal—" I almost said *me*, but then I switched to "—us all. But you were totally different. Nothing like the guy I knew. Nothing like Max, either. Nothing like this school or its values. And now I don't know what to do because now everything that mattered to me is falling apart—and it's not *all* because of you, but you are certainly not helping—and it's so much worse now because I just used to be so totally—"

I stopped myself from saying *in love with you*.

I tried again. "You were just so—"

I stopped myself from saying *lovable*.

Finally, I said, "It's *worse* than if you were just some random, or-dinary, pencil-pushing, form-loving administrator. It's worse than if you were just some run-of-the-mill douchebag. Because I know who you used to be. And he was so much better than the guy you've become."

In the process of, you know, speaking my truth, I had stepped closer and closer to him, and by the time I finished, I was just inches away, and he was looking down at me.

The wind tugged at my straw hat, so I put a hand on top to hold it in place.

For a second there, I felt like I'd made a pretty good argument.

And then I realized I'd just called my boss a douchebag.

He realized it, too.

In the silence that followed, it was like he shuttered himself back up. He took a step back. He gave a single nod. Then he said, "Noted."

We'd forgotten ourselves for a second there. His utter surprise that I'd thought he'd married the long-forgotten Chelsey and fathered a litter of kids had disarmed him. For a few minutes, he'd relaxed into his natural self. We hadn't been fighting, or disagreeing, or sparring. We were just talking. Like people do. Not cast in roles as uppity librarian and hard-ass administrator—just two people catching up on old times.

But I'd been so afraid of saying something foolish, that I'd done something foolish instead. I'd tried to argue him into staying like that.

Surprise! It didn't work.

He took another step back in the sand, composing himself. Then, he turned back toward the group—all of whom were staring at us, by the way. And, as he made his way back toward them, I had no choice but to follow.

The teachers' eyes shifted between the two of us as they watched for a verdict.

When he arrived at the group, he let out a long sigh.

Then, in a tone of voice like *he* was the one who'd been defeated, he finally said, "Everybody back to school. Right now. Or the kids all have D-halls and the teachers all have to proctor them."

The teachers hesitated for a second.

But then, when Duncan added, "Don't make me take the Keurig out of the faculty lounge"—they jumped into action.

eleven

That moment on the beach left me on an emotional seesaw about Duncan.

He was still acting like a warden, and systematically dismantling everything I loved about my school, and by extension my job, and by extension my life.

But that little human moment we'd shared together on the beach wouldn't let me give up on him entirely. Worse: it had cracked open a little leak of longing in the dam of my heart. And I could feel the crack growing a little bit every day.

In response, mostly, I avoided him. Things had been easier when I could see him as nothing but a jerk. It wasn't *fun* to see him that way, but it was easier.

That taste of honey wound up being worse than none at all.

Just like the song says.

Now, I was having to master the art of looking at him but not looking. Because now, I wanted to look as much as I didn't want to look, and that state of tension was infused with agony. So I'd look at things near him. I'd find a reason to glance in his direction without actually focusing on him. I'd try to give in just enough to satisfy the urge without actually doing it. Like biting the corner of a chocolate bar.

It only made things worse. You could've told me that.

This was the crux of it: Yes, he was the enemy, and yes, he was ruining my life, and yes, I was in the process of trying to get him fired . . . but he was also really fun to talk to.

Irresistibly fun to talk to.

You know those people? Those very rare, very special people who just play a kind of counterbeat to yours? It was like the way we talked had a rhythm, like he was the bass drum and I was the snare. He was doing his thing and I was doing mine, but the two of us together were just super danceable.

And the more we talked to each other, the faster we fell into that rhythm, and the more I just wanted to stay there.

But of course, it was all forbidden. I shouldn't joke with him, or banter with him, or even talk to him unless I had a good reason. I sure as hell shouldn't walk through the hallways with him.

The other teachers wouldn't approve. Heck, *I* didn't even approve.

So, for a couple of weeks there, I found myself looking for "legitimate" reasons to pop by his office, or ask for his help, or stay late after school in case he might be walking out around the same time that I was walking out and we could walk together and crack each other up without, you know, getting in trouble with myself.

Chuck Norris turned out to be a great resource for this because he kept coming to the library and gnawing on the books when he should have been on patrol. He really loved to eat books. So I'd walk him down, hand the book to Duncan to add to the growing pile, and then, as I turned to leave, Duncan would say, "Great outfit today, by the way."

I'd look down at my kelly-green circle skirt and my striped, multicolored knee socks below. "Thanks," I'd say. "These are clown socks, actually. Got 'em at the party store in the bargain bin for a dollar."

"Wow. Clown socks."

"Yeah. But . . . cool ones."

"They're less cool now that I know they're clown socks. Remaindered clown socks."

"False. Now they are *more* cool. Because now they have my stamp of approval."

"Yes, but you are a person wearing clown socks. So you're not qualified to judge."

And before I knew it, I'd spent twenty minutes trying to tear myself away.

I can't explain it, but talking to him—about anything—just felt good. The way singing feels good. Or laughing. Or getting a massage.

I've never been addicted to anything, but I suspect it might feel a little bit like this: You know you shouldn't but you just *want to so bad*. That was conversation with Duncan: illicit, indefensible, and wrong, wrong, wrong—but also blissfully, hopelessly impossible to resist.

And so I thought we were going to have one of those moments on the last day of school before winter break as I reported for lunch duty. Like, I walked along the cloister and saw him holding the door for people, and my heart did a little illegal shimmy in my chest. I almost felt nervous as I got closer—a feeling in myself I did not endorse—and then when it was my turn to go through the door, I looked up at him from under my eyelashes to say thank you, and just as I did, Chuck Norris came bounding toward us from behind me and knocked me right into Duncan's arms.

Totally legitimate.

I smacked against Duncan's chest with an *oof*, and the next thing I knew, he'd caught me.

It was the first time we'd touched in any way since I'd grabbed his arm on the beach—and now here I was, in his arms. The moment seemed to shift into slow motion and all my senses seemed to ramp up: I heard the swish of fabric, felt the rumble of his voice, the tension in his muscles as his arms clamped down to catch me.

He lifted me back to my feet, and it wasn't until I was standing on my own that time caught up. I looked around and saw the room staring at us.

"Chuck Norris!" I said, all scoldy, to prove to everyone that I would never have voluntarily crashed into Duncan's chest like that. But Chuck Norris had wandered off to try to drink from one of the sprinkler heads in the courtyard.

So I just kept moving, stepping on into the cafeteria, my whole body giving off invisible sparks from the impact.

It was a moment that made me feel dizzy and girly and stupid, and who knows what kind of giggling I might have done afterward if circumstances had been different. But as it was, as I arrived in the cafeteria, I looked up to see something that wiped the memory of Duncan's chest clear from my mind.

The butterfly mural on the cafeteria wall—the floor-to-ceiling, full-sized, gorgeous, epic, legendary mural that Babette and I had spent an entire summer painting—was gone.

In its place was a gray wall.

I gaped.

Then I turned to look around the room like maybe it had . . . *moved,* somehow?

But all the walls were gray.

Everything was gray.

Even the floor, which hadn't changed and was still a yellow-and-white checkerboard of slick industrial squares, looked gray. Like all the gray around it had soaked into it. The room—always so sunny and bright—suddenly looked dingy, and dirty, and sad. Just like a prison. Just like I'd warned him.

I looked around for Duncan.

He'd walked in after me.

He always prowled the perimeter of the cafeteria during lunch duty, standing at military attention and watching all entrances and exits. He never actually ate during lunch. I wasn't sure I'd ever seen him eat anything at all. Did he eat? Maybe he just plugged himself in at night like a Tesla.

I spotted him, standing stiff as a soldier, on guard.

I don't even remember closing the space between the two of us. I just remember showing up.

"Where's the—" I started to ask, but then I couldn't say it. I started over and forced out the words. "Duncan . . . what happened to the mural?"

Maybe I haven't properly described to you how awesome this mural was. Babette had designed it so the butterflies were the same size as the kids. So that when you walked in and saw it, you felt like you were among the butterflies. The plants were supersized, and the butterflies were hyperrealistic. All native plants, too, and native butterflies, and we'd labeled them—in pretty cursive script—so that the kids would come to know them—so that when they saw them out in the real world, around town, or fluttering over the dunes, they'd be able to say, "Look! A Gulf fritillary!"

It was all Babette's design. I'd just helped to fill in the colors, like paint-by-number. It had taken full working days, all summer long. But we had put on music and Max had brought us tacos for lunch. And I'm not exaggerating when I say it was a masterpiece. Breathtaking, colorful, and alive somehow—filled with sunshine.

And I never appreciated that more than when it was suddenly . . . gray.

I knew Duncan was planning to paint over the stripes and the hopscotch patterns and the accent walls. But it had never occurred to me that the mural was in danger.

I'd assumed it was too beautiful to destroy.

Wrongly. Apparently.

I was out of breath now—feeling urgent and panicked—like there was an emergency. But there was no emergency anymore. Everything was already done. I was just witnessing the aftermath.

Duncan hadn't answered.

"Did you paint over the mural?" I asked, now just openly staring at the gray wall.

"Not me," Duncan said, like this was any kind of a valid point. "The painters."

"How could you?"

"In my defense, I thought they'd start with the hallways."

"You have no defense. There is no defense."

"You got the memo. It's for—"

"Visibility," I finished in a hollow voice.

"Look how much better we can see now."

Now I turned to stare at him. "Is that a joke? Do you really think this is better?" Of all the changes he'd forced on us since he'd arrived, this one—*this one*—broke my heart.

"I understand," Duncan said, sounding like a robot.

"No. You don't."

"The mural was beautiful, but—"

"The mural," I interrupted, my voice shaking as I worked to hold it back, "wasn't just beautiful. It was magic. It was irreplaceable. It left you in awe. It made you feel like you were part of something bigger than yourself. And it was Babette's. And Max's. And mine. And all the children in this room. And it wasn't yours to destroy."

I saw his shoulders sink a little at that. How dare he look disappointed? How dare he have any feelings about anything?

"Look—" he started, but my eyes snapped to his, and whatever he saw in my face stopped him cold.

I could feel the tears in my eyes as I stepped closer to him. "You. Are. Killing. This. Place."

"No," he said flatly. "I'm protecting it."

"I've been rooting for you," I said. "I've been hoping you'd come around. But all that ends now. I officially give up hope. And I'm going to fight you like crazy."

I started to walk away.

"Hey," Duncan called after me.

I turned back. What could he possibly have to say?

"You still have lunch duty."

I walked right back over to him, my face shiny with tears and my eyes blazing—and I pulled him down by the shoulder so I could get my mouth right next to his ear. Then, because we were in a room full of children, I cupped my hand to constrain the sound, and then, right up next to him, I whispered, "Fuck lunch duty."

twelve

And then it was winter break—and man, oh, man, did I need it.

This was Babette's year of firsts—her first Thanksgiving without Max, her first Christmas. We'd decided to spend every one of those firsts that we could somewhere else. We'd driven to San Antonio for Thanksgiving, and now, for Christmas, we'd made reservations at a resort near Austin.

Babette and Max had always hosted a giant feast on Christmas for "anybody who didn't have somewhere to be," and Babette was worried that all those people who counted on her would feel adrift without her. But she needed to get away. And so did I.

"Is this about Duncan Carpenter?" Babette asked.

"Don't say that name in this house," I said.

Babette smiled. It was her house.

But this wasn't a smiling matter.

I had told her about the butterflies, and she had shrugged, and said, "Nothing lasts forever." But she hadn't gone back to the cafeteria after that. She'd eaten every lunch alone in the art room.

"Fair enough," Babette said. And then she gently, and without irony, listened to me complain for a good long while about how the last thing I wanted to think about, or focus on, or talk about—ever again—was Duncan Carpenter.

See what I did there?

And then, just when I thought I was truly done with him, just when I thought I'd finally shut it all down . . . the very next day, I ran into him on the beach.

It was a bright, sunny, fifty degrees out, and I'd decided to take a long, calming Duncan Carpenter–free walk by the ocean. The winter beach was mostly empty, and my plan was to get lost in the sound of the waves and the wash of the wind. A jogger went by, and then a lady walking her bulldog, and then a couple appeared on my horizon: a man and a woman strolling just at the edge of the waves, and as they got close enough for me to see who they were, it turned out to be Duncan, with . . . a woman.

And just like that: I wasn't done with him anymore.

A very pretty woman, I should mention. Not that I was being weird about it. But it was a thing that was hard to not notice. Anyone would have noticed.

Okay, fine. It bothered me.

A noxious gas of jealousy seeped into my lungs as they came closer.

The woman was wearing a smart black winter coat with a ruby-colored scarf. And Duncan . . . well, Duncan's hair was windblown into a messy, bed-head, Old Duncan–style, and he was in jeans and a red, cheerful Norwegian sweater . . . and get this: He was smiling.

He dropped the smile as soon as he saw me, though.

I dropped mine, too, on principle.

That's when Chuck Norris came leaping out of the dunes and went streaking past us—fast as a greyhound, skittering over the wet sand at the water's edge.

"Hello," I said.

"Hello," the woman said back—and then Duncan, lingering behind, said, "Hello."

A pause.

Finally, the woman said, "The two of you must . . . know each other?"

"From work," Duncan confirmed.

"I'm Sam," I said, holding out my hand to shake. "The librarian from Kempner."

Her eyes got big, and delighted at that—and maybe a little bit . . . teasing? "Sam!" she singsonged. "The librarian! From Kempner!" Then she turned in an exaggerated way to Duncan—who looked, in turn, defeated.

"Sam," Duncan said to me, "This is Helen. My sister. Who hates me."

His sister.

I released a breath.

What *is* it about a man in a Norwegian sweater?

Helen turned to me and looked me up and down—at my pom-pom scarf and my knitted hat with earflaps and braided ties hanging down. Then she gave me a very quick hug, said, "You're adorable!" and spun herself around to start dragging the both of us back the way they had just come. "Let's take her to meet the crew!" she said, as we fell into step and Chuck Norris led the way.

I couldn't think of a polite way to tell her that her brother was a mural murderer—and that I had just decided he was my mortal enemy forever. She was just so . . . cheerful. I couldn't find a way to work it in.

"And what are you doing for Christmas?" she asked me.

"I'm going to Austin. With a friend. Whose husband died last summer." I glanced at Duncan like that was somehow his fault.

But this lady Helen was not picking up my bitter tone. "That's sounds fun." She took off jogging toward Chuck Norris, who'd found a tennis ball. She took it and pelted it farther ahead, toward a group of people down the beach.

"That's your sister," I said, as we watched her run off.

"Yeah."

"I thought she was your girlfriend."

Duncan burst out with a laugh. "No. No girlfriend. Not since—a long time."

I shrugged. "That seems like a shame."

That landed wrong. Duncan was quiet for a second. Then he said, "Hey, I'm glad we ran into you."

"Yeah?"

"I want to tell you something. About the mural."

"Nope," I said. "Not talking about that."

"Yes," Duncan said. "It's important."

"I'm trying to be pleasant right now, but I swear if you get that started, I might seriously drown you in the ocean."

"Just give me a second to explain—"

But I was shaking my head, turning away.

"Listen!" he shouted.

That got my attention. I turned back.

He pushed out a hard sigh. "The mural's not gone."

"I don't know what that means."

"It means . . . they painted over it, yes. But the paint they used—it washes off. It's water-based. It comes off with a sponge."

My mouth fell open—and then I just stood there, blinking.

"It's still there. It's not gone. I just wanted you to know that."

I shook my head for a bit before I could pull it together. "Why didn't you tell me?"

"Uh. Because you are terrifying when you're that mad. Not even kidding."

And then I just . . . started laughing. The relief of that news was physical. It was like my whole heart just unclenched.

"I do think neutral colors are better for safety. But that mural was all the things you said. It was sunshine. It was magic. So I researched paints until I could find something temporary. They were supposed to paint it over the break—and I was going to warn you, and explain it all before you saw it. But they got things out of order. I'm sorry."

I just stared at him.

"When the world is a safer place, we'll bring it back."

And then, I couldn't help it. I hugged him.

"Thank you," I said. Then I took what felt like the deepest breath of my life. "I was so angry at you, it was physically painful."

Duncan nodded. "Are you less mad now?"

I thought about it. The relief left me almost tingly. "I'm less mad."

Just then, down the beach, Helen started jumping, and waving her arms, and calling for Duncan, so we started walking in her direction.

"So," Duncan said, as we fell into step. "While you're less mad, I have a kind of odd favor to ask. I've been meaning to call you about it."

"Okay."

He took a breath. "I know that we do not always see eye to eye on Kempner-related issues."

I let out a bitter, "Ha!"

"But . . . it turns out that, these days, you are the one person in this town that I'm closest to."

"That is very sad," I said, "given that we're mortal enemies."

"And," he went on, "it turns out, the week before New Year's, I have to have a quick surgery."

"A *quick* surgery?"

"It's outpatient. No big deal. But they're going to sedate me—hopefully heavily—and so I'm going to need a ride home. I scheduled it for when Helen would be here, but it turns out they have to go back early."

I nodded. "So . . . you need a ride home?"

"I said I could just take an Uber, but they want to release me to a known party."

"Um. I don't drive."

"You don't drive?"

"Nope."

"Why not?"

No way was I telling him the real reason. "Just eccentric, I guess."

"You can use my car."

"No—I don't drive at all. Like, ever."

"Oh." He looked disappointed.

"But I could call a car service, if that works."

He nodded. "That would be . . . really helpful."

"What's the surgery for?" I asked then.

He shook his head. "Just . . . breaking up some old scar tissue. It's called cryosurgery, actually. They freeze you with liquid nitrogen."

"Cool," I said.

He sighed like "cool" was the last word he would've used. Then he said, "Not really."

When we caught up to Helen, she had her arm around the waist of a tall, cool guy wearing a peacoat and aviator glasses—and they had two little girls running in circles around them, now throwing the tennis ball for Chuck Norris.

"Sam," Duncan said. "This is my best-friend slash brother-in-law, J-Train. J-Train, meet my . . . employee. Sam Casey."

J-Train stuck his hand out in my direction. "Great to meet you, Sam."

I took his hand and shook it. "Great to meet you, too—" and just as I was trying to decide if I should actually say J-Train, Duncan slapped a hand on J-Train's shoulder and said, "He also goes by J-Money, J-Town, J-Dog, and J. J. McJayJaykins."

"Among others," J-Train concurred, grabbing Duncan by the neck as he did and pulling him into a noogie. "But Jake works, too."

"Jake. Gotcha," I said, but the words were lost as Duncan tackled him, and they hit the sand and started wrestling.

"Jake!" Helen called out. "Glasses!"

Both boys held still for one second while Jake pulled off his aviators and handed them to Helen.

"Careful of the left side," Duncan said to Jake during the pause.

"Careful of the eyes," Jake said to Duncan.

Then they got back to wrestling.

Helen stepped over closer to me and we watched them for a minute. "They're basically just human puppies," Helen said.

"Huh," I said.

Helen and I turned toward the girls, now a little farther down the beach, turning cartwheels while Chuck Norris barked at seagulls. Helen pointed. "That's Virginia. She's six. And that's Addie. She's four."

We walked a few steps toward them.

"So," Helen asked then, "how's Duncan doing?"

"I can hear you!" Duncan called from behind us, where Jake had him in a wrestling hold. "Don't ask her how I'm doing."

"The grown-ups are talking," Helen called back with a dismissive wave. Then, back to me: "How *is* he doing?"

"Um . . ." I wasn't really sure what to say. "Fine? I guess? I don't really know him that well."

Helen glanced back at the boys. "You don't?"

"I mean . . . we're—"

"Helen!" Duncan shouted—Jake now sitting on his back. "We're just work colleagues."

Just as I said, "Work colleagues."

"Oh," Helen said. "That's all?"

I shrugged. I could have added "mortal enemies," I supposed. But it didn't seem to fit with the wrestling-in-the-sand energy of the moment.

"Huh," Helen said. "I got a different vibe."

"Helen!" Duncan shouted, now overtaking Jake. "Shut up!"

Helen turned back and eyed Duncan. "How much does she know about you?"

"Nothing!" Duncan shouted. "And keep it that way!"

"I wouldn't say *nothing*," I said. "But he does keep to himself." Plus, I didn't add, I was still trying to get him fired, washable paint or no.

"Yeah," Helen said. "We've been worried about that. Maybe you and I should go get coffee."

"No! No getting coffee!" Duncan shouted, breaking free from Jake at last and launching himself up into a run toward Helen, looking dead set on tackling her. She held still as he came at her and then, at the last second, she darted away like a matador.

So Duncan wound up tackling me, instead.

He was covered in sand, and when we landed, there was another

spray of it. I squeezed my eyes closed, and in the background, I heard
Jake say, "Did Duncan just tackle somebody?"

"Yes," Helen answered. "His work colleague."

Then Jake said, "That's a lawsuit waiting to happen."

I opened my eyes, and there was Duncan, backlit by the sky, looking
straight down at me. "You okay?" he asked.

"Fine," I said.

We hesitated there for a second, the wind fluttering the hair over his
forehead, and I felt suddenly so elated that I didn't have to be mad at
him anymore. Or, at least, not *as* mad.

"Close your eyes," Duncan said then.

"Why?" I said, but I closed them. For one crazy second, I thought
he might be about to kiss me—there in front of his family, and God,
and the whole Gulf of Mexico.

But the next thing I felt wasn't his mouth on mine—it was the tips of
his fingers, brushing sand off my cheekbone. "Keep 'em tight," he said.

I squeezed them tighter.

"Not *that* tight."

I tried to relax.

"Man, you got sand all over the place."

"Um," I said, eyes still closed. "*You* got sand all over the place."

"True enough." Then he was quiet as he brushed my hairline, my
forehead, my chin, and my ears. The softness of it was a stark contrast
from getting tackled, I'll say that. At one point, Chuck Norris tried to
come over and lick us, but Helen snapped his leash on pretty quick and
walked him over to Jake to hold.

Then, Duncan paused. After I hadn't felt his touch for a few seconds, I opened my eyes.

He was looking at me, like there was something he wanted to say.

Finally, his eyes crinkled in a wry way, and he said, in a faux-scold,
"Be more careful next time."

"You be more careful."

That's when Duncan looked up and saw his sister and brother-in-law watching us intently. "Sorry about that," he said then. "I was aiming for my sister." And at the word "sister," he launched himself up and went chasing her off down the beach.

I sat up. *Was* I fine? I took an inventory.

Fine enough, I decided.

I stood up to brush myself off and noticed that Jake had put his aviators back on and was doing the same. I walked a little closer to him. "They have a love-hate thing," Jake said, still brushing. "In a good way. Most of the time."

The girls took off running after their mom and uncle, and then Chuck Norris, wrenching the leash out of Jake's hand, took off after them like a blur.

"He's chasing them?" Jake asked.

"Do you want me to go after him?" I asked.

"Nah."

I watched him run, his gray fur undulating with each leap. "Chuck Norris is the worst security dog in the world."

"That makes sense," Jake said. "He failed out of training school for 'overexuberance.'"

"That sounds about right."

"Duncan was sure he could fix him," Jake said.

"He hasn't managed it yet," I said.

Jake went on, bending over to shake sand out of his hair. "It's good for him, though. We tried to get him to move home to Evanston after everything, but he wanted to come here."

But I'd stopped listening to what he was saying—distracted instead by the way he was saying it. I turned to stare at Jake. "Can you say something else?"

"Like what?"

"Anything. Pledge of Allegiance? Recite a poem?"

"Um. Sure?"

"Because," I said, "your voice sounds so familiar to me." Then I said, "The more you talk, the more I keep thinking I recognize it."

"Oh," Jake said, stamping sand off his shoes now. "Then you probably want me to say something like, 'Hey, friends and neighbors—and welcome to yet another hour of the Everything's Invisible podcast.'"

Oh, my God.

I felt a thrill of recognition like a flutter. I *did* recognize that voice.

I turned and stared at him. "Shut up!" I shouted, and just as Duncan and Helen and the girls came jogging back, now much slower, I said, "You're Jake *Archer*?"

Jake just smiled, so I turned to Duncan, who had collapsed on his knees in the sand nearby, and I pointed at Jake. "Is this Jake Archer from Everything's Invisible?"

Duncan frowned at me like I was funny. "Yes," he said.

"Wait—you're *friends* with Jake Archer?"

Duncan gave Helen a little smile. "I can hardly believe it, myself."

"Hardly friends," Jake said. "He's more like an obsessive and troubled fan."

Duncan kept his eyes on me, but called over to Jake. "Don't make me hurt you." Then, to me, he said, "I named that podcast, in fact."

"You named it?"

Duncan nodded. "Jake over there wanted to call it, 'What's Essential Is Invisible to the Eye'—you know, that line from *The Little Prince* about how 'it is only with the heart that one can see rightly.' But that was way too long. So I shortened it."

I turned to Jake. I was freaking out. I was fangirling.

"I *knew* I knew that voice! I've heard every episode—multiple times. I'm in the library all the time, stamping books and cataloging and restocking and doing inventory. I listen to a ton of podcasts and audiobooks—and yours is in my top three. It's actually my favorite. Sometimes I get to the end of a show, and just go back and start it again. But I'm not going to say that out loud for fear of sounding like a . . ."

"An obsessive and troubled fan?" Duncan suggested.

I shrugged. "Too late?"

"Let's treat that like a rhetorical question," Jake said, but now he was teasing me, too.

I turned to Duncan, and said, almost like I was giving him some great news: "Your brother-in-law is *Jake Archer*!"

"Does that make you like me better?"

"It doesn't make me like you *less*, that's for sure."

"This is why you pay me the big bucks," Jake said to Duncan.

Then I turned back to Jake, and as I did, I remembered an article in *Variety,* or *Vanity Fair,* or *Vogue*—something with a V—about America's new favorite podcast host, and how he always insisted he was so good at interviewing people, at reading their voices and asking the perfect questions, because he was blind.

Duncan saw me looking at Jake and seemed to know what I was thinking. He took a few steps closer to Jake and wrapped him up in a bear hug. "Love ya, buddy," I heard Duncan say, just as Helen, who had been brushing sand off of Jake this whole time, said to the guys, "I'm calling a moratorium on wrestling."

Then she turned to the girls. "I think it's time for hot chocolate."

The girls cheered and jumped around, but Duncan charged toward them. "Ugh! Hot chocolate is the worst!" He swooped down, scooped them up, and spun around, one in each arm, until centrifugal force pulled their feet out sideways.

I had never—not once, in all the days since he'd come to Kempner—seen him goof around with kids like that. Mostly, he ignored all children. But here he was, *playing*. Here he was, looking and acting so much like Old Duncan that it made me sad. I felt my smile fade, even as the girls kept squealing and giggling in palpable delight.

After they'd gone, I regretted not getting Jake's autograph. Maybe I should have gotten all their autographs, for good measure.

I couldn't stop thinking about them as I walked back up the beach. Thinking how radically different Duncan was in their presence. Was he faking? Or did they open up some part of his psyche that he normally kept bolted shut?

It was so thrilling—and heartbreaking—to see Duncan happy, given how rarely that ever happened. It was like this glimpse into a parallel universe where he was okay. Maybe not exactly as exuberant as he had been all those years ago at Andrews . . . but close.

Where was that Duncan when we were at school?

When they'd left in search of hot chocolate, I'd wanted to go with them so badly—and they had tried to convince me to go. I don't know why I said no. Maybe I didn't want to interrupt their family time together. Maybe their easy camaraderie was intimidating in a way.

But as I walked home, I had to admit: The more glimpses of the old Duncan I got, the more I wanted. I hadn't gone with them, in part, because I'd wanted to go with them so badly. The version of him on the beach today was so close to the version I'd always found so irresistible— the mischievous, playful version. Seeing it made me long for more of it so intensely, it was physical, like an ache.

I didn't want to want him. Or long for him. Or yearn.

Since my epilepsy had come back, I'd tried very hard not to want things I couldn't have.

And I feared now that Duncan fit easily into that category—in part because of how he'd changed, and in part because of how I had.

Deep down I knew that even if the old Duncan resurrected himself tomorrow, I shouldn't let myself want to be with him. Because I wasn't the same person now. I was better in so many ways—but I was also worse.

I'd gone a whole semester without having a seizure—without collapsing in the library in front of the kids, or in the cafeteria line, or on the playground at recess. I was passing as a person who was perfectly fine.

But I wasn't fine. I had this . . . condition. One I couldn't hide forever. It wasn't the worst thing in the world, but over and over in my life, people I cared about had acted as if it were. The more time I spent with Duncan, the more desperately I wanted him—and the more I wanted him to want me back.

And also: the more I feared that he wouldn't—couldn't—once he knew the truth about me. Or, more specifically: once he'd seen it.

That was the crux of it, just like I'd feared all along. He was making me want something I couldn't have. Him.

Better to stay away. Better not to go to a cozy diner and spend a whole afternoon laughing and joking with them in a big semicircular booth with my thigh grazing against Duncan's. Better not to feed the addiction.

Better to shut it all down, and fast—before it got worse.

thirteen

I didn't wind up going with Babette to Austin for Christmas.

In fact, I wound up spending Christmas alone. Mostly because just as we were packing up Babette's SUV, Tina showed up—with Clay. And two suitcases.

Tina parked right behind me as I was loading my bag into the back.

For a minute, I thought maybe Tina had left Kent Buckley.

Tina's face went sour when she saw me, but Clay dropped his suitcase and hugged me around the waist.

I worked very hard to make my voice pleasant. "Hey, buddy. Are you here for Christmas?"

"Yes," Tina answered for him, and then she turned to Clay. "Go find Baba and tell her we're spending the night."

After he ran off, I turned to Tina, glanced at the suitcases one more time, and said, "Did you leave him?"

Tina frowned. "Leave who?"

"Kent Buckley," I said, like *Who else?*

She looked affronted. "Of course not. He went on a last-minute work trip to Japan."

Oh. Oops. "Japan," I said, nodding. "Wow."

Just then, Babette and Clay came clomping down the porch steps and out to the car, rolling Babette's suitcase behind them.

"You're coming for Christmas!" Babette cheered when she reached Tina, holding out her arms and pulling her into a big hug. It was the happiest I'd seen Babette since summer.

"We're coming for Christmas!" Clay echoed, and they pulled him in, too.

This was what it must be like to belong. You could utterly ignore people, and not be there for them, and let them down, and forget about them—but then, when you finally showed up, they were happy.

I didn't have anyone in my life like that.

And if I did, I thought, I wouldn't abuse the privilege. If I had anybody anywhere who loved me like that, I would be grateful every day. I would meet all that love with the same amount in return. It made me wish I didn't have to try so hard with everybody all the damn time. It made me miss my mom—again, as always. It made me wish I had somebody—anybody—in my life who would love me no matter what.

Did this mean our weekend in Austin was off?

I stood by awkwardly, watching how unreasonably happy it made Babette to see Tina. And then it hit me: Tina showing up here meant *my* trip to Austin was off.

I turned and pulled my suitcase back out of the car.

Babette noticed. "What are you doing?"

I threw Clay's suitcase in the back. "These two should go with you," I said.

"No!" Babette said. "We'll all stay here."

But I shook my head at Babette. "You need to get away." Then I gestured to all three of them. "And you all need some time together."

"We'll just get a room of our own," Tina said, not meaning it.

But I shook my head. "It's fully booked," I said. I had no idea if it was booked or not. But here's what I did know: Nothing could be better for Babette than a little time with her real family. Nothing could be better for all of them than to make good use of Kent Buckley being halfway around the world. And nothing could possibly be worse for me than a whole weekend with Tina.

I'd rather spend my Christmas all alone watching Hallmark movies.

And that's exactly what I wound up doing.

A few days later, I took a car service to pick up Duncan from surgery.

As promised.

It wasn't a hospital, it was an office building—with Cryosurgery Associates taking up the entire third floor.

I wasn't even entirely sure what cryosurgery was.

They were rolling Duncan out of recovery in a wheelchair just as I arrived.

Are you wondering if he'd worn his suit and tie to have surgery?

Because that's a yes. Though the jacket and vest were off now, and lying across his lap, the shirt was open at the collar and untucked, and he was wearing the tie outside his collar, lying there loose—as if he'd just slipped it back over his head like a lei. There it was. He looked good neat and pressed, but he also looked good mussed up.

He squinted when he saw me. "Are you who I think you are?"

"Who do you think I am?"

"The librarian with the clown socks."

"That's me. You asked me to pick you up."

"I did?" He turned to the nurse behind him for confirmation. She nodded. "That was smart of me," he said.

Wow. What had they dosed him up with?

The nurse gave me a stack of discharge instructions and a small batch of "hard-core" painkillers, saying he could switch to Tylenol tomorrow, but to definitely stick to the hard stuff through the night.

"My name's Lisa," the nurse said next, circling her name on the discharge instructions, "and you can call me with any questions."

"Okay," I said, nodding. "I'm Sam."

"Oh," she said then, turning to take in the sight of me. "You're Sam!" Then she just smiled.

"What?" I asked.

"He was telling us all about you."

I frowned.

She smiled again and nodded. "Don't worry," she said. "Good things."

"Like?" I prompted.

"Oh . . . I feel like you must already know."

"I definitely do not."

"And if you don't know," she went on, "then he should be the one to tell you, not me."

Well, that was unsatisfying.

Lisa helped me wheel Duncan out to the parking lot, where the driver was waiting. "He sang about you, too," she said as we walked. "In recovery."

"He sang about me?"

"You know," she said. "The 'Oh! Susanna' song—but adjusted for 'Samantha.'"

"Do a lot of people sing in recovery?" I asked.

She shook her head. "Never. No one. He's adorable. How long have you two been"—she gestured between us with her hand—"ya know?"

"Oh!" I said. "No. We're not . . . we're just work colleagues."

She laughed like I was joking. Then she stopped walking when she realized I wasn't. "Wait—you're not even dating?"

I shook my head. "Not even close."

She opened her eyes wide, like *Whoa*. "He has got a thing for you, lady."

I shook my head. "He doesn't even like me. Like, at all."

"I'm telling you," she said, "he does." Then she added, "The opiates never lie."

At the car door, Lisa flipped up the footrests on the chair so Duncan could set his feet on the pavement. Before we hoisted him up, she said to be careful of his left side—hip to ribs. He was harder to lift than I was expecting—so much dead weight. I wedged myself up under his armpit and clamped his arm over me as I rotated him.

He was bigger than I'd realized.

I maneuvered him into the backseat with a plop, and he was so out of it, I had to lift his feet up for him, and lean across him to buckle him. He kept his eyes open the whole time, watching me without helping—like his brain was in slow motion and couldn't catch up.

"You smell like honeysuckle," he said, while I was clicking the buckle.

"That's my shampoo," I said, and just as I pulled away, he leaned in closer to take a deeper sniff—and his face collided with the back of my head.

"Oh, God," I said, leaning closer to see if he was hurt. "I'm sorry! Are you okay?"

He just smiled up at me. "I'm fine."

Do you know what love-struck looks like? It's so hard to describe—something about the eyes, just open and admiring and maybe even a little bit wonder-filled, like they're drinking in the sight of you. That's the only word I can come up with for his expression.

Safe to say, it was not a look I got very often—especially not from him.

He looked down at my blouse. "I knew you'd be wearing polka dots."

Lisa watched me as I closed the car door. "He'll sleep a lot today, but he should be pretty normal tomorrow," she said. "And the painkillers cause nausea for most people, so he won't want to eat, but he needs to do it, anyway. Especially before the next round of pills."

"Gotcha," I said.

"He should sleep in a loose T-shirt tonight—or shirtless if the skin is irritated," she said. "It's all in the instructions. And you might want to put him in some sweatpants when you get him home," the nurse said. "He was supposed to arrive in something comfortable, but he showed up in a suit."

"He really loves suits," I said.

"They really love *him*," she said, giving me a wink.

"Noted," I said, with a nod.

She snagged one last glimpse of him through the car window and shook her head. "Adorable."

On the drive home—I swear, this is true—as I sat beside him in the backseat of the car, Duncan held his empty hand as if there was a phone in it, peering at it and saying, "I'm sorry. I think we're lost. My phone's not working."

I didn't even know how to begin to correct him, so I just said, "Don't worry. I know the way."

He shook his head. "But you've never been to my place."

"But our driver has the address."

Duncan frowned and blinked. "We have a driver?"

I pointed up at the guy in the front seat. Then I said, "They really doped you up, huh?"

"Yes," Duncan said. "It was nice of them. They know I don't like . . . surgeries."

"Does anybody like surgeries?" I asked.

"Probably not," Duncan said. "But I don't like them the most."

He tried to check his phone again.

He didn't seem drunk, exactly. He wasn't slurring his words. He just seemed really, really relaxed. And, also, like the world he saw through his eyes and the actual world were not exactly the same thing.

Next, partly to distract him, but mostly because Lisa had made me curious, I said, "The nurse said you were talking about me."

He gave a big nod. "Yes. Yes, I was. I told them about the day we met."

Oh. "That," I said, "was not my best day."

"Are you kidding me?" Duncan said, squinting over at me to see if I was serious. "I thought you were the most beautiful girl I'd ever seen. Like, ever."

"Oh," I said, frowning. "Really? 'Cause—"

"Oh, yeah. I'm talking, ever. And that's really saying a lot because—I don't know if you've noticed but this whole entire planet is just crawling with girls."

I shrugged. "Well, we are fifty-one percent of the—"

"They're everywhere! You can't even get a donut without running into at least one! Sometimes five or ten. That's what I'm saying. In my whole life of being constantly bombarded by girls . . . you"—he pointed at me—"are the prettiest one I ever saw."

This had to be the drugs talking. I was absolutely nothing special. Not a head turner or a showstopper. Just a perfectly ordinary human.

But what else was there to do but play along?

"Okay," I said. "I did not get that vibe."

Duncan nodded. "Yeah. Well, you've gotta hide it, right? You can't just drool all over people. I remember it exactly. It was your first day."

"It was *your* first day," I corrected.

"Nope. You were wearing . . . I don't know. All gray. And your hair was different then." He looked up at my pink bangs. Then he reached out and patted them. "No pink."

Wait—*what*?

"And remember we had those cubbies in the faculty lounge, but yours was jammed—and I walked in to find you just beating the shit out of it." There was admiration in his voice. "And then I came in and showed you the exact place to smack it, and it popped right open like Fonzie."

He was talking about *Andrews*. He was talking about four years ago. He was talking about the old me. The mousy me. The forgettable me.

And then I suddenly felt . . . nervous. Or maybe more like . . . alert. Like every nerve in my body had been called to attention.

Duncan was neither nervous nor alert. He leaned his head back, savoring the memory. "That was a cool moment for me. Wasn't I so badass in that moment?"

"You were," I said, still taking it in.

"That might have been my life peak," he said then, blinking. "It might have been all downhill from that day."

"I thought you were talking about when we first met here. At Kempner."

"Oh. No. But I played it cool then, too."

"Yeah," I said, "kinda more like 'ice-cold.'"

He nodded, like *Yeah.* "I've never been great at gauging that stuff. And now I'm a tough guy all the time, so it's even harder."

A moment of quiet, then he added, "But, yes. It would be safe to say that I had a thing for you. *Have* a thing for you."

Some of it had to be real at least, right? The drugs couldn't make him remember something he didn't remember.

"At Andrews?" I had to ask. "You had a thing for me?"

"Oh, yeah. So bad. But you really couldn't stand me, so . . . I gave up. Eventually."

"I could stand you," I said, like he was crazy. And then, wanting to emphasize but too flustered to do it properly, I said, "I could stand you very much."

Duncan frowned.

"I didn't hate you is what I'm saying."

"Oh," Duncan said. "That's surprising. But you sure hate me now."

I didn't hate him now, but I wasn't confessing to that. "You're very different now," I said.

Duncan laughed. "No shit."

Then he leaned back against the headrest and watched the beach houses go by—all their pinks and aquas and yellows.

"Man, I had such a thing for you," he said, thinking about it like we were reminiscing. "But of course," he said, pointing at me, "I'll never tell you that."

"You're telling me that right now."

"Yeah, but you'll forget it all by morning."

"No, you're the one who'll forget it by morning."

"Huh," he said, frowning at that news. "I guess it's the medicine talking."

"Fair enough," I said. "We should probably drop the subject."

"Good idea," Duncan agreed. "Because I do *not* want you to know how into you I am."

"Good plan."

A minute later, he started up again.

"It's just hard to hold it in though, because when something like that happens to you—like when you just see someone and a part of your heart just clicks into place like a little puzzle piece you didn't even know was missing—and you don't even think it in words, but something in you just knows, like *that's my person,* somehow. Or at least, *that person could be my person.* You know—if they liked the idea, too. If they looked at you and by some crazy miracle thought the same thing back." He looked over. "Did you by any chance think the same thing back?"

"Even if I did, I wouldn't tell you."

"Good idea, good idea. Keep a poker face. Don't tell me."

He tried to check his phone again. Then he said, "Besides, I wouldn't want you to go out with a guy like me."

"Why not?"

"Don't tell my sister," he said. "But I'm pretty much ruined."

The school had rented a waterfront beach cottage for Duncan in a fancy, West Beach neighborhood.

Not too shabby.

I paid the driver, opened Duncan's door, unbuckled him, and put his right arm over my shoulder again, careful not to touch his left side, where they'd done the cryosurgery. He felt heavier this time, and even on that short walk from the car, he lost his balance more than once.

West Beach houses were all up on stilts, so we had a whole flight of stairs to climb. When we reached the base of them, Duncan stopped at the first one, head bent down as he stared at it, and pawed several times with his foot before he hit his target.

Needless to say, we took it slow.

Halfway up, he turned to me like he'd had a great idea and said, "Hey! I've got it! Let's get married!"

"Brilliant," I said. "I'm in."

I'd forget everything by tomorrow, anyway.

Chuck Norris practically knocked us both over when I finally got the door open.

Then he ran in circles around the living room, engulfed in delight, for at least ten minutes before finally habituating to the idea that Duncan had come home.

"That dog is really happy to see you," I said, as we made our way across the living room and Chuck Norris ran laps around us.

Duncan nodded. "Don't tell him I said this," he said, "but he's a terrible security dog."

"Agreed," I said.

Inside, things were . . . ascetic. It was a furnished rental—simple wood floors, minimal furniture, nothing too wild or wacky. There was almost nothing personal about it. A few apples in a bowl in the kitchen area. A laptop on the coffee table, a pair of running shoes by the front door, and a dog-eared copy of *Lonesome Dove* on the sofa. Other than that, there could have been no one living here at all.

"Where's all your stuff?" I asked.

"Back bedroom," he said, waving. "In boxes."

Next, Chuck Norris tried to jump up on Duncan, but I blocked him.

"I just have to make myself ignore him," Duncan said, as we kept shuffling. "No human affection," he said, like he was reminding himself.

I knew Duncan wasn't denying that dog human affection. I spied him throwing toys for him in the courtyard all the time. Not that I was watching.

"But he's so fluffy and cute," I protested.

"Exactly," Duncan said. "He controls your mind with his cuteness. He stares at you with those big doggie eyes until you do his bidding."

We'd worked our way back toward his bedroom. I leaned Duncan against the bed, and he perched there for a minute. When Chuck Norris saw Duncan sit, he settled down in the corner, watching us, eyes bright, front paws crossed.

"See that?" Duncan whispered. "He's doing it right now."

"I'll be in charge of Chuck Norris tonight," I said. "You be in charge of resting."

Later, I'd take Chuck Norris to the beach and throw his toy for him, and get him fresh water, and fill his food bowl. But right now, I needed to get Duncan settled.

"Okay," I said, looking around. "The nurse wants you out of that suit. What were you doing wearing a suit to surgery, anyway?"

Duncan shrugged. "Respect for the occasion."

"Wait here."

I located his dresser, looking for soft sweatpants. I found a drawer of T-shirts. I might have expected all neatly folded, identical, heather-gray ones—to match his suits—but, instead, I found colors and jokes: A green tee with a hedgehog on it that said, HEDGE OR HOG? *YOU DECIDE*. A blue shirt with a logo that said, TAUTOLOGY CLUB: IT IS WHAT IT IS. A shirt with a picture of Bill Murray's face that read, DON'T MESS WITH ME, PORK CHOP.

Shirts belonging—clearly—to the former Duncan.

I pulled out an extra-soft red one with an image of a hammer that read, THIS IS NOT A DRILL. Then I kept rummaging for the sweatpants.

Duncan waited obediently, legs bent, eyes closed.

I set the folded clothes on his lap.

"Can you handle this on your own, buddy?" I asked.

"Oh, yeah. Sure," he said. He gave me a thumbs-up. "I got it."

But when he stood up and bent over to take off a shoe, he lost his balance, fell—on his right side, fortunately—and hit the floor with a *whomp*.

"Whoa!" I said, squatting down after him, just as Chuck Norris decided to come over to see what the ruckus was.

"Whoa is right," he said, as I leaned in to hook my arms under him and hoist him back up.

He was not light.

"Lift with the legs," he called out.

"You could help," I said.

At that, Duncan got his feet under him, and shoved us upward with a burst that sent us reeling sideways against the bed until we fell back on it.

He landed on top of me.

Again. Just like on the beach.

But less sand this time.

We froze there—me looking up, him looking down, his chest pressing against mine, and his hands on either side of my head as he braced himself against the mattress.

"I'm afraid we're hurting you," I said then.

"I'm not."

Time slowed down. Everything fell quiet except the sounds of our breathing. Everything slid out of focus except his eyes, which seemed to brighten and darken at the same time.

His chest against mine. His breath across my neck.

I didn't look away, and neither did he . . . until he dropped his gaze to my mouth. And then, I just knew that he wanted to kiss me. I could read it in his expression as clearly as if he'd said it out loud.

Was it a good idea? Was it the right thing to do? Was it proper? Was it prudent? Was it even . . . medically advisable?

I had no idea.

But I could feel it was going to happen before it happened. I could sense his intentions. And I could have done something to discourage him, or distract him. I could have turned away, or started to scramble up, or pushed against his chest to get him moving in the other direction.

But I just didn't.

Instead, I watched him bring his gaze up from my mouth, and when our eyes met, I held mine there, open and willing, and vulnerable.

And then he dropped his head—just as we'd both wanted him to— and he put his mouth on mine. And I pressed mine to his, right back.

And that ache of longing I always felt when I was around him?

The moment his mouth touched mine, it melted away.

Duncan's kiss was all warmth—firm and soft and urgent all at the same time, and I'll bet anything that mine was all those things back, but what I remember most was this impossible combination of opposites: it felt dangerous and safe at the same time. Shocking and soothing. Electrifying and relaxing. Impossible and inevitable.

Like we'd left the ordinary world and landed in a place where everything could happen.

And I just gave all the way in—and let myself be everything: alert and relaxed, awake and dreaming, lost and found.

He dropped to one elbow to free a hand to roam over my hair, my neck, my shoulder as he pressed, and pulled, and touched, and—I don't know—*explored* and *excavated* and *ignited,* and I let him. I wanted to soak him in.

Until.

Duncan shifted position—and then he caught his breath and pulled away.

I opened my eyes.

He was wincing.

"Oh, my God," I said, instantly pulled back to reality. "Are you hurt?"

"I just—shifted the wrong way."

Carefully, he transferred his weight back to a better position, and his face relaxed a little.

I edged out from under him. "Oh, my God!" I said. "What are we doing? We can't do this!"

"Just a cramp. It's practically gone," Duncan said, but his face was still tight. "I'm fine."

"You're not fine," I said. "You've just had surgery—"

He snorted. "*Cryo*surgery."

"None of this is fine!"

"I fully disagree."

He pushed into a sitting position at the edge of the bed again, like before—clearly defeated by whatever pain he'd just felt—and pressed his hand to his side.

I climbed off the bed and came around to face him. "Did we just hurt you?" I asked. "Should I—call the nurse?"

"Just a cramp," he said, shaking his head. "I'm good."

Then, as if to prove it, he opened his eyes and smiled at me. His hair was all messed up, falling over his forehead. Old Duncan. Right there.

I might have swooned a little—before I came to my senses.

"Oh, my God! I took advantage of you! You're on drugs!" I was supposed to be looking after him, not—whatever this was.

That made him burst out with a laugh. "You couldn't take advantage of me if you tried."

"I'm so sorry," I said.

"Hey," he said. "None of this is your fault. I'm just irresistible."

I flared my nostrils at him.

And then he did look better, and then he gave me a delighted smile. "You just kissed me!"

"Um. *You* kissed *me*, pal."

His frown at this gave way to a grin. "Yeah, but you kissed me back."

"Only because you fell on me."

"I should fall on you more often."

But he was shaking his head, like he couldn't believe it.

"Don't get too excited," I said. "You're going to forget it, anyway."

"I won't forget it," he said. "Even if I don't remember, I'll remember."

But then I shook my head to clear it. "We just need to stay focused," I said. And then this came out spectacularly wrong: "We just need to get your clothes off and get you to bed."

He gave me a wry smile. "Sold."

I let out a growly sigh. "You know what I mean."

Safe to say, I had never been in a situation even remotely like this one. We still needed to get him out of that suit. "Can you . . . change your own clothes?" I asked, hoping his answer would be, *No problem.*

Duncan gave a big nod. "No problem," he said.

But then he didn't move. Just stared at the sweatpants like he wasn't sure what to do with them. "Or maybe I could use a little help."

I sighed.

No big deal. This was a medical situation. I'd taken men's clothes off before. It wasn't rocket science. I frowned to get into an all-business mind-set, then said, "Hold still. I'm going to help you."

He was still sitting on the edge of the bed. Swaying a little.

I untied his tie, my fingers nudging at the silk knot until it released— unable to not notice how sexy even the most mundane action seemed in the wake of that kiss. Then I slid it from around his neck with a *zip* and tossed it on a chair nearby.

Sexy.

"You smell good," he said then. "But I knew that already."

"Just . . . focus."

Next, I shifted to those stiff leather oxfords of his, tossing one and then the other with a *clomp* across the room. Then I peeled off his black dress socks, and he wiggled his toes at me, as if to say hello. Then, I stood. Frowning harder, I said a quick prayer that he'd be wearing underwear, and I stepped closer to unbuckle his belt, unhook his pants at the waistband, and unzip his zipper, all in quick succession. Then he had to stand up a little so I could work his pants down over his—thank God—boxer briefs, and then I helped him step into the sweatpants.

All of it: inescapably sexy.

Once all that was done, I figured we were through the hard part.

"Okay, pal. Can you get your shirt off on your own?"

After the pants, the shirt really should have been a breeze.

Duncan nodded, but then his fingers were too rubbery to do the buttons. I watched until I realized the attempt was doomed, and then I stepped in to help. At one point, he put his hands over mine, met my eyes, and said, "Thank you."

"Of course," I said.

"I never get taken care of," he said, like it was a fascinating fact he'd just noticed. "It's nice."

"Me, neither," I said.

He shrugged his dress shirt off, and I got a whiff of his deodorant, which reminded me of a scented candle I used to have called Winter Beach. Time for the undershirt. I reached down and pulled up the hem as he lifted his arms obediently. I raised his undershirt up and off—and that's when I saw his torso.

That's when I saw what he meant by "ruined."

Because the whole left side of his body, armpit to hip, was covered in scars.

fourteen

I gasped, and I pushed back a little—the shock of the sight reverberating through me.

I didn't mean to, but I did.

He looked like he'd been chopped up with a butcher knife and then stapled back together.

At my reaction, he remembered it. "Don't look!" he said—dopey enough that he put his own hand over his own eyes. "Pretend you didn't see."

I'd expected *something*, of course. I knew he'd just had surgery on that side to reduce some scarring. I'd skimmed the post-op instructions on the ride here. I'd been expecting . . . a sterile gauze pad, maybe?

I don't know. Something . . . smaller. Not . . . *this*.

He had a thick, fifteen-inch incision scar running along the contour of his ribs from just under the armpit to the bottom of his rib cage. It was not a clean line—it was dark red and jagged, puffy and stippled, angry and chaotic. He had red marks along both sides where they'd stapled him back together. Below that, closer to his hip, was another, shorter incision with round scars underneath it. And around toward the front, on his chest, just under his nipple, there were two round discs of scar tissue that I thought . . . as soon as I saw them . . . had to be—

"Duncan, what happened?"

"You don't know?" He blinked at me.

I was holding him by the shoulders now. "I don't know anything. Tell me."

"Yeah. I got shot."

"When? How? Who shot you?"

"At my last school. It wasn't just me, though. It was . . . a few people."

"Duncan—" I shook my head. "*What?*"

"Yeah. I didn't want them to tell you. I tried to keep it quiet. Hoping for a fresh start, I guess."

It was all coming together. "A school shooting?"

Duncan nodded. "The Webster School. One killed, two wounded."

"I think I heard about that one."

Duncan seemed to tense up. "Yeah. Well. It's hard to keep track of them all these days."

"I just didn't know you were even teaching there."

"We really lost touch, huh?" Duncan said, more to himself than to me.

"Does it hurt?" I asked him.

"Yes and no," Duncan said. "Mostly now it's just that the scar tissue inside has kind of hardened, and that was uncomfortable . . . so that's what this surgery was for. They had to go in lap—" He paused, like he couldn't make his mouth say the word. "Lap—"

"Laparoscopically?"

He gave an approving nod. "You're good at that."

"So, no stitches."

"The nurse said it'll feel like a bruise. A really big, bad bruise."

"Can I take another look?" I asked.

"If you can stand it."

Duncan lifted his arm over his head. I bent to follow the sight of the scar around his ribs and to the back. It was hard to look—to see the evidence of how badly he'd been injured—and that definitely held my focus in the moment, but I couldn't help but be aware of other things, too, right there: how close I was to his bare shoulder, his body heat rising toward me; the sound of his breathing as he waited for me to finish looking; his muscles and his smooth skin and his living presence right there, so close, all that energy and movement contained so quietly just inches away.

How had I not suspected something like this? Of course he had a past I knew nothing about. Of course he was full of contradictions. Of course his life contained layers and layers of history. Wasn't that true of everyone?

"I should have died," Duncan said, when I stood back up. "That's what everybody said. They all thought I was going to. I even thought I *had* died for a little while there."

I stood back up so I could meet his eyes. "I'm glad you didn't die," I said.

"Me, too," he said. "Most of the time."

"What happened?"

But Duncan shook his head. "I never talk about that."

"Never? To anyone?"

"Nope. Can't. Not even on all these drugs that cause aphrodisia."

"Amnesia?"

"Yeah. That sounds more like it."

He was still sitting on the side of the bed, feet apart, and I was standing between them. He was still shirtless, and now, I really noticed that for the first time.

There he was. Shirtless.

I took in the sight of him—starting up high, at the dip above his collarbones and the square bulk of his shoulders, and then descending down, and to the side, where everything disintegrated into chaos.

I met his eyes again. What could I say? What was there to say? My voice, when it came, was saturated with emotion. "I wish I could make it better," I said, at last.

Duncan's eyes were steady and fixed on me. And then, deliberately, without breaking the gaze, he put a hand on each of my hips and pulled me toward him.

I stepped between his knees to get closer. He clasped his arms around me and leaned in to rest his head against me as he held on. I rubbed his shoulder with one hand and let the other hand stroke his hair. The buzz cut on the back of his head felt velvety on the skin of my palms.

Why not? We'd forget it all by morning, anyway.

After a few minutes, he said, "I thought this would make it better, but I think maybe it's just making it worse."

"You're okay, you know," I said.

"Am I?" he said, sounding like his eyes were closed. "I'm not sure that's right."

"You need to lie down and rest."

"Fair enough," he said, but he didn't let go.

I didn't let go, either.

The weight of his arms felt steadying, and comforting, and I let myself just stand there and enjoy it.

This moment would change everything.

I didn't know how, exactly, but I knew it would.

When his breathing started to get steady, like he might be dozing off against me, I laid him back on his bed and pulled a blanket up over him. His eyes were closed as he relaxed back onto the pillow. I couldn't help it: I stood there a minute longer and stroked his hair.

But it was okay. He was already asleep.

I pulled his bedroom door mostly closed and then went to root around in his kitchen to make sure he'd have some food when the time came for the next round of painkillers. I checked the time and reread the discharge instructions. I'd have to wake him later for a pill to stay ahead of the pain, and he'd need to eat before he took it.

I found a can of soup in the pantry, set it by the stove, and then I half-snooped around his apartment, both scolding myself and justifying my behavior at the same time.

The scars had thrown me, that was for sure.

The sheer size of them. The unfaded, saturated color of them. The anger.

I walked around his apartment, just trying to let it all sink in.

This was why he was so obsessed with safety. This was how he could call our sweet, sunny school a nightmare. He'd seen the worst-case scenario.

He'd lived it.

There was a collection of little succulents on his kitchen windowsill that looked like they were dying, and I found myself wondering how it was possible to kill succulents.

Just then, his phone rang.

I wasn't going to answer it—but then it kept ringing. I found it on his bedside table, and as I was pressing buttons to silence the ring, I saw it was Helen.

So I answered.

"Hey!" she said. "How is he?"

"Good, I think. He's asleep."

"Are you staying there tonight?"

"I just read the post-op instructions, and it looks like I'm supposed to. Just in case."

"You're the best."

"It's fine. I'll sleep on the couch."

"He's so lucky to have you there. I was supposed to do it, but our ninety-year-old grandma got sick."

"Oh. I'm sorry."

"Just a touch of pneumonia," Helen said. "She's tough as a boot."

"Hey . . ." I said. "I saw the scars."

"Oh," Helen said. "Well, I'm glad. I never thought he should have worked so hard to keep it from you in the first place."

"Well he's not hiding anything right now. They doped him up like crazy."

"I bet."

"So . . ." I said, wanting the full picture, but not sure what questions to ask. "It looks like it was really bad."

"It was really bad," Helen confirmed. "He was hit three times. One just grazed him, but another pierced his abdomen, and another punctured his lung. It would have been bad with regular bullets, but these were military, and so they were designed to do as much damage as possible."

"The scars are . . ." I paused to look for the right word, but I couldn't find it. "The scars are awful."

"They're from the exit wounds," Helen said. "The shot to the abdomen destroyed part of his intestine. He wound up getting a blood infection that almost killed him. The shot to his chest punctured his lung—but that's not even the right way to describe it. Going in, it punctured it, but going out, it pulverized it. They had to cut out a square section of his ribs with a saw to get in there and take out all the bone and tissue, then repair what was left."

"I'm amazed he didn't die."

Helen's voice was shaky. "He survived, yes."

"But he's different now," I finished for her.

"He can't talk about it. He won't come home. He doesn't want help."

"He definitely doesn't."

"I want to believe that he's getting better. But I worry he might be getting worse."

"I'll keep an eye on him," I said. "I'll do what I can."

"Thank you for being there," Helen said. And then she added, "Hey—how are the succulents doing?"

I frowned. "You mean—on the windowsill?"

"Yeah."

I walked over to the kitchen window and assessed the plants on the sill. Even I could tell they were mostly dead. "They are not exactly long for this world," I said.

"Totally dead or just mostly?"

"I'd say ninety-nine percent dead," I said. "How do you kill a succulent? They don't even need water."

"That's just it," Helen said. "He keeps watering them."

"Doesn't he know you're not supposed to water them? Once a month—max."

"That's exactly the problem."

"He's watering them too much!" I said, getting it now. "He can't stop watering them. He's not neglecting them. He's drowning them!"

"Poor Duncan," Helen said. "Can't escape it. He's a nurturer."

I considered that for a second. "I really miss the guy he used to be," I said.

"Oh, God, so do I," Helen said. "And you know what? I think he does, too."

When it was time, I brought Duncan a mug of soup and a heavy-duty painkiller.

He was all wrapped up in his blankets, shirt still off, curled up on his side.

"Hey," I said, gently, touching him on the shoulder. "Time to drink some soup and take your medicine."

He sat up, slowly. I tried to hand him the mug, but instead he shuffled off to pee, and then spent some time brushing his teeth. The door wasn't entirely closed. Through the crack, I could see his elbow moving.

"Why do you have a whole windowsill of dead succulents?" I asked.

I saw him lean down and spit. "They're not dead. Yet. Not quite."

"I mean, how do you kill a succulent? All you have to do is just *not water them*."

"You make it sound so easy."

"It is easy."

"Not for me," Duncan said, leaning his head back to gargle.

"Here's my advice," I said. "Every time you feel the urge to water them . . . don't water them."

He spat in the sink, rinsed his mouth, washed his face, and shuffled back into the room. He was shirtless still, and the sight of him as he perched on the bed's edge, lit from the side by the light in the hall, was so dissonant: his shoulders and arms just covered in muscles, and his side covered in scars. A picture of health—and destruction.

"Thank you for being here," he said.

I handed him the mug of soup. "Drink as much of this as you can."

Duncan took it. Then he said, "My sister keeps sending me the succulents. I know I shouldn't water them. But I keep doing it anyway."

"Watering them to death."

"Pretty much."

"What if you moved them to another part of the house?"

He took a swig of soup. "Tried it. Didn't work."

"Maybe you should get some different plants. Ones that like to be watered."

"Too late."

He gulped the rest of the soup down, and then I handed him his pain pill. He knocked that back with the last sip.

Then I helped him get under the covers, and I tucked him in like he was a little kid.

He patted the bed next to him, and said, "Sit for a second."

He'd be conked out again soon. "Just for a second," I said, sitting to face him.

He held my gaze for a second. Then he said, "I hate nighttime now. I can never sleep anymore. Every tiny noise makes me jump."

I leaned over to get his phone off the bedside table. I thought he'd closed his eyes again, but when I looked up, he was watching me.

"I'm going to download this white-noise app I love for you."

Duncan kept watching me.

I played a couple of sounds for him. "What do you want?" I asked, trying to stay all business. "Ocean? Waterfall? Bath faucet?"

"You choose."

But I kept going. "Car motor? Dishwasher? Campfire? You can combine them, too."

"I trust you."

In the end, I gave him what I had: thunderstorm, city trucks, and cat purr.

"This is going to change your life," I said, turning it up a little.

"Perfect," he said, eyes still closed. "I always knew you'd do that."

"You should get some sleep now," I said, setting his phone on the bedside table.

"Sam?" he asked.

"Yeah?"

"I'm so sorry about your butterflies."

Oh. "I am, too," I said.

He let his eyes close again. "I just have to keep everybody safe."

I couldn't help it. I reached out and stroked his hair. "Nobody can keep everybody safe."

He was half asleep. "I have to try."

I watched him a minute, until I thought he was out, but when I shifted to stand, he took my hand and pulled me toward the bed. "Stay here with me," he said.

"I can't. I'll be right nearby."

"Stay here," he said. He closed his eyes. "We're never going to remember it, anyway."

"*You're* never going to remember it," I said.

"Oh. Yeah."

I stayed close by until he was truly out. And I could have walked back to the living room and curled up on the couch there. He never would have known the difference.

But I didn't.

I edged around to the far side of the bed, kicked off my shoes, and let myself curl up beside him. And when Chuck Norris jumped up on the bed to sleep at our feet, I decided to just add it to the long list of things Duncan would be forgetting . . . and I let him.

fifteen

By the next morning, when I woke up at six, slipped my shoes back on, loaded up all of Duncan's succulents into a grocery sack for a rescue-op, and snuck back down under the house to call a car, I had a lot to process.

Fact: I had slept with Duncan Carpenter.

In a manner of speaking.

It wasn't quite as great as it sounded, but it was still pretty great.

I blamed the shirtlessness. And all his confessions. And the way he kept looking at me like he was in love.

Oh, and that epic, transformative, metamorphic kiss.

Jesus. I'm only human.

On the ride home I texted an APB to Babette and Alice to meet me in Babette's kitchen.

Alice showed up first, which felt counterintuitive. But Babette was not much of a morning person.

"What's up?" Alice said, when I let her in the back door.

"Shocking plot twist!" I announced. "Duncan Carpenter kissed me."

Alice was not shocked. "You didn't see that coming?"

"No! Did you?"

"We've been placing bets in the teachers' lounge for weeks."

"Alice! You can't tell anyone."

"Don't worry, polka dots. I'm a vault." Then, shaking her head: "I can't believe it took so long."

"Alice!" I scolded again. "He's my boss."

"Max was Babette's boss."

"No comparison!" I said.

"I'm just saying. Extenuating circumstances."

"Alice! He's the enemy! He painted over the butterflies."

"With removable paint."

"So he claims."

Alice looked me over. "Are you trying to say it was a bad kiss?"

I shook my head. "It was an amazing kiss."

She smiled, like *That's better.* "Who kissed who?"

"He kissed me. But he fell on me first."

"Case in point. You two had a spark from day one."

I shook my head. "It's a disaster."

"Incorrect," Alice declared. "Mathematically, it was almost unavoidable."

"Alice," I said, "there was no math involved. Trust me. This comes from a lady who never finished learning her times tables."

But Alice started counting off points in support of her theory: "You're both adorable. You're both single. You're both lonesome. You're drawn to each other like magnets. And you're exactly the polar opposite of his misery. So were you one hundred percent guaranteed to pair bond? No—"

"*Pair bond?*" I interrupted, like *Really?*

"But looking at it statistically, yes. Mathematically, it works."

"None of that is math."

Alice gave me a look like I was pitiably naïve. "*Everything* is math."

I sighed.

"I'm just saying," Alice said, suppressing a little smile, "if I plotted your slopes on a graph, they'd intersect."

I pointed at her. "Nope."

But she was having fun. "If you were geometry, you'd have proved yourselves weeks ago."

"Alice!"

But she couldn't resist one more. "If you were algebra, you'd both be solving for X, if you know what I mean."

"Cut it out!"

She straightened, hearing something real in my voice. "I'm sorry."

"It's bad," I said.

She shifted gears. "Why is it bad, again?"

But I didn't know how to answer that question.

Because it was too good. Because it made me want him even more, and there was no way wanting him was going to end well. Because he would never remember that kiss, and I would never forget it.

"It's bad," I finally said, "because it was so good."

"Oh, Sam," Alice said.

Did she understand? Could she? I wasn't even sure that I understood. All I knew was this feeling I had—like I was carrying a terrible secret about myself . . . a secret that would always ruin everything.

"If you never let yourself want anything," I said, trying to explain it without saying it, "then you're never disappointed. But if you want something . . . *someone* . . ."

Alice leaned in, her eyes soft with sympathy now. "Are you afraid he won't want you back? Because—I promise you—he does."

"It's not that," I said.

I didn't know how to explain. But this was why I hadn't even tried to date anyone since my epilepsy came back. I said I needed stability, and that was true—but it was deeper than that.

The truth was, there was something wrong with me. Something I couldn't fix.

Something disqualifying.

On the night my father had left my mother, when I was eight, I'd overheard them arguing. I'd had a grand mal seizure that night—I'd had them constantly back then—and this was a particularly bad one that made me lose all bladder and bowel control at a country-club party for some of my father's clients. Back home, after my mother had cleaned me up and put me to bed in my favorite flannel nightgown, I had slept— you always sleep after a seizure—but the sound of them arguing woke me up a few hours later.

I listened for a little bit, but when it didn't stop, I crept to the edge of the stairs, where I could peer down at the entryway.

They were just out of view, standing close to the front door. I could only see their shadows, but I could hear the voices loud and clear.

"I didn't sign up for this," my father was saying.

"None of us did," my mom said.

"She's not getting better, she's getting worse."

"We're doing everything we—"

"I couldn't believe my eyes tonight. I've never been so humiliated. You can't take her anywhere."

My mother's voice broke. "Steven—"

"It's too much for me," he said, his voice tight. And then I heard the click of our front door handle.

"Don't you dare walk out that door," my mother said, her voice low and threatening.

"I can't take it anymore," my father said. "I never wanted this."

"You did want this! When we decided to start a family."

"You were the one who wanted to start a family. You pushed and pushed for a baby. And look what we got. I never should have given in."

"How can you say that? She's our daughter!"

"She's also the thing that ruined our marriage."

There was a long pause, and when my father spoke again, his voice sounded like it was made of wood. "I just can't live like this anymore."

Next, I heard the door shush closed behind him.

Then, it was quiet for a long time. I started to wonder if maybe she'd gone, too. If maybe they both had. I edged down a couple more steps, and from that angle, I could see my mom. She was pressed up against the door, totally still, almost like she wasn't even breathing.

Mama, I mouthed—but without sound.

And then a deep, otherworldly sound started to fill the room, as she slowly sank to the floor, and I realized she was crying out—a kind of long, lowing, desperate sound of agony, like nothing I'd ever heard. When she reached the floor, she beat against it with her open palm until she started to cry for real—dark, ragged, body-racking sobs like I didn't even know existed.

I hesitated for one second—unsure if I should go to her, if seeing me would make her feel better or worse. But then I couldn't stand it. I skittered barefoot down the steps and across the Persian rug, and I threw myself down beside her.

She looked up, surprised.

"I'm sorry, Mama," I said.

And she just knew in that instant, the way mothers always know, that I'd heard it all. She pulled me tightly to her chest and wrapped her arms around me. "It isn't you, sweetheart," she said, her voice still thick. "It isn't you."

But, of course . . . she was lying.

It was me.

She knew it, and now so did I.

I never thought about that night now. I hadn't forgotten it, exactly, but I kept it somewhere at the distant edges of my memory. What was the point of replaying it? Nothing could change. Nothing could work out differently. My father would leave, and I wouldn't see him again until my mother's funeral, two years later—and even then he would look at me with bitterness.

He didn't take me in after that. I'd go to live with my mother's sister, and my father and I would spend the rest of our lives ignoring each other's existence.

All because of this one thing that was wrong with me that would never be fixable.

Anyway, how could someone like Alice—cheerful, logical, tea-drinking Alice—ever understand something like that?

I couldn't even understand it, myself.

She wanted to know why my falling in love with Duncan was bad—and for a second, I thought about trying to explain it to her.

But words failed me.

In Alice's world, love was mathematical. Every problem had a solution.

But in my world, solutions had always been a hell of a lot less easy to come by.

sixteen

When Babette showed up in the kitchen, still in her robe, she took one look at the two of us and said, "What did I miss?"

"Sam kissed Duncan," Alice said.

"Finally!" Babette said. "Maybe it'll fix him."

"One kiss can't fix a person."

"Maybe it'll inspire him to try to fix himself."

I meant to lay it all out for them very carefully, but instead, here's what came out: "He was so doped up after the surgery it was like a truth serum, and he wound up confessing that he'd had a thing for me back in California, and then I had to take his clothes off for him and he fell on top of me, and then he stared into my eyes until we were kissing, and then he told me he was lonely and he asked me to stay with him, and now I'm afraid I have no choice but to fall back in love with him."

Babette took that in.

"Wow," Alice said.

I nodded. But I was tired of thinking about what it all meant for me. Now that Babette was here, I added: "And there's one more thing. He was shot. In a school shooting."

Babette and Alice both set down their coffee mugs, leaned in, and said, "What?"

Maybe I shouldn't have told them. Maybe it was private information that he'd only disclosed under the influence of drugs. But I trusted them.

And I really, really needed advice.

I nodded to confirm. "He almost died. The scars are . . . massive. Shocking. I mean. Disfiguring."

Babette sighed. "That explains a lot."

"And so now I'm very conflicted," I said.

"I can see why," Alice said.

"Because I'd already given up on him. And we've hatched a plan to get him fired. And there's no doubt that for the sake of the school, he needs to go. But . . ."

"You want him to stay," Babette said, with a little smile.

"But, now, after seeing the scars . . . I can see why he's acting like he is."

"He's afraid." Babette nodded.

"Yes, and I don't think he's dealt with any of it—whatever that would even mean. I mean, how would a person even do that? How would you even start?"

"You feel like there's hope for him?" Alice asked.

I nodded. "I've been trying all this time to figure out what changed. And now that I know, I feel like maybe instead of trying to fire him, we should try to help him."

Babette and Alice thought about it.

I looked back and forth between them. "What do you think?"

And that's when Babette gave me a big smile—the first real smile I'd seen from her in months. Then she said, "I think it's the best idea I've heard in ages."

Babette had never really been too jazzed about the idea of getting Duncan fired.

But the idea of helping him?

That really lit her fire.

Right then, we started brainstorming on one of Babette's yellow pads. We titled the list The Duncan Project, and Alice made tea while we shouted out ideas and I wrote them all down. Our motto was "No idea too dumb," which we decided we wanted on T-shirts, and we listed every single crazy thing we could think of that might help Duncan remember who he'd been before, reconnect to joy, and "deal with it," whatever that meant.

We put down everything, from "throw oranges at him to see if he'll accidentally start juggling them," to "do a fake teacher raffle where he wins free sessions with a therapist," to "bring in guest speakers about PTSD."

"Is he in therapy?" Babette asked.

"I don't think so."

"He needs to be."

"Good luck with that."

In the end we wound up sorting the ideas into several categories:

- Help him remember his old self
- Help him make connections with humans
- Remind him what it was like to be happy
- Expose him to risks
- Soften his tough-guy outer shell
- Nurture him physically
- Help him build a mental framework for thinking about resilience
- Therapy

Under each category, we listed everything we could think of to help accomplish that thing. Under "Help him remember his old self" we listed things like: trick him into wearing a Hawaiian shirt; get him to dress up in costume; make him teach a yo-yo class; and dare him to walk on his hands. Under "Help him make connections with humans" we listed: game night at Babette's; go fishing with the guys; kissing booth; and massage.

And as far as helping him build a framework for resilience, we listed: keep a journal; see the documentary about the 1900 storm; talk about Buddhism; study post-traumatic growth; and get him talking.

A lot of spitballing going on.

We really didn't know what we were doing.

But we made up for that with ideas. Pages' and pages' worth.

Babette asked me about how I'd coped when my epilepsy came back. "Were you depressed?" she asked.

"Very," I said. "It felt like a prison sentence. Like I'd spend the rest of my life alone, never knowing when disaster would strike."

"Kind of like Duncan."

I thought about it. "Good point."

"So how did you cope?"

I thought about it. "Max helped me," I said. "He told me to pay attention to the things that made me feel better—and then to do more of those."

"Sensible," Alice said.

"It made me feel better to walk on the beach, so I walked on the beach. It made me feel better to drink cups of warm tea, so I drank them. Bubble baths made me feel better. Riding my bicycle. Flying kites. Listening to audiobooks. Reading. Baking. Candles. Wearing the flower hat."

"And then I gave you that book on color theory," Babette said.

"And I started filling up my world with color. Because Max promised me that joy was the cure for everything. And the more I learned about how it worked, the more I felt like joy was cumulative. That it wasn't about finding one big thing—but about collecting as many tiny pieces as you could."

Alice pointed at me. "See what I'm saying? *Math.*"

"It worked for you?" Babette wanted to confirm.

"Life is still *life*. But it has definitely helped stack the deck in my favor."

Maybe that was why Duncan's attack on the school felt so personal.

It was more than just bad for the faculty and bad for the kids—it was specifically bad for me.

My epilepsy had gone away when I was twelve. It just . . . resolved itself. All through middle school, the seizures were less and less frequent, and then, six months had gone by, and then a year. And the relief I'd carried—for years after the seizures stopped—was profound. It was like I'd been broken my whole life, and now was fixed.

I worked very hard at pretending the epilepsy had never even happened—and did a very thorough job of forgetting.

So when it came back—out of nowhere, in my midtwenties—I had some feelings about it. Dark feelings. Hopeless feelings. Self-hating feelings. Lots of those.

That first seizure brought the feelings all back—and maybe even bigger. Maybe worse. Almost as if ignoring it all for so long had allowed all those emotions and assumptions to fester and mutate and grow.

But I'd coped.

I'd found a way to drag myself out of a very dark place back into the light. I'd worked to fill up my world with flowers and sunshine and color. It wasn't theoretical for me—it was very practical. If Duncan erased those things from the school, he erased them from my life.

And what if the darkness took back over?

I couldn't let that happen.

It wasn't just the school that was in danger. It was me.

But we weren't going to think about that now. We were going to figure out some way to bring this guy back to life. For his sake, as well as mine—and everybody else's.

"This is going to work," Alice said.

"I think he needs to have some good, old-fashioned fun," Babette said.

I frowned. "Fun?"

"You should take him dancing—what about that line-dancing bar by San Luis Pass? Or that secret disco on Post Office Street? Or even just to the Pleasure Pier. You could ride the merry-go-round, hit the bumper cars . . . Or—don't overthink it—just go swimming in the ocean. Go walking down Seawall Boulevard."

Alice was nodding. "We have to start confronting him with joy."

"*Can* you confront someone with joy?" I asked.

"You know . . ." Alice said, trying to rephrase. "*Pelt* him with joy. Attack him with it. Joy-bomb him."

"*Joy-bomb* him?"

"Yes," Alice said, like *Duh*.

"And get him into therapy," Babette added. Then she made me circle "therapy" on the list twice and put stars all around it.

She wasn't wrong. We weren't professionals. It seemed pretty clear that he was dealing with some hefty post-traumatic stress disorder, and none of us were really qualified to cure that. So therapy would be a cornerstone of this plan.

"Good luck with that," Alice said, and as I pictured Duncan's stony face, he did not strike me like a willing candidate for therapy, either.

But Babette wasn't worried. "Trust me," she said. "I've got a guy."

It was so fun to see Babette taking on a project. The fog around her seemed to burn off at the prospect of helping someone. And of course, helping Duncan meant helping all of us. And the school, too. And potentially putting everything—well, almost everything—back the way it should be.

When the flow of ideas finally started slowing down, it hit me that I had no idea how we were going to make him do all these things

"Babette," I said then, feeling suddenly worried. "How exactly are we going to get him to cooperate?"

"Oh, that'll be easy," Babette said, with a little wink.

"Nothing is ever easy with Duncan," I said.

"Now it's time for me to share a little secret," Babette said.

"Okay," Alice and I said, leaning in.

"After Max died," Babette said, "the board asked me to take over."

Alice and I looked at each other.

Babette went on, "But I refused."

"I knew it," I whispered.

"Actually," Babette said. "They didn't just ask. 'Begged' would be a better word."

"But you were too overwhelmed by grief to take it on?" Alice asked. Babette nodded.

"So you let them hire Duncan," I said, nodding.

"Honestly, right then, I was too numb to care who they hired."

"I get it," I said.

Babette pulled her reading glasses down her nose. "But that doesn't change who I am. Max and I built this school. And nothing happens here without my say-so."

"Are you saying things aren't as bleak as they seem?"

Babette gave me a smile.

"Are you saying Kent Buckley is not the final word on everything?"

Her smile got bigger.

I smacked my hand on the table. "I knew Max wouldn't have left us with that dude in charge," I said.

"Here's what I need you to know," Babette said. "I could have both of them fired tomorrow."

"You could?" Alice asked.

"But I'm not going to."

"You're not?" I asked.

Babette shook her head.

"Why not?" Alice asked.

Babette glanced up at the heavens. "Because Kent Buckley is married to my daughter, and so that could make things awkward. And because you like Duncan. And I like Duncan, actually. And I think he's got potential. And he needs our help."

"So if there's a way to fix things amicably, that's what you prefer?" Alice asked.

"Exactly," Babette said.

I nodded. I got it.

"And frankly," Babette added, "I wouldn't mind a project. Something to redeem this whole, inexcusable year."

"Fair enough," I said.

"So here's how it's going to work," Babette said. "You're going to tell him that he has to do one thing I ask of him every day—maybe a small thing, maybe a bigger thing—and that if he agrees to all my demands, I won't fire him right away." She smiled. "But I still reserve the right to fire him later."

Alice looked at Babette in awe. "So we're blackmailing him."

She shrugged. "In a good way."

"What if he says no?" I asked.

She shrugged again. "Then he's out."

"Babette," I said, in a state of besotted admiration, "you are an absolute genius."

seventeen

Here's the thing: when they called the drugs they'd given Duncan "amnesia-inducing," they weren't kidding.

He didn't remember *anything*.

I didn't hear from him again after that night we spent together, even though I'd written my number on the post-surgical instructions and written "Call me if you need anything"—with "anything" underlined twice.

I did half-expect to hear from him again, if I'm honest.

Minus the whole surgery thing, it had been a very pleasant time.

I found myself thinking about him. Wondering how he was. Picking up my phone to call, but then deciding against it. Thinking about the moment when he'd said, "Even if I don't remember, I'll remember."

What would he remember, if he didn't remember?

It was the feeling you get after you've had a great date. A kind of rising, excited feeling of anticipation . . . like, even if the moment itself was over, the connection still lingered.

One part of trying to control epilepsy for me was trying to keep my emotions in check. Like, I tried to avoid the extremes when I could.

Which is one of the many reasons I didn't spend a lot of time in the dating pool. Dating was hard. Dating was tense. For all the bliss people felt about love and romance, it was stressful, too. And potentially destabilizing.

I didn't want to be destabilized. Any more than I already had been.

I was all about being the opposite, in fact.

So as I walked over to school that first morning after break, I had a wild sense of uncertainty. What would it be like to see Duncan again after all that? Would he be friendly with me? Flirty? And if he felt drawn to me like I did to him, what then? What on earth was going to happen next?

I had no idea.

But I felt almost hungry to see him. My last two encounters with him had been so very Old Duncan, I'd almost forgotten what New Duncan was like.

Until I saw him there.

He was in the courtyard, as the kids arrived, standing at attention in that gray suit, like nothing had ever happened. Hair swooped up and back. Navy tie knotted tight.

New Duncan, for sure. There he was.

Because when I walked over to him with a slightly goofy smile, the way you do with people you feel close to, people you've kissed, for example, or people whose *pants you have removed*, for Pete's sake—he blinked at me like I was a total stranger.

"Hey," I said, settling in pretty close next to him.

I could be wrong, but I thought I felt him edge away. "Hello."

Just days before, I'd had my hands on his shirtless torso. I'd stroked my palms up and down over the velvet of his hair. I'd let myself melt under the weight of those arms. I'd slept beside him in his bed.

Not to mention: the kissing.

Today, that suit might as well have been made of metal.

He didn't meet my eyes. "Thank you for the ride home the other day."

"Oh!" I said. "You're welcome! For a second, I thought you didn't remember."

"I don't remember," he said, all just-the-facts-ma'am. "But I know you agreed to come. And I woke up at my house. So, I figure you must have gotten me there somehow."

"Oh," I said, deflated. "You don't remember anything?"

He shook his head. "I remember that I asked you to drive me home. And that you agreed to do it. But I don't remember it happening."

Oh.

It gave me a tree-falls-in-the-forest feeling. *If a guy kisses you on painkillers, and the next day he doesn't remember, did it really happen?* Or, just as important: *If a guy confesses having a thing for you but then, the next time you see him, he looks for all the world like he couldn't care less . . . how can you possibly know what to believe?*

Honestly, based on his expression, I'd have sworn he was utterly indifferent to me.

Indifferent—with maybe a touch of nausea.

What would he remember if he didn't remember?

Nothing. Nothing at all.

"How are you?" I asked then. "Any trouble with the—?" I touched my palm to my side.

"No. All fine. Just some bruising." He could have been talking to his doctor.

"You fell over a couple of times," I said, watching to see if it sparked anything. "Once when you were trying to get undressed."

Duncan frowned.

"So, no complications? You're all good?"

"Yep." He nodded, not meeting my eyes.

"Any pain?"

"Some."

"And did you remember to text your sister?"

Now he looked over at me. "My sister?"

Two words. An improvement. "Yeah. She called a bunch of times. You told me to tell her you'd text her later."

He frowned. "How did that happen?"

"When your phone rang, I answered it."

"You talked to her?"

"Yes, I talked to her. For a while."

"What did she say?"

Now it was getting fun. She'd said a lot of things, actually. "She told me about that time in high school you and Jake accidentally mooned your math teacher and got suspended."

Duncan closed his eyes for a second, and I won't lie: it felt good to get a reaction out of him—any reaction at all.

But not good enough.

Being around a warm, doped-up version of Duncan had been good—and I didn't even really register how good until that guy was gone. Being around the robotic Duncan just made me want the human version back even more. I'd been unable to stop thinking about him, feeling a glow of affection that had stayed bright all week. Until now.

I missed the other Duncan.

It created a tightness of frustration in my body.

And so I decided to mess with him a little.

"Thank you for all the hugs, by the way."

Duncan held very still at that idea.

"And thank you," I went on, "for being so open and honest about your feelings."

I gave him a second to ponder what feelings, exactly, I might be referring to.

"And thank you for giving me your succulent collection."

That got his attention. He looked over at me. "Is that—? You took them?"

"For safekeeping. You'll be pleased to know I haven't watered them all week."

Duncan nodded, like he wasn't sure if he was pleased or not.

"Also," I added then, "I saw your scars."

Duncan got very still.

"But you wouldn't really talk about what happened."

Duncan nodded. "I never talk about it."

"Don't you think maybe you should?"

"Nope." Then he turned to me and said, "I will never talk about that. Okay?"

"Not with me," I said. "But maybe with a professional."

He gave a curt head shake. "Nope. Not my style."

I tried to make my voice sound pleasant and informational. "I get it. But I need to tell you something. Babette wants you to get into therapy."

"Babette?"

"She does," I said. "And she's very . . . all-powerful. She doesn't make a big thing of it, but she's basically God around here. She owns this school. And she owns the board of directors."

Duncan waited.

"Everybody thinks that the board passed her over for you. But that's not what happened. They begged her to come run the place. She just declined."

"Understandable," Duncan said, thinking.

"That's right. Right? Bad timing."

Duncan nodded. "Very."

"But she explained something to me the other night that I didn't know. They wanted her to run the school then, and they still want her to run the school now. And all she has to do is say the word, and you're out."

Duncan turned to look straight at me. "What about Kent Buckley?"

"Kent Buckley only thinks he's in charge. The board is loyal to Babette. They'll do anything she says."

"So, what are you saying?"

And here's where I had to work really hard to be convincing: "I'm saying your job is on the line. And she's very tempted to fire you. But she won't . . . if you agree to some simple terms."

"What terms?"

"Well, one: She wants you to get into therapy." I handed over the business card of Babette's guy.

Duncan took it. Looked down at it. Read it.

Wow. Life sure was easy when you had Babette in your corner.

I nodded. "Two, she wants you to lay off with the changes to the school—for now. Just put all that stuff on the back burner. No more painting things gray."

Duncan studied me for a second, then let out a breath, and said, "Okay."

Looking back, it was maybe a little too easy to get him on board.

But at the time, I just thought, *Everything in life should go this smoothly.*

"And three," I said, "she wants you to promise that every single day, you will do one thing that she asks you to do."

"Like what?"

"Probably something small, like eat a bowl of ice cream."

"Babette wants me to eat a bowl of ice cream?"

"Or do other things. Maybe something bigger."

"Bigger, like what?"

I shrugged. "I don't know. Swim in the ocean, maybe? Go fishing? Play mini-golf?"

Duncan frowned.

"Nothing terrible. She's not going to ask you to murder anyone or anything."

Duncan considered it.

"Not to be pushy, but I'm not really sure you have much choice here."

"Because if I don't agree to her terms, she'll fire me?"

I wrinkled my nose in sympathy. "Kinda. Yeah."

Duncan closed his eyes, then looked at me. "Is this for real?"

I suppose, if you hadn't been at the brainstorming session, this might seem a little random. I shrugged. "It's not forever. Just the spring semester."

"What happens after that?"

"Good question. She reserves the right to fire you, anyway. But maybe she won't. She'll definitely fire you right now if you don't go along with it, though. So: worth it to take the deal."

"What is this called? Is this extortion?" He thought about it. "Bribery? Blackmail?"

"I think they call this 'the kindness of strangers.'"

"Doesn't feel all that kind."

"Babette wanted me to mention that she's a benevolent ruler."

"Great," Duncan said, giving me a look.

"So?" I said. "Are you in?"

"Well," Duncan said, "given that I don't have a choice . . . I guess I have to be."

eighteen

And so began Operation Duncan.

We had a chance to rescue him—and possibly ourselves, as well.

And oh, man, was it fun.

We told Duncan to eat a frozen custard? He ate a frozen custard. We told him to do a handstand in the courtyard? He did a handstand in the courtyard. We told him to tell cringe-worthy math jokes over the school intercom (that one was Alice)? He told math jokes over the intercom.

It was true we had him boxed in—hard. But he sure didn't put up much of a fight. As far as I know, he never even thought about trying to expose us to Kent Buckley, or anyone else. On some level, I think, he was glad to go along with it.

Maybe even relieved.

For our part, Babette and I did a lot of strategizing about how to structure his journey. We wanted to push him to open up, to try forgotten things, to relax, to feel some feelings, and a million other things—but we didn't want to push him so hard he got spooked.

We started with small things—easy things.

Every morning, I'd pop by his office with his "thing" for the day. That first week, it was: eat a hot fudge sundae (to help him remember pleasure), jump on a pogo stick (to help him remember who he used to be), take a hot bath (to help him relax), watch a Bill Murray movie of his choosing (to get him laughing), and, on Friday, to juggle something—anything—for the kids at lunchtime (because juggling used to be his favorite thing to do). Duncan's rented house didn't have a bathtub, so Babette made him come to her house after school that evening, and then, while he was there, she insisted he stay for dinner (human connection). Likewise for the Bill Murray movie (Duncan chose *Meatballs*). Babette required that he watch it at her place so we could confirm the task was done. And since he was there, anyway, we fed him dinner and then joined him on the couch (friendship).

Alice came, too.

Babette and I took this project very seriously. We made a color-coded chart for all his required tasks—I'm not even kidding. Laughter was yellow, relaxation was pink, his old self was blue. We had four months, roughly, not counting spring break, and we wanted to make the most of them. On top of that, we read self-help books about overcoming trauma, about PTSD, about finding ways to move forward in life. We read, we highlighted, we took notes and discussed.

At no point did it occur to us that we might be doing any of this for ourselves.

But of course, it helped us, too.

We all needed to move on. We all needed to overcome trauma. We all needed hot baths and good laughs. Granted, I couldn't juggle, but watching Duncan finally do it that Friday at lunch in front of all the kids—was just as good, if not better.

"It's juggling day," I said to him pleasantly, during lunch duty.

He did not fight me.

"Kids!" he shouted, standing up to get their attention. "Who wants to see me juggle?"

A great cheer went up in the room.

Duncan walked around the room, snaking between the tables, picking up items off the kids' lunch trays. He took a red apple from a fifth-grader and started tossing it up and down as he kept walking, prowling for other things to gather.

"What should I juggle?" he asked the room over and over, as the kids watched him and shouted out suggestions: *A salt shaker! A glass of milk! A cupcake!*

"I'm choosing round things," he called out to the room, "because they're easier. And it's been a long, long, long, long . . ." He paused to look around the room, and then kept going: "long, long, long time since I've juggled anything."

The kids were spellbound, watching him.

So was I.

"Not even a spaghetti noodle!" he shouted. "Not even a square of Jell-O!" He was still tossing that apple up and down, barely even looking at it. "Not even," he said at last, lowering his voice, "a piece of belly-button lint."

A ripple of laughter from the kids.

"Some of you," Duncan went on, turning all around the room, pointing at the kids, "were barely even born the last time I juggled."

The kids cheered.

"So I'm sticking with easy," he said then, lifting up the apple, and saying, "Like this donut!"

"That's not a donut!" the kids called out.

Duncan was standing near Clay, and, with that, he leaned over and picked up an orange off his tray. He held it up for the kids. "You might think this watermelon is too heavy," he said next, as the kids launched into giggles and protests, "but I'm telling you, as long as it's round, I got this."

"That's not a watermelon!" the kids shouted.

"Now, I just need one more round thing," Duncan said, and the kids quieted to see what he was going to choose. "What should it be? A pomegranate? A tomato? A cactus?"

"A cactus isn't round!"

He sidled his way over toward the faculty tables now. "It'll be hard to top the watermelon, but I'll try."

That's when Duncan noticed an unpeeled kiwifruit on the lunch table in front of me. He met my eyes and started walking my way.

Quietly then, just to me, under the din, he said, "Who packs an unpeeled kiwifruit in their lunch?"

"Ran out of time," I said, tapping the paring knife I'd also brought.

Then Duncan winked at me and turned back to the room.

"I've got it!" he shouted. And the kids quieted to see what it would be.

He stepped closer to me, leaned over, picked up the kiwi, held it up, and shouted, "An avocado!"

The kids went nuts.

Duncan made his way back toward the stage at the far end—never breaking his rhythm with the apple and the orange. He climbed the stage steps without stopping.

He had their attention now. Lucky for all of us, he had not forgotten how to juggle.

And once he let himself start, it was like he'd never stopped. At first, it was just a simple circle, but then he started adding in pops and surprises, syncopating the rhythm. I left my table and moved closer to the stage, mesmerized by the sight, lost in the easy rhythm. He tossed the orange up high and caught it. He Hacky-Sacked the kiwi with his shoe. He tossed the apple between his legs and behind his back.

He created a marvelous, transcendent little moment of magic.

And then, once it was all over, he went back to the edge of the room, reassumed his military posture, and reapplied his poker face like it had never happened.

But it had happened.

And I'll tell you something. Even as I eyed him for the rest of lunch, looking stern again, and boring again in that same-old-same-old identical gray suit with that identical navy tie . . . I knew something was different.

Because when he'd caught that kiwi on his shoe a few minutes before, his pants leg had flipped up, and I'd seen something hidden under
there. Something I couldn't unsee.

The socks he was wearing today? They had polka dots.

The next night, our activity was to walk downtown to the movie theater that played the documentary about the Great Storm of 1900. "It's
very tragic," Babette had warned me, and I had explicit instructions to
stress themes of resilience in conversation afterward.

On the walk there, I couldn't stop talking about the juggling.

"You're just . . . so good," I kept saying.

"I used to perform on street corners. That's how I made money in
college."

"Juggling?"

He shrugged. "Other things, too."

"Like what?"

He sighed, like *So many.* "I can walk on stilts. I can do magic tricks.
I can solve a Rubik's Cube in under five minutes. I can blow a bubble
inside a bubble. I can burp the alphabet. Oh, and I'm a yo-yo champion."

"You're a yo-yo champion?"

"Well," he corrected, kind of aw-shucks, "state champion."

"That's a thing?"

He gave me a look. "Trust me. I could mesmerize you."

I flared my nostrils at him. "I'm not easily mesmerized."

"You only think that 'cause you've never seen me spin a yo-yo."

We strolled on for a second. Then I said, "How did you learn how to
do all that stuff?"

He thought about it for a second. "Do you remember when you were
in school and you came home every night and did homework?"

"Yeah . . ."

"Well, I never did that homework."

I smiled. Of course he didn't.

"I taught myself mumbley-peg instead. I read comic books. I taught myself Morse code. And knife-throwing. And cracking a whip. I memorized the name of every bomber that flew in World War Two. I built a working radio from scratch. Basically, I was wildly enthusiastic to learn everything they *don't* teach you in school."

"And now you're a school principal."

"They didn't hire me for my brains."

Our whole idea was to lure him in gently with easy things, and get him hooked, and then build from there. As the weeks went on, we upshifted slowly: making him read a favorite *Garfield* of Clay's choosing, making him wear a Hawaiian shirt and flip-flops on casual Friday, making him serenade Mrs. Kline in the courtyard on her birthday, making him eat a quarter-pound of fudge at La King's candy shop, making him play charades, and making him read a psychology book about post-traumatic growth.

Oh—and let's not forget the therapy. Babette's guy had confirmed that Duncan had, in fact, started attending sessions twice a week.

It had almost been too easy.

Maybe he'd known he was struggling. Maybe he'd wanted some help.

Maybe, on some level, he was grateful that Babette and I were bossing him around.

Was that possible?

I was, of course, the designated companion slash chaperone on all these outings. Babette always planned her biggest events for Friday nights and then gave him the rest of the weekend off. They weren't dates, of course, but since we did them together, just the two of us, they definitely resembled dates. Babette sent us to the movies, and to the aquarium, and bowling, and out to dinner.

It was confusing, to say the least.

For me, anyway.

The more time I spent with him, the more time I wanted to spend with him. And the more I thought about him when he wasn't around. And the more I looked for him in the hallways.

It wasn't . . . *not* agonizing. I'll say that.

I definitely felt like we were helping Duncan. And the kids. And the school.

I just wasn't quite so sure what we were doing to me.

nineteen

One Friday, Babette's task for us was to go to an amusement park that was built on a pier out over the Gulf. It was just a few blocks from school, and Duncan left Chuck Norris dozing on a dog bed in his office and walked over to meet me around sunset.

Before we'd made it to the pier, the sun had gone down, and the lights had begun to glow—neon ones on the rides, and string bulbs in graceful scallops all up and down the pier. We bought our tickets and strolled along.

Unable to resist a teachable moment, I said, "Wouldn't this place be so sad if someone had painted it gray?"

Babette actually had a specific ride that she'd designated for us, and it was a roller coaster called the Iron Shark.

Important note: roller coasters are not exactly safe for people with epilepsy. Some people did fine on them, and some people did not—and I was not exactly sure which category I fell into.

Duncan was clearly a fan of roller coasters. "I hear it has a ten-story, face-down, vertical drop," Duncan said, like that was a good thing. He'd done a lot of things on Babette's orders so far, with varying degrees of reluctance, but he actually seemed excited about this one.

He was about as excited as I was nervous.

What the hell was I doing?

To be honest, I just wanted to hang out with Duncan. I didn't want to skip one of our tasks. I wanted to keep things going and not lose momentum. I couldn't resist a chance to spend time with him.

You know that feeling when you just click with somebody—when something about that person just lights you up? It's so rare. When it happens, it feels like a little miracle—and all you want is more of that person. I wanted more of Duncan. *This* Duncan.

And if I had to ride a roller coaster to get it, fine.

I put what we were doing out of my mind—and just gave in to being there.

Before I knew it, we were seated side by side in the very first car, and I was starting to question my life choices. I pushed the restraint down and clicked it into place at my waist.

"Wait—" I said, turning to Duncan. "There's no shoulder harness? Where's the shoulder restraint?" I reached up behind my head and mimed pulling an imaginary shoulder restraint down over me.

"There is no shoulder restraint," Duncan said.

I felt a tightening of alarm. "Just—*waist*? A '*waist restraint*'? That's not a thing."

"It works," he said. "It's fine."

But I shook my head. "So the top half of your body is just loose?"

"Well, yeah. That's part of the fun."

"Oh, my God," I said. "We're going to die." As I said those words, I looked straight in front of me and saw—really saw, for the first time—the vertical wall of tracks ahead.

A black hole of fear opened up in my stomach. This was happening.

"You okay?" Duncan asked.

I had a clear view of the tracks: They eased out about thirty feet from the loading dock and then curved in a right angle straight up. And up. And up.

"This maybe wasn't a good idea," I said.

"Oh, yeah," Duncan said. "It's a terrible idea." He said it with relish—as if the fact that it was a bad idea made it awesome.

"I think I need to get off," I said, tugging at the waist restraint—which, of course, didn't budge—just as another coaster car whooshed over our heads and muffled my words.

I turned to look for someone to signal on the platform . . .

But that's when we started moving.

"No turning back now," Duncan said

He wasn't wrong. We were in motion. This was happening. How long did this ride last, again? Three minutes? Four? I felt my fingers get cold and then a sandpapery tingle of fear spread through my body.

How had I let myself wind up here? My heart rate had doubled—or possibly tripled—like it was not just beating, but more like *convulsing* in my chest.

I squeezed my eyes closed, but that was worse. I opened them again just as we tilted back and back on the tracks until we were fully sideways, and gravity pulled every unharnessed part of me back against the seat. It felt so vertical it seemed like we were tilting backward, and I decided to argue with the fear. *All you have to do,* I said to myself, *is wait for it to be over. Just sit tight, and wait, and don't die of a heart attack.*

I'll say this: they really draw out the anticipation during that ten-story climb.

"Are you okay?" Duncan asked.

But I couldn't answer.

The anticipation was the worst part, I told myself.

But, actually, no.

The worst part was yet to come.

Because just as we reached the tippy-top of the ten-story-high scaffolding, just as we were barely starting to tip up to start the U-turn that would send us plunging back toward the earth . . . the coaster car stopped.

Like, stopped moving entirely.

Just went dead.

After a second, I said, "Is this part of the ride?" Maybe they were trying to intensify the anticipation.

"No," Duncan said.

Not what I wanted him to say.

"What's going on?" I said, my voice sounding like it was somebody else's.

But next, a voice sounded through a speaker between our seats.

"Nothing to worry about, folks," the voice said pleasantly.

"What the hell is going on!" I yelled at the speaker, as if it could hear me.

"We're experiencing a normal pause of the system. The system is not broken, and there is no reason for alarm. Our computer sensors are highly calibrated to detect the presence of any foreign objects on the tracks. If the sensors detect an impediment, they immediately stop all rides until our technicians can resolve the issue."

I met Duncan's eyes. "What kind of foreign objects?"

The loudspeaker barreled on. "Foreign objects include, but are not limited to, newspapers, kites, beer cans, and pelicans."

Duncan shrugged at me.

"Please sit tight and enjoy the view until the situation is resolved."

The loudspeaker shut off, and for a second, there was only wind.

Wind, and nothingness. Because there was nothing at all around us. We were at the tip-top, perched at a slight angle like a jaunty hat, with nothing but sky in every direction.

That's when the panic really hit.

"Duncan?" I said then.

"Yeah?"

"I'm freaking out."

Duncan angled his head so he could stare at me. "You look fine. Great, even."

"I am not fine. Or great."

Then, forcing a chuckle, he said, "Why? Because there's a pelican on the tracks?"

But that's when I started hyperventilating.

"Hey," he said, leaning closer. "What's going on?"

"I want to get down," I told him—and saying the words made it worse.

"Hey. This is a modern roller coaster—it's not like there's some old geezer in a choo-choo hat pulling a rickety old lever."

"That's not helping."

"I'm right here," he said, his voice now all business. "I'm right here with you, and we are safe. We are safely strapped into a ride that hundreds of people ride every day for, you know—*for fun*. I'm sure this pelican thing happens all the time. No big deal. We'll just wait for them to shoo it away, and then we'll get this done."

"That's just it, though," I said, panting now. "I don't want to get it done. I want to get off."

"We can't get off," he said. "But the good news is, this scary roller coaster seems about average for scary roller coasters."

"That's not comforting."

"I'm just saying, once we get going, it won't be so bad."

"I don't ride scary roller coasters, okay?"

"What? Ever?"

"Pretty much never."

"So why are you here?"

"It just kind of happened, okay? I was having fun. I wasn't paying attention."

Silence from next to me. Then: "You're only here because of me?"

"Yes," I said, in a voice that was half frustrated sigh, half eye roll. And then my explanation came out fast: "Babette told us to do it, and you seemed excited about it, I got caught up in the moment, and I wasn't really thinking."

"That might be the nicest thing anybody's ever said to me."

"Okay. But I think I'm having a panic attack."

"What makes you think that?"

This came out sarcastic: "Um. Might be all the panic I'm feeling."

"Fair enough."

"Hey," I said then. "I need to warn you about something."

"Okay."

I sucked in a tight breath, and said, "It's possible that at some point I might wind up having . . . a seizure."

"A *seizure*?"

"Yes."

"When?"

"Anytime, really." Then I amended: "Probably not now. But possibly. Who knows?"

He said, "Could you elaborate, please?"

I looked up at the sky while I said the words. I watched the stars, and they watched me back. "So . . ." I said then, keeping my face turned up, "I have epilepsy."

"Okay."

I sped up a little, to get it over with. "I mostly had it in grade school. It was very bad then—I had a lot of seizures—like at least one a month—and sometimes they happened in school, and if you're wondering if little kids think epilepsy is cool . . . they do not."

"You got teased."

"Teased. Ostracized. Shunned. All of it. Everything. The worst part was—with a grand mal seizure, first you go completely rigid, like everything in your body goes as tight as it can go, and then you go completely limp, like a rag doll. And when I was little, though this doesn't actually happen to me anymore, I used to lose all control of my bodily functions."

"Oof."

"Yeah. Not great in a school situation. I basically had no friends. At all."

"I'm sorry."

"But when I got older, the seizures went away. We found a medicine that worked, and then we slowly weaned me off of it, and I was fine. Middle school—less frequent; high school, college—nothing. Totally normal. I thought I was cured. But then it came back just after I moved here."

"Why did it come back?"

"Nobody knows. Just happens sometimes. And it's much milder now—like once or twice a year. I don't even take medicine for it, because the medicine has lots of side effects." I glanced over. "That's why I don't drive."

Duncan nodded.

"I just try to control it by getting enough sleep, and eating right, and . . . you know . . . making good choices."

"Are those things enough to control it?"

"No. Yes. Kind of."

Duncan nodded.

"Eating no carbohydrates at all helps some people, so I eat that way. And I don't drink. And I get enough sleep, and drink enough water, and basically try to keep my life pleasant and drama-free. Because one of the biggest triggers for seizures?"

"Roller coasters?" Duncan offered.

"Stress," I said.

Duncan shook his head. "What the hell are you doing on this thing?"

"Not my best-ever decision."

Duncan nodded, like he was really getting it all now. "Because if you were to rate the stress-inducing level of the Iron Shark on a scale of say, one to ten—"

"Twenty."

"Gotcha."

"So. If it happens, don't freak out."

"I'll try not to."

"I'm not going to swallow my tongue or anything—that's not a real thing. After it's over, there's a phase where I go limp. Please just make sure I'm okay to breathe. And when all that's over, I get really tired— just sleepy and exhausted beyond belief. If you could just help me home, that would be awesome."

"Shouldn't I take you to the hospital?"

"Nope."

"But you had *a seizure*."

"If *you* had a seizure, we'd go to the hospital. But it's normal for me. Same-old-same-old. No big deal."

Duncan frowned at me. "Okay. I'm going to help you not stress. I'm going to distract you."

"How?"

"Did you know I invented a dance?"

I tilted my head back and looked up at the sky. Deep breaths. I could work with this. "You invented a dance?"

"Yep. A dance called the Scissors. Look." He put his elbows together. Then he moved his hands up and down, like his forearms were scissor blades.

I watched him for a second, then turned my eyes back up to the stars. "I'm not sure that's a dance."

"It's totally a dance."

"Is it a dance other people know?" I asked. "Or just you?"

He gave me a look. "It's a dance other people know. It's all over YouTube."

I looked over at him, then back up to the stars, still breathing. "How did you invent a dance?"

"I used to have a job as a party motivator. I worked the bar mitzvah circuit."

"I can't imagine you in that job," I said. "I can imagine you as a drill sergeant, maybe. Or maybe, like, a museum guard. Or one of those guys at Kensington Palace in one of those crazy hats."

"A Beefeater," Duncan supplied.

"Something stoic. Something solemn. I absolutely cannot in any life-time see you as a dance instructor."

"Well, that's your loss," Duncan said. "Because I am a legendary dancer."

This actually made me laugh out loud.

"I'll take you dancing one night, and you'll see."

"Oh," I said. "I'm not a big dancing-in-public person."

"You don't dance?"

"In public," I specified. "I dance, but only alone in my house with nobody around."

"That sounds really sad."

I shrugged. "I just have a mortal fear of humiliation."

"The trick to dancing is that it's voluntary humiliation. You have to lean into it."

"No, thank you," I said.

But now I was smiling. The idea of Duncan as a dance instructor was too funny not to.

"You don't believe me," he said, shaking his head.

"I believe that you once had that job. I don't believe you were good at it."

"I was *a legend*. In the Chicago-area bar mitzvah community, I was a god. A dance god. That's what I'm saying. It's been almost ten years, and kids still do this dance. It's everywhere. It's popping up in California and Florida and New York. Kids are doing it at clubs."

"Why would you make up a dance called 'the Scissors'?"

"I made up hundreds of dances. It was just to keep the room going. Seriously—anything that popped into my head. The Palm Tree. The Blender. The Seesaw. The Get Over Here. The Don't Look at Me. The Gummy Bear. The Stub Your Toe. The ThighMaster."

Now I was smiling. "Those can't be real."

"I'm telling you, they are."

"Why didn't you just do regular dances?"

"I didn't know any regular dances. I fell into that job by accident."

"And now you'll forever be known as the inventor of the Scissors."

Suddenly: a voice came through the loudspeaker. "Great news, folks. The tracks are clear, and your ride will recommence as soon as we reboot the system. Please be patient a few more minutes."

"Oh, shit," I said, the panic revving back up in my voice. "I don't want the ride to recommence."

I started feeling cold and hot at the same time, and a rushing sound welled up in my ears, and then for a second I thought the ride was shaking, but then I realized it was just me, breathing in and out in staccato bursts—way, way too fast.

Duncan was peering at me. "You look really green."

"I might be about to faint."

He grabbed my hands and enclosed them in his. They felt big, and warm, and strong, and dry—not clammy and moist and pathetic like mine. "Hey," he said, "look at me."

I turned and looked at him, at those eyes fixed on mine in an intense way I'd never seen from anybody before.

"I'm going to help you breathe."

"I know how to breathe," I said, panting.

"Not at the moment."

Next, he put a hand against my face to hold my gaze right on him. "We're going to breathe together, and you're going to start to feel better."

He made me look straight at him—into his eyes—and breathe in for five counts and then back out for four. Then again, and then again. We breathed in together and out together, in sync, while he counted in a quiet voice. I watched his mouth moving. I heard his breath rustling the air. I let my hands stay wrapped up inside his.

What was it about eye contact that was so intense? Or was it just that face of his? Something about the shape of his nose, maybe, or the line of his jaw, or the plumpness of his bottom lip. I didn't know. I might never figure it out.

"Just keep your eyes on me," Duncan said.

No problem.

I liked being that close to him. I liked having his full attention. I liked the curve of his neck and the way that long, vertical tendon pressed out and curved down and around as he kept his head turned to me, face to face, focused in a way that people never, ever are—unless they have a reason to be.

I was a tiny bit glad I had a reason to be.

Everything had its upside.

And that's when the Iron Shark revved back up, and we started to move.

Then we tipped up, and then forward, and then went stomach-lurchingly, heart-twistingly, death-facingly over the top . . . and then, in impossible, helpless slow-mo, we plummeted face-first back down toward the earth.

twenty

Back on the boardwalk, I had to sit down and put my head between my knees.

Duncan, clearly at a loss, rubbed my back like a boxing coach, which was not nearly as soothing as I think he intended. He kept saying, "Can I get you anything?" and "You're all right, right? Do you need a funnel cake?"

When I could finally sit up, Duncan's first suggestion was chocolate, but I was too nauseated for that. Next, he suggested we "dance it out" down by the music stage where a country band was playing, but that was also a *no*. His final idea was a kind of hair-of-the-dog approach, suggesting we ride the Iron Shark again.

Which left me no choice but to charge toward the exit, leaving him behind on the bench.

I wasn't leaving him behind on purpose. I just had to get out of there.

Duncan followed me. "Hey!" he said. "Hey—wait!"

"I think I just need to walk," I called back, not slowing.

He caught up pretty fast, and we made our way out. The music and the lights and the people and the cyclical rush of the rides going by, which had all seemed so delightful and objectively fun at first, suddenly now seemed crazy-making.

At the exit, without ever agreeing to, we started walking along the seawall, leaving the chaos behind.

The seawall is seventeen feet high—built after the Great Storm of 1900 to protect the city from storm surges. A boulevard runs alongside it that—and this has always struck me as a bold choice—does not have a guardrail. So, as we walked, on our right cars were zooming by—folks in top-down Jeeps blasting music, and Harley hogs, and the occasional cute red trolley—but on our left was a seventeen-foot drop-off down to the beach.

I noticed Duncan repositioning himself between me and the edge of the sidewalk, as if I might just kind of veer off and over the edge.

Gentlemanlike of him.

Almost in response, I took hold of his arm as we walked. And then the ballast of his weight there just felt so steadying and comforting, I didn't let go.

"Thank you," I said as I held on.

Duncan nodded. "My arm is your arm."

"I'm not sure that works," I said, "even metaphorically." But I let myself hold on to him for a few more minutes before I made myself let go.

It was much quieter after we left the pier, and it wasn't until we'd made it some distance, when it was just kite stores and pizza shops and tattoo parlors on the right, and the quiet, steady, eternal ocean on the left, that I started to recover.

The moon was out, too.

Duncan kept watching me—closely. "Are you sorry you told me?"

"Of course. It's embarrassing."

Duncan nodded. "What if I tell you something embarrassing about me? Then we'll be even."

"That works."

After a pause, he said, "So many to choose from."

"I'm not picky," I said.

"Okay, got it," he said then. "Here's one: I plan my funeral."

"You *what*?"

"Yeah. I keep notes on a document on my computer."

I frowned. "That's actually a little disturbing."

He turned to me then, like I might get the wrong idea. "I'm not suicidal, understand. I don't *want* to die. I'm just aware that I *could* die. At any moment. And, if I do . . . I want a kick-ass funeral."

Of course, now that I knew he had almost died, the whole thing made sense. I could see why he might have started thinking about it, anyway. Why he *kept* thinking about it was another question.

"What is a kick-ass funeral, exactly?" I asked. "Are we talking like a New Orleans marching-jazz-band parade? Or, like, skydivers? Fireworks?"

"Those are all great ideas." He gave me a little sideways smile.

"What, then?"

"Just a normal funeral . . . but cool. I don't like organ music, for example. So I made a playlist. You know, of favorites."

"Like?"

"Oh, you know. Maybe some Talking Heads. A little Curtis Mayfield. Some Johnny Cash. A little hint of James Brown. And, of course: Queen."

"Sure," I said, "Queen goes without saying. At a funeral."

Duncan gave me a look.

"I guess 'Another One Bites the Dust' is too on the nose."

Duncan pointed at me. "Great rhythm-guitar line, though."

"Is your funeral a sing-along?" I asked. "Wait—is it karaoke?"

"No, but that's not a bad idea. I've got some poems set aside, too. One I found about harvesting peaches and, you know, the cycle of life, and another one about the death of the spider in *Charlotte's Web*."

"You've really thought about this."

"Nobody wants a shitty funeral."

I thought about Max's funeral. "Aren't they all ultimately kind of shitty, though?"

He shook his head. "We've set the bar too low. We can do better."

I lifted my hands in surrender. "Fair enough."

He nodded. "And, then, you know . . . I typed up a few words."

"You wrote your own obituary?"

"Eulogy."

"What does it say?"

"It stresses how handsome and heroic I am—"

"Naturally," I said.

"And mentions my Nobel Prize and my Pulitzer."

"Fair enough."

"And then, at the end, there's a dance party."

"In the church?"

He frowned at me like I hadn't been paying attention. "None of this is happening in a church. This is a *beach* funeral."

"Oh," I said, feeling a little sting in my heart as this theoretical scenario suddenly shifted to feeling far too real. More quietly, I said, "Max had a beach funeral."

"Did he?"

"It was packed. You wouldn't think you could pack a beach, but he did."

Duncan recognized my shift in perspective. "I wasn't here yet. For that."

I let out a long breath. "You would have loved Max so much." I looked over, then added, "He would have loved you, too."

Suddenly, I couldn't help but think about how sad this conversation was. Not just remembering Max, and the unbelievable day when we'd all said goodbye to him, but the idea of Duncan planning his own funeral. As funny as he was being about it, it said a lot about what life had led him to expect.

We fell quiet for a bit. The wind off the Gulf—that steady current washing over us—was relaxing me. It was almost like a micro-massage. The stress was draining away, but in its place was something like sorrow. But not only sorrow. Companionship, too. I let go of his arm and fell into the comforting rhythm of just walking side by side with somebody.

We had survived the Iron Shark. And so many other things, too.

That really should have been enough.

But of course, I wanted more from him. Couldn't help but notice how our hands kept accidentally brushing past each other as we walked. Each time it happened I felt a little jolt. It would have been so easy to edge a little closer and just give mine permission to find a way into his.

But what if he said no? Or—worse—what if he said yes?

I was in an impossible situation. One I had no idea how to get out of. Mostly because I wanted to be there so badly.

After a while, Duncan said, "Thank you for telling me about your epilepsy."

I pointed at him. "That's need-to-know information, by the way. Don't use it against me."

"I won't," he said. "I wouldn't."

He did look serious. "Yeah, well," I said, walking on, "I'll believe you when I believe you."

"You've been through some hard things," he said.

"Sure. Who hasn't?"

"It's just—you kind of seem like someone who doesn't have any problems."

"Is there anyone in the world who doesn't have any problems?"

"What I mean is, you seem like a person life has been kind to."

I frowned. "Why?"

"I don't know. You wear all those crazy polka dots and stripes and pom-poms. You wore *rainbow suspenders* the other day." He looked down. "You are literally wearing clown socks right now. You're just so . . . weirdly *happy*."

"You think I'm happy because I don't know any better?"

"I don't know."

"Dude—I'm not happy because it comes easily to me. I bite and scratch and claw my way toward happiness every day."

Duncan squinted at me, like that almost made sense.

"It's a choice," I went on, feeling like I needed to make him see. "A choice to value the good things that matter. A choice to rise above everything that could pull you down. A choice to look misery right in the eyes . . . and then give it the finger."

"So it's a hostile kind of joy."

He was mocking me. "Sometimes," I said defiantly.

"Is that a real thing though?"

"It's a deliberate kind of joy. It's a conscious kind of joy. It's joy *on purpose*."

Duncan squinted like he really wasn't sold. "In clown socks and a tutu."

"I'm telling you. I know all about darkness. That's why I am so hell-bent, every damn day, on looking for the light."

twenty-one

That night changed everything.

Nothing like a near-death experience, a walk on Seawall Boulevard, and a little adrenaline-inspired oversharing to promote interoffice
bonding.

When I got to work on Monday, Duncan was friendly.

Friendly.

He greeted me pleasantly, the way nice people greet each other, and
then he walked with me toward the courtyard. And that's when things
got really crazy.

The courtyard . . .

Was full of children . . .

Blowing bubbles.

I froze. I frowned at Duncan. "What is going on here?"

Duncan just smiled.

I reached over and poked my finger into his shoulder, as if to check
that he was not a hologram.

Confirmed: flesh and blood.

I had woken up that morning with a terrible oversharing hang-

over, aghast at the amount of talking we'd done, the things I'd confessed to. I didn't go around *chatting* about my epilepsy. It wasn't
something I shared with people—especially not people who were . . .
complicated.

I'd wondered what it would be like to see him again.

Duncan was truly impressive at compartmentalizing. No matter
how much fun we had doing Babette-mandated activities outside of
school, he remained totally wooden and impersonally professional at
school. Sometimes, after we'd had an especially fun time, he'd be extra
cold the next day, as if to get us back to neutral.

Fair enough. As long as he didn't paint anything else gray, I wasn't
going to complain.

Getting dressed that morning, I went extra cheerful, as if to confirm
visually that he couldn't get me down: a pink-and-red sweater set and a
blue-jean skirt—and red knee socks with little pom-poms on them.

I'd spent the whole morning holding my shoulders back and bat-
tening down my emotional hatches to prepare myself for whatever
glacial, stoic, all-business expression I was about to encounter on Duncan's face.

He wasn't going to disappoint me, dammit. I was going to be un-
disappointable.

But now here he was, *smiling*. And waiting for me to smile back.

Standing in a courtyard full of bubbles.

Every single kid had a colored bottle—red, blue, orange—and a
little wand. Some were blowing, and some were running around, trying
to harness the wind. The teachers were there, too.

And, of course, Chuck Norris was running around like a lunatic, trying to catch the bubbles in his mouth.

"What is going on here?" I asked.

Duncan shrugged, suppressing a smile, and said, "We're blowing
bubbles," almost like *What about bubbles don't you understand?*

"Am I still asleep?" I asked Duncan.

He smiled. "If you are, then I am, too."

"Why is this happening?"

Duncan said, "The teachers asked if we could have a bubble party during homeroom."

"And you said yes?"

"I said yes."

"You never say yes."

"This time, I did."

"But . . . why?"

Duncan looked away and surveyed the kids. Then he gave a little shrug. "I don't know. You convinced me."

"What—the other day?" I asked. "How, exactly? All we did was almost die!"

He shrugged. "I guess you reminded me of something. Something important. And that was enough."

"What did I remind you of?"

Duncan lifted a bubble wand toward his lips and blew a steady stream of bubbles in my direction. Then, when the wand was empty, he lowered it, shifted his gaze to my eyes, and said, "You reminded me what it felt like to be happy."

And that, right there, was the tipping point.

The rest of the spring semester just floated by on a cloud of pleasantness.

Babette and I felt like maybe we had done it. Maybe we had fixed him. Or, more specifically, maybe we and six weeks of twice-a-week therapy had fixed him. Could it have been that easy? That fun? He really did seem a lot better.

He didn't turn back into Old Duncan, exactly. He still wore his suit, still coiffed his hair, still stayed serious a lot of the time.

But there was warmth to him now. He let himself give in to play. He gave in to crazy socks. He accepted that Chuck Norris was never meant to be a security dog and started letting the kids pet him.

He let himself relax. A little.

There was no hope of resisting him after that, and I let him take my heart completely hostage. I settled into a comfortable-uncomfortable life of pining. I never found the nerve to ask him if the things he'd said on drugs had been true, and he, of course, never brought it up. He continued doing Babette's daily tasks, and I joined him if he needed a partner, and he seemed to actively like my company . . . but he never tried to kiss me again or take anything to another level.

It told myself it was fine. I tried to focus on the upsides.

Babette was doing better—and making (mostly failed) attempts to learn how to cook. Alice—her fiancé still deployed until midsummer—joined us lots of nights. We played board games at Babette's kitchen table, and gossiped about our coworkers, and analyzed Duncan's progress.

It was good to settle into a little holding pattern, I decided. It gave me some time to practice self-care. That seizure that had been threatening never did come, and I wanted to keep it that way. I meditated, took walks by the water, and got plenty of sleep. It started to feel like maybe things could find a way to be okay.

Until one day Tina Buckley showed up in the library. My library.

"I need to talk to you," she said. "It's about Clay."

I stopped.

"He's having trouble with his reading."

This got my attention. Sweet Clay, with his big, owl-like glasses, was one of my most voracious, enthusiastic readers. I could not imagine him having trouble with his reading. With Clay, in fact, the challenge was finding enough books to keep him busy.

"What's going on?" I asked.

"He's had a book on his nightstand for a week, and he's barely read any of it."

That definitely didn't sound like Clay. "What's the book?" I asked.

Tina looked straight at me and said, *"The Sound and the Fury."*

I coughed. "I'm sorry, what?"

She nodded. "Yes. He did fine with *Of Mice and Men,* but he's faltering with this one."

"Clay read *Of Mice and Men?*" I asked.

Please note: we were talking about a third-grader.

"Yes," Tina says, "and he aced his reading comprehension quiz. But now it's like he's backsliding."

I had to step back.

"Why," I asked then, "is your third-grader reading Faulkner?"

Tina gave me a look. "You've seen him. You know what he can do. His father and I think he needs to be challenged."

"Challenged . . . by Faulkner?"

"His dad and I want him reading the classics."

"In the third grade?"

"He can handle it."

"Maybe he can. But should he have to?"

It wasn't shocking to talk to a parent who was pushing difficult reading on her kid. Parents at this school did that all the time. No matter what culture or socioeconomic group they came from—and we had a wide variety here—they were all, uniformly, people who valued education. They were hard-working, driven, goal-oriented people, and most parents, I've found, have some level of anxiety about their kids' relationship with reading. It's beyond common for parents to equate reading with success—and difficult reading with more success.

I spent a lot of time trying to convince overeager parents that *harder* didn't always mean *better*. So a conversation like this wasn't all that surprising.

What was surprising, though, was that this was (A) Max and Babette's daughter (who should know better), talking about her (B) third-grader and his interest—or lack thereof—in (C) reading Faulkner.

Faulkner.

"We also have another issue," Tina said, lowering her voice to a whisper. "Last night, I found some disturbing materials in his backpack."

I frowned. What were we talking about? He was a little young for *Playboy*.

"Disturbing how?" I asked.

"I found them—but I hid them in the pantry behind the cereal boxes before his father could see."

"Hid what?" I prompted.

Tina took a breath, then let it out. She leaned in a little closer. Then she whispered, "*Garfields*."

I frowned. *Garfields*? "I don't understand," I said.

She nodded, like we were on the same page. "Four compilations. The big, fat ones."

I knew about those *Garfields*. He had checked them out yesterday. I'd let him go one book over the limit, even. "What's wrong with *Garfield*?"

She looked at me like I was nuts. "It's cartoons."

"Not animated cartoons, though. Not Porky Pig."

"Close enough. His dad and I want him reading real books."

As far as I was concerned, *any* book was a real book. "So . . . no comics? No graphic novels? No *Archies*?"

She made a disgusted face. "Good Lord, no. His dad doesn't want him reading kid stuff."

"You do realize that Clay *is* a kid?"

Tina glared at me. "Look, my husband went to Princeton—and so did his father, and so did his grandfather. Kent is very concerned with making sure that Clay also goes to Princeton. And from every study he's seen, reading can really give a kid the competitive edge." Then she added, "Real reading, we mean. *Garfields* are not going to cut it."

Okay. Got it. I mentally added to my to-do list: *Find Clay a secret cubby where he can keep his* Garfields.

I glanced up at the wall clock.

Then Tina Buckley said this: "You may have noticed that Clay is . . . not an athletic child."

I waited to see where she was heading.

"My husband was a Division One athlete, so you can imagine how disappointed he is about that."

No, actually. I couldn't imagine anyone on earth being disappointed in Clay.

"If Clay can't be an athlete," Tina went on, "then his academics will have to be extra strong."

"Aren't they already?" I asked.

"Kent doesn't want to take any chances."

I wanted to stop her right there and beg her not to crush her child's love of learning—but I could feel she was building to a question, so I waited.

"So I was wondering," Tina went on, the muscles in her face tight, like she was deeply uncomfortable, "if I might be able to volunteer in the library. So I can be near him. And check in on him. And help him make better choices."

The easy answer to that was not just *no*, but *hell, no*.

The last thing a kid with parents like that needed was his mom hovering over him in here, judging him and shaming him about totally normal kid stuff. This library was supposed to be a safe place where kids could follow their own reading compasses—without grown-ups watching, micromanaging, and judging them.

Seriously. Show me a kid who hates to read, and I'll show you a kid who got shamed about it, one way or another.

I was here to protect kids from that kind of crazy. But, I just couldn't bring myself to say no to her in that moment. She must have really wanted it bad to make the ask in the first place. I was the last person on earth she'd want to turn to.

Of course, *she* was the last person on earth I'd want in *my* library.

She couldn't stand me, that much was always clear. And any hope I'd had that we would've closed ranks around Babette after Max died and find ways to stitch back together that empty hole he'd left in each of our lives was long gone. But it was also clear that for some reason— maybe one I didn't even understand yet—Tina really, really wanted me to say yes.

So I said yes. Of course.

For Max and Babette—and Clay, if not for Tina herself.

"Of course you can," I said, offering her a smile that was more like a twitch. "You can sign up for shifts on the website."

There was a good chance that I was going to let her into the library and she'd find some way to burn the place down. Metaphorically. Or maybe even literally. I wouldn't put it entirely past her.

But there was also a chance that our sunny little library would do for her what it always did for me: make her feel better. Be that little source of joy she so clearly needed. And that might have some kind of butterfly effect on the people around her. And for their sakes—especially since I was one of them—I just felt like I had to take it.

Even though, remember: this woman had *kicked me out of Max's funeral*.

She looked down, like she'd suddenly remembered it, too.

"Thank you," she said.

I had no idea how this would play out. But here's what I knew for sure:

I wouldn't be giving Clay a secret cabinet of *Garfield*s at school, after all.

I'd be giving him a *super*-secret cabinet of *Garfield*s.

Then, in late April, on the Friday of the near-the-end-of-year faculty party, Duncan closed the cafeteria for the day and sponsored a lunch picnic in the courtyard for the kids.

Mrs. Kline had taped big signs on the cafeteria doors that said, CLOSED FOR DECORATING.

It seemed like a lot of decorating.

But when I showed up at the party that night, I figured out why.

Duncan had brought back the butterfly mural.

Before I noticed the room strung with bulb lights and lanterns, and the round tables covered in festive cloths and candles, the first thing I saw—the only thing I saw, for a while there—was the butterflies. They were even more beautiful than I remembered.

I stared up at them for a while before I looked around for Duncan.

He was across the room, chatting with Mrs. Kline, but as soon as

I spotted him, he seemed to feel my eyes on him. He looked over and watched me walk toward him.

"The butterflies are back," I said, unable to disguise the tenderness in my voice.

"Yes."

"The paint really was removable," I said, shaking my head. "You scrubbed it off."

"You didn't believe the paint would come off?"

"I believed that you believed it."

We both turned toward the mural.

My eyes stung a little bit. "But, if I'm honest, I didn't really expect to see it again."

Duncan gave me a little smile. "Surprise."

"Thank you," I said, my voice like a whisper.

Duncan nodded.

"Does this mean you think the world is a better place now?"

Duncan gave me a little sideways smile. "I think my world is better when you aren't mad at me."

"Fair enough," I said. Though I hadn't been mad at him in a good while.

There were twinkle lights strung across the ceiling, and quiet music on the speaker system, and drinks and food all around. Mrs. Kline had brought a lemon cake, and Coach Gordo had brought home-brewed beer. The teachers were showing up and filling the room—ready to bring a long school year to a close.

For a second, I found myself thinking about how I hadn't been to a party since Max's birthday, and I wondered if it might be hard for Babette to be here. And that's when I remembered I had a message for Duncan.

"By the way," I said, "Babette says you're done with your tasks for her, as well. So you're a free man. Now. Mostly. As long as you don't . . . relapse."

Duncan held very still, and I couldn't tell if he was disappointed or just stoic. "The tasks are over?"

I shrugged, like *Yep*. "In fact, she instructed me to tell you that she's very pleased with your work."

"Huh," he said, nodding, like it was taking a minute to sink in.

"She just has one more task for you. A grand finale."

"I knew there'd be a catch."

"Babette is nothing if not surprising."

"What is it?"

And then I shrugged—because I truly didn't know. I reached into my purse and pulled out an envelope she'd given me for Duncan. A sealed envelope. She'd even put a gold sticker on the back, like at the Oscars.

I handed it over.

"What's it going to say?" Duncan asked, shaking his head.

"Let's find out."

Duncan opened the envelope and looked at the card inside for a minute. Then he blinked and looked up. "She wants you to dance with me."

I felt a familiar tightness in my chest. "When? Now?"

"Right now," Duncan said. "Right here."

"I can't do that," I said.

"Neither can I."

"So don't even think about—" I started, but then I stopped. "Hold on. You can't do that?"

He shook his head.

That wasn't right. At Andrews, he had danced all the time. He danced in the lunch line, and at car pool, and while teaching. You almost couldn't stop him. "But you're a dance instructor," I said. He had dances on YouTube.

Duncan shook his head. "Not anymore."

A whole montage of Duncan doing endless goofy dances flashed through my head. Me refusing to dance? That was fine. That was reasonable. But Duncan refusing to dance? It was an outrage.

"Duncan," I said, "you can't not dance."

"Sure I can."

"No." I shook my head. "You have to do this." And as I spoke the words, something shifted in me. I became more interested in making Duncan dance than in avoiding it myself.

A world where Duncan Carpenter refused to dance just didn't make sense to me.

Babette wanted Duncan to dance? I would find a way to make that happen.

"We're doing this," I said. I held my hand out

But Duncan shook his head. "I can't," he said.

"You can," I said. Then I added, "Babette's orders."

I was still holding my hand out, but he wasn't taking it.

He shook his head. "I really can't."

All the teachers were staring at me now—at us.

I let my hand fall to my side. This was getting embarrassing.

"What's the problem?" I asked, stepping a little closer.

"I haven't danced in a long time," Duncan said.

"I haven't danced *ever*," I said, "except in my living room. But that's not stopping me." Actually, it might stop me. I wasn't sure what I was going to do if he didn't take charge.

Duncan shook his head, like *Don't do this*.

Should I do it?

I took the card out of his hand and read it. "Final task," it said. "Dance with Sam. Right now. Mrs. Kline has a song queued up for you."

I looked around. Mrs. Kline was watching us, at the ready. The room was watching us, too, trying to figure out what was going on. Duncan was watching me, wondering what I was going to do next.

What *was* I going to do next?

I hesitated.

And then I remembered something Max used to say. *Do something joyful.*

And so I just knew. We were doing this. He didn't want to, and I sure as hell didn't want to, but we were doing it anyway.

I looked over at Mrs. Kline, and I gave her a little nod.

Then I said, "Well, if it's really been a long time, I bet you miss it."

Duncan blinked.

"I can't make you dance with me," I said. "But I'm kind of hoping I can tempt you."

Duncan shook his head.

"I bet that you can't resist whatever Babette's got queued up."

Duncan shook his head. "I can resist anything. I resist things every day. I am a world-champion resister."

I raised my eyebrows, like *Touché*. "So this is a very low-risk proposition for you."

I could sense his competitive spirit rising. "It's not low risk, it's *no* risk."

"You don't know what the song is yet. Maybe it's irresistible." I didn't know, either, but he didn't know that.

"Don't worry about me."

"I won't."

"Worry about yourself."

Actually, I should have been worrying about myself. Because I'd just chosen a path that I'd have no choice but to dance my way out of.

Not good. At all.

But this was happening.

"Hey!" I shouted then to the room, before Duncan could stop me. The few teachers in the room who weren't already watching us looked over. "Principal Carpenter thinks he can resist an irresistible song!" I pointed at him exaggeratedly. "And so I dare him *not* to dance!"

The room cheered me on.

I glanced over at Duncan. Was he hating this? Or kind of liking it?

Little bit of both, maybe.

Kind of like me.

His face was stern, but his eyes had a challenge-accepted look. "Get ready for disappointment," he said.

"Get ready to dance," I said right back.

"Mrs. Kline," I said, "will you please do the honors?"

Mrs. Kline gave an efficient nod and hit play.

Just percussion at first, a kind of slinky, syncopated, almost tropical sound. The kind of rhythm that just takes hold of your hips and starts swinging them for you.

Duncan cocked his head. "Is this George Michael?"

I pointed at him. "Good ear."

Then came deep, chunky piano chords underneath. Big. Loud. Filling up the room. The sound system definitely worked.

Duncan looked around for Babette and found her watching from over by the butterflies. "You could pick any song in the world, and you picked 'Freedom! '90'?"

"Alice picked it, actually," she said, pointing at Alice, who waved. "She read an article that said it's the best dance song in the world. Mathematically."

Duncan snorted.

"According to Alice, it's neurologically irresistible."

Duncan looked back at me, like *You minx*. Then he spread his feet shoulder width and closed his eyes.

He thought he could resist *music* by closing his *eyes*?

Oh, I had this thing won.

The teachers were all watching to see what was going to happen.

It was time to make this work.

The best thing I could possibly do to get Duncan dancing was to do it myself. Dancing was contagious. But that familiar hitch at the thought—that deer-in-the-headlights compulsion to stand very still— had me paralyzed.

I needed to give myself a pep talk, I decided. A good one.

It wasn't that I couldn't dance, I reminded myself. I loved to dance. I just didn't like people to watch me.

But that's the thing about joy. You don't have to wait for it to happen. You can make it happen.

And doing this for Duncan? Getting him to have fun? Reminding him of this essential, forgotten part of himself? It would be worth it.

As Duncan stood there, stiff as a board with his hands and eyes squeezed tightly closed, I forced myself to give in to the tug of the song.

I had to trick myself into it. I bargained with myself: just do the arms. It's not really dancing until the booty gets involved.

So I lifted my arms and started moving them around to the rhythm.

Did I look ridiculous?

Oh, for sure.

But as Duncan squeezed his eyes tighter, the urge to win did battle with the urge to hide—and started to get the upper hand.

Once the arms were going, the feet wanted to follow.

All I had to do was let them.

Well, that—and force myself to ignore the part of my brain that really, desperately didn't want to look ridiculous. In fact, I had to *lean in* to looking ridiculous. Duncan had said it, himself: that's part of the joy.

So I closed my eyes, too—and tried to pretend like I was just home in my living room.

Which helped a lot.

Once I'd started, I'd done the hardest part.

Now all I had to do was keep going.

The music helped. It *was* irresistible.

This was working. I was doing it. Success gave way to more success. I shook my booty a little. Then I spun around. Then I stretched my arms out. Bravely. Defiantly. Even though Duncan couldn't see me, I knew he could feel me.

So I just did it. Anything that popped into my head, I made myself do.

The easier it got, the easier it got—and before I knew it, I'd opened my eyes.

It was an accident at first. I'd just forgotten to keep them closed. But when I saw all the faces in the room, I realized I didn't need to keep them closed. The crowd wasn't cringing, or looking on in horror—which was the usual vibe when a crowd was staring at me. They were smiling. They were rooting me on. They were shaking their own booties, too.

When the lyrics began, I sang along—even though I didn't know all the words.

I started doing a kind of Charleston, stepping forward, then back, then forward again—close enough to Duncan that he could feel my presence.

At one point, I got so close, Duncan couldn't resist opening his eyes to look.

The second he did, I crooked my finger at him, like *Come to the dance floor.*

"What are you doing?" he asked.

"I'm dancing."

"You said you never dance!"

"It's a moment of personal growth."

He squinted and shook his head, but he kept watching me.

Once he was watching, I got sillier. I put a big theatrical smile on my face, like *See, buddy? Doesn't this look fun?* I added some jazz hands. Then I shifted into the robot. Then I did some "King Tut" moves. Before I knew it, I was flapping my elbows like chicken wings.

That's when Duncan broke a little. "Oh, God. Tell me that's not the Funky Chicken."

"Well," I said, waggling my wings at him. "It's a chicken. And it's clearly funky. So I think we all know what's happening here."

"Stop flapping."

"Make me."

He frowned and recommitted to holding still.

"Resistance is futile," I said. "They did a whole study on it. The science doesn't lie. Just give in."

I shifted into a kind of salsa thing where I was also spinning an imaginary lasso above my head.

"Why be miserable?" I cajoled. "You've got all night to be miserable. Give yourself five minutes to feel good."

"This song is actually six minutes and thirty-four seconds."

I frowned at him, but I kept dancing. "That's awfully specific."

"I used to be a DJ. So. I know some things."

I did a jumping-jack kind of thing. "So this is extra torturous for you—because, as you've stated, you actually really know how to dance."

Duncan confirmed, "I actually really know how to dance."

"Which truly begs the question of why a guy who can really dance would choose not to."

Duncan flared his nostrils.

"And it doesn't make you want to dance when I do this?" I pretended to spank myself.

"Um. This is a PG event."

"Or this bad backward Moonwalk?" I slid my feet backward in the worst Moonwalk ever performed.

"Actually, the Moonwalk *goes* backward. So that's technically a bad *forward* Moonwalk you're doing right there."

I turned to the crowd, pointing at Duncan over and over in rhythm. "He used to be a dance *instructor*!" I switched into a terrible version of the Running Man. "So seeing me do this is probably almost physically painful for him."

Duncan wanted to give in.

I could feel it.

Before the song started, he hadn't even wanted to hear it, but that irresistible backbeat had shifted his mood. The hardest part was already done. Now the only thing holding him back was the idea of losing the bet.

Or, more specifically: the idea of me winning it.

So I kept going. I could feel the expression on my face: one part triumph, one part gloating, and one part just genuine joy of my own. I crouched down into a little *West Side Story* position and dance-walked toward Duncan, snapping. It was so goofy, he couldn't *not* smile.

He tucked his chin to try to hide it.

"Give it up, Duncan," I said. "You've already lost. Might as well enjoy it."

Duncan shook his head. "This song is cheating. They sampled that beat from James Brown. And they definitely took the chorus from Aretha Franklin."

"So you're not just fighting one musical titan—you're fighting three!" I spun around. "You're doomed."

Duncan flared his nostrils and pushed out a sigh like he was blowing smoke. "This is so wrong."

"How can it be wrong," I said, "when it feels so right?" And with that, I spun away and launched into the Hustle. Step, step, step, clap—out and then back. Then I threw in an Egg Beater. Then a few John Travoltas.

"Please tell me you're not doing the Hustle," Duncan said.

"I most certainly am."

"You're doing it wrong."

Spin, spin, spin, clap. "If it's so wrong, then get over here and do it right."

He shook his head.

"You realize that you are shaking your head to the beat." I pointed at his head and turned toward the group, nodding. "Is that dancing, y'all?" I demanded.

The room cheered.

Duncan froze.

I dance-walked up to get in his face. "Some people would say you've already lost."

"Nope." He squeezed his eyes closed again.

"Hey," I said, trying to get him to peek. "I'm doing the Scissors."

He peeked.

I moved my arms up and down—totally wrong.

"That's totally wrong," Duncan said.

"So you claim," I said, switching into another dance. "But who's to say? What else did you invent? The Blender? I'm going to guess that looks like this." I spun myself around.

"Incorrect!"

"What else?" I said, still dancing. "The Bring It On!" and I dance-walked toward him, motioning with my arms for a hug. "Making up dances is fun!"

Duncan shook his head. "Don't make up dances."

But I just said, "Here's one: the *Matrix*." I leaned all around like it was bullet time.

"Are you Keanu Reeves right now?"

"Or how about the *Terms of Endearment*?" I waggled my hands in a boo-hoo motion in front of my face.

"Nothing about that works."

"How about this?" I pointed at him and then started flapping my arms. "The Jonathan Livingston Seagull."

"You are the actual worst." Duncan squeezed his eyes closed. Again. But I could see that smile trying to burst through.

"He's tapping his toe!" Alice yelled with delight.

"He's nodding his head!" Carlos called out.

And then Babette stepped up with a triumphant announcement: "He is shaking his booty!"

The booty made it official: victory. I put my hands on my hips in mock shock and said, "Principal Carpenter, are you shaking your booty?"

And so, at last, four minutes into a six-minute-plus song, he sighed, shook his head like I was a plague upon humanity, and then lifted his arms to wave me closer.

I raised my arms in victory as I stepped closer, and I was just about to say, "Told you," when Duncan grabbed my hand and pulled me into a partner dance, a kind of Swing-Hustle hybrid. Before I knew it, he was pushing me out and pulling me back in like a yo-yo.

"This," Duncan said, "is how you do the Hustle."

I'm not going to lie.

It was a pretty sexy move.

The whole room cheered, and I looked around to realize that everybody was dancing now—with wildly varying levels of ability. But nobody cared. Even Mrs. Kline was clapping along. It was like a faculty production of *Soul Train* in that room.

And now Duncan was teaching me, locking his arms with a hand on my lower back. "Just forward, then back, then rock back." I watched his feet, and mirrored them, and we repeated for a few bars before he spun me out again. Next thing I knew, he was leading me around, and as soon as he realized everyone was watching us—just as George Michael was dying down—he turned to Mrs. Kline and said, "Mrs. Kline, you beautiful traitor . . . would you be willing to put on 'The Hustle'?"

Mrs. Kline nodded, and as she walked away, Alice called after her, "It's on that same playlist!"

Duncan and I turned to Alice. "You have 'The Hustle' on a playlist?"

She nodded, like *Of course*. "The One Hundred Most Mathematically Booty-Shaking Songs of All Time."

We both blinked at her for a second, and then she shrugged. "Told you," she said. "Everything is math."

And so, Duncan taught us the Hustle. His version was definitely better. We did it mostly like a line dance, but every now and then he'd pull me into his arms and dip me, which made everybody, even me, cheer.

And then later, when Duncan spotted Babette watching us from off to the side and he shimmied over to take her by the hand and pull her into the group, she let him. And when Duncan pulled her into his arms and spun her back out, I found myself falling still on the dance floor, just watching them. It was Babette's first dance with anybody since the night Max had died, and for a second, I wasn't sure how it would go.

But I'd underestimated Duncan.

Babette's face bloomed into a smile.

Later, she might go home and miss Max even more, reminded of all she'd lost. But I suspected that Babette knew better than to let a little pain hold her back. She knew that joy and sorrow walked side by side. She knew that being alive meant risking one for the other. And she also knew, as I was starting to understand in a whole new way, that it was always better to dance than to refuse.

twenty-two

That night of dancing in the cafeteria was without question the best, most delightful, most joyful night of my entire school year. And it was followed, just a few days later, by an afternoon in that exact same space that very quickly became the worst.

Because, at the final faculty meeting of the year, Kent Buckley had an announcement for us.

He arrived at the meeting twenty minutes late. Talking on that douchey Bluetooth.

Duncan showed up late, too—just behind him.

"Okay, people! Listen up!" Kent Buckley said as he strode in, alienating everyone in the room.

We watched him as he took the stage and turned on the microphone at the podium.

"Great end-of-year news," he said, as the mic gave a scream of reverb.

Kent Buckley tried again, more carefully.

"Duncan Carpenter—where are ya, buddy?"

Duncan hesitated, but then when it started to look like Kent Buckley might literally wait all day for him, he went ahead and mounted the stage.

At last, Kent Buckley went on. "My good friend Principal Carpenter and I have been hard at work on a super-secret project all year that it's my pleasure to reveal to you today. We've got all the pieces in place to start moving forward at the start of summer. It's been a difficult year for the school, but, as you know, I never see difficulties. I only see opportunities."

By this point, we were all looking around at each other, like *What?*

Duncan had been working on a super-secret project with Kent Buckley?

Kent Buckley flipped the switch on the projector screen, and it slid down behind him. I present to you . . . *Kempner School 2.0!"*

Up popped an image of a sleek, black, glass-and-chrome building.

Everybody stared at it.

Everybody, that is, except Duncan, who stared only at the ground.

When Kent Buckley didn't get the response he wanted, he launched into salesman mode. "Meet your new school! Gone is the sad old building with the peeling paint and rusty windows. Gone are the sagging steps and drooping shutters and missing roof shingles and cracking walls. We're upgrading! Welcome to the newest, fanciest, most state-of-the-art educational facility in America. We're going to make history with this building, folks. Remote video surveillance, automatic locking doors and panic buttons, bulletproof doors and windows. Hi-tech everything."

At this point, people were starting to look around. What the hell was Kent Buckley talking about?

"This is . . . what?" Alice asked.

"The new school building," Kent Buckley said, like *Try to keep up!*

"Whose new school building?" Carlos asked.

"Kempner's," Kent Buckley said, already impatient.

This couldn't be real—but it couldn't be a joke, either. Kent Buckley didn't know how to joke.

Plus, one look at Duncan's stricken face made it clear: this was real.

"We're remodeling the school?" Mrs. Kline asked.

"No," Kent Buckley said. "We're building a new one."

Murmurs all around—and not happy ones—as people tried to figure out what the hell was going on. Kent Buckley, never the most perceptive guy, went on talking like we were all gearing up to throw him a parade.

"Genius, right? I've gotta give a lot of credit to this guy"—he gestured at Duncan with his thumbs—"because when I was grilling him last fall on upping our security game, he did a pretty thorough assessment and finally came back and said, 'You'd be better off building a brand-new school.' So I said, 'Hold my beer,' and the next thing we knew, we had a potential buyer for this broken-down old place and a very promising pad site in an office park down on West Beach."

When Kent Buckley stopped talking, it was dead quiet.

"You want to sell this place," Carlos said then, "and build . . . the Death Star?"

Kent Buckley laughed and said, "You know, it's funny—that's exactly what we've been calling it."

"It doesn't have any windows," Emily called out. "Just little slits."

"It doesn't have any plants," Anton said.

"It's in an industrial park," Carlos said.

"Very observant," Kent Buckley said, flashing a thumbs-up. "That's all for visibility."

"There's no outdoor space," Coach Gordo said.

"True," Kent Buckley said. "Not a problem if you've got a wimpy kid like I do. But I'm working on arranging off-site sports facilities we can bus the jocks to after school."

My head was swimming. What was happening?

"You've already had plans drawn up?" Lena asked.

"Not yet," Kent Buckley said. "This image is from the website of the company we'll hire. They used to be a defense contractor, but now they build schools. And great news: I'm an investor, so I can get them for cheap."

"Has this—been approved by the board?" Carlos asked.

But Kent Buckley shook his head. "The board is excited. I've got all the board approval I need. We will be a go."

That's when I stood up.

Just . . . stood.

Kent Buckley turned in my direction. "Librarian," he said, pointing at me. "Question."

But my question was not for Kent Buckley. I turned and scanned for Babette.

She was at the back of the room.

"Babette," I said. "Can you do me a favor and shut this guy up?"

There were gasps around the room.

Babette met my eyes, but she didn't move.

I took a few steps closer. "I mean, don't you feel like we've all had to put up with enough bullshit this year?" I looked around at the room. "Is there anybody in this room who wants to hear this dude waste any more of our time? I mean, there's no way we're doing this. We're not selling our beautiful, historic building so that we can move to a sensory deprivation chamber." I looked around. "None of this is happening. Why let him keep talking?"

Mrs. Kline was staring at me like I'd lost my mind—and was about to lose my job, too.

I came to a stop next to Babette. "It's time to shut this down, don't you think?"

But Babette looked at me through her glasses and then—just barely—shook her head.

But I didn't understand. I leaned in closer. "What are you waiting for?" I whispered. "Fire him."

But Babette just gave that same, imperceptible head shake again—and then, from her expression, I knew.

I took her hand, squatted down next to her, and very softly I said, "You can't really fire him, can you?"

Her eyes had tears in them now. Just barely, she shook her head.

"But you told me you could because . . . ?"

"Because I knew Duncan would only believe it if you believed it. And you are a terrible liar."

I nodded. I kissed her on the cheek. I gave her a little hug. And then I turned around, and I marched right out of the room.

I didn't even know where I was going. I charged my way through the courtyard, and shoved the school gates open. I didn't even have my purse with me. I was so angry, it was like rocket fuel. I needed to move or it would burn me up.

I hadn't even finished listening to Kent Buckley's plan. I didn't even know if there was a way to fight it. I didn't know if this was a done deal or a foregone conclusion or what.

But that wasn't the point.

The point was Duncan.

The point was he'd been in some kind of cahoots with Kent Buckley this whole time. He'd been hanging out with me—acting like a friend— when all the time he'd been working with the enemy. He'd been helping Kent Buckley *sell the school*? Of all the worst-case scenarios I'd pictured, this wasn't even in the running. I'd thought we'd cured him. I thought we'd solved it. I thought the threat was over.

Apparently not.

I was two blocks from the seawall when I heard running feet behind me.

"Sam! Wait!" It was Duncan.

I did not wait.

The sun had gone down. It was dark. I kept moving.

"Sam!"

I knew Duncan's legs were longer than mine, and I knew he'd eventually catch up with me, but I sure as shit wasn't going to make it easy for him.

I didn't even know where I was going. I was just . . . going.

When Duncan finally caught up with me, I wouldn't slow, and I wouldn't look at him, and I wouldn't wipe the tears off my face. What I would do was yell: "Are you kidding me right now? You've been in cahoots with Kent Buckley this whole time? You've been eating Babette's food, and hanging out with me, and bonding with the teachers—letting us all like you, and root for you, and help you—and you've been some kind of enemy spy all along—for *Kent Buckley*? Of all the douchebags in the history of douchebags—*that guy*? Really?"

These weren't even questions that needed answers. I was just talking. Just making noise. Just attaching words to the primal yelling.

But Duncan tried to respond. "No! No. I didn't even know about this until today."

I kept charging forward, not looking at him.

"Okay—technically, I knew last fall. I knew when I started that Kent Buckley wanted to turn the place into a fortress. And at the time I was all for it, honestly. When I first got here, I totally agreed with him about the Death Star. I couldn't believe you guys were teaching kids in that crumbling old building with nothing but Raymond for security. It offended me, honestly. It made me angry that you would be so willfully ignorant of the world we're living in right now."

When we hit the seawall, I didn't even break stride, just turned and kept going, crossing my arms against the sea breeze. But my pace was slowing some. At first, I'd only wanted to yell, but now, I couldn't help but listen, too.

"So yes," Duncan went on, "I helped him. That's what he told me the job was—that's what he said the school wanted—a total security revamp. That's why I walked in with that water gun last fall. Kent Buckley had told me this group was super pro-guns."

"One look at us should have cleared that right up."

"Yeah. But this is Texas."

"Literally nobody wanted any guns anywhere except Kent Buckley."

"But I didn't know that. And it was only as I spent more time with him that I started to realize that he was . . . kind of . . . off."

"Duh," I said, still charging on.

"That—and once he got the idea for the new building—the way he obsessed over it, it felt kind of personal."

"Max did not like Kent Buckley."

"I got that impression. And then once he got this idea for the new school, he realized that he could make money off of it."

"Why?"

"Because he's a part owner in the company that builds those Death Stars. Plus, he owns the pad site on West Beach. So if the school buys it, they buy it from him."

"He told you that?"

"He did. Winter break. He called me and told me to put all that on hold—that we might be selling this building, and he wanted to save that money for the new school."

My pace slowed now, as I thought about it. "So . . . you didn't stop painting everything gray because of Babette?"

Duncan shook his head.

"So were you just—playing along?"

"At first. Yeah."

"And when Babette told you to get into therapy?"

"I'd been planning to do that anyway, so Babette just made it easier. My sister was overjoyed."

"And . . . me? All the stuff we did together? What was that about?"

A pause. "I knew Babette was bluffing."

"How?"

"I'd read everything. I'd read my contract. I'd read the bylaws and guidelines and rules for the board. Babette wasn't anywhere—not in the paperwork, anyway."

"That can't be right. Max wouldn't just leave Babette out."

"Maybe he didn't think about it. Maybe he thought he'd live forever. Maybe he wasn't a paperwork guy."

"He definitely wasn't a paperwork guy."

"Maybe he was too busy dreaming up playgrounds to get into the nitty-gritty of the power structure of the board."

That sounded about right. That sounded like Max.

"But Kent Buckley?" Duncan went on. "He is all about the power structure of the board. And after Max died, during all the shock and chaos, he was working to bring his friends on to the board, he was re-writing bylaws and pushing them through when nobody was focusing—and pretty soon, he'd executed a good old-fashioned power grab."

"Did you know about it?"

"Some. He'd take me out sometimes, back at the beginning, and drink quite a bit and tell me too much."

"So you knew what he was up to."

"Yes, but in his version of reality, he's the hero and everybody loves him. So it took me a little time to get that sorted out."

I kept walking.

"At first," Duncan said, "I was just doing the daily tasks to *not* call Babette's bluff. I didn't want her to know I was onto her. But then the weirdest thing happened . . ."

I waited, but he didn't go on. Finally, I said, "What? What happened?"

Duncan took a breath. "I started to like them."

For the first time, I looked over.

"I mean, I started to really like them. I started looking forward to them, wondering what was coming up next. I looked forward to the moment in the morning when you would swing by my office and give me some nutty assignment, like 'eat a bowl of udon noodles,' and I looked forward to actually doing it. Most of all, I just looked forward to you."

I sighed. "I looked forward to you, too."

"And the more time I spent with you, the more I started seeing the world through different eyes."

"We were trying to wake you up. We called it Operation Duncan."

"Well, it worked."

"Not well enough."

I thought of our school building. Its butterfly garden, its court-yard, and its cloisters, and the way it felt like another place and time. I thought of my library and its book staircase and our sunny cafeteria and our butterfly mural.

Then I said, "Is there anything you can do to stop him?"

Duncan didn't answer right away. I looked over and saw a funny expression on his face.

"Oh, my God," I said. "You don't want to stop him."

"I didn't say—"

I started walking faster. "Oh, my God, here I was thinking we were friends."

"We are friends."

"You can't be friends with a person who wants to put you in prison."

"Come on. It's not prison!"

We'd just come to a fishing pier that jutted out over the Gulf. I turned and started marching out along it, over the water. "It's pretty damn close," I said. "You can't live your whole life in fear. You can't insulate yourself from everything. Kids get hurt all the time—but we don't make them wear bicycle helmets everywhere. You take reasonable precautions, and then you hope for the best. That's all you can do."

"This is bigger than a bump on the head," Duncan said.

But I didn't break stride. "And even if you make us all move to that tragic Death Star building—if you really make the kids give up natural light, nature, play, color, and joy, and hope to lock them away all day in some hermetically sealed, unearthly environment all their lives—even still . . . they could still step outside and get shot. They could go to the movies and get shot. They could go to the beach and get shot. They could go to a concert and get shot."

"But it wouldn't—" He stopped himself.

"It wouldn't what?" I stopped walking to meet his eyes. We were out over the water now, waves beneath us. "It wouldn't be on your watch?"

Duncan looked away.

"That's all about you, friend. That is not about them."

"It's not just about me!" Duncan said, his voice loud. "It's about you. It's about all of you. It was hard for me to see you in danger when I first got here—but it's even harder for me now! Because now

I know you—and the kids, and the teachers—and now I've spent time with you, and now I care about you! Before, it was theoretical. Now it's real."

He had just told me that he cared about us—about me—but I couldn't even hear it. "We are not in danger!" I shouted. "No more than anybody else is any other minute of the day. Life is full of danger. Terrible things happen all the time. That doesn't mean you live your life in fear."

Looking back, I want to grab that version of myself by the collar and yell at her to shut up. Who was she to lecture Duncan? Who was she to talk about fear? Who was she to dole out life advice?

Something shifted in Duncan's eyes then. He stood up a little straighter, too. Then he said, "Ask me why I didn't want to dance with you."

"What?"

"The other night. At the party. I didn't want to dance. I said I don't do it anymore. Ask me why not."

I hesitated, and I felt my righteous irritation drain away. I suddenly knew he was going to have a hell of an answer to this question. When I did it, my voice was much quieter. "Okay, Duncan," I said. "Why don't you dance anymore?"

He nodded, like *Right. Here we go.* "Because when I got shot, we were right in the middle of having a dance party in class."

I put my hand over my mouth.

He took a deep breath to continue. Then, without letting himself pause, he told me. "We'd been reviewing for finals all week. It was Friday, which was always Hat Day—so the kids were all wearing top hats, and cowboy hats, and hats that looked like sharks, and traffic cones, and roasted chickens. We were burned out and just needed to laugh like crazy and jump around.

"We heard the gunshots down the hall over the music—so much louder than the music—and silliness shifted to soul-blazing terror in one second. I mean, that sound is unmistakable. Even if you've never heard it in real life—even if you've only seen it in movies. We all knew in an instant what was happening.

"My classroom was a square—there was no place to hide. I even had a window in my classroom door, but I locked it anyway and got my kids down behind my desk, and then I shoved the bookshelf in front of it. Some of the boys jumped in to help, and I'm telling you, it was like a war zone—we could hear the shots and the screaming—and you think you've heard screaming before, but you have never heard anything like that. It ripped my soul in half. I will never forget that sound until the day I die.

"Anyway, I was still piling things—a computer cart, a bunch of student desks—in front of the kids, when a kid named Jackson appeared at my door window, and he started trying to get in. He was rattling the handle and beating on the door and shouting, 'He's coming! He's coming!' And that's when a girl who'd been behind the barricade—her last name was Stevenson, so we all called her Stevie—she darted out toward the door, unlocked it, let the kid in, and shoved it closed again. She got it locked in time, and the kid made a break for the barricade, but before Stevie had a chance to get away from the door, the shooter just . . . got her. Just shot right through the door itself like it wasn't even there. Just riddled her with bullets, and the force of the impact actually jerked her backward, and when she hit the floor, she just . . . turned red—like she'd sprung a hundred leaks."

Duncan was shaking now—his voice, his hands, his breath.

He shook his head. "Stevie, you know? *Stevie*. She made origami butterflies all the time and gave them to people—out of gum wrappers and notebook paper decorated with highlighters. She was wearing a crown for Hat Day, and she'd forgotten to take it off—but it flew off on impact and dragged a streak of blood across the floor. I started to go to her, but that's when he shot out the window, and that's when he got me. I was halfway to her when I felt it like burning acid all up and down my side. And then I just collapsed—facedown on the classroom tiles. Watching my own blood seep out and pool around me, the sound of my own breath swallowing me up. And that's the last thing I remember before everything went black."

Oh, God.

"Did Stevie make it?" I finally whispered.

He shook his head.

"What about—" I started, but my voice caught. "What about the kid she saved?"

"He got hit, too, as he dove for the barricade. But he made it."

"That's good," I said—though "good" felt like the wrong word in reference to anything about this.

"He made it . . . but I don't know if he'll make it in the end."

I shook my head. "What do you mean?"

"He's tried to kill himself twice since it happened."

I put my hand over my mouth.

"They were eighth-graders," Duncan said then. "They were kids. But Stevie . . . was his girlfriend." He squeezed his eyes tight, then rubbed them. "First girlfriend. First love. They were always passing notes. Half the teachers thought they'd wind up getting married."

I didn't know what to say. I reached out and took Duncan's hands.

"You said one time that you miss the guy I used to be. But I'm not that guy anymore. I can't be him. I can't know what I know now and be who I was then. I can't go back. Sometimes I really hate that guy— how naïve he was. How happy he was. How he was filling kiddie pools with Jell-O when he should have been working harder to look after the world." He took a deep breath. "I'll never be that guy again, and if you're waiting for it, you're going to be disappointed."

All I could do was nod.

Duncan fell quiet for a second. Then he said, "You keep telling me not to live my life in fear. But I need you to understand that you don't know what fear is."

And do you know what? He was right.

I'm not even sure I can identify all the emotions that submerged me right then. I felt sorry, and wrong, and embarrassed and cowed for having been so judgmental. I felt angry at myself, and angry at the world— and angry at Duncan, too.

It was more feelings at once—all at maximum intensity—than I knew how to handle. And I have no way of explaining, or justifying, or even understanding what I did next—other than just to confess that in the moment after I'd realized how stupid I'd been, how I hadn't even understood him all along or what he'd been through, I felt this over-whelming, truly suffocating feeling like I just needed to *do something*.

But I had no idea at all what to do. There was nothing to do. So, in a millisecond decision that I've never been able to explain or understand or take back—I just turned, right there on the pier, and took off run-ning.

Not back toward the seawall, though. Away from it.

I knew this pier. I knew that there was a break at the far end with a ladder down to the water. I knew there were Polar Bear Clubs that jumped off the end every New Year's, and Mermaid Clubs that dove off it wearing sparkly costume tails. Like all bad decisions, it didn't seem too bad at the time. Who was I to tell Duncan to be brave? Who was I to judge anybody at all? I wasn't a risk-taker! I was a librarian. The scari-est thing I'd done in years was the Hustle. But I could change that. I could change that right now.

This might be the worst decision I'd ever made, but it was my decision. I ran faster.

I heard Duncan behind me. "Sam! Sam! Hey! What are you doing?"

It's possible that if he hadn't taken off after me, I might have stopped at the edge. There's a very good chance I would have come to my senses and rightly chickened out.

But he did take off after me.

I heard his feet behind me on the boardwalk. I felt him gaining on me. And it sparked that feeling I remember from childhood games—what must be an ancient human instinct—of realizing you're being chased . . . and running faster. You know that feeling. It's like a prickly feeling on the back of your neck. You can't let them catch you. Some deep part of your lizard brain wipes out every thought except: *don't get caught*.

I didn't even think the words. I just felt them.

I am not a risk-taker or a thrill-seeker. I am the opposite of those things. That moment on the Iron Shark was enough fear to last me forever. I blame the adrenaline. I blame my frustration with Duncan. I blame the fact that every single thing I'd tried to do lately had failed.

I just ran.

And when Duncan chased me, I ran faster.

And when I got to the end of the pier, I ran right through the opening in the railing, launched myself off the end, and plunged down toward the water.

twenty-three

I regretted it instantly.

The very second that I passed the railing, the second there was no turning back, I wanted nothing more in my whole life than to turn back.

My life that might not last very long.

The fall took forever and gave me plenty of time to review my idiocy. There could be pilings down there, or jetty rocks, or a shipwrecked boat. There could be an oil slick, or a whole school of jellyfish, or even a patch of flesh-eating bacteria. Anything was possible.

No matter what, this was the dumbest thing I'd ever done.

My arms spun involuntarily, by the way, as if they might find something to grab on to in the empty air. And my legs kept pumping, as well, as if their efforts might inspire some solid ground to appear underneath them.

And I'll tell you something: I knew a sudden truth in those dead-silent seconds before I met whatever gory death awaited me below.

I definitely didn't want to die.

I'd known it in a casual way before. But now I knew it in a hundred new ways.

So there it was. You can't know what you don't know.

Mid-plunge into whatever blackness awaited me below, I felt many of the things you'd expect a person to feel in that situation. But I felt one thing that really surprised me: empathy for Duncan. I'd been so judgy with him. I'd rolled my eyes at his suits and his color schemes and his rules. But would I give every single one of those moments back for one chance to find myself standing safely back up on the pier with him?

Hell, yes.

This was what it felt like to be truly scared. This was what it felt like to feel like you might really, truly die.

Duncan knew that feeling, and he remembered it, and he carried it around with him every day.

I regretted it all—everything about this foolish, insensitive, self-satisfied moment—with utter vehemence.

And then I hit the water.

Or more like *it* hit *me*.

I'd tilted a bit on the way down—and so I smacked the surface pretty hard on my side. It felt like a weird combination of plunging into water and getting smacked by a wooden board.

I could have anticipated that, if I'd thought to anticipate anything.

I hit the surface, then plunged below it, then continued downward and downward, knowing, very clearly, in my wide-awake brain, that I needed to stop that downward momentum and start kicking my legs and pumping my arms to fight my way back up to the surface.

But I couldn't.

I couldn't move.

It made no sense. I knew I had to kick. I knew I had to swim up toward the surface, where all that air was waiting for me. But for longer than I could possibly believe, I let myself sink farther and farther down into the black ocean.

How long can you go without breathing? A minute? Five? I had no idea. I was still frozen, still sinking, when my lungs started screaming for me to breathe.

Underwater.

And it was the desperate act of stopping them—of ordering my diaphragm to *stop*—that put me back in motion. *Your lungs are balloons,* I remember thinking. *And balloons float.*

It was a wildly unscientific notion. But it turned out to be exactly the encouragement I needed. My beautiful, air-filled lungs were going to float me back up to the surface. All my arms and legs had to do was help.

I kicked and pulled and fought my way toward the surface while my diaphragm cramped and stung. Everything stung, actually—like the oxygen deprivation was individually hurting every cell in my body.

I had no idea how far it was up to the surface. It wasn't like I could see a finish line. It could be five feet up or half a mile. I had no clue, and I was just starting to think it was hopeless, that I was too deep to ever get there, that I was going to drown before I reached the surface, when I broke through.

Hitting the air was just as surprising to me as hitting the water had been.

But this time my body knew what to do. The second I touched air, my lungs drank it in, panting and coughing in desperate heaves.

Before I had my bearings, I heard Duncan's voice somewhere nearby at the surface of the water. "I've got you," he said.

I felt his arm wrap around my rib cage.

Duncan said, "Lie back. Be still. Keep breathing."

He leaned us both back so we were floating faceup. Then he started kicking us back toward the beach.

All I could do was stare up at the stars and breathe like crazy until he got us back to the shore.

I had salt water in my eyes—in my mouth—stinging the back of my nose.

In the shallows, he left me kneeling, breathing hard, in part just because I could, knees digging into the wet sand and waves rolling over my thighs, as he rose from the water and paced away. As my breathing returned to normal, I looked up and watched him.

It's hard to describe what I saw, but let's just say that the version of

Duncan that had found me in the water and kicked us back to shore had been patient and calm. Almost peaceful, in a way.

But the version of Duncan now pacing the shore as the waves crashed against his calves?

That guy was pissed.

"Are you bleeding?" he shouted at me from ten feet away.

It sounded more like an insult than a question, but I answered it, anyway. "No."

"Are you hurt in any way?"

There were a lot of ways to answer that question, but I went with, "No."

Then, as a kind of grand finale of his questioning: "Are you *fucking kidding me?*"

At that, I stood up. My legs were shaking—and so was pretty much everything else—but I did it, anyway. We faced each other in the surf. Duncan was hunched over, like he was clenching every abdominal muscle. His hands looked clenched, and so did his arms and shoulders for that matter. He wasn't looking directly at me, just near me, as if he were so mad, he couldn't even see.

"*What*"—he demanded, his voice tight with rage—"*in the hell were you thinking?*"

It didn't sound like a question that wanted an answer.

"What the hell"—he said again, this time louder—"could you *possibly* have been thinking?"

"Not my best decision," I said.

But Duncan was now telling himself the story of what had just happened, every word incredulous, as if every single moment of what I'd just done had been impossible. "You took off running down the pier—and then you *flung yourself off the end of it.*"

"I regret that last part," I said.

He wasn't listening. "Was it idiocy? Was it a suicide attempt? Are you on some kind of drugs I don't know about?"

These were all rhetorical questions.

"I can't even believe what just happened. I can't even believe you just did that. Is this a nightmare? Am I trapped in a nightmare right now? That was, hands down—with only one horrific exception—the stupidest thing I've ever seen anybody do."

I didn't argue.

"You could have died. You should have died! Do you have any idea how many pilings are down in that water? How much debris floats up under those piers? Logs and construction boards and crap from offshore rigs? There could have been barbed wire! There could have been fencing! People *perish* jumping off this pier!"

"People jump off this pier all the time!"

"*Crazy* people! And even if you weren't killed on impact, do you have any idea how close we are to the port? There are riptides all along here!"

I raised my hand a little. "I wasn't thinking about riptides—okay? I wasn't thinking at all."

"You sure as hell weren't!" he shouted. "You could have been swept out to sea in minutes—at night—so far I would never have been able to find you!"

I'll grant that he was pretty much right about most of this stuff—and maybe this is just a quirk of my personality—but I can only get yelled at for so long, even by someone who's right, before I start yelling back.

"I wasn't thinking, okay?" I yelled back. "I was trying to be brave. I was trying to help!"

I sloshed my way closer to him in the water. Now he was watching me—the first time I'd seen his eyes since we made it to shore.

"Don't help!" he shouted. "I don't want you to help!"

But I charged after him. "Somebody has to!"

I'd forgotten how good it could feel to really yell. How satisfying it could feel to let yourself burn clean with anger like a flame. Duncan turned away, but I came after him and edged around to get up in his face. "You're living some kind of half life, and you're dragging a whole school full of terrified kids with you. You said I didn't know what fear was, and I thought maybe you were right—but I'll tell you something!

I almost killed myself just then—but I still think I was right all along. You need to wake up and live."

He was breathing hard. "Every morning, I get up and go to school. I shower and put vitamin E on my scars and shave and get dressed and shine my damn shoes and I walk into that place and spend all day every day watching out for those kids and keeping them safe and not curling up in the fetal position on the floor of the men's room. I keep it together! I meet all my responsibilities! How the hell is that not enough?"

He turned away—like that was some kind of argument-winning rhetorical question.

But it wasn't rhetorical. I ran after him. "Because it isn't!" *Great point.* "I want you to be alive. I want you to feel something!"

"I feel something!" he shouted. "I feel everything!"

But then, it was like in the wake of that declaration, he could suddenly see clearly. It was like, for the first time since we hit the water, he really saw me there, just feet away from him, drenched and shivering and defiant in the water, my hair in wet strings against my neck.

I was still staring at him with burning, self-righteous eyes.

But whatever he saw in that moment seemed to break his anger. He sighed—almost deflated—and his posture shifted, and then he started sloshing back toward me through the waves. "I feel things," he said, his voice hoarse and quieter now, a little breathless from all the shouting, his gaze unwavering on mine.

He kept pushing toward me. His pace didn't slow—just step after step through the water in his sopping wet clothes like he might not stop at all.

I stood my ground.

The anticipation of it was as physical as if it were a gust of wind—impossibly fast but in slow motion at the exact same time, and I held absolutely still—my gaze fastened to his, my whole body alert and humming, seeing him clearly now, too, for what felt like the first time.

He felt things.

He'd just shouted that at me, but I could feel it now.

He was angry, and aching, and lost, and lonely. Exactly like the rest of us.

Also, he was totally ripped, with his drenched white oxford grasping and clinging to his torso.

So there was that.

I've never felt such intense anticipation—wanting him to hurry up and get to me, hoping like hell I was reading him right, longing to be closer to him so badly. Feeling like I finally understood him at last.

Duncan made it to where I was, and then he stopped short.

We stared at each other, wet and breathless, until I could only think of one thing left to do.

I took the final steps that separated us, and I reached up, clasped both my hands behind his neck, and then brought his mouth to mine. In that same smooth motion, as our bodies collided, he clamped his arms around my waist and pulled me close.

I could write a book about that one moment in my life: the pressure and drag of my wet clothes against my skin. The breathlessness of exertion and surprise. The tug of the waves at my calves. The feel of his chest against mine—cold with salt water and warm with body heat at the same time. The sense of safety I felt inside his arms. The ravenousness of his hands as he ran them all up and down, almost like they would never find a way to touch me that would be enough.

The relief of being connected at last.

The only sounds were the rush of waves and breath and air. Just motion and touch and closeness.

We kissed each other in the water for a long time.

Though I'm not sure "kissed" is the right word.

"Devoured" might work better.

Or "consumed."

Or we might need to invent a new word.

I reached up, pressed myself closer, and kissed him harder. Whatever he was starving for, I wanted him to have. Because I was starving, too.

I brushed my tongue against his. I traced my fingers into the velvet of the back of his hair. I breathed him in. I pressed as close to him as I could get. I could feel his heart beating through his rib cage, and I wondered if he could feel mine, too.

I was cold, but I didn't care. I was sticky with seawater, but it was fine. Somebody wolf-whistled us from up on the seawall, but we ignored it.

Whatever he was doing, I did it right back. I clutched him just as tightly as he was clutching me. We were cold, and still dripping wet, but his mouth was warm, and his chest and the tightness of the way he was holding me seemed to steady my trembling. He was like the only solid thing in the world. I wanted to melt into him.

I wanted to never, ever stop.

And just as I had that feeling, he stopped—and pulled back.

"The first time I saw you, I knew you were going to be trouble for me."

"You did?"

"Yeah. I saw you banging on that broken locker, and I thought, 'Oh, shit. That girl is going to ruin my life.'"

I pulled him closer. "The first words you thought when you saw me were, 'Oh, shit'?"

"Pretty much."

"What do you think when you see me now?"

"The exact same thing."

I gave him a little smile.

"Don't ever fucking do that again, okay?" he said.

"I won't. I swear."

"You scared the hell out of me."

"I'm sorry."

"I feel things, okay? You have to believe me."

"Okay."

"I feel everything."

"I believe you."

And I had one last thought before he kissed me again. The world keeps hanging on to this idea that love is for the gullible. But nothing could be more wrong. Love is only for the brave.

After that, we kissed our way back to my place.

I'm not even entirely sure how we got back. But there was kissing involved.

Kissing as we walked.

Kissing at crosswalks as we waited for the light to turn.

Kissing pressed up against the sides of buildings before remembering to keep going.

Kissing back in my apartment, after we worked the lock open with the key, still kissing, and stumbled in. Kissing as we fell back onto my bed and tried to peel off each other's sticky, salty, seawatery clothes.

Good kissing. Life-changing kissing. Kissing so intense, my whole body tingled.

Kissing so intense, I saw flashes of light.

Kissing so intense, I could smell honeysuckle and roses.

And that's when I realized: It wasn't just the kissing.

I was having an aura.

twenty-four

Yep. I was about to have a seizure.

For a minute, I wondered if maybe I'd just swallowed too much seawater earlier when I'd almost drowned. But that wasn't it. You get pretty good at knowing.

Perfect timing.

But not all that surprising. It's not usually in the middle of the stress that the seizures come. It's usually right after. Just when you start to relax.

I pushed back from Duncan.

"You okay?"

I nodded, but then I shook my head. "I think I might be about to have a seizure."

He frowned. "Oh."

"And I'd rather not do that with you here. Like, I'd really, really rather not."

"You need me to go?"

"Yeah," I said.

"I'd actually kind of like to stay."

I shook my head. "Can't happen."

"I'd really like to be here for you," Duncan said.

"That's a nope."

"Why not?"

I didn't know what to say. "It's . . . private."

"Having a seizure is private?"

"Yeah."

"If you don't control when they happen, how can it be private?"

"It's private *if at all possible*."

Duncan frowned.

"I'm just going to lie down after you go," I said. "Stay in bed. No big deal."

It was clear that he thought it was a big deal. "I feel like you shouldn't be alone."

"I'm always alone," I said, before I realized how sad that sounded.

I didn't know how to explain why I was kicking him out. "The thing is," I said, taking a breath, "it's not pretty when these seizures happen. It's me at my absolute worst. And I just can't bear the idea of you seeing that."

Duncan nodded.

Then he did something I was not expecting. He lifted up his shirt to show me the scars on his side—pink and purple and mottled as ever, and so much more heartbreaking now that I knew how they'd happened. "You saw these before, right?" he asked.

I nodded.

"This is *me* at my absolute worst. And I wish you'd never seen it. But you did. On a night when you looked after me. And Chuck Norris. And apparently rescued my dying succulents."

I gave a little smile.

"You were there for me, is what I'm saying. I want to be there for you."

"That's sweet, but no."

I needed to get him out of there.

"You think I can't handle it?" he asked.

Well, yeah. Kinda. "You shouldn't have to."

"What if I want to?"

"Nobody wants to."

"I would have told you nobody could see my scars without fleeing the country, but here you are."

"It's not the same."

"Why not?"

I tried to think. "You got shot by someone else. It wasn't your fault. But my seizures—they're *me*. I'm not doing them on purpose, but I *am* doing them. My own malfunctioning neurology. I'm the problem. That's different. Plus, they're never over. They don't fade away."

"What do you think that means?"

What did it *mean*? It meant that I couldn't promise him that it wouldn't get worse—or start happening all the time. It meant my life wasn't in my control. It meant that we didn't have a future together. It meant that if he ever saw me like that, he'd be disgusted.

And maybe that was the first time I'd put that into words.

He was waiting for an answer. So I sat up and edged to the side of the bed. The I turned to him and said, "You know all those after-school specials where kids mistakenly think their parents split up because of them—but then they learn the healing lesson that it had nothing to do with them after all?"

"Okay," Duncan said, not sure where I was heading.

"I was the reason my parents broke up when I was eight. My dad left because of me. I overheard him actually saying it that night. Then, when I was ten, my mom died. And he wouldn't take me. I went to live with my aunt instead. When I graduated high school, she gave me a trunk of my mom's old things, including some diaries, and they confirmed everything I already knew—in intricate detail. He hated my seizures. He was humiliated by them. I drove him away. I was the reason my mom's life fell apart. Why she had to work two jobs. Why she died alone. And that's not a false conclusion. That's the straight truth."

Duncan nodded, but just barely. Then he said, "You think your dad left because you were too much. But what if your dad was *too little*?"

"What do you mean?"

"I mean . . . a better man would never have left you. A better man would have stayed."

I tilted my head. "Maybe you've just never seen one of my seizures."

Duncan sighed.

Sitting up had helped a little. I felt slightly better. Encouraging. "And it wasn't just him, by the way," I added then. "I wasn't just teased at school, I was a *pariah*. I was the butt of every single joke. Utterly cast out of grammar-school society."

Duncan shook his head.

I went on. "Do we need to talk about the time I woke up to find the kids throwing the spilled peas from my lunch tray at me? Do we have to talk about the bag of spare clothes the school nurse kept in the supply closet for the inevitable moments when I would need to change my pants? Do we have to cover all the years when I ate lunch by myself, sitting across from Richard Leffitz as he ate his own boogers?"

"Fair enough," Duncan said. "But those were kids. And—all due respect—kids are assholes."

"Spoken like a guy on the verge of summer break," I said.

But it was true: after elementary school, I'd blamed it all on the epilepsy and never looked back. Which was fine. Until the epilepsy returned. And then it turned out I had a whole truckload of unquestioned assumptions about my worth as a human being.

Assumptions that, perhaps, I had not examined too hard.

And would not be examining tonight.

Being around Duncan . . . there was no question it was glorious, and powerful, and hypnotic. The kissing-in-the-waves portion of the evening left me in no doubt of that. There was no doubt that he was a good thing. Too good.

Because: *what if?*

What if I had a seizure, and he was horrified? Disgusted? Creeped out?

He felt things. He'd said so. He'd kissed me like he meant it—again and again.

But what if I had a seizure—and that killed it for him?

I'd never once dated a person who had seen me go through something like that. Besides my mom, and later my aunt, and a few health-care professionals, everybody who had ever witnessed me have a seizure had decided irrevocably to avoid me.

I'm mostly talking about grade-schoolers here, but the point still stands. How could Duncan be any different?

But Duncan was still focused. "I wish you'd give me a chance to prove you wrong."

"But what if you don't prove me wrong? What if you just confirm my worst fears—again?"

"That's not going to happen."

"You don't know that."

"But didn't you just yell at me in the ocean and tell me not to live my life in fear? Didn't you just literally hurl yourself into a black ocean?"

"That's different."

"How?"

The aura was intensifying. The nausea was coming back stronger. "Because," I said, standing up to move him toward the door, "this is scarier than that."

"It doesn't have to be."

I shook my head. "I can't be brave about this."

"Yes, you can."

The nausea was intensifying. I was running out of time. I stood up and led him toward the door. "Anything in the world—except this."

"Sam—"

"You need to go now," I said.

"Let me stay," he said. "You don't have to be alone."

Would I have liked to let him stay?

Would I have liked him to take care of me?

Of course.

But I'd rather be alone forever than let him see me that way. I could bear loneliness. I could bear disappointment. But the one thing I absolutely could not bear was Duncan changing his mind.

I hated that he was arguing with me. I hated that he was still here.
I hated that he was right.

I pushed him toward the door with a rising feeling like I didn't have much time.

He had to leave. He had to go.

But then, before he could—the world disappeared.

twenty-five

I woke up alone, hours later, in my bed, in the dark.

I checked the clock on the nightstand. Two in the morning.

What had happened?

I knew I'd had a seizure—but only by deduction. Not from memory. Seizures always involve amnesia. Your brain can't exactly make new memories when it's short-circuiting.

I was pretty sure I hadn't gotten him out in time. I was pretty sure he'd been there. And I was pretty sure right now I was completely alone.

I sat up. Listened for sounds of life in my apartment. If Duncan were still here, but not asleep, what would he be doing? Insomniac activities, I guessed. Making tea? Reading a magazine? Or maybe he'd taken himself out to sleep in the living room.

But there was no rattle of a kettle boiling, no swish of magazine pages turning. No rhythmic snoozing of a passed-out man on my sofa.

It was so quiet the silence was practically ringing.

"Duncan?" I called, just in case. "Hey, Duncan?"

Nothing.

I flipped on the bedroom light, then followed it out to the living room. No one. Empty.

I'd been so sure he would leave—but I had also wanted so badly to be wrong.

Now I had my answer.

He wasn't here. He'd split. He'd seen me at my worst—and taken off. I had stayed the night for him, but he hadn't done the same for me.

I felt hollow.

I'd been right all along.

I stepped into the bathroom to brush my teeth and wash up, and then I just stood there, looking at myself in the mirror. My hair was down, my bangs were mussed up, my eyes were puffy. I washed my face again. I flossed for a while.

You see? This was exactly why I'd tried to send him away. This was exactly why I'd argued with him about staying. To avoid exactly this moment—exactly this undeniable truth about the world and my place in it. If Duncan took off—despite all his cajoling and platitudes—who else on earth was there even hope for?

At least, before, I'd been able to hold on to the hope that I was wrong.

I should go back to sleep, I supposed.

But I was wide-awake now.

So I paced around my place for a while—looking for a note, maybe, that said, "Be right back!" Or any clue anywhere that could prove me wrong.

I milled around, looking for way too long.

There was no note. No sign that he'd been here at all.

Nothing at all to argue me away from the only conclusion I could see. There had been a question at the center of my life ever since my seizures had come back—and now, pretty much against my will, Duncan had given me the answer to that question.

An answer I would much rather have avoided for the rest of my life.

❁   ❁   ❁

No going back to sleep after that.

Just pacing. Muttering to myself. Spasms of humiliation.

Just a shame-fueled spiral of misery that could easily have lasted until dawn—but, in truth, lasted only about a half an hour.

Until I heard a key in my door.

Duncan. Right? Had to be. Who else?

On instinct, I fluffed my hair. Like an idiot.

The door opened, but it was not Duncan. It was Alice.

"Hey!" she said. "You're awake!" She was wearing a T-shirt that said, MATHLETE.

"Couldn't sleep," I said, nodding like it was just ordinary insomnia.

She came and sat on the side of my bed. "Babette texted me to come check on you. I was just going to peek in and then sleep on the couch."

"Babette texted you?"

"She said you had a seizure."

Huh. Maybe Duncan had told her?

Now I was irritated. Did we really have to wake people up about this? Were we putting a notice in the paper—or driving the streets with a bullhorn?

"I'm fine," I said. "I don't need to be checked on. This is not a huge deal. This is just my life."

My tragic, hopeless, profoundly disappointing life.

I could feel the pull of hopeless thinking. It exerted a force on me like gravity—that temptation to come to simple and very dark conclusions: It was useless. I was hopeless. I would always be alone.

But "dark" wasn't Alice's thing. "Okay, then." She shrugged. "I'll make us some coffee."

"It's two thirty in the morning. We don't need coffee."

"Decaf," she corrected, like *Duh*. She walked to the kitchen.

"I'm fine," I said, not following. "You can go home."

She turned to look at me and gave a little shrug. "I'm awake now," she said. "And so are you, apparently."

"Not because I want to be."

Alice was reading my voice. She was super even-tempered, and almost nothing flustered her, but she was perceptive, too. "Do you want to talk about it?" she asked.

"What?" I was stalling.

"Whatever has you feeling so . . . brittle."

"No," I said. Then: "I don't know. Maybe. Not really. Never mind."

"Cool," Alice said. And she went ahead and busied herself with the coffeemaker.

Correction: the *decaf* maker.

Next, as it brewed, she turned around to look at me with such a sympathetic face that I just completely broke.

I could feel my body sinking, giving in to the weight of the truth. I said, "Duncan was here when the seizure happened."

"Oh."

"And then he . . . left."

Alice nodded, taking it in.

"Like, completely split. Vanished. Disappeared."

Alice studied me like I was a sudoku puzzle. Then she said, "Kinda like your dad."

"Yeah," I said, feeling a sting of anger at the connection. "And I tried to warn him, but he wouldn't listen, and now the exact thing I predicted would happen has happened—except it feels so much worse than I imagined. Maybe if he'd just listened to me, we wouldn't be in this mess. Except there is no 'we' in this mess. There's just me. Alone. Like, apparently, I will always be."

"Um. You are hardly alone. You are hanging out with your BFF."

"I mean—romantically alone."

Alice's voice went high and squeaky with manufactured hopefulness. "Maybe there's some other explanation?"

"Yeah, I can't come up with one."

But Alice was forever finding the upside of things. "Well," she said. "If you are right—and I'm not convinced that you are, but just for argument's sake: probably better to know now. Right?"

"Right," I answered, defeated.

"I mean, at some point, he was bound to witness you"—and here, she searched for a euphemism, which struck me as very kindhearted, given my fragile state—"*not at your most graceful.*"

True.

"Better he disappear now than after you'd had, like, ten kids."

"Ten kids?"

She nodded, all deadpan. "Two sets of twins, and two sets of triplets."

"That's a lot of kids," I said.

"See that? You've averted disaster. How could you ever reach your potential with all those kids? He did you a favor, really. And the kids, too."

"Sounds like it," I said, giving her a thanks-for-trying smile.

She gave me the exact smile back. *Thanks for letting me.*

Then she shook her head, as if to clear the whole subject away, turned her attention to the now-perked decaf, and said, "We should take a line-dancing class."

And just as she said that, as if to punctuate, our cell phones dinged at the exact same time.

My phone was in my bedroom, but hers was in her pocket.

She pulled it out, checked, and then looked up. "It's from the school. A kid has gone missing. They're calling us in for a search party."

twenty-six

It was Clay Buckley.

When we got there, we found Tina in tears, Babette drained and anxious, and Kent Buckley prowling around like an angry animal, growling at people.

The school was awash with cops and detectives. They were setting up a makeshift headquarters for the search in the cafeteria. Mrs. Kline was already there, at a folding table, organizing search packets and working from a clipboard.

Alice and I asked her what happened.

"It was Clay's birthday," Mrs. Kline said. "His dad was supposed to pick him up after school and take him to some pirate ship museum down toward Matagorda Bay. But his dad never showed up. From security tapes, it looks like Clay went to visit with Babette—and she confirms that he told her he was going to the library to read—but, instead, at four thirty-seven, he let himself out of the back gate."

"But those gates are locked!" I said.

"He had the code," Mrs. Kline said. "Or he figured it out. The video shows him pressing the keypad and then swinging it open."

"Which way did he go?" I asked.

But Mrs. Kline shook her head. "It doesn't show. You can just see him leaving."

"So . . . he's been missing since this afternoon?" Alice asked.

"He's been missing since about four thirty," Mrs. Kline said, "but they didn't figure out he was missing until eleven thirty. At night."

"Holy shit," Alice said.

"Language, please," Mrs. Kline said. Then she added, "His mother thought he was with his father—that he'd picked him up at car pool and the two had gone off on their adventure. But apparently"—Mrs. Kline glanced around and lowered her voice—"Kent Buckley forgot about the whole thing. Entirely. And so he stayed at work late and then went for drinks with some clients, and he didn't get home until after eleven. When he got home and didn't have Clay with him . . . that's when they called the police."

"She wasn't expecting them home until eleven?"

"She wasn't expecting them home at all. It was supposed to be an overnight trip."

Alice was nodding. "So that explains why Kent Buckley is so red-faced and angry."

Mrs. Kline frowned and nodded, like *Oh, yeah*. "Tina's angry, too. She's absolutely on the edge of losing it."

"Understandable," Alice said.

"They've already had several shouting matches since I've been here."

"How long have you been here?" I asked.

"Since about two. The police searched likely places he'd be first—the school, Babette's—before deciding to call everybody in. They've re-called all their officers, and we've texted everybody on our notification system. As people come in, we're sending them out in teams—giving everybody a grid section of the city to search."

This was Mrs. Kline at her multitasking best. She gave us an assignment—to walk the seawall heading east for ten blocks. If nothing turned up, we should report back to her by text, she'd send us a new section. Before we headed out, she told us to check in with the officer by the door, who was giving each team instructions.

Alice and I headed that way. A few other people were already waiting. Emily and Donna had their packet already and seemed antsy to get going. Carlos had been paired up with Coach Gordo, who was wearing his reflective car-pool safety vest. Everyone had that look—of being awakened from a dead sleep and hurtled straight into a state of maximum adrenaline.

Just as Alice and I arrived for instructions, Duncan came around a corner and saw me. He was walking with one of the officers, and at the sight of me, he slowed to a stop and stared for just a second.

There are no words to describe the sting of humiliation I felt at the sight of him—and, specifically, at the sight of him seeing me. It hijacked my entire body so tightly I felt like one big charley horse. It was physical. It was agony.

And then it was over.

There were bigger things going on. Another officer came up to Duncan with some new piece of urgent news, and he turned and walked off.

Fair enough. We had a situation.

As I watched him walk off, I had to mentally remind myself to *breathe* and *relax*.

He was still in the suit he'd been in yesterday, the suit he'd been wearing as he plunged into the ocean after me—probably still damp. His oxford shirt was dry, but stippled the way shirts are when they haven't been pressed. His navy blue tie was nowhere to be seen. His shirt was open at the collar.

I couldn't entirely read his reaction to seeing me—partly, I'm sure, because *my* reaction to seeing him was so intense. The moment was over almost as soon as it started, but the aftereffects lingered, aching for a long while after.

I knew he'd be there, of course. He was the principal. He was in charge—on the school end of things, anyway. But I hadn't had time to plan. At minimum, I'd hoped to avoid eye contact. I'd figured he'd be off in some far corner working in some kind of makeshift headquarters, not just wandering around loose like that making random eye contact with the lovelorn.

What was that eye contact, anyway? What had I seen in his eyes? Surprise, maybe? Or maybe fear? God, was I that scary?

I had just about refocused my attention on the moment at hand, when I saw him walking back toward me. He was holding up a hand, like *Be right back,* to the group of officers he'd left behind

He came up beside Alice and me. She looked at him, then at me, like *What's going on here?* But, to her credit, she didn't say anything.

Duncan gave Alice a nod, and then he turned to me. "Hey. You're here."

The stinging of humiliation came back and took me over. I almost couldn't look at him. I stayed totally still. "As are you."

"I just—wasn't sure if you'd be up for it."

"There's nothing that could have kept me away. Clay might be my favorite kid on the planet."

"Where are they sending you?"

"Seawall."

"Okay," he said, like he was making a note of it. "Be careful."

And that's when his tone shifted a little, and rather than just being all business, he edged a little closer, like he was going to say something more personal. "Are you—" he started.

But that's when the officer giving instructions to the search teams barked, "Okay, folks, listen up."

Duncan gave a quick nod and stepped back.

The officer went on. "Cover your area and your area only. Text or call any of the numbers on your sheet if you see anything. Mostly, you'll be walking, using your flashlights to check for anything out of the ordinary. The child was in gray uniform pants and a white shirt. He had black sneakers. He had a blue backpack with school items in it, and also several comic books and some kind of reference book about marine life. You're not just looking for the kid himself. If you see a shoe, if you see a backpack, if you see a book lying in the street. Do not touch it. Take a picture. Note your location. Call us and we'll send officers to determine the next step."

"Are we worried he's been abducted?" Carlos asked.

"Right now, he's just missing," the officer said. "He left of his own will. But he's a nine-year-old on the streets at night. Anything could have happened since then. We have to consider every possibility, and we need to move fast, so be thorough but stay focused." His tone changed, as he added, "Bad things happen to kids at night."

The entire briefing took two minutes, and somewhere during it, Duncan left, but I barely noticed. By the time the officer was done briefing us, I was staving off panic, and as soon as we got the green light, we were on the move. The school had a stash of heavy-duty flashlights we'd used for camping that they were handing out at the door. We each grabbed one, and as soon as we were out the gates, we started running toward the seawall.

Most of the search grids were square city blocks, but ours was just that narrow strip of beach. Alice and I decided to split up. She walked up high—at the top of the wall—and I took the steps down to the beach level, working along the water's edge. I kept my flashlight trained on the waves—looking for Clay out in them.

Or a backpack. Or a book. Or—God forbid—a shoe.

Alice shined her light down and examined everything on the beach and near the wall—bushes and plants, driftwood logs, litter—looking for the same stuff.

We called for him, too. "Clay!" we shouted over and over. "We're here!"

The hope, of course, was to find him safe and sound—maybe sitting pleasantly on a bench, reading a book and eating a bag of chips. Carlos and Coach Gordo had been assigned a fishing pier. Maybe he'd snuck out onto one and gotten trapped behind the gate when they hadn't noticed him at closing time. It was possible, I kept telling myself, that there was some reasonable, not-at-all-tragic explanation for what was going on.

He'd be fine, I told myself. He'd be fine. He'd be absolutely fine.

But the longer we walked with no sign of anything, the harder it felt to believe that. The officer's words, *Bad things happen to kids at night,* kept echoing through my head, and every now and then, I'd feel a swell of panicked tears squeezing my throat, threatening to rise up and take over.

But I'd shake it off. I couldn't—wouldn't—fall apart.

Clay was counting on us to find him and help him. He always seemed like such a little grown-up, but, of course . . . he was a kid. Despite his vocabulary, and his serious vibe, and his encyclopedic knowledge of pretty much everything, he had just as much right to make crazy mistakes as any other kid in the world. And just as much right to be totally overwhelmed by their consequences.

I tried not to think about how terrified he must be right now, wherever he was.

He was a kid. He was a kid who had lost his grandfather—probably the best person in his life—just weeks before the trip they'd planned together, one he'd been waiting for, looking forward to, reading up on, and planning for months. He'd read every shipwreck book in the library. He'd been keeping notes in a Moleskine of important questions to ask the museum staff.

I don't know who pressured Kent Buckley into agreeing to take Clay on that trip, but I swear even a casual observer could have warned you that it wouldn't end well.

That said, nobody could have imagined this.

The police weren't totally sure if he'd run away—or been abducted.

My hunch was that he'd run away. My hunch was that he'd finally had enough of that father of his. A father who'd forgotten all about him—on his birthday. Any kid could make some bad decisions in the wake of a moment like that.

It was high tide now, and dark down by the water.

"Clay!" I kept calling. "Clay!" But the roar of the surf seemed to swallow the sound.

We were supposed to turn around at Murdochs—a gift shop built off the seawall on stilts over the water. That was the end of our ten-block range, and our plan was to switch positions on the walk back.

But when I reached the pilings underneath Murdochs and started sweeping the area with my flashlight, I saw something odd. It looked like a capsized motorboat that had washed up near the shore. Oh, God. Had Clay tried to take out a boat somehow? Had he tried to head out to sea? Where would he have even found a boat? Most boats were on the bay side, or in the ship channel. The Gulf side of the island was too shallow for boating.

I called for Alice to come down, and I walked closer—out into the waves. I looked harder.

And then I realized, it wasn't a boat.

It was slick, and gray.

And it was . . . a fish of some kind.

A really, really big fish. A fish the size of a sedan.

And that's when I saw, standing beside the fish, up to his rib cage in the waves: Clay Buckley.

It was a hell of a sight.

For half a second, I couldn't speak, or move, or respond in any way. All I could do was take it in—until Alice arrived behind me.

"Clay!" I shouted, as Alice hooked her arm around me and propelled me forward.

"Holy shit," Alice said, as we made our way closer. "Is that . . . ?"

It sounded too crazy to say out loud. But we both could see what we saw.

"It's a whale, right?" I said.

"Sure looks like one."

"A baby one, maybe."

I'm shaking my head in disbelief even now at the memory of it.

It was impossible.

But it was also unmistakable. It couldn't really be anything else.

Not only was a whale washed up under the pilings of Murdochs gift shop, but it looked like Clay—our nine-year-old Clay—was talking to it.

We got closer and then paused for a second, just . . . *flabbergasted* by the sight—and then I trained my flashlight beam on Clay. He looked up and squinted at it, clearly aware that he was the subject of somebody's scrutiny, and then, I swear, he lifted a finger in front of his mouth, and he shushed me.

Then he turned his attention back to the enormous creature beside him in the water.

Alice fell back to call and report that we'd found him, as I continued sloshing my way closer to Clay in the water.

As I closed the distance, I could see what was going on—though I could hardly believe my eyes. The massive animal beside Clay, which was half-submerged in the waves, was tangled in a fishing net. And Clay was standing right beside it with his pocketknife open, sawing at the rope of the netting.

"Clay, you need to step back!" I said, though he had clearly been there for a good while—and the idea that he would step back now just because some grown-up came along and told him to was pretty laughable.

I mean, this mammal was taller than he was. And there was skinny little Clay, right there, in the waves, risking getting crushed with each shift of the tide—and he absolutely didn't care. Also, he seemed to be singing.

"Are you humming a Christmas carol?"

Clay didn't look away from the net, but he nodded. "'Silent Night.' It's the softest song I know," Clay said.

And that's when I knew. Clay wasn't scared, and he wasn't traumatized. He was helping. This kid knew exactly what he was doing right now in the middle of this crazy situation. He was trying like hell to make things better.

What would Max do?

"Do you have a knife?" Clay called. "Do you have anything sharp? Scissors even?"

But all I wanted to do was get Clay out of there.

I started walking toward him, thinking I was going to rescue him somehow—pull him back to the sand where it was safe. "Clay, it's not safe for you to be here."

Clay didn't even look up. "We don't have a lot of time," he said. "The tide brought him up this far, but it's going back out now. It'll be gone by morning."

I shone my light over toward Alice and she gave me a thumbs-up.

"The police are on their way now," I said. "They're bringing your mom, and Babette—"

But Clay was suddenly staring straight at me, looking stricken. "Tell them to keep their sirens off!" he said. It was the first moment I'd seen him stop sawing at the net.

I gave a little shrug. "I'm not sure if we can—"

"Please!" Clay shouted. "Don't let them run their sirens." He looked over at Alice.

Alice blinked at him.

"His whole head," Clay explained urgently, "is a supersonic hearing device. He's already in distress. A sound like that could kill him."

Alice nodded, and got back on the phone.

Clay went back to work.

For the first time, I really saw the animal. Its otherworldly gray skin, its deep, black eyes. The blocky shape of its head.

"Wait—Clay, is this a sperm whale?"

"I think so," Clay said.

"There are sperm whales in the Gulf of Mexico?"

Clay sighed. "We've already been over this."

"Is it . . . a baby?"

"It could be a baby. Or it could be a pygmy sperm whale."

Wow. "Don't worry," I said. "The police will get him fixed up."

"They need to bring knives to cut this net away," Clay said. "And they have to hurry."

"Probably easier to work by the light of day," I said gently, trying to lay the groundwork for the inevitable moment when the cops dragged Clay away out of the ocean and back to the safety of the beach.

"We can't wait for daylight. If the tide goes out, he'll die. Marine animals of this size can't handle the weight of gravity outside the water. His bones and organs will collapse."

"But people save whales all the time."

"No," Clay said, breaking through a section of net and grabbing another one. "Not this kind of whale. They never make it. They all die."

"All of them?"

Clay nodded, still sawing at the net. "But," Clay said, "this might not be a normal stranding. If it's just the net—if he's not sick—he might be okay. If we get him back out there fast enough. But if the tide goes out, there'll be no way we can get him back in the water until the tide comes back in—hours and hours. By then, he'll be in organ failure."

"I'm sure we could figure out some way to get him back in the water."

"Yeah?" Clay challenged, still sawing like crazy at the net. "He probably weighs a thousand pounds. Name one way to drag him back to the ocean that wouldn't kill him."

"Bulldozer?" I offered.

"Now you're just being insulting."

Good God, I felt like I was talking to Jacques Cousteau.

"If we don't free him before the tide goes out, he's a goner."

I took a look at the net. Clay still had a long way to go.

"How long have you been here?" I asked.

"A long time," Clay said.

That's when I noticed the blisters on his hands. He was wet and shaking—more from exhaustion than hypothermia, I suspected, since the Gulf water is warm this time of year in Texas. Either way, he'd been out here a long time.

"Let me take a turn," I said, stepping closer and putting my hand out for the knife.

Clay turned to read my face, deciding if he could trust me or not.

He could trust me. I hoped he knew that.

Then he nodded, so solemn, and handed me his knife. "You have to sing to him," he said, before he moved away. "He's frightened."

"How can you tell?"

But Clay just met my eyes. "Haven't you ever been frightened?"

I sighed.

"Go explain all this to Alice," I said, "so she can warn the officers."

And then I started sawing at the net with everything I had.

By some miracle, the police got the memo and did not run their sirens.

They all had utility knives anyway, and as soon as they arrived, about ten different guys waded right into the water to start working on the net.

Clay didn't protest, and neither did I. Clay's pocketknife was pretty dull. I'd been sawing like hell, and I'd only managed to cut two strands.

Plus, if I'm honest, it was a little scary to be so close to this giant beast out in the black water all alone. I could feel the whale's essential gentleness. Its wise, regal otherworldliness was palpable. I was humbled in its presence.

But I also knew that I was about one big wave away from getting crushed.

And something, too, about being so close to the blowhole, being able to feel its slow and ancient breaths, about suddenly having such intimate access to one of the most inaccessible creatures on the earth . . . it was intense.

When Clay's mom showed up, she was almost hyperventilating with sobs. She fell to her knees in the sand as she clutched hold of Clay. He put his arms around her, too, but he kept his eyes on his charge in the water. And when the paramedics—Kenny and Josh, the same paramedics who had tried to save Max—wanted to evaluate Clay and check for hypothermia, he let them. They cleaned and bandaged his hands, and they changed him out of his wet shirt into a too-big Galveston Fire Department T-shirt they'd had stashed somewhere in the truck.

One of the guys put his bunker coat on him. "That'll keep him warm," he said, ruffling Clay's hair.

Clay kept giving me instructions to relay to the team—and they followed them. A mass of giant men, working frantically and taking instructions from a nine-year-old: Make sure not to let water into the blowhole.

No shouting or scary movements. Keep their voices gentle and calm. Don't forget to sing.

When Clay spoke, they listened, and that's how, as the rescue wore on, a whole crowd of adults, chest deep in the water, huddled around a hulking creature and fighting like hell to beat the tide—on Clay's instructions, slow and gentle—wound up singing "Silent Night" to a whale.

Some of them even harmonizing.

I will never forget the sight of it—of so many people trying so hard to help. To rise above themselves and do the right thing. *See that?* I told Duncan in my head. *This is what it means to be fully alive. To feel it all—the joy and the sorrow, the hope and the fear. This is what life demands of us. You just have to stay, and try, and let life break your heart.*

Mrs. Kline notified the search teams that Clay had been found, and they made their way to the beach in pairs as they all heard the news and gathered on the shore to watch the rescue. Carlos and Coach Gordo went back to the school to gather buckets, and the group formed a bucket brigade, sloshing salt water over the whale's exposed skin as the rescue team worked.

Once he trusted that we were following his instructions, Clay allowed the grown-ups to take over. He was clearly exhausted, and he was, after all, *a child*.

When the Marine Mammal Stranding Network arrived, they agreed with Clay's assessment, his rescue strategy, and the calls he'd made—especially the urgency of the whale's situation: Yes, this was probably a pygmy sperm whale. Yes, there might be hope for this one. Yes, time was running out. We had another hour or two at most before the tide would be too low.

The hope became that if we could just get the whale free from the net, it might be able to use its tail to power back out of the surf. And while half-submerged in the water wasn't ideal, it was certainly better than fully beached.

The scene was undeniably inspiring: Police and firefighters working together to cut away the net—and taking gently spoken instructions from a lady marine biologist, no less: the ranking member of the Marine Mammal Stranding Network. Teachers faithfully working to slosh the whale with buckets of water. The exhausted Clay wrapped up safe in his mother's arms. And all of us now gently humming "Silent Night."

All of us on the same team, desperately coming together to work toward the same meaningful, important thing, in a way that human beings almost never do.

I want to tell you that all of this was enough to completely hold my attention—that I was 100 percent dedicated to Team Whale.

And I was.

But I confess that part of my brain was also wondering about Duncan. Where was he? Shouldn't he be here by now? I kept checking the crowd. I wasn't worried about him. I just felt like he ought to be here. That he would want to be here. That this remarkable moment somehow wasn't quite complete without him.

Even though the thought of seeing him again was not appealing.

Even though the humiliation of it felt like liquid agony.

I still didn't want him to miss it. I still couldn't help but think about how good it would be for Duncan to see humanity doing something good for a change.

How good it was for me to see it, too.

How much I wanted to share it.

The news crews showed up—but the firefighters wouldn't let them turn on their spotlights. Vacationers staying in nearby condos and folks who lived in the surrounding area appeared with coolers of water and boxes of cookies to help fortify the rescuers. As the crowd grew, newcomers either added their voices to the humming, or just stood gazing at the sight—everyone seeming to sense instinctively how important it was to stay quiet.

That is, until Kent Buckley showed up.

"What the hell is going on?" he shouted from the top of the seawall. "Nobody texted me!" He clomped down the concrete steps to the sand and then pushed through the crowd, his face red and flustered.

By this point, the firefighters had brought some beach chairs to Babette and Tina, and Clay had curled up on his mother's lap—totally unwilling to leave the beach, but fighting to stay alert. When Tina saw Kent Buckley, she defiantly stayed seated, tightening her arms around Clay a little.

"You were supposed to let me know when he was found," Kent said. "I had to hear the whole story on the news!"

"Shh," Tina said.

The onlookers hummed a little louder, as if they could drown him out.

"You couldn't send me one text?" Kent Buckley demanded.

"I was busy," Tina said.

"He's my son," Kent Buckley said, sounding notably petulant. "I've been just as worried as you."

"No," Tina said. "Because you're the reason he ran away in the first place."

"I've already told you, my secretary didn't remind me!"

"She shouldn't have to remind you."

"You try it!" Kent Buckley said. "You try working as hard as I do and see if you can remember every tiny piece of minutiae!"

But Tina was shaking her head. "This wasn't minutiae," she said. "This was your son's birthday. It was a trip you'd rescheduled three other times. He never complained. Every time something came up, he forgave you. But this time . . ." She shook her head like she was too angry to even keep talking. "No more."

But Kent Buckley wasn't really one to take criticism. Right? He wasn't just going to sign up for personal growth. He wasn't going to have an epiphany right here on this beach that he'd ignored all true sources of nourishment in his life in the relentless pursuit of status.

No. He was going to attack back.

"And what kind of mother are you?" he demanded. "This child has literally been out all night. He's wet, he's half-unconscious. He should be home in his bed, fast asleep. And yet here you sit, in a beach chair, like it's some kind of all-night party."

Then Kent, who, I suddenly noted, had not apologized to Clay for forgetting him in the first place, reached his hand out to Clay and said, "Come on, son. Time to go."

But Clay just blinked up at him for a second. Then he shook his head and said, "No. I need to stay."

Friendly hadn't worked, so Kent Buckley shifted to mean: "Get over here. Right now."

But Clay shook his head. Then he climbed out of Tina's lap, and stood to face his dad, looking so young and so small. "No," Clay said.

And then we all watched as Kent Buckley leaned over his nine-year-old son and hissed, "Come with me. Or I'll make sure you regret it."

But Clay, steady and calm, said, "They need me, and I'm staying."

It was a hell of a David and Goliath moment. I guess once you've befriended a whale, humans don't seem quite so scary anymore.

And that's when Tina got up and stepped forward.

"He wants to be here. He doesn't want to go with you. And I'm not going to make him."

"You will make him, if you know what's good for you."

"And guess what else I'm not going to do?" Tina said, standing up taller and moving toward him. "I'm not going to let you sell my parents' school."

"You don't get to 'let me' do anything."

"Are you really going to fight me?" Tina said, stepping closer. "Because I think you're forgetting something."

Kent Buckley's face said, *Oh, yeah?* "What would that be?"

Very deliberately, like she was saying much more than she was saying, Tina said, "I know all your secrets."

Kent Buckley's face froze.

Tina went on. "I've let a lot of things go. I've looked the other way, and put up with your demands, and kept quiet. Mostly, I did it for Clay. I did it because I thought he needed a father. But you know what? He doesn't just need any father. He needs a good father. And I've tried so hard for so long not to believe it, but you're not a good father." She shook her head and then said it again, like the act of saying it was empowering. "You're a terrible father. And you're a terrible husband. And you're a terrible person. My dad was the kind of person who made everything better . . . but you make everything worse. I didn't want to know that about you. I didn't want it to be true. But the truth is, Clay would be a hundred times better off without you. And so would I. Now that I see that . . . I can't not see it. That's it. I've backed down from you a thousand times, but that's not going to happen today."

Kent Buckley's tone shifted then, as he realized he needed to manage her a different way. "Look, it's been a long day. Let's go home, get a good night's sleep, and talk it all out in the morning."

He sounded suddenly so reasonable. I had a flash of worry that Tina might fold.

But then she said, "No." Then she shook her head. Tina said, "I want a divorce."

Let's just say it was a statement that wasn't going to go down easy with Kent Buckley. He stood up straighter. He took a step closer. And then he shouted, "You bitch!"

A gasp from the growing crowd of teachers on the beach.

"Dad!" Clay said. "You'll scare the whale."

Kent Buckley glanced at Clay before turning back to Tina with a lower, even more threatening tone. "You can't divorce me."

That's when Babette stepped up next to Tina. "Sure she can."

And then I stepped up, too. "She absolutely can."

Alice stepped up after that, and then Coach Gordo, and then, one by one, the rest of the teachers. A silent army of support.

And the last person to step up—and wasn't it just like him to appear just as soon as I'd stopped looking—was Duncan.

That's when Kent Buckley decided he was outnumbered and stepped closer to grab Tina's hand and pull her away from the group. In response, Clay ran up to break his grip and push him back—though Clay was hardly strong enough to do it.

Kent Buckley shoved his son out of the way, and Clay hit the sand.

In a flash, Duncan was between them. "Hey," he said to Kent Buckley. "Take it easy."

"Back off, pal," Kent Buckley said. "This is not about you."

"Why don't you take a walk—and a few minutes to calm down?"

"I don't need to calm down!" Kent Buckley shouted.

He was definitely upsetting the whale. The crowd hummed a little louder.

"Kent!" Tina said. "Just go home."

"Don't tell me what to do!" Kent shouted.

"Okay, buddy," Duncan said, stepping closer. "That's enough." And Duncan was putting his arm around him, presumably to lead him to the seawall steps for a little distance, when Kent Buckley turned around and slugged him right in the gut.

I was standing a few feet away when it happened, just one in the still-humming crowd that had shifted its attention from the whale to the real-time divorce happening before our eyes.

As soon as Kent Buckley's fist connected, Duncan doubled over and hit the sand.

All questions—of whether Duncan had freaked out over my seizures, or whether he had let me down, or whether or not we were even still friends—disappeared. I ran to him without thinking, without deciding to, just as two of the cops from the harmony section grabbed Kent Buckley and cuffed him.

Something Kent Buckley didn't take too kindly to.

"What are you doing?" he bellowed.

"That's assault, pal," one of the officers said. "We're taking you to the station."

And with remarkable efficiency, they maneuvered Kent Buckley to the seawall steps and up to the squad car. Tina watched them go, not protesting, as they pushed him into the backseat and then drove away—no siren.

I don't want to say it wasn't big news for Max's daughter to demand a divorce from the chairman of the school's board, and then for that chairman to punch the principal before getting hauled off to the slammer. On any other day, it would have been the biggest news we could imagine.

But today, it barely registered. Before he was even off the beach, we'd turned our attention back to the majestic creature in peril before our eyes. We had work to do. A rescue attempt to complete. And let's not forget Christmas carols to sing. Everyone turned back to the whale—all except me, and Chuck Norris, who was now on Duncan's other side, licking him.

Duncan was still panting and coughing.

"Did he get your scar tissue?" I asked.

Duncan gave a wry head shake. "It hurts like hell . . . but I'm fine. He's stronger than he looks, though."

"Can you get up, do you think?"

"Only if I have to."

I helped him to his feet, and he tried to look into my eyes, but I turned away. I stepped closer to the water, as if to say that the whale needed all my attention. Which felt, actually, kind of true.

The rescuers were still in the water, still working on the last section of net.

The water levels were lower with each roll of waves.

The sun was rising, and we were running out of time.

I watched Duncan move past us all, out toward the rescuers, and pull out a utility knife of his own to get to work, helping.

I told myself to stay focused. That my personal heartbreak could wait.

It was not looking good for the whale. And I didn't even realize I was crying until Alice showed up beside me and put her arm around my shoulder.

There wasn't anything left I could think of to do, so I prayed.

I'm not even a praying person, but I prayed for the whale. I stood right there, ankle-deep in the waves, and I just prayed like hell for something good to come out of this day. For all this human kindness to amount to something. For somebody on this beach to get a happy ending.

Even if it was a fish.

Clay would later correct me with an eye roll and explain, again, that you can't call a marine mammal a fish. "It's insulting."

But nomenclature aside, my praying worked.

Fine. Maybe I should give a little credit to the rescuers who actually cut the net away. Or the Marine Mammal Stranding Network. Or the nine-year-old boy who started it all.

Just as I was starting to give up hope, the last piece of net came free.

There was no time to lose. The rescuers pushed a little bit on the whale's tail to turn him, and get him facing back out to sea, and then they gathered behind him, and, on the count of three, they gave a shove from behind.

They might not have been able to do it on their own, but—on *three*, just as they pushed, as if it was following the count, too—the whale lifted its flukes, pumped them down, and launched itself off toward the open water and disappeared beneath the surface.

We all stopped singing.

We all stood in awe—alone now, with just the *shh* of the waves.

An officer and a firefighter got knocked over, but they bobbed back up, laughing

And then, with nothing left to do, the whole beach erupted into cheers. Babette and I hugged. Clay and I hugged. Even Tina and I hugged. The teachers all hugged. The officers all hugged—and then they came to grab Clay and raise him up on their shoulders.

All the noise we'd been holding back all that time came erupting out, and we cheered, and jumped around, and waved our arms—completely exhausted and absolutely wired at the same time.

And then, just as we were winding down, Clay called out, "Look!" and we saw a set of flukes rise up out of the water, off near the brightening horizon.

And then we saw another set of flukes.

And then two more.

"It's a pod of them," Babette said.

"They were waiting for him," Tina said.

"They're waving at us," Alice said then, waving back. Then we all waved, too.

"Do you think they're saying thank you?" I asked.

But Clay shook his head, still on the shoulders of one of the medics. "Nah," he said. "I think they're saying goodbye."

twenty-seven

Tina took Clay home after that, with plans to sleep for a week.

The police headed off, too—except for one car, waiting for Duncan to come back and wrap up the paperwork.

Before he left, he came to find me.

I was standing under the pier, pausing to gaze out at the water, waiting for my brain to catch up with everything that had happened.

He walked up to me with his hands in his pockets.

He swallowed when he saw me.

"You should go home, Duncan. Go to bed."

"Yeah," he agreed. "Crazy night."

"Yep."

"I just . . . had a question."

"What?"

"What's going on?"

"I don't know," I said. "The usual. We found a missing kid. We sent the chairman of the board to the clink. We rescued a whale. Pretty ordinary night."

"But are you . . . angry at me?"

"No!" I said. "No." Then I added, "It's fine. I get it. I really do."

There was no point in talking about it now. It was what it was.

"What's fine?"

I tried to keep my voice light, like it was all vaguely amusing. "You. You know. Leaving. Earlier. I get it. I mean, I warned you. You can't say I didn't warn you. But you were so busy arguing with me, you kind of missed your chance to escape. That's on you."

But Duncan was really frowning now. "What are you talking about?"

"Earlier," I said, gesturing back toward town, "I had a seizure, and you finally saw what I'd been warning you about, and you freaked out, and you took off. And it's fine. Told ya so."

Duncan shook his head. "Is that what you think happened?"

I gave a little shrug. "Well, I woke up alone in my bed in the pitch-black in an empty place, so . . . yeah."

"How do you think you got to your bed?"

So he'd dragged me over there before he left. "Thank you."

I really was too tired for this. My whole body felt shaky. I felt a tightness in my throat like I might be about to cry and blow my cover.

"Sam," Duncan said. "I didn't run away. I stayed."

"The me-waking-up-alone part contradicts you."

He gave a frustrated head shake, then he said, "You did have a seizure—and it absolutely was a little scary to witness only because it was new, and it doesn't look like the most relaxing thing a person could ever do, and it's hard to watch someone you love go through something that looks like agony. But I did not freak out, and I did not leave you. What kind of an ass do you think I am? I stayed—*of course* I stayed. I looked after you and did everything you said to do. And when you came to after, I helped you to your bed, and tucked you in, and curled up next to you on your bed. And I would still be right there right now if I hadn't gotten a call at midnight that Clay had gone missing."

"You only left because of Clay?"

"I only left because of Clay."

I tried to take that in.

"I told you I was going," Duncan went on. "But you were so out of it. And you'd said that seizures make it hard to remember things. So that's why I sent Alice—Babette texted her for me because I was in a meeting with the cops."

I let all of those pieces settle into place in my head. "You didn't . . . leave?"

He stepped a little closer.

"You stayed?" I asked. "Voluntarily?"

He nodded and stepped closer. "And now I'm back again. Trying to continue not leaving."

I couldn't look at him.

Somehow, knowing that he hadn't left seemed to hurt worse than thinking that he had.

It sounds crazy, I know.

But it was like, I'd spent the entire day just trying to hold my heart together, and I couldn't bear the idea of breaking it open again.

"I'm not a guy who runs away," Duncan said. "I'm a better man than that."

He was. He absolutely was. And suddenly my eyes had tears in them.

"You are a better man than that," I said.

He leaned closer, like he might kiss me, but I stepped back.

I shook my head.

Duncan frowned.

"I can't," I said. "I can't ask you to do this. It's not fair to you. You've got enough to cope with as it is. I can't ask you to be my caretaker."

"Hey." He reached out to try to take my hand. "Sam—"

But I edged away. "Don't," I said.

It was too much. The way I felt about him was too much. I was afraid to care that much for anybody. I knew now, after waking up alone, how vulnerable I was. And I just couldn't stand it.

I pushed away from him, and then I broke into a run across the sand to the steps of the seawall.

I climbed them without ever looking back.

But I didn't have to.

This time, he didn't chase me.

It turned out, Alice and Babette were waiting for me up at the top of the stairs.

They came at me like I was a wild animal they needed to trap.

"What are you doing?" Babette demanded, looking almost angry.

But I shook my head. "I can't."

"Didn't you hear him?" Alice demanded as the two of them followed close behind me. "He didn't leave you. He stayed."

"What—were you eavesdropping?"

"We were just waiting for you!" Babette said.

"So you heard that whole thing?"

"Yes, and you're an idiot," Alice said.

"Okay," I said, turning to march away along the seawall. "We really don't have to call each other names."

But Alice wasn't going to let me distract her. She followed. "You chickened out!"

"I didn't chicken out! It was self-preservation!"

"The thing you want—the person you want—was right there for the taking, and you just walked away."

Now I could feel my throat thickening. My face got wet with tears I didn't condone. They just made me angrier. "It's too much, okay? Hasn't anything ever been too much for you?"

"Yes!" Alice grabbed my arm to stop me and turn me around. "Every single deployment Marco goes on is too much for me. Every time I say goodbye knowing I might never see him again is too much for me. But guess what? I do it anyway."

She had me there. I looked away.

Alice went on. "I do it anyway because it's worth it! Because I refuse to let fear make me small. Because being brave is good for you."

"Great," I said, turning to keep walking. "Awesome."

Alice and Babette followed me. Alice went on, "You've been telling Duncan ever since he got here that he can't let fear control his every move. That he can't live in a prison to stay safe. But that's exactly what you just did. You put yourself in a prison. How are you going to face him day after day like this? How are you going to work with him knowing that he stayed—that he did everything you asked—and you still couldn't find the courage to say yes?"

"I'm not," I said then, slowing to turn and face them. "I'm not going to work with him. I'm quitting."

Alice and Babette fell quiet.

"I always knew this was going to happen," I said. "I always knew his coming here would run me out of town. Fine! I'm a hypocrite! I'm the one who's afraid. I'm the person who has lived her whole life in fear. I'm the one who talks about being courageous without any idea at all what that even means. So, yes—I'm going to chicken out. And get the hell out of here. And give the hell up."

"No," Babette said then.

"No? 'No' what?"

"No, you're not leaving. And no, you're not quitting. And no—you are not giving up on Duncan. Or on yourself. Or on love."

As she hit the word "love," her voice broke. But in her dignified way she stood up straighter and took a step closer. "Life doesn't ever give you what you want just the way you want it. Life doesn't ever make things easy. How dare you demand that happiness should be yours without any sacrifice—without any courage? What an incredibly spoiled idea—that *anything* should come easy? Love makes you better because it's hard. Taking risks makes you better because it's terrifying. That's how it works. You'll never get anything that matters without earning it. And even what you get"—she lifted her chin in defiance—"you won't get to keep. Joy is fleeting. Nothing lasts. That's exactly what courage is. Knowing all that going in—and going in anyway."

There were tears on her face now, but she held my gaze. I thought about everything she'd lost. I thought about what kind of courage it must have taken just now for her to search a darkened city for her missing grandson—to know that anything could have happened, to face down the terror of all of it, but to show up, anyway. To go looking and to keep looking—all through the night and into the dawn.

How exhausted she must be.

And yet, here she was. Standing on the seawall in her housecoat, her eyes red with exhaustion—and stubbornly, insistently, caring about me and all my stupid choices.

This was what it meant to be alive. This was what it meant to let the beauty of it all break your heart. I got it in a new way, looking at her right then. And I got something else, too. This is what it meant to be part of a family.

I wasn't going to quit. For better or for worse, I belonged here—on this island in this sea-battered old city. These were the people I'd chosen to love—who had chosen to love me, too. I wouldn't turn my back on them. And they weren't about to let me turn my back on myself.

"You're right," I said then, nodding. I stepped closer and squeezed Babette's hand. Then I turned to Alice. "You're right, too."

"I'm always right."

Then I looked back the way we'd come, toward the pier at Murdochs. Would Duncan still be there?

Then I looked at Babette and Alice, and both already knew what I was thinking. Then Babette reached out and gave my shoulder a little push just as Alice shouted, "Go!" And that was everything I needed.

I took off running.

I made it back to where we'd started in seconds, it seemed.

There were still a few cop cars parked on the boulevard. Maybe not everybody had gone.

I reached the edge and looked down the steps toward the beach, breathing hard, hopeful to find him.

But the beach was empty—like none of us had ever even been there at all.

I turned around, still breathing. Where was he? Back at the station? Back at school? I had no idea. I turned in a kind of panoramic sweep, hoping to spot him somewhere.

But that's when the passenger door of one of the squad cars opened, and Duncan climbed out.

I ran over to him and stopped just short of throwing myself into his arms.

"I'm sorry!" I said.

Duncan just stared, like he was trying to figure me out.

"You stayed," I said, "and that really matters. You stayed, and I'm so grateful to you."

He shook his head. "Of course I stayed."

Then, not sure if this was a statement or a question, I said, "The seizure didn't . . . change how you felt about me."

He shook his head even more. "Of course it didn't."

This time, the words—the fact of them, and what they meant—hit me differently. This time, I didn't deflect them. This time, I let them in.

They swirled in my chest in a way that almost made me dizzy.

I closed my eyes.

Duncan took a step closer. "Actually, if I'm honest, it did change how I feel about you."

I opened my eyes to find his.

And then he said it almost sadly. "I think it made me love you more."

"You love me," I said.

He nodded. "Hope that's okay."

And so I reached up around his neck, pulled him to me, and kissed him.

The cops, still waiting to take Duncan back wherever they were going, all honked their horns.

When Duncan pulled back, he looked intensely into my eyes. "So it's okay, then?"

And then, because joy is fleeing, and nothing lasts, and even what you get, you don't get to keep, I didn't waste any more time. "I love you, Duncan," I said. "I've loved you for a long, long time." I said it to be brave. I said it to be better.

But more than anything, I said it because it was true.

And then Duncan leaned down again, and I stretched up, and even though the cops were waiting, we let ourselves have a simple, easy, perfect kiss.

But we sure had earned it.

Halfway through, Duncan broke away, held a finger out to me like, *one second,* and then trotted over to tap on the passenger window of the closest cop car. The window rolled down, and Duncan poked his head in.

When he stepped back, the cop cars all pulled away.

"What did you say?" I called.

He shrugged. "I just asked if we could finish up the paperwork later."

And so he walked me back to my place, and we slept together.

Actually slept.

Because man, oh, man, were we tired. And man, oh, man, what a hell of a day-slash-night. But it was okay. Better than okay, even.

It was, in fact, the most better-than-okay either one of us had been in a very long time.

epilogue

Tina really went through with it. She did divorce Kent Buckley. We'd all worried that the momentum of her old life might make her chicken out, but she did it. And while in theory, a divorce is a sad thing—the real sad thing was the marriage that came before it. The divorce itself turned out to be a happy solution.

What I mean is, things got a lot better for Tina Buckley once she was free of Kent and all his demands. Tina and Clay wound up moving in with Babette for a while, which suited Babette just fine, while Tina went back to school to finish her degree.

Turned out one of Tina Buckley's wifely duties had been to cook gourmet meals for Kent most nights, so Babette ate very well after Tina came home and started teaching her some skills in the kitchen.

And so did I. Because Tina—of all people—invited me to join them.

It turns out to be a funny thing about moms: once you help their children rescue whales in the middle of the night, they stop hating you so much. Or, maybe, once they get rid of the husbands they should have been hating all along, they can give you a break.

Either way, we made up.

She turned out to be a much nicer person than I'd given her credit for.

Tina did stop Kent from selling off our school. She must have had some really great dirt on him. He didn't even put up a fight. His behavior at the beach—specifically, assaulting the school principal—also prompted his removal from the board.

Guess who took his place?

The beautiful Babette.

Kent Buckley moved to New Jersey, after that, and he turned out to be the kind of divorced dad who did not make a large effort—or, frankly, any effort—to see his kid.

And while we can all agree that it's good for boys—in theory—to have a father around, we also agree that it really depends quite a bit on the father.

Which was fine. Clay wound up with a better family, anyway. Between Tina, Babette, and me, he had more than enough loving adults looking after him. I even gave him his own CLAY RECOMMENDS shelf in the library. Not to mention the Texas Marine Mammal Stranding Network, which gave him a medal and honored him at their annual fundraising dinner (he wore a little tux), as well as got him volunteering with them almost every weekend.

After Babette took her rightful place on the board, Kent Buckley was quickly forgotten. We moved forward with the Adventure Garden, at last, and built the most astonishing pirate-ship tree house. Babette continued to boss Duncan around—in part because now she really could get him fired—but mostly just because it was fun.

He liked it more than he admitted, I think.

We did wind up making security changes at the school. The goal became to do enough without doing too much. Duncan brought us into the sad, modern age where schools have to think about these things, but he wound up trusting the instincts of the collective wisdom of the faculty when it came to figuring out where to draw the line. He changed the school a little bit, but he also worked to change the world a little bit, too, volunteering for a gun-sense group and trying to make the world safer.

And in the meantime, despite all the worries and tragedies and injustices in the world, we remembered to have fun when we could.

We remembered to have dance parties, and sand-castle building contests, and cookie-decorating competitions. We remembered to do karaoke, and have school-wide movie nights in the courtyard, and take long walks on the beach. We let the kids write stories about the school ghost at Halloween, we played hooky from school on pretty spring days, and we brought back Hat Day.

We made a choice to do joy on purpose. Not in spite of life's sorrows. But because of them.

And it really did help.

Not that our lives were all magically fixed. Babette still missed Max, and grieved for him, and would for the rest of her life. Tina still—inexplicably—missed Kent Buckley, or, at least, the idea of him. Alice still had to live much of her life with Marco deployed half a world away. Clay still had kids at school calling him Brainerd.

And even after Duncan and Chuck Norris moved into my little carriage house with me, Duncan still had nightmares, and I still had seizures.

We didn't fix everything for each other—but we didn't have to.

We just made a choice to be there.

Which counted for a lot.

Max had always joked that if anyone ever made a statue of him, he'd want it to be a fountain—of him peeing. But the board, even with Babette at the helm, just couldn't run with that idea.

We held on to his memory in other ways. We decided to hold an annual, disco-themed dance party in his honor. We hung a painting Babette had done of him in the office. And Babette painted a colorful mural on the playground fence with everybody's favorite Max-ism: "Never miss a chance to celebrate."

Did we miss chances to celebrate after that? Did we get caught up in our worries and our petty arguments and ourselves?

Of course. We were only human.

But we tried our best—again and again and again—to choose joy on purpose. Just like Max would have wanted.

And, of course, I didn't quit my job, or leave my island, or give up on courage. I stayed, and I chose the people I loved over and over. For better and for worse.

But mostly for better.

acknowledgments

I need to thank many people who generously helped me coax this story into existence.

Much gratitude to all the librarians in the world for doing the soul-work the world so badly needs—as well as to the particular teachers and librarians I consulted with: my mom (who would say she only "barely" worked as a librarian before having kids, and then took over her dad's company after he died—but she has an MLS degree, and she gave me a love of books from the very start, so she counts!); my sister, teacher Shelley Stein; librarian Mary Lasley; and librarian (and former Duran Duran fanfiction-writing childhood friend) Julie Alonso. I should also mention that my husband, Gordon, a seventh-grade history teacher, was basically the model for Duncan in this book. The crazy pants? The ties? The "Defense Against the Dark Arts" name tag? The drowned succulents? That's all him. He's seriously a teaching legend—and I'm so proud of his kindness, his wisdom, and the way he always makes everything better.

I'm also deeply grateful to my friend Dale Andrews and her daughter

Izzy for being such phenomenal resources and talking with me so openly and honestly about the challenges of living with epilepsy.

Many thanks also to Veronique Vaillaincourt, LCMSW, and Gerard Choucroun, MSW, for their help as I researched PTSD and its treatment. I also want to acknowledge Dr. Patricia Resnick's work on Cognitive Processing Therapy. Thanks as well to Norri Leder, former chapter division head for Moms Demand Action for Gun Sense in America, for talking with me so thoughtfully about the effects of gun violence in our schools and communities.

I'm also so grateful to Wayne Braun, Corey Lipscomb (Hi Heather!), and Philip Alter for helping me research issues of building design—and I owe a great debt to the fascinating book *Joyful: The Surprising Power of Ordinary Things to Create Extraordinary Happiness,* by Ingrid Fetell Lee, for its insight into how design can impact our experience of the world.

FYI: The poems that Duncan would like to have read at his funeral are two of my personal favorites: "From Blossoms" by Li-Young Lee, and "Wondrous" (a poem about *Charlotte's Web*) by Sarah Freligh. Look 'em up! And also, before I forget, I need to thank Makenzie Minshew, a girl I met while doing "research" on the real-world Iron Shark, who described our collective fear just perfectly when she said, "It's like your stomach's inside out." Heartfelt thanks, also, to Lizzie Kempner McFarland and Babette Hale for letting me use their names.

And can I just take a moment to thank all the Bookstagrammers, and bloggers, and online reviewers and . . . just . . . readers out there who took a chance on my books, and then loved them, and then helped spread the word in one way or another?! Books live or die on word of mouth. If you have ever done anything to encourage anyone to read something I've written, thank you. It mattered. I'm still here because of you.

I need to send the most heartfelt thanks to my beloved writing teacher from Vassar College, Beverly Coyle. I will never forget—and will always cherish—the moment when she said to me, "I can count on one finger the students I've taught who can write like you." Encouragement is so vital, and so precious, and that one little sentence saw me through some long valleys of self-doubt.

I am grateful beyond human description to my beloved publisher, St. Martin's Press, for all the ways they've believed in me and supported me and become the most wonderful home. I'm so thankful to be there, and so lucky to get to work with the most amazing people on the planet: Jen Enderlin, Sally Richardson, Lisa Senz, Olga Grlic, Jessica Preeg and Katie Bassel, Brant Janeway, Erica Martirano, Tom Thompson, Sallie Lotz, Natalie Tsay, Elizabeth Catalano, Anne Marie Tallberg, Lauren Germano . . . and so many more, including, in a way, my dear friends Katherine and Andrew Weber! I also—always—want to thank my agent, Helen Breitwieser, for all her unwavering support over so many years.

Most of all, I need to thank my fun, loving, astonishingly supportive family—most especially, my hilarious husband, Gordon, my delightful kids, Anna and Thomas, and my phenomenally awesome mom, Deborah Detering—for all the ways that they keep encouraging me to get out there and try like heck to reach my potential. There's no way I could ever thank you enough . . . but I'll always keep trying.

WHAT YOU WISH FOR
by Katherine Center

About the Author

• A Conversation with Katherine Center

Keep On Reading

• "The Guy at the Wedding" by Katherine Center

• Recommended Reading

• Reading Group Questions

Also available as an audiobook
from Macmillan Audio

For more reading group suggestions
visit www.readinggroupgold.com.

 ST. MARTIN'S GRIFFIN

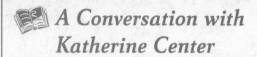 *A Conversation with*
Katherine Center

What You Wish For *has been called a book about* *"love, loss, and finding joy on purpose." Why did you want to write about joy?*

My understanding of joy has changed a lot as I've grown up. I used to think of joy as something that had to be big—a huge, monolithic emotion that you couldn't miss. But the older I get, the more I see it as less like a roaring bonfire than little twinkle lights. One little light might not make much of an impact, but hundreds? Thousands? Suddenly, the world is different. More and more I feel like joy is *cumulative*—that the more of it you notice, and pay attention to, and savor, and remember, the more there suddenly is all around you.

For me, that means trying to fill up my life with whimsy, and jokes, and kitchen dance parties, and good food. It means wearing stripy rainbow socks (like Sam), and singing a lot, and trying to notice flowers and breezes and little tiny blessings. The smaller joy is, the easier it is to overlook—but also: the easier it is to find. So part of living a happier life is training yourself to notice the joy that's already there, and another part of it is working to create more of it in your life. I'm endlessly fascinated by joy because being happy has never come easily to me. It's something I work at consciously. But working at it works!

Choosing joy on purpose is something I've learned to get pretty good at, and I wanted to write about a character who's learning to do it, too.

What You Wish For *is set on historic Galveston Island. What made you want to write about Galveston?*

Galveston Island is an hour from my hometown of Houston, and it's the main beach I grew up going to. My mom has a little beach shack down on the island, and that's the place where I write most of my books, so it's become a very special place to me. Galveston's like nowhere else in the world. It used to be the biggest city in Texas before the 1900 storm that devastated the city and killed over six thousand people in one night—and so it has this very proud history. The city still has tons of remaining Victorian architecture that's gorgeous and picturesque, but it's also a town that has known vast amounts of sorrow. Nowadays, it's somehow both touristy and real, both fancy and dilapidated, both triumphant and sad. Between all those opposites, the place just feels *woven* out of stories. There's a lot of magic there.

You write and talk a lot about reading for joy. What does that idea mean to you?

Reading for joy is about giving yourself permission to read what you want to read—instead of what you think you *should* want to read. It's about getting to know yourself as a reader—learning to follow your own compass about the stories that are going to resonate for you. I have a theory that finding the right story at the right time is one of the most nourishing things you can do for yourself. Stories have this magical way of going straight to the heart—and if the right story finds you at the right time, it can change your life. It can teach you things you didn't even consciously know you needed to learn. We all come out of school with a certain amount of baggage about reading and stories. We've absorbed other people's opinions about what stories are "good" or worth our time. Reading for joy is about learning to decide for yourself what a good story is for you at any given moment in your life—and letting joy be your guide. Because if a story captivates, delights, or just works for you, that's a good story. Period.

Duncan Carpenter is a character who also appears in your novel Happiness for Beginners. **How did he come to be a main character in** What You Wish For?

The thing is, I just kind of fell in love with Duncan. In *Happiness for Beginners,* he was only supposed to be an idea. He was the irritating younger brother of the main character, Helen. He existed to annoy her. But the more I wrote about Helen, the more I couldn't help but love her little brother. He was a disaster, but he meant well. He kept messing everything up, but he was trying so hard. He was such a goofball, but he was so good-hearted. By the end, he wound up playing a big part in that story, and he just stole the show, as far as I was concerned.

After that, I wanted to give Duncan his own book—and I kept holding that idea in my head, that someday I would. And then suddenly, as I was starting up *What You Wish For* and hearing Sam in my head talking about how she couldn't *believe* who they'd hired as the new principal at her school, I was like, "Wait—is it Duncan?" Last time

I saw Duncan, he was dancing "like Animal from the Muppets" at the bar mitzvah of a kid he didn't even know . . . but now here he was again—totally changed, wearing a three-piece suit, and acting like the toughest of tough guys. And I was just so curious about what happened to him. And even after I knew that, I wanted to see if he could find a way to be okay again.

How did you come to write the bridge story, "The Guy at the Wedding," that connects What You Wish For *to* Happiness for Beginners?

That story just *hijacked* my brain. I didn't have an assignment to write it, or permission, even, and I didn't even know when I started if there would be a place to publish it. But none of that mattered, because as soon as I got this idea—that I could write the story of the first night Helen and Jake met, all those years ago—the story took off without me. I hoped we could include it here, in the trade paperback edition of *What You Wish For,* but I didn't know for sure—and it didn't matter. I wrote it for love. I wrote it for joy. I wrote it because *I wanted to read that story.* I wanted to know what happened! And I also just couldn't resist the opportunity to hang out with the two of them again. It's one of my favorite things I've ever written.

What's next for you? What are you working on now?

I'm just finishing up a new book with all-new characters that's a total barn-burner! When I first started thinking about this story, I worried that it might be *too fun.* I was like, "Can I do that? Would that be too fun?" But then 2020 came along and convinced me that there's no such thing as too fun. The book doesn't have an official title yet, and it's not even finished, but every page so far just crackles with energy and purpose. If it's half as much fun to read as it has been for me to write, y'all are in for a serious treat.

THE GUY AT THE WEDDING

A bridge story between
What You Wish For
and *Happiness for Beginners*

by
Katherine Center

DUNCAN

The first night Jake met Helen, I punched him in
the jaw so hard I dislocated my thumb.

By accident. Kind of.

I was in trouble anyway because I'd snuck him
into the wedding uninvited, and I'm not saying that
Helen was a bridezilla, exactly, but let's just say she'd
planned everything herself, paid for everything
herself, and worked out deals with the venue and
the caterer to fit a tight budget . . . and her tolerance
for me screwing things up on her wedding day was
particularly low.

Plus, she'd had to fight our grandma GiGi
every step of the way, as GiGi—eccentric as ever—
suggested endless ways to make the whole thing
more fabulous.

Live peacocks wandering around, for example.

GiGi was in a book club with a part-time peacock breeder.

An X-rated book club, actually, but that's a story for another time.

"We'll just borrow them," GiGi kept saying. "Judy's fine with it."

"No. Nope. No peacocks," Helen kept saying.

Helen knew the manager at the Kemp Hotel, and he'd given her a deep discount off the ballroom that opened out to the pool.

"They'll stay outside," GiGi said.

"That's got to be a health code violation."

"That's not for us to decide."

Sometimes, with GiGi, you had to run through a list of objections. Helen tried again. "People are going to step in peacock poop."

"I don't think peacocks are big poopers."

"All birds poop, GiGi."

"But, I mean . . . comparatively."

"Why don't you research peacock poop and get back to me?"

"This feels like a lot of negativity."

"Yeah. That's because I'm not having feral birds roaming loose at my wedding."

"They're not feral. They even know some tricks."

"No, thanks."

"If it's money you're worried about, darling, then don't. She won't charge us a cent."

"I just want a normal wedding. Like normal people have."

That was the crux of it. GiGi wasn't a big fan of normal.

Or maybe I should say that what was normal to GiGi—wearing silk pajamas to the grocery store, drinking champagne at breakfast, carrying an unlit

cigarette in a rhinestone-encrusted holder even though she'd quit decades ago because she "couldn't give up the glamor"—wasn't the same normal as most other people's.

GiGi's normal was different from *normal* normal.

And I don't want to say that GiGi was judgmental, but she definitely considered anything normal a synonym for "boring."

Boring might be fine for other people. But not the grandchildren she had hand-raised herself.

This wedding was personal.

If we were boring, what did that say about her?

So the idea of a plain vanilla wedding for Helen with no peacocks anywhere was tough for her.

"How about just one," GiGi attempted, nodding like, *Yes, this is right,* "at the entrance?" She'd come a long way from proposing the peacock as the ring bearer.

But, back then, Helen was all about normal.

GiGi had tried for a speakeasy-themed, Scott Joplin–style wedding, then a forties USO vibe, then a New Orleans jazz theme with gumbo and jambalaya.

All rejected.

Helen wanted a strapless white dress, and men in shawl-collar tuxes, and white linen tablecloths, and candles. Nothing weird. Nothing nutty. No peacocks. The words she kept using over and over were "simple," "elegant," and "classic."

The word GiGi kept using was "generic."

And so they agreed to disagree.

And that meant Helen did everything herself. GiGi was being difficult, our dad was remarried in California, and we hadn't seen our mom in years. And I—Helen's sixteen-year-old, pain-in-the-ass little brother—certainly wasn't going to contribute anything useful.

That was a given.

And don't get me started on the groom.

I get it now. When it's just you, you can get fixated on the details. Maybe to the point where the details are all you see. Helen knew the cost of each guest down to the penny, and so she wasn't just tossing out invitations to anybody. She was parsing cousins and old friends from high school. She was ranking friends in tiers.

Cuts were made. People were snubbed. But the budget was not breached.

Which is why me showing up—late, as usual—in her dressing room with my new best friend, Jake, and declaring he was my 'plus one' . . .

It really, really pissed Helen off.

Really.

Of course, back then, the "empathy" quadrant of my brain was totally underdeveloped. I couldn't have stepped into Helen's emotional shoes if I'd tried.

But of course I didn't try.

I mean, *I* was happy to have Jake there, so I couldn't imagine that Helen wouldn't also be happy about it. That was the sophistication of my thinking at age sixteen: if something was good for me, it was good for everybody.

I was happy that Jake had come. Because I'd learned at lunch the day before that today—the day of Helen's wedding—also happened to be the one-year anniversary of Jake's mother's death. And even with my underdeveloped empathy skills, I could figure out that much: his dad was out of town on business, he'd just moved to a new school in a new town, and if I didn't do something, he'd spend a

very sad day totally alone.

So right there at lunch, I chugged a root beer, burped like a champion, and invited him to the wedding on the spot.

He didn't think it was a great idea. He said something like, "Your sister doesn't want some teenage weirdo crashing her wedding."

"You're not a weirdo," I said. "You're the poster boy for an upstanding citizen."

"I'm still not crashing."

"But here's the thing, though," I said, winding up to spin a convincing lie. "The numbers are down."

"What numbers?"

"A lot of people said no. Like, she sent out all these invitations, and then, at the last minute . . . an *avalanche* of regrets. So now there are going to be all these empty seats, and the biggest day of my sister's life will kind of be the Charlie Brown Christmas tree of weddings. Just sad and crooked and unwanted."

Jake frowned at me.

"You'd be rescuing her, is what I'm saying."

As Jake started shaking his head, I countered with nodding mine.

"You'd be doing her a favor," I went on. "Really. She was just worrying about all the empty chairs last night. Couldn't sleep, even. You don't want to leave my sister alone in a ballroom full of empty chairs, do you?"

Jake considered this. "Everybody just—canceled? At the last minute?"

I nodded, like an emphatic *yes,* even as I said, "In a manner of speaking."

None of it was true.

Jake was pretty sure he didn't believe me. But he didn't have enough evidence to know for sure I was lying, either. Nowadays, he can tell if I'm lying *in one glance*. But back then, he was still the new guy. We were barely friends yet. All he really had to go on was my word.

"You wouldn't abandon my sister, would you?" I demanded. Because even back then, I already could tell that much about him.

He wouldn't.

JAKE

I definitely knew he was lying. I just couldn't prove it.

It just didn't sound feasible that a huge number of wedding guests would RSVP "no" at the last minute and leave a bride with an empty ballroom. I didn't know much about weddings, but that just didn't track. Plus, Duncan's face was so earnest it felt like a tell.

But I guess the damsel-in-distress narrative worked on me.

Though Helen would turn out not to be in distress. And she was anything but a damsel.

The point is: I went.

I wore the same dark gray suit I'd worn to my mother's funeral. Same blue tie. Same shoes. Same belt with the broken buckle.

A year had passed, and now the pant legs were like an inch too short, but I told myself nobody would notice.

Needless to say, me following Duncan into Helen's dressing room—a teenage stranger she'd never laid eyes on—as she was slipping into her fancy shoes just minutes before the ceremony began . . . it might not have been the smartest choice I've ever made.

Or maybe it was.

Duncan opened the door without even knocking and strode right in. Five minutes sooner—and I've thought about this a lot—we could have walked in on her half-dressed, stepping into her gown in her strapless bra and garters.

Lucky for her we showed up just when we did.

Keep On Reading

Less lucky for me.

For years, I reflected dolefully on that timing, thinking I'd missed my one and only chance to ever see Helen less-than-dressed.

But of course, catching her that way would have been even more incapacitating for me than walking in just when we did.

When all that was left was the shoes.

She was bent over, her hands pulling back the folds of her silk gown so she could land her feet properly in the white pumps. All I saw at first was the top of her head, and of course, just below that, her cleavage, with her hair dangling down in ribbons on either side. Right then, she paused and slid both hands up her thigh to readjust her bridal garter.

Even now, just remembering, I can almost feel the nylon of her stockings—that slick, delicate, geometric texture.

Then she got back to business: one shoe, then the next. Then she stood up to square her shoulders—and that's when she saw us.

There were some other women—bridesmaids, I think—deeper back in the room by the makeup table, but they seemed a thousand miles away.

Everything seemed a thousand miles away.

For me, it was a love-at-first-sight thing—something I didn't even believe in until right then. I stood in awe of it all. Helen herself, the sight of her, the way she seemed to glow in that white silk gown, the way every curve and dip and angle of her seemed luscious and inviting and hypnotic.

That one second before she spoke seemed to last for an hour. Everything slowed down and got sharper and I could hear my own breathing and my own heart thumping, and I felt genuinely woozy

for a second, the way you might if you were just walking home from school and ran into, say, Athena.

Or Aphrodite.

The best way I can ever think of to describe it is this: it felt like all my blood got replaced with warm, sparkling honey.

Though, to be fair, the sight of me did *not* do the same thing to her.

At first, Helen only seemed to see Duncan. Her expression went from something soft and vulnerable to something hard and irritated. Her posture shifted. Her shoulders tensed. Almost like Duncan showing up meant she had to get into character.

She pushed out a hard sigh. "Don't you know how to knock?"

Duncan frowned like the idea of knocking would never have occurred to him. "Fair point."

"I could have been half dressed. I could have been *naked*."

The thudding in my ears got louder.

I tried not to picture that. I really did.

But that's when she noticed me. Her eyes shifted from Duncan's face to mine.

Then a flash of irritation as tangible as sandpaper. She spoke to Duncan but kept her eyes on me. "Who's this?"

"This is my friend Jake. He's new. He just moved from Texas."

I wanted to look down so bad, but I held steady.

Helen looked me over. When she got to the too-short cuffs at my ankles, she paused. Then she turned back to Duncan. "Please tell me," she said, with a voice like she already knew the answer, "he's not here for the wedding."

Duncan gave her a big grin. "He's my plus one."

Helen glanced near me, but not at me. "Nope. Get him out of here."

"Seriously?"

"Yeah. I'm not hosting strangers at my wedding."

"He's just here for the reception."

"The reception is a hundred dollars a plate."

"So he won't eat anything." Duncan gave me a wink.

"You can't just bring random people to my wedding."

"He's not random. He's my friend."

She didn't buy that for a second. "What's his last name, then?"

She had him. Duncan had no idea what my last name was, and I didn't know his either. But Duncan was unfazed. "He doesn't have one. He's like Madonna. He's just"—and here, he spread out his hands like we were looking at a marquis—"Jake."

"Duncan. This is not a birthday party at an arcade. This is *my wedding*."

"You get a million friends and I don't get anybody?"

"I'm paying for all those friends! A—"

But Duncan jumped in. "A hundred dollars a plate."

"That's right," Helen said. "So we're not bringing in random teenagers off the streets."

"Come on, Hells Bells. He put on a suit and everything."

From the look on her face as soon as he called her "Hells Bells," I knew he was toast. She went from irritated to venomous.

But, just then, deus ex machina, an old lady in a red dress with peacock feathers in her hair called from across the room. "Helen?"

Helen turned.

"Sweetheart, it's time."

The old lady held out her hand, and Helen, forgetting us entirely, walked over to take it.

I tried to leave after that, but Duncan wasn't having it. "It's fine, man. She's too busy to notice us." He opened the door to the next room, which was set up for the ceremony with chairs and flowers. It was packed.

I closed it again.

"I thought you said nobody was coming to this," I said, now self-conscious about my too-short trousers.

"I might have been misinformed on that," Duncan said.

"You tricked me."

"Fine. Yes. I tricked you."

Looking back, knowing Duncan like I know him now, I know why he wanted me there. Because I'd told him at lunch that my plan for the night was to just "walk around on the train tracks"—and I wouldn't be his friend much longer before learning he was way too big-hearted to let that happen.

I asked him about it straight-out one time, actually: "Did you trick me into showing up just so I wouldn't be alone?"

And Duncan just gave me a big, goofball shrug. "Of course."

But now I had a bigger problem.

"Duncan," I said. "I'm going to need you to punch me in the face."

He looked at me, like, *Interesting.* Then he said, "Why?"

"I think I just fell in love with your sister."

"You do need to get punched, then."

"That's what I'm saying."

"I've never punched anyone before, though."

Keep On Reading

"How hard can it be?"

"Fair point." Duncan squared to face me.

"Make it hurt, okay?"

"I'll try."

I was hoping getting punched might break my momentum.

And it did. Kind of.

It also broke Duncan's thumb.

He got me right in the jaw, and it hurt so bad the world went white for a second.

As soon as I'd recovered enough to focus, I walked out the dressing room door.

But Duncan followed and grabbed my arm. "Where are you going?"

"Home. She told me to get out of here."

"You can't go."

"I can't *stay*."

"She'll never notice, man. She's kinda busy right now."

We were standing now in the room set up for the ceremony. All the guests had taken their seats. The pianist, who had been playing softly up front, suddenly shifted gears into what sounded—alarmingly—like a processional.

Duncan startled and turned to look at the front of the room.

There was a gap in the line of groomsmen, and Duncan took off running down the center aisle to pop himself into place and fill it.

I should have left right then.

That was the perfect time to leave.

But I didn't.

Duncan was barely gone before the doors behind me opened—and then there was Helen, looking more . . . more *everything* than she had even minutes

before. She held onto the arm of the peacock lady, and as the two of them lifted their heads and started processing, I stepped back to let them pass.

I knew the bride didn't want me there.

But I just wanted a few more minutes to look at her.

And then "a few more minutes" turned into the whole ceremony. And then the ceremony turned into the reception—outside, by the pool—and while it felt morally imperative not to consume any of the hundred-dollar plates of food, I did drink a couple of the rum and Cokes that Duncan kept bringing over, and let's just say that the question of how the bride felt about my presence there started seeming less and less important.

Before I knew it, the night was over, and almost all the guests had gone. Just a few lingered near the valet.

Duncan and I were splayed out on the sofas of the lobby—him icing his hand with a bag from the fifth-floor ice machine, and me doing the same to my cheek—with Duncan trying to convince me to *go eat something, for fuck's sake,* as the hotel staff was breaking down the tables and the caterer was boxing up the leftover food.

"Nope," I said, again, shaking my head for drama. "I promised I wouldn't eat."

Duncan was somehow much drunker than me. "You said you wouldn't eat the primary food. But this is the leftover food."

"Same difference."

"Everybody's gone, buddy. Somebody has to eat it."

"Well, it's not gonna be me."

"If you don't eat it, I'll eat it for you."

"Be my guest."

"That doesn't solve our problem, though."

"It's fine. I'm not even hungry." I was definitely hungry.

"They're just going to throw it away. Do you wanna see that happen?"

"It's not about what I want. It's about what your sister wants."

"Helen?" Duncan asked, like he'd forgotten all about her.

"Helen," I said, nodding. Her name felt good in my mouth. I said it again, noting how the "l" and the "n" were almost the same motion of my tongue.

I leaned my head back against the sofa. Then I asked, "What's the boyfriend like?"

"What boyfriend?"

"Helen's boyfriend." Helen. *Helen.*

Duncan flipped his head my direction to give a pointed look. "Helen's *husband.*"

"Right. Is he any good?"

"He's okay, I guess."

"Do you like him?"

"*Like* him?" Duncan said, like the concept was irrelevant. "He's like thirty."

An old man. "Is your sister thirty?"

Duncan shook his head. "She's twenty-six."

"He's too old for her. He's a grandpa."

"Too late now."

I was all set to argue with him—to say it's never too late—when I opened my eyes and saw Helen herself standing right in front of me.

She was still in her wedding gown, but everything about her seemed looser now—her veil was gone, her hair was coming unpinned, the fabric of her dress seemed more . . . flowy . . . after a reception's worth of doing the Macarena and

sipping champagne.

She looked right at me—right into my eyes in a way that I felt all the way down in my stomach. "You didn't leave."

I panicked. Then, after a second: "Correct."

She nodded. "That's a good thing."

I sat up. "It is?"

"What happened to your face?"

Duncan raised his hand like a pupil who knew the answer. "I punched him."

"Duncan! What the hell!"

"He asked me to."

Just then, the peacock lady showed up beside her and looked at me. "You're Duncan's friend?"

I nodded.

"I'm GiGi," she said, taking my hand. "Don't you think this wedding would have been more majestic with a flock of peacocks?"

I glanced at Duncan, moving only my eyes.

He gave a tiny head-shake.

"Um . . ." I said.

But GiGi went on. "Either way, we're so glad you could make it."

Helen turned to her. "GiGi! You knew about this?"

"Of course. Duncan tells me everything."

"You didn't stop him?"

"Why would I?" GiGi held her arm out toward me. "Look how handsome this kid is!"

"But you didn't know he was handsome until right now."

But before I could enjoy being called handsome, Helen pushed on.

"Are you on Duncan's side?" she demanded.

"I'm on both sides. At all times," GiGi declared. Then she looked at me. "I hope you ate something."

I kept my eyes on Helen and shook my head.

"Nothing at all?" GiGi demanded.

"I tried!" Duncan called from his spot on the sofa. "But he told me it was morally wrong."

"It *was* morally wrong," Helen said, giving me a nod of approval that felt weirdly triumphant to receive.

"Starving people is morally wrong," Duncan countered.

"He's not starving. Nobody that handsome is starving."

Handsome again. Noted.

We were all clearly a little tipsy.

Except for GiGi, who was eyeing us all. "Who is the *least* drunk here?" she asked, setting her hands on her hips.

Duncan and I pointed at each other.

"Stand them up," GiGi ordered Helen, and then, as Helen pulled me into a stand, GiGi did the same to Duncan.

They both studied us, then pointed at me, in unison, with a nod.

"You take that one," GiGi said, of me, "and I'll take this one."

Helen came right at me, cleavage and all, grabbing one of my hands and tugging me along behind her. GiGi grabbed Duncan and hauled him off in the other direction.

My lucky day.

"Where are we going?" I asked.

"GiGi's taking Duncan and all the leftover food back to her house."

At the mention of food, my stomach gave a little squeeze.

Helen went on, "And I'm taking you—the bigger,

less drunk one—to go get the groom."

I pulled up beside her to walk side by side. "The groom?"

She didn't meet my eyes. "He passed out. Behind the dance floor."

"Ah."

"He'll be fine," she assured me.

Even though I hadn't asked.

"This happens sometimes," she said, in a tone like, *No big deal*.

"Sure," I said. "Of course."

"I just need you to help me get him up to the bridal suite."

"Aren't you supposed to be on your honeymoon right now?"

"We fly out tomorrow."

"Guess that's a good thing."

"Guess so."

At the dance floor, we evaluated the groom's motionless body for a minute. "Did he hit his head?" I asked.

Helen shook her head. "He landed on the carpet. He's okay."

So I shrugged. Then I leaned down and worked his arm around my shoulders. Helen got under his other arm, and then we stood.

That roused him a little. Enough that he could stumble along between us toward the elevator bank. He didn't much question what was happening, like maybe this wasn't the first time he'd done this.

We rode the elevator in silence and then maneuvered him down the hall to the bridal suite, through the doorway, and onto the king-sized bed. Helen went to get a blanket for him from the closet, and while she was gone, I evaluated him.

He looked like a man who had no idea how to count his blessings.

Even the way Helen spread the blanket out over him involved more tenderness than he looked like he deserved.

Of course, from the angle she happened to be at, I could see straight down her strapless dress—again—and so, because I was a gentleman, I shifted my gaze to the side—where I saw a bucket of champagne chilling on the table. When she stood back up, she saw me eyeing it.

"Not much of a wedding night," I said.

She gave me a look like I was as annoying as Duncan, and then walked toward the door like she was about to kick me out.

I followed, head down. Fine. I'd overstayed everything, anyway.

But at the door, she stopped and looked me over. "Did you really not eat anything all night?"

I shook my head, holding her gaze.

She stifled a smile. "Okay. Hang on."

She disappeared to the kitchenette and then came back with a neatly folded and stapled grocery sack in one hand and the bottle of champagne in the other.

Then she turned to check on the husband one more time before saying, "Come on."

Next thing I knew, we were sitting out by the pool, side by side on a long chaise, and she was pulling plastic containers out of the bag.

I frowned at her when she handed me one.

"It's food," she said.

I looked down at the container and opened it up. Sure enough, it was fried chicken.

"This is a thing that happens," she explained.

"Caterers always box up food for the bride and groom, since they're so busy being congratulated all night they never get to eat."

"Did you get to eat?" I asked.

She shook her head.

I held out the container to her and she took a piece.

Then I said, "I can't believe you had chicken fingers at your wedding. That doesn't seem very fancy."

"These are pecan-encrusted chicken *goujons* with a sriracha-infused hoisin sauce, thank you very much."

"Ah," I said, not sure if I was being reprimanded.

Then she added, "Also known as chicken fingers." She took a bite. "Just three times more expensive."

We opened all the boxes and set out the food. Mashed potatoes, green beans, rosemary dinner rolls, roast beef slices, stuffed mushrooms. The caterers had packed it all up like a picnic for two—silverware, napkins, plates, sauces.

I didn't want to ask, but I felt like I ought to. "Should we save some for your boyfriend?"

"Mike?" she asked.

Mike. I guess I hated that name now. "Yeah."

But she shook her head. "He'll be out cold all night. It's fine." Then she popped the cork on the champagne and took a swig from the bottle. "None for you," she said, shaking the bottle at me by the neck. "You're underage."

I decided not to mention all those rum and Cokes. "Fair enough."

With that, there was nothing left to do but eat. We ate straight out of the containers like hungry animals, sharing, and licking our fingers, and leaning over each other to grab containers. For a

*Keep On
Reading*

few minutes, we did nothing else. Me in the suit I wore to my mother's funeral, and her in a strapless wedding dress that seemed to hold itself up like magic.

The pool had what seemed like hundreds of candles floating in it, and we watched them while we chewed.

It was a while before we got full enough to talk. "I think that was the best food I've ever had," I said.

"Food always tastes best when you're hungry."

I reached across her to dunk a chicken finger in the hoisin sauce. "I guess it does."

"You really should have eaten something," she said.

"You told me not to."

"Do you always do what you're told?"

"It depends on who's telling me."

She gave me a little smile with just her eyes. Then she said, "Watch out for Duncan. He's a troublemaker."

"Noted."

"He's lovable, but he's high-maintenance."

"Everybody's high-maintenance if you're paying attention."

She blinked at that, and then seemed to see me for the first time. The feel of her eyes on me was physical, almost like heat on my skin.

I let it happen as long as I could stand it. Then I said, "Good wedding, by the way."

She frowned like that was funny. Then she said, "Yeah. I think it was."

"Are you excited to be married?"

She thought about it. "I don't think it's sunk in yet."

"Is that guy the love of your life?"

"Yes," she said. But then she looked like she was

thinking about it.

"We're both drunk," I said. "You can tell the truth."

"You're not supposed to be drunk," she said, pointing at me. "And I don't think I'm drunk. I don't feel drunk."

"I don't feel drunk, either."

"You probably don't even know what it's like to be drunk."

"Sure I do."

"But what are you—like twelve?"

"I'm almost seventeen. And I was drunk a lot after my mother died."

She turned toward me then and took that in. No automatic, knee-jerk "I'm sorry," like you usually get. Just a quiet moment of understanding.

Then she said, "But you're not drinking anymore, right?"

I shook my head. "Not for a few months now."

"You're okay?"

"I'm okay."

"It takes a while to be okay."

For some reason my throat tightened. I'd been waiting all day to feel something about my mom— for the *missing her* to hit me—but I hadn't felt anything so far. I wasn't sure if that was a good thing or a bad thing. But now, at last, I felt it.

Though it wasn't as bad as I'd been fearing.

"When did she die?" Helen asked.

"A year ago," I said, watching Helen's eyes, which stayed steady, focused on mine. Then without overthinking it, I added, "A year ago today."

Helen drew in a slow breath. Then she nodded. Then she reached over, took my hand, and pulled it onto her lap to clasp it between both of hers. She turned her eyes back toward the water then, toward

Keep On Reading

the warm light of the floating candles, and so I turned and did the same.

Before I knew it, my face was wet with tears.

Helen kept my hand in her lap, like it was something precious, stroking the back of it with her palm. "It's okay," she said.

I think if she'd been looking at me, it would've been too much.

But she wasn't. She didn't. She let me have my side of the pool chaise, and she kept to hers, and nobody said anything until the stinging in my chest had subsided and my breathing had settled back down.

"Don't worry," Helen said then, after a while. "You'll be okay. I promise. All you have to do is just keep going."

"That's harder than it sounds."

"I know."

Then, when we'd been quiet long enough, she said, by way of lightening the subject, "Tell me about the constellations."

I looked up, but the stars weren't there. So I looked over at Helen, and I realized she was watching the candles in the pool.

"The *pool* constellations," I said, studying the candles now. "Well, *that* one," I said, pointing to a clump in the far corner, "is pretty legendary. Irving, the dentist."

Her mouth pressed into a little closed-lip smile.

Man, it felt good to see that smile.

I went on, pointing at a new clump. "And once you've found that one, it's easy to find Melvin, the accountant. And then Fred, the barber. And then, of course, Bubba the plumber. There's his crack."

Now she was laughing.

Actually laughing.

So I went on. "That," I pointed, "is the Golden Croissant. And over there are the Big Burrito and the Little Taco."

"What about there?" she asked, pointing at a clump in the middle.

"There? That's Pickle the Wonder Dog. But I'm sure you already know that story."

"Of course I do. I definitely do. It's the story about the big dog—"

"Tiny dog," I corrected.

"The *tiny dog* that managed to find its way—"

"Rescue," I corrected.

"Managed to *rescue* a whole group of—"

"A lone woman," I said.

"A *lone woman* when she . . ." Helen turned to study my face, like it might tell her the rest.

I nodded, like she was totally getting it. "When she fell into a swimming pool in her bridal gown. Exactly. Great job."

"Great story," Helen said. "Who doesn't love that story?"

"A classic."

"Of course she fell into the pool because she . . ."

"Was rescuing someone else. A boy who'd fallen in before her."

"That's right, and without Pickle, who . . ."

"Heroically dog-paddled them both to the steps . . ."

"Exactly. She might never have . . ."

But now I had just started gazing at her.

"She might never have . . ." Helen prompted.

But I was looking at the sheen of her lip gloss, and I'd lost focus.

Finally, she smacked me on the shoulder. "She might never have?"

Keep On

Reading

"Become a goddess," I answered.

She liked that answer. Her whole face seemed to glow. "That's right. She's the goddess of brides. And swimming pools. And rescues."

"And boys who fall by accident."

"A small but proud community."

"All thanks to Pickle the Wonder Dog."

Helen gave a decisive nod. "Who has nothing to show for it but his own constellation."

And then she smiled at me.

And that's when I knew that smile was going to be a problem. Because I had no idea how to make myself lose interest in that smile.

I just knew right then that smile could ruin my life.

But it was already too late.

HELEN

I blacked out that night, apparently.

I don't remember a thing.

One minute, I was doing YMCA on the dance floor, and, the next, the sun was prying open my eyelids on a sofa in the bridal suite, and I was fully clothed in my wedding dress, tucked neatly, *meticulously,* under a hotel throw blanket—with a glass of water and two Tylenol waiting neatly for me on the side table.

Huh. Uncharacteristically thoughtful of Mike.

But I'd take it.

Was I hungover? You bet I was.

But Mike was fine. Up and showering. We had a plane to catch by noon.

Anyway, I didn't even know you could black out just randomly like that—but I Googled it later and, apparently . . . *yes.* If you drink on an empty stomach, or drink the wrong type of alcohol, or if you've taken anti-anxiety meds recently, it can happen.

And to that, I confess: *all of the above.*

I spent part of my honeymoon researching this from the hotel, in fact. You don't even have to be all that drunk. You can be walking around seeming almost normal. But if you get the wrong combination of chemicals hitting you in just the wrong way, it can slam the memory center of your brain and just . . . shut it down.

Until I did the research, I'd always thought you had to be falling-down drunk to have a blackout. Or be a habitual, out-of-control alcoholic. But it turns out you can just combine bad choices with bad timing.

One of my specialties.

And then, *boom*: everything that happened never happened.

I didn't drink again for years after that. That's how scary it was to *not remember my own wedding night*.

But I'll admit: even though I knew I forgot part of the night, it never once occurred to me that it might be the most interesting part.

I assumed that Mike and I finished dancing, said goodbye to everybody, went up to our suite, and conked out pretty quickly. I did notice the caterers forgot to provide the after-reception picnic bag they'd promised. And the hotel had set out the chiller for the bridal suite champagne but forgotten the champagne itself.

But I just chalked it up to the world being habitually disappointing.

Oh, well.

I held that version of events in my head for years.

And nobody corrected me. Not Duncan. Not Jake. Not even GiGi.

In case you don't know, my marriage to Mike didn't work out.

For lots of reasons, in lots of ways.

And then—long story short—six years later, when I was thirty-two and newly divorced, and Jake was twenty-two and out of college—I wound up accidentally going on a hiking trip with him and accidentally falling in love.

Man, I could write a whole book about that.

The long and the short of it is, three months after that hiking trip, Jake asked me to elope with him in GiGi's backyard, and I couldn't manage to stop myself from saying yes.

A week later, we were hitched.

That's all it took.

Six years, three months, and one week.

What can I say? He's persuasive.

I tried to make my impromptu backyard wedding different from my first one in every way—for luck, if nothing else—up to and including allowing GiGi's yard to be overrun with peacocks. Although GiGi was considerably less ornery about planning my second wedding than she'd been about my first one. Partly because there just wasn't time. But mostly because, as she later explained, she'd been "rooting for Jake all along."

One notable exception to the "make everything different" rule was the wedding dress. Jake wanted me to wear the one from last time.

"The same one from before?" I asked when he suggested it.

"Yep."

"The dress I wore last time? When I married someone else?"

"Yep."

"Why?"

"I like that dress."

"But . . ." There were so many things wrong with reusing that old wedding dress, I hardly knew where to start. "But you've seen it already."

"Exactly."

"But . . ."

"Seeing you in that dress is what doomed me to love you."

I thought about it. "Okay."

"But back then, you were somebody else's. And now you're mine."

I guess I could see it. Sort of.

"That dress deserves a happy ending," Jake said then. "It never hurt anybody. Quite the opposite, in fact."

"It was complicit in some very bad choices."

"Maybe it deserves a shot at redemption."

So I didn't fight him. Maybe he was right.

I wasn't opposed to redemption.

After the wedding, and the reception, and helping GiGi round the peacocks back up, Jake said he was going to take me "somewhere romantic," but then wound up driving me to the Kemp Hotel, instead—the site of my first wedding.

"*This* is 'somewhere romantic'?" I said.

"Just you wait," Jake said.

"You really do want to redeem this dress."

"What I want," Jake said, as he led me by the hand through the lobby, "is to show you something."

"But—here?"

"You don't trust me?"

"It just seems like we're looking backward instead of forward."

"Don't worry," Jake said. "We're doing both."

We passed the mirrored lobby for the elevators, and then a candlelit dining room, and then we stepped outside to the pool area where I'd held the reception for my last wedding. There was dinner service on the patio, and folks at the tables turned at the sight of a bride and groom walking by.

"Why are we here?" I asked, when my eyes fell on the pool itself . . . and it was full of floating candles.

"Oh," I said.

"Pretty, huh?"

I nodded. "I had candles just like this at my wedding to Mike."

"I know."

"You do?"

"Of course."

He led me to a pool chaise down by the shallow end and sat us down side by side. "I want to tell you a story," he said then, as we both watched the floating lights, "about one of the constellations."

I looked up at the sky, but it was empty.

Jake pointed down at the candles. "Those constellations," he said.

"Of course," I said, all wry, "the *pool* constellations."

"Exactly," Jake said. Then, "See that batch in the middle?"

I nodded.

"That constellation is a very famous one called Helen, the Goddess."

Now I gave him a look that somehow combined *"please," "come on,"* and *"you're awesome"* all at once.

"There's a story about that constellation. Want to hear it?"

"Sure."

"On the night she got married, Helen the Goddess met a scraggly teenage kid. A very sad scraggly teenage kid. A kid so sad, just all the time, that he thought—no, he just *assumed*—that he'd never be happy again. And this kid, being a genius . . . he fell in love with her on sight."

"He did?"

Jake nodded. "Want to know why?"

"Because he peeked at her cleavage?"

Jake pointed at me. "Partial credit."

"Wasn't she mean to him, though?"

"She was epically mean! She tried to kick him out of the wedding. But he didn't go."

"He didn't?"

*Keep On
Reading*

"He wanted to go. He thought he should go. He even asked his new friend Duncan to punch him in the face in the hopes that it would hurt enough to make him *want* to go. But guess what?"

"What?"

"He stayed."

"He stayed? The whole time?"

"He couldn't make himself *not* stay. So he stayed. But he didn't eat anything, because she'd told him not to."

"Wow. She really was mean."

Jake nodded in appreciation. "Wasn't she?"

"Bet he got pretty hungry."

"He did, but it was worth it."

I held Jake's gaze.

"Anyway," he went on. "She married this horrible guy that same night. And by the end of the evening, the horrible guy had insulted a bridesmaid, knocked over a buffet table, and passed out behind the dance floor."

"Wow," I said. "I bet she was really panicking about her life choices."

Jake gave a nod. "But there was an upside: she asked the scraggly kid to help her carry her new idiot husband up to the bridal suite."

"Wait—what?" I said. "Wait! She did?"

Another nod. "Helen and the kid laid the groom out on the bed, and then the kid was about to leave and go back to his lonely life, but Helen stopped him."

"She stopped him?"

"Yeah, because she felt bad he hadn't eaten anything. So she grabbed some leftovers from the caterer and guess where they went?"

"Where?"

Jake patted the chaise we were sitting on. "Right

here. They ate overpriced chicken fingers, and she drank champagne straight from the bottle like a badass, and the two of them watched the floating candles for so long they started to look like stars. And that's when the kid confessed something to her that he hadn't planned to."

I leaned closer. "What did he confess?"

"He confessed that *that* day—her wedding day—was the one-year anniversary of the day his mother died."

I caught my breath. "Was it, Jake? It was?"

"Probably a terrible thing to tell a bride. Probably something he shouldn't have said. But guess what?"

"What?"

"She took his hand, and she held it. And it was the first time in that whole, long year that he didn't feel completely, utterly, endlessly alone. And something about not feeling alone for the first time in so, so long made him start to cry. You know? Like, the kind of crying that's like a thunderstorm. And guess what she did?"

"What?"

"She let him. She just let him. And she kept him company. And held onto his hand. And they watched the floating candles. And even after he was all cried out, even in the midst of all that sorrow, he had the craziest feeling that he loved her. And that no matter what happened from then on out, he always would."

I watched the candles. "That *was* a crazy feeling. He'd known her for like an hour."

"Four hours," Jake corrected. "And guess what?"

"What?"

"He wasn't wrong. He did love her. And he never stopped."

"Even though she forgot everything?"

Jake nodded. "Man, she really did. The next time he saw her, it was like they'd never met. And that went on for years. Him just loving her like crazy, and her just not even registering his existence."

My mind flashed back through all those Thanksgivings and Christmases he'd spent with us at GiGi's house—and how he always helped me do the dishes and made runs to the store for last-minute supplies. And the way, as GiGi had once told me, he always switched the place cards so we wound up sitting together.

"Until one day," Jake went on, "he fooled her into kissing him. And that turned out to be the trick to it all."

This part, I remembered. "That was all it took?"

"He's a very good kisser." Jake buffed his fingernails on his tux jacket. "Some say legendary."

"That must have been quite a shock for her."

"For him, too. He waited six years for that kiss."

"That's a long wait."

"He wanted to kiss her that first night, but he didn't."

"Hello? Appropriately! Since he was jailbait."

"And she was . . . married."

"That, too."

"So, instead, he just walked the newly married love of his life back up to her bridal suite, and tucked her in on the sofa, and set out a glass of water and some Tylenol for the morning."

I took a breath. "That was you?"

"Of course it was me."

I nodded. "Of course it was you."

Jake squeezed my hand.

"All those years," I said. "Why didn't you ever tell me?"

Jake just shrugged. "I guess I just remembered it well enough for both of us."

I shook my head, trying to call up even the tiniest memory of any of it.

But nothing.

"I tried to move on," Jake said. "But, as you can see," he looked down at his tuxedo, "I failed."

"You sure did."

"One of the best nights of my life."

I nodded. "I'm so mad at myself for forgetting."

Now he was looking into my eyes. "It was good. But wanna know what would have made it better?"

Very slowly, without breaking eye contact, I nodded.

Jake leaned close enough to rest a hand on my back, and then, he slid it down the silk of my dress to my hip and pulled me closer to him, leaning in all the while until his mouth was almost touching mine.

I looked into his eyes. "Are people watching us?"

He nodded. "Do you care?"

I shook my head.

And then he pressed in closer and kissed me— soft at first, then harder, tightening his arms around me like all he wanted was to touch in every possible way. And when it started to feel like we needed to upgrade locations from the pool chaise, I said, "Did you happen to reserve us a room at this hotel?"

"I did," he said.

"Good thinking."

"The bridal suite, in fact."

"That seems very cheeky."

"I figured we could redeem it, too."

"Are we already checked in?"

"We are."

"So could we go there? Like, now?"

"We could."

"So what, exactly," I asked then, "are we waiting for?"

In answer to that, Jake just stood, lifting me up in his arms and carrying me in toward the elevators. And as he did, the outdoor diners broke out in shy applause.

Next: Jake kissed me in the lobby, pressed up against a mirrored wall. And then he kissed me in the elevator, pressed up against the buttons. And then he kissed me halfway down our hallway, pressed up against somebody else's door.

And, of course, I kissed him back all the while.

And by the time we finally made it to our room, and fumbled with the key fob, and stumbled toward the bed, and fell back onto it, I didn't care anymore about all the things I'd forgotten, or all the moments I'd squandered, or all the joys that were lost to time.

We were here now.

Whatever we'd miss in the future, and whatever we'd lost in the past, we were here right now.

And I made myself a little secret promise right then, as Jake kissed my collarbones, and fumbled with the zipper on my dress, and thanked me over and over for being crazy enough to marry him.

It's a promise I break all the time, the way people do. But I keep it a lot, too. And either way, I still think about it every single day:

I would be grateful.

I wouldn't forget to be grateful.

I'd remember. I'd remember. *I'd remember.*

Joyful: The Surprising Power of Ordinary Things to Create Extraordinary Happiness by **Ingrid Fetell Lee**

This is the book that inspired *What You Wish For*! I got so obsessed with this wise, insightful book about how the world around us can spark (or not spark) joy in our lives, I started actively trying to think of a story idea that would lend itself to talking about joy. Ingrid Fetell Lee looks at how the world around us impacts our emotional lives, and it's the kind of read that changes the way you see everything. After reading this book, I decoupaged polka dots on the ceiling of our guest bathroom, started planting succulents around the house in little teacups, and taught myself to make origami butterflies, among many other whimsical things. It'll inspire you to see and appreciate the joy already around you—and galvanize you to create more of it.

Keep On Reading

Isaac's Storm: A Man, a Time, and the Deadliest Hurricane in History by **Erik Larson**

This true history of the Great Storm of 1900 is an up-all-night page-turner. It takes you through the night the storm killed over six thousand people in one night—still the highest death toll for a natural disaster in U.S. history—in harrowing, gripping, heartrending detail. If you know Galveston, once Texas's largest port city and a kind of Ellis Island for the South, you will absolutely never see the city in the same way again. If you don't know Galveston yet, it will become a real place to you, one you'll love all the more knowing everything it endured. This is the kind of story that will stay with you.

Galveston: A City on Stilts by Jodi Wright-Gidley and Jennifer Marines

After the Great Storm of 1900, Galveston—the wealthiest city in Texas at the time—decided to raise the grade of the entire city to protect against future storm surges. No kidding. The city built a nineteen-foot retaining wall, the Seawall, to buffer it against the gulf, and then pumped sand in to raise the elevation of the city. It was a massive undertaking that involved lifting entire houses and filling in beneath them, and you'd never know that the short little fences you sometimes see around town now used to be the tops of very tall fences. During this project, a commercial photographer named Zeva B. Edworthy documented the process with his tripod and large-format camera . . . only to later move away and take his photos with him. Fast-forward to the end of the century: his daughter learns of the photos for the first time when she inherits them from her mother . . . and then sends them home to the Galveston County Historical Museum, almost a hundred years after they were taken.

The Wisdom of Anxiety: How Worry & Intrusive Thoughts Are Gifts to Help You Heal by Sheryl Paul

In *What You Wish For,* both Sam and Duncan are dealing with forms of anxiety and worry in their lives. *The Wisdom of Anxiety* is one of the best books I've ever read on how the worries that come after us can serve as *teachers* in our lives, rather than tormentors. I, myself, am a world-champion worrier, and this book taught me to relate to those worries more with curiosity than hostility. It caused

a shift in the framework of my thinking that has been genuinely useful. That's a heck of a read!

Craftfulness: Mend Yourself by Making Things by Rosemary Davidson and Arzu Tahsin

In _What You Wish For_, Max tries to teach Sam that she doesn't have to just wait for joy to happen: she can make it happen. She can _do something joyful_. The book _Craftfulness_ is all about doing joyful things—about the powerful intersection between making things, positive psychology, and caretaking. So worth a read if you're hoping to incorporate more joy-making in your life.

The Unhoneymooners by Christina Lauren

Here's a novel that could be a great follow-up to _What You Wish For_ the next time you're in the mood for a page-turning, delightful read. I devoured this one in a day. It's the hugely addictive, romantic story of two people who are not exactly fond of each other who wind up taking someone else's honeymoon in Hawaii. It's dreamy, perfectly paced, overflowing with witty banter, and genuinely laugh-out-loud funny. Delicious.

_Keep On
Reading_

 *Reading Group Questions*

1. On page 59, Sam recalls Max telling her to "Pay attention to the things that connect you with joy." Did reading this also remind you to pay attention to what makes you happy? What are some things in your life that make you feel connected with joy?

2. What did you make of how affected Sam is by the news of Duncan coming to her school? Why do you think the idea of Duncan, and Sam's feelings for him, have so much control over her and her thoughts?

3. What was your initial reaction when Duncan doesn't recognize Sam? Did you suspect that he did and was keeping it a secret? Why do you think he did?

4. Sam knows that Duncan coming back into her life would be hard and stressful for her, but it turns out to be, in a way, entirely different from what she expects. Have you had any situations in your life where you similarly thought something would be challenging, but it turned out to be so in a completely different way? How did you handle it?

5. On page 144, Duncan talks about painting over the butterfly mural and says, "When the world is a safer place, we'll bring it back." What did you make of that comment? Did you believe Duncan and his motives? Did you begin to wonder why he is so concerned about safety?

6. At one point in the novel, Sam says that she doesn't have anyone in her life with whom she feels like she truly belongs. Did you see this come across as you were reading? How does this change over the course of the novel?

7. Sam makes it clear that her epilepsy has held her back from doing things like driving and dating. Do you think some of Sam's past trauma with her epilepsy, and her father walking out on her and her mother, has affected her in other ways?

8. Duncan confesses his true feelings to Sam after his surgery, but he doesn't remember doing so. Why do you think Sam doesn't tell him what he told her? Why do you think she never has the nerve to when she has such strong feelings for him?

9. The library is a safe place for Sam that brings her joy. She also works very hard to make sure her students feel the same. Is there a place like this for you in your life? Was there one when you were a child?

10. As cruel as Tina Buckley is to Sam, we know that she has faced a lot of challenges in her life. What do you make of her evolution over the course of the novel and the evolution of her relationship with Sam?

11. This story has a lot of lessons about how to live a more joyful life, even in the face of hardship. What insights from the book

stood out for you? Are there ways you might approach your own life differently after reading this novel?

KATHERINE CENTER is the *New York Times* bestselling author of *How to Walk Away* and *Things You Save in a Fire,* as well as five other bittersweet comic novels about facing life with compassion and grace. *BookPage* calls her "the reigning queen of comfort reads." The movie adaptation of her novel *The Lost Husband* hit #1 on Netflix. Katherine writes laugh-and-cry books about how life knocks us down—and how we get back up. She's been compared to both Jane Austen and Nora Ephron, and the Dallas *Morning News* calls her stories "satisfying in the most soul-nourishing way." Her books have made countless best-of lists, including *Real Simple*'s Best Books of 2020, Amazon's Top 100 Books of 2019, Goodreads' Best Books of the Year, the Indie Next Great Reads List, and many more. Katherine lives in her hometown of Houston, Texas, with her husband, two kids, and their fluffy-but-fierce dog.